Jessica Rosenberg

1

Aloha Also Means Goodbye

Jessica Rosenberg

Aloha Also Means Goodbye

Copyright ©2014 Jessica Rosenberg
Published by Blue Octopus Press
www.BlueOctopusPress.com
(831) 471-7028

Library of Congress Control Number: 2013949631
Library of Congress Cataloging-in-Publication Data
Rosenberg, Jessica
Aloha Also Means Goodbye / Jessica Rosenberg
ISBN: 978-1-7367229-0-9

Cover design by Jeroen ten Berge

For my husband, whose love and support always give me the courage to soar beyond my comfort zone, and my dad, forever the voice of my inner editor, who kept my feet firmly planted in in reality.

Aloha Also Means Goodbye

Aloha Also Means Goodbye

Jessica Rosenberg

Aloha Also Means Goodbye

1. Jo

"He's here," Sadie hissed. "He's here. Right now. In the hotel."

Jo ignored her for a moment while she looked around to see where the driver had gone. Her overstuffed duffel was still in the back of the hotel's airport shuttle and, tug as she might, it wasn't coming out.

Sweat poured down her back, pooling in the dip just above her cotton capris. What had she packed that could possibly weigh so much? She tugged some more before realizing that the strap had snagged itself on a hook in the back of the seat. Jo leaned into the van to free the bag and called back to Sadie.

"Who's here? What are you talking about? Why are you whispering?"

"Shhhhhhhhhh!" Sadie hissed again, "He'll hear you!"

"Who? Who is here and going to hear me talk about him?" Jo asked. One final yank and her dark green canvas bag was out. It hit the ground with a loud THWACK, causing a few hotel patrons to gaze their way.

"Shhhhhhhhhh!" Sadie hissed again.

"Okay! What is the big deal?" Jo asked, turning to pay attention to her plump best friend. Sadie's curly red hair was disheveled and sticking out in every direction, same as always, though maybe a bit more frizzy than usual. Jo pushed back her own sticky hair and wiped some of the sweat from her forehead. It was hot. Much hotter and more humid than she had anticipated. A dip in the hotel pool would feel like heaven.

Jo wondered if Sadie's hair looked like that because she'd already been swimming. Her friend was looking uncharacteristically frazzled. Her usually relaxed and happy face was creased with concern making the freckles on her forehead mass together in an alarming way.

"What's going on?" Jo asked again. She searched for an answer in Sadie's worried eyes and reached for her shaking hand.

"He's here," Sadie said again, as though that explained everything.

"Who? Jordan? No, he's not, he doesn't get here until Thursday." Jo watched as the porter, who had finally materialized, took her bag to the front desk. She had no idea who Sadie was going on about, but she didn't want to lose sight of her bag. Her bathing suit was in there and right now all she could think about was hitting the pool.

"No. Not Jordan. *Andy*. Andy is here. Right here. In the hotel."

Jo's heart stuttered. She reached for Sadie's arm to steady herself as her chest constricted, and she struggled to take a breath. She gasped, her hand flapping at her throat, wedding ring clinking against the pendant nestled in the hollow. Jo stared at Sadie. There was nothing but concern written all over her friend's face. Concern that was increasing by the second.

Jo forced herself to calm down by focusing on the sound of the surf and ignoring the mounting hysteria of her thoughts. Finally, her throat unclenched, letting in a thin stream of air and letting out a strangled whisper.

"What do you mean, he's here? How is that even possible? This is a pretty remote island, even for Hawaii? What is he doing here?"

"I don't know." Sadie shrugged. "I spotted him at breakfast this morning. At first I thought I was mistaken, but then I saw him again in front of the elevator bank. There's no mistaking that hair. And that voice. It's definitely him."

Jo listened to Sadie and concentrated hard on breathing. She was not going to pass out here in the hotel lobby. She just wasn't going to.

"His voice? I thought you barely saw him? How did you manage to hear his voice?" Jo could hear herself getting shrill but couldn't stop the hysteria from breaking through. Shrill seemed inevitable, but it was better than fainting and making even more of a scene.

His voice. There was a time Jo would have done anything to hear his voice again. Now the mere thought was sending cold sweat cascading down her back. And yet, it was all she could hear – his voice in her head. And, oh, now his voice behind her!

No Emily! Freeze! You cannot run into the parking lot like that. Come hold Daddy's hand right now!" The once familiar rich timbre shook Jo to the pit of her stomach, but the words caused both her eyebrows and Sadie's to shoot straight up.

"Daddy?" They both mouthed at each other? "Daddy?"

"Emily?" Jo thought to herself. "He named his daughter Emily?"

2. Jo

Paris, France

They had walked hand in hand along the Seine, watching the sunlight glint off the water like jewels playing hide and seek in murk. They had been on vacation, their first alone, and they were heady with the joy of being together in the city of love. The cost of the flight and the cheap tiny hostel had stretched their budget to its utmost limit, so they had spent their days just walking around the gorgeous city, eating bread and cheese at pretty much every meal. They were so wrapped up in each other that they'd barely noticed any of the architecture that they had supposedly flown so far to see. Intricate doorways and ornate stonework went unnoticed as they meandered from arrondissement to arrondissement passionately discussing everything under the sun from their mutual love of olives to the life that they were going to build together.

"We'll have just one child. A daughter. She'll have big blue eyes and soft blond curls," Jo had said dreamily.

"Oh, will she?" Her dark haired boyfriend had

replied. "Blond with blue eyes, you say?" He'd laughed and poked her ribs before pulling her towards him. He'd gathered her in his arms, his deep blue eyes locking onto her own bright brown ones and kissed her tenderly on the lips. "If she's half as beautiful as you, she'll be a lucky girl and we'll have to beat the boys off with sticks." Jo had laughed and kissed him back and after a moment they had walked on.

"She will be gorgeous and smart," Jo had continued, in love with the image of this baby they would create together. "We'll call her Emily."

"Emily? Why Emily?"

"No reason, except we were just kissing on Rue Emile Zola."

He had laughed and they had walked on, but from that moment on they'd always joked about baby Emily, born in a kiss on a crowded street in the heart of Paris.

3. Jo

"Sadie!" Jo hissed. "I cannot be here. He cannot see me like this! How is this happening? Why now?" She ran her shaking hands through her tangled frizzy mop, damning airplanes and their overload of stupid static electricity. Why couldn't she ever look like one of those super sleek models; each strand of hair always in place, face unlined, clothes perfectly pressed? Jo glanced down at her stained and wrinkled cargo capris, covered in sweat spots, and took in her chipped home pedicure. Most of the toenails were visible around the glittery red, but the surrounding skin was still stained from her pathetic attempts at doing the job herself. Sadie grabbed Jo's hands frantic hands and pulled them from the wrinkled front of her grubby white button-down shirt.

"Calm down," she said, squeezing hard. "It's okay."

"No. No it's not." Jo's voice shook as she fought back the flood of tears that threatened to break free. "It is the opposite of okay. There might have been a time when this might have been okay, but this is not it. The last thing I needed this week was to see Andy again." Jo yanked her shaking hands out of Sadie's grasp and fumbled for the carry-on bag the porter had left at her feet. She just managed to grab the strap before breaking into a run.

Jo reached the safety of the hotel lobby just in time, barely taking in the double story ceiling, marble counters, and how the whole space opened out onto a massive balcony that overlooked the beach and the ocean. The automatic doors slid shut behind her, almost protecting her from hearing what she imagined was taking place where she'd left Sadie. She shuddered at her best friend's shrill greeting, and her shoulders sagged when she also recognized the true delight buried in the pretend surprise of the greeting.

"Andy! Is that really you? Oh my god! What are you doing here! It's so good to see you!"

4. Andy

"Sadie! Is that really you?" He reached down and scooped her into his arms, surprised by the overwhelming need to hold her close. She hadn't changed much over the years. Her hair was still as crazy as he remembered and she had the exact same smile, right down to the dimple in the right cheek. Holding her in his arms felt like stepping back in time and he had to swallow hard to dislodge the lump that was forming there. He hugged her hard before easing her back to the ground. "It's good to see you too. What brings you to Ha... OOF." He swooped down to pick up the little girl who had just careened into his legs.

"Emily, can you say hi to Daddy's friend, Sadie?" In response Emily nuzzled her face into his neck, whimpering quietly. Typical. The kid was always bouncing off the walls, except when he needed her to be sociable. "She's shy," he apologized. "And she needs her nap. Are you staying in the hotel? Can we have coffee later and catch up?"

"Sure thing! I'm here for the whole week, Room 704. Just give me a call."

He watched Sadie walk away, slight hop in her step. He hadn't seen her in years. He let himself wonder if maybe, just maybe... but Emily's shrill "Who dat?" interrupted his train of thought before he had time to look around to see who was with her.

"Dat, was an old friend of Daddy's. An old, old friend."

"Hawow!" Emily called out to Sadie a second too late. The shining elevator doors had just engulfed her and Sadie never saw the small fist open and shut in a wave.

"Let's get you to bed kiddo," Andy said to his daughter, "we have lots of swimming and fun waiting for us when Hunter gets back from camp."

5. Jo

Jo jammed the flimsy plastic key into the lock over and over again, but the red light stubbornly refused to turn green and she finally had to admit that it just didn't work.

"Damn. Damn. Damn. Damn." She rested her forehead against the wooden door and tried hard not to cry. How on earth was this happening? This was supposed to be fun. A week on an island with all her favorite people, with a party thrown in for the heck of it. Fun. That's what it was supposed to be. Fun and relaxing. There's no room for closet skeletons in fun and relaxing, no room at all. There's room for sunscreen and sand. There's room for friends, and fun, and wine, lots, and lots of good wine, but there's. Just. No. Room. For. Exes. Who. Broke. Your. HEART! Jo banged her head against the door in time with her thoughts until her forehead started to hurt. She looked down at the hotel key still grasped in her hand and stifled a shriek.

Jo threw the offending piece of plastic on the floor and stomped on it for good measure. She knew she was acting like a brat, but just couldn't stop herself, this was all just so damn unfair!

Voices at the other end of the hall squelched her

escalating tantrum. Jo picked up the card sheepishly and wondered what she should do. Did she dare head back to the lobby for a new card? What if Andy was still down there? And where the heck was Sadie? She'd have another key to the room, no?

Just as the voices came closer, the elevator, so conveniently located in front of the door to Sadie and Jo's room, opened. Jo jumped behind the potted plant right next to it seconds before the sliding door came to a stop. She held her breath, waiting to see if anyone would come out, pulling her carry-on bag a little further out of view. She didn't think she could handle another chance encounter.

Jo chided herself silently. Was she really going to spend the whole week hiding from Andy? Sadie was wrong. This was so not okay. So not okay at all.

Jessica Rosenberg

6. Andy

The door opened and Andy reached for Emily's hand. "Come on kiddo, time to go."

Emily balked and pulled against him, straining to reach the elevator buttons again. For the third time that day Andy cursed the hotel Kid Club for only accepting kids who were 3 and up. What kind of stupid rule was that? Weren't parents of two-year-olds allowed to relax a bit too?

"Come on Emily, I'll let you put the key in the door," Andy cajoled with all the enthusiasm of a used car salesman trying to convince a reluctant buyer that the wreck they were looking at was really a Lamborghini under all the rust.

At the promise of her other favorite hotel activity Emily deigned to leave the confines of the elevator and skipped out. She broke into her awkward toddler run and raced away down the hall towards their room, careening out of sight for a moment. Andy heard her kicking a door and hoped that she'd gotten the room right this time. Yesterday she'd woken up their neighbor mid nap and now the guy kept giving them the stink-eye when they ran into him.

He caught up with her in front of their room and

21

hoisted her up so she could slip the key into the lock. The door opened right away, and they tumbled into their suite.

"Okay, tootsie-pop, shoes off. Nap time for you!"

Emily kicked off her sparkly sandals and clambered onto the bed. As soon as she flopped onto her back her eyes started to close. She was so tired. The time change and all the upheaval that they'd been through was wreaking havoc with her sleep at night. She was making up for it with marathon naps during the day. Andy yanked her shorts down and wrestled her soggy diaper off her small body. He worked fast and soon had her ready to drop into her crib. She instantly curled herself around her beloved stuffed duck and popped a pacifier into her mouth. He watched her for a moment, wishing he could fall asleep as fast, but he hadn't been able to sleep easy in years. He brushed her hair from her face and whispered a quiet sleep tight before tiptoeing away to his adjoining room, leaving the door cracked open so he'd hear her if she woke.

7. Sadie

Sadie pounded on the door again.

"Open up, Rox! Come on! I know you're in there!"

After an eternity, the door finally opened a crack and she pushed it wide open. A gust of stale air greeted her, and she wrinkled her nose in disgust. She stepped into the dark room as her friend slipped back into bed and tried to pull the covers over her head. Sadie was having none of it. She yanked the covers back down and walked over to the window.

"Dude! We need to talk. NOW." She barked after throwing the curtains and the window open. She gulped at the fresh air that billowed into the room and turned to face Roxie's hidden form again.

"What time is it?" Roxie grumbled from under the pillow where she'd taken refuge. "It feels way too early."

"It's 11am. You're missing the whole day! Did you seriously come to Hawaii to sleep all day?"

"Be nice, I'm jet lagged." The muffled retort made Sadie snort. They had arrived at the exact same time and she wasn't feeling the effects of the time difference.

"You're hungover, that's not the same thing. Get

up." She grabbed the pillow and pulled it away.

Roxie sat up and dragged her hands through her wavy hair. She instantly looked adorable, like a movie actress playing this exact scene. She peered up at Sadie and pouted.

"Fine, I'm up. What's going on?"

Sadie handed her the hot latte she'd thought to bring up and Roxie grabbed at it like a lifeline. She sipped at it hungrily, blowing on the hot liquid between sips, and waited for Sadie to speak.

"Okay? Awake? Do I have your attention? Put down the coffee."

"Noooo," Roxie whined, tightening her grip on the paper cup.

"Yes. Trust me. Put down the coffee."

Sadie waited until the paper cup was on the nightstand and continued. "He's here. Right here. In the hotel."

"Who? Who's here?" Roxie rubbed at her face, not really focusing on the conversation.

Sadie stifled a sigh and answered. "Andy. Andy is here, in the hotel."

She didn't get the reaction she'd expected. There was no shocked expression, no frantic arm waving, no jumping up in horror. Instead, Roxie looked thoughtful and sad. "I was afraid of that," she murmured, reaching for the coffee she'd just put down.

"WHAhhh?" Sadie managed to say. "What do you mean 'you were afraid of that'? Why are you not surprised?"

Roxie looked embarrassed for a moment, then she whispered, "I knew Andy was coming to Hawaii."

Sadie's jaw dropped open and she stared at Roxie

who squirmed under her unwavering gaze.

"How on earth did you know that Andy was coming to Hawaii?" she finally said.

"He contacted me on Facebook a few months ago. We've been emailing a bit ever since." She took a swig of hot coffee and looked embarrassed for a moment. "I might have maybe told him to come."

"You WHAT?" Sadie yelled. "Why would you do that?" She stared at Roxie, mouth hanging open. They had both been there to pick up the pieces when Andy left Jo. They had both witnessed the devastation of that breakup. She couldn't fathom why Roxie might have thought bringing him to Jo's wedding could possibly be a good idea. "What were you thinking?"

"He deserves to be here. He deserves a second chance. Jo deserves a second chance. Plus, I miss him. And anyway, it was a long time ago. His vacation was already planned; I just let him know we'd also be here."

Roxie's words stopped Sadie mid rant. There was something she didn't know here.

"A second chance at what exactly?"

"We've been chatting. Things didn't end the way we thought back then. There's a lot more to the story. Jo..." She paused, looking down at her hands. "Jo deserves to know everything before..."

"Before she gets married?" Sadie shrieked, throwing her hands up in the air. "No, before she renews her vows. Did you take that into account here? She's already married. No matter what storybook reunion you had in mind it's too late. She's already married to someone else!"

Roxie cowered and let Sadie rant.

"I'm sorry. I've missed him. He was my friend

too. And the way it ended... it was wrong."

Sadie's shoulders slumped forward, and she sat down heavily on the side of the bed.

"Yeah, I've missed him too," Sadie admitted, sitting down on the bed and lowering her head. "It was good to see him this morning."

"You saw him? You talked to him?" Roxie asked, perking up a bit. "How does he look? How is he?"

"He looked good, really good. He had his kid with him. A little girl called Emily. But that's neither here nor there, is it? What are we going to do?"

"What do you mean?"

"Uh, hello! Don't you think we have a situation here? Did you have a plan?" Sadie hated to admit it, but a tiny piece of her was thrilled that Roxie had been so daring. Andy and Jo... They had been a great couple. Jordan was a lovely man, but Andy had been the love of Jo's life.

The two girls looked at each other for a moment then Roxie shrugged.

"I have no idea what comes next. Let me take a shower. I think best in the shower, I'll think of something."

"Hey?" She called back as she pulled the bathroom door open, "Is Jo even here yet?"

"Oh! Crap!" Sadie cried, jumping up from the bed. "Jo! She must be wondering where I went!"

8. Jo

Jo heard Sadie's voice before she saw her come into the room. She'd finally thought to use the phone in the hallway to call the front desk. A sweet hotel employee wearing a bright Hawaiian shirt and flowers in her hair had hurried up from the lobby with a fresh key card. She had let Jo into her room and checked that the room was well stocked with clean towels and cold water. Then, without making a show of waiting for a tip, had quietly excused herself and left Jo to enjoy the calm of her hotel room. She was still lying on the bright bedspread watching the palm leaf fan spin around hypnotically over her head when Sadie burst into the room.

"Jo? Jo? Are you in here?"

"I'm right here," Jo called out to her without moving.

Sadie threw herself onto the much more rumpled twin to Jo's bed, groaning.

"Ugh, when are we getting those massages?" She asked. "Can it be now?"

Jo laughed. The quiet and the fan had helped calm her down and she was feeling a bit more in control. Plus, she kept hearing the cheery sounds of people laughing as they headed to the beach or the pool. It was making her remember why she had chosen Hawaii in the first place.

"No massage yet! First we have to go swim, and see the beach, and, and... Oh! First we have to get some breakfast. I'm starving!" She sat up abruptly.

Sadie lifted her face from the pillow she'd buried it in and stared at Jo. She raised an eyebrow and cocked her head to the side.

"What?" Jo asked her.

"Why are you so cheerful?" Sadie asked slowly.

"Why wouldn't I be? I'm in Hawaii, it's beautiful, and warm, and this hotel is stunning." Jo gestured around the bright room decorated with cheery plumerias and splashes of primary colors. Then she waved at the bright blue sky out the window. "It's a gorgeous day out there!"

"Well, for one, you're getting married in three days," Sadie said.

"Re-married, confirming vows, whatever we're calling it. I'm already married." Jo blushed and hoped that Sadie would think her cheeks were flushed from the heat in the room.

"Ohh-kay," Sadie replied, clearly not convinced by the calm demeanor. "How about the fact that your ex, the guy who broke your heart, the 'one that got away,' is staying here in the hotel, where you're sorta-kinda-maybe-not-really getting married in three days?"

Jo winced at her use of air quotes and shrugged. "Whatever. I'm not going to let that bother me. He moved on and had a kid. I moved on and got married." Plus, she added to herself, with any luck she'd soon be having kids of her own. An Emily of her own. Soon enough. Then they'd be completely even.

"Really? You're really OK with this?" Sadie asked, the worried crease in her forehead smoothing out.

"Yes, I'm fine. Now, how about we go out and enjoy this paradise before my husband and my mother arrive tomorrow to torture us with wedding details?"

9. Jordan

Jordan shivered; he couldn't wait to be in Hawaii relaxing on the beach. He was so done with summer in the city. It was days like this that he longed to be back in Zambia. He wished he could throw open the windows to get some fresh air, but the AC was going full blast and the windows were blocked by the screens anyway. He still hadn't figured out the ridiculous central air console for the house and he didn't have the patience to try again right now. Instead, he reached for a sweatshirt and glared at the vent in the ceiling. Ninety-eight degrees outside and in here his nose was dripping from the cold. So absurd.

The collection of photos on the mantle caught his eye. He and Jo in various poses, dressed in muddy shorts and t-shirts, holding equally muddy shovels, babies, or each other's hands. It was never cold in Zambia he thought. He moved towards the photos, drawn by the memories that they brought back. If he looked closely at Jo's frozen face he could still see the haunted look that had always been present when he had first met her. It had faded slowly over time and he hadn't seen it in a long time. She rarely, if ever, cried in her sleep anymore. He gazed longest at the photo of Jo holding a small orphan. Jo's thin arms encircled the young child and her cheek rested lovingly on his round head. The child was completely oblivious to her embrace, too intently focused on the necklace hanging around her neck to notice. This photo never failed to mesmerize him; the combination of the innocence on the tiny child's face and the peace in Jo's eye was irresistible.

They had found a loving home for that little boy, like they had for so many others. It was the most rewarding part of their jobs, knowing that they had really helped a child find a home where he would be safe and loved. But he had seen how bittersweet it was for Jo to hand these babies off to their new parents. She had felt each loss keenly and needed days to adjust after each departure. He had so hoped that they would finally conceive their own child, a child they would never have to say goodbye to.

He sighed and gave the photo a little tap before finally putting the silver frame down and moving away from the fireplace. He still had a lot of packing to do before the cab came to get him early the next morning.

10. Jo

"Oh, this is the life," Jo mumbled to Sadie, not even bothering to lift her head from the plush towel the pool boy had spread out for her on the lounge chair.

"Mmmmm."

"What time did you say lunch was?"

"I didn't. We just ate our weight in bacon and pancakes. How can you possibly want more food?" Sadie replied more clearly. Jo looked up in time to notice that Sadie had sat up and was frantically waving to someone on the other side of the pool. Jo's heart skipped a beat as her stomach lurched into her throat.

"Ugh, I'm so full of it," Jo thought to herself. "Where's all my bravery when faced with reality? Huh?" She held her breath and forced herself to look in the direction Sadie was looking. A familiar svelte figure was making her way gingerly towards the pool, shielding her face and golden head of wavy curls from the sun with a magazine and a scowl.

"ROXIE!" Jo shouted as she jumped to her feet. "Sadie! Why didn't you tell me she was already here?"

"I wanted it to be a surprise," Sadie answered with a smug look on her face.

Jo bounced towards her tall, gorgeous friend and

hurled herself into her arms, well aware that every eye at the pool was on them, wondering if Roxie was famous or just looked like she should be.

"It is so good to see you!" Jo said, then when she noticed Roxie wincing she murmured, "You look amazing. I've missed you so much!"

Roxie hugged Jo back hard, lifting her off the ground and spinning her around.

"Careful girls, you're going to fall into the pool," Sadie warned from the safety of her chair, where she'd retreated with a huge sloppy smile.

"Sadie, seriously, how did you pull this off? I thought Rox couldn't get here until the day before the wedding?" Roxie's job as a model took her to exotic locations all over the world and she'd been overseas ever since Jo had come home. It was a miracle that she'd been able to get away for the wedding, let alone arrive early.

Both Roxie and Sadie laughed. "Come on, it wouldn't be much of a bachelorette party without the other maid of honor, right?" Roxie teased and then laughed even harder at the face Jo made.

"Come on, people, I'm an old married woman. I'm not exactly entitled to a bachelorette party."

"Hey, lady. Your mom gets a wedding, we get a party. Fair's fair," Sadie said.

Jo laughed this time and acquiesced. "Fair enough. Why should she have all the fun, right?"

"Right!" The girls answered in tandem.

"Not that either of you look like you waited for me to party," Jo teased, making a pointed reference to the way Roxie was trying desperately to shield her eyes from the glare of the sun. "Did you two have fun last night?"

"Ugh," Roxie groaned. "You know what I need? I need a little hair of the dog. Excuse me sir," she called towards the nearest pool boy, "Could I please have three Mai Tais?"

"Three?" Jo asked.

"What? You didn't think I was going to party alone, did you?"

Jo laughed again and leaned back onto her lounge chair. She looked at her two closest friends and then at the gorgeous view spread out in front of her. It was just maybe possible that this was going to be okay. Wait. No, it was possible that this was going to be better than just okay. In fact, with these two by her side this had the potential to be a memorable week, not quite the week she'd anticipated, but memorable nonetheless.

11. Jordan

Jordan's phone bleeped and he struggled to get it out of his jeans pocket before the caller hung up. He still hadn't gotten used to having the thing with him. At least not enough to remember to take it out of his pocket before he buckled himself into the car. He also couldn't get used to being constantly reachable and in fact frequently "forgot" to turn it on. As rebellions went it was feeble, but it made him feel a tiny bit in control.

"Hi Maryanne, what's up?" He asked into the phone after finally getting it out and flipping it open.

"Jordan! Have you left yet?" His mother in law was breathless and he could picture her caught in a last minute packing frenzy.

"I'm on my way. I'll be in front of your building in fifteen minutes."

"Oh, darn. I was hoping I had a few more minutes. I'm all out of sunscreen and I wanted to run to the corner store." Her anxiety echoed down the line, making him smile. She worried about the littlest things sometimes.

"I'm sure it'll be okay. You know, it's Hawaii, not the moon. They'll have sunscreen. They know all about sun protection. In fact, I bet that the hotel even has a convenience store. You won't have any trouble finding good sunscreen."

"Oh, I'm sure you're right. Right then, I'll be outside waiting for you when you get here." He wasn't convinced that he'd appeased her in the least and with a glance at the clock, relented. They had a bit of time to spare.

"It's okay. Go to the store. I'll pick you up there and drive you back home so we can get your bags."

Jordan smiled as he snapped his phone shut and dropped it in the center console of the car. Her tangible relief at this new plan had flown through the phone line. He knew she was a nervous wreck. If buying some sunscreen helped her to relax it was no skin off his nose. He'd factored in extra time for them to get to the airport. He'd had a hunch they'd be running late.

12. Jo

This is so good. I mean so, so good," Sadie said. Roxie and Jo laughed. She'd had all of half of her Mai Tai and she was already clearly drunk.

"I can't believe what a lightweight you are," Jo teased her. "Seriously, did we not eat enough alcohol absorbing carbs for you this morning?"

"'Parently not," she mumbled, putting her drink down on the ground and lowering her head. "I need a widdle nap." Roxie pelted her with a wet towel, but Sadie never looked up, which made the other two, also a little worse for the wear, laugh hysterically.

"Lightweight!" Jo said again, but all she got in reply was a light snore. "Hey, Rox, ready for a dip?" She'd been eying the sparkling blue water of the hotel pool ever since they'd sat down and couldn't wait any longer to see if it felt as good as it looked. Jo's main goal for her time in Hawaii, aside from getting remarried and all that, was to spend as much time in the water as possible. Swimming was something she rarely got to do now that she was back in the States and she missed it terribly.

"Oh, you go ahead," Roxie said looking off somewhere in the distance. "I'll hold the fort over here with our friendly neighborhood lush."

"Got your eye on some hottie already?" Jo teased as she turned to look at what Roxie was staring at on the other side of the pool. The chuckle died in her throat.

Andy.

Still breathtakingly handsome after all this time.

"Breathe Jo," Roxie murmured. "Just breathe."

Jo closed her eyes and took in a deep breath. "I can do this," she thought to herself. "I'm over him. Our story ended badly. He hurt me. But all that was in the past. The way, way past." The image of his bright eyes looking lovingly down at her popped into her mind and her heart jumped in her chest. She reminded herself sternly that she was a happily married woman, here to proclaim to the world that she was head over heels in love with her husband and proud to yell it on the rooftops. She breathed in again and steadied herself.

"Emily! NO! You wait for Daddy before you get in the pool! And you, hurry up would ya?"

That name again. That voice again.

"Jo, you okay?" This time it was Sadie's soft voice that Jo heard. Roxie must have prodded her awake. She nodded briefly and focused on her breathing.

"Here he comes," one of them whispered.

Jo forced herself to open her eyes and act as normal as possible. She lifted her drink to her suddenly parched lips and tried not to drain the glass in one gulp. Her legs felt like jelly and she was relieved that she hadn't had time to get up before noticing Andy on the other side of the pool. This was torture, but there was no way she was going to let Andy see that his mere presence still tore her up inside. Crumbling to the ground would have been a dead giveaway.

By the time Andy had made his way to their side. Jo was more or less composed and to anyone but her two closest friends she looked the picture of a happy, relaxed woman enjoying her Hawaiian vacation. They, of course, could hear her heart pound, and see how hard she was clutching at her glass. They even knew that the beads of sweat lining her face had nothing to do with the heat. Jo took another swallow and hoped the extra alcohol would kick in soon enough. She forced her fingers to relax a bit.

Andy, entirely focused on the toddler hell bent on following her brother into the water, hadn't even noticed the festive trio. In fact, he'd dumped all of his family's belongings on a lounge chair one away from theirs without even looking in their general direction. He sat down with a thump and pulled the squirming child towards him.

Jo couldn't tear her eyes away from the little girl. Her golden curls glinted in the sunlight and her pink cheeks looked like tiny ripe apples. When she turned to speak to her father Jo noticed a neat row of tiny white teeth and an enchanting smile. The stress melted on Andy's face as the smile worked its magic on him.

Her heart ached as she watched the two interact. That should have been her baby making his face soften like that. Her heart skipped a beat and the air suddenly felt solid. She felt a scream building, fighting with the air trying to make its way in. She couldn't stand to be there any longer. She had to get away from them.

She looked to Roxie, hoping for a possible escape route, but her friend just shrugged and looked over at Sadie, who just looked a bit panicked and green around the gills.

Unable to get up and run, Jo settled for taking in shaky breath after shaky breath, willing her heart to slow down, unable to tear her eyes away from Andy despite the physical pain it was causing her. She'd been wrong earlier, she thought, as little details started to appear. He had changed. There was more gray in his hair and a fine network of lines on his forehead. His shoulders stooped a bit more than she remembered. A stab of pity ripped through her. The years hadn't been easy on him either.

"No! I will not feel sorry for him! What he did was despicable and unforgivable! He brought this on himself!" Anger gave Jo the guts that the alcohol had failed to provide. She sat up and took a deep breath.

"Hi Andy," she said, just barely loud enough for him to hear. Jo hadn't counted on how hard he was concentrating on the wriggling child he was trying to squeeze into some sort of flotation device. Even though she was less than a foot away he still hadn't noticed, or even heard her.

Jo took an even deeper breath and waited until he was done. As soon as Emily was safely encased in multiple layers of inflated plastic and foam, he let go of her arm and she bounced towards the pool. They both watched her stop at the edge and gingerly sit on the edge. After a moment she delicately dipped her toes in and pulled them back out hastily before tucking them under her. After all that fuss, she was afraid to get too close to the water.

A slightly hysterical giggle escaped Jo's throat and she finally had Andy's attention.

"That kid..." His voice trailed away as he turned his head and took in her face. His jaw dropped, closed, dropped again. Color drained from his face. His throat bulged as he gulped. And finally, he was able to speak. "Jo... Joanne..."

She winced at the use of her given name. Jo hated that her mother had essentially named her after herself. Andy should have known that.

"Oh. Sorry, I forgot." He grimaced and Jo smiled wryly back. "How is the delightful Maryanne these days?" He asked with a pained frown. "Oh, sorry. I guess I should ask you how you are first."

"She'll be here tomorrow. You can ask her yourself. And me? Well, yeah, that would have been a more appropriate question." Jo's anger flashed brighter. That's what he came up with first? Seriously? Her mother? What about sorry? What about her? What about... GAH! She clenched her hands into tight fists and resisted the urge to throw her drink in his face. No way was she going to make this easy on him, no matter how many glares Sadie and Roxie sent her way.

13. Andy

Andy looked at Jo, shocked at her anger and hostility. Wasn't he entitled to a bit of compassion from her? Considering the way he'd been treated she should be groveling right now, not shooting daggers at him with her eyes. The anger that threatened to overwhelm him ran head on into the emotions that flooded him as he took in the face he had loved for so long.

He had missed her for years. He had no desire to turn this dream encounter into something he'd eventually regret.

He took a deep breath and pushed the anger away, "Fine, then. How are you doing? What brings you to Hawaii this summer?"

He knew full well why she was there, but he didn't want to seem like a pining loser who'd kept up with her every movement since they'd last seen each other. He had some pride still.

"Well, if you must know," she replied, shoulders hunched and fists clenched, but still meeting his gaze. "I'm getting married."

He knew she was married, knew why she was on the island, but her words still ripped open the gaping hole in his heart that he had thought finally healed. He took in a sharp breath and forced himself to look at Emily, still kicking her feet in the water, splashing Hunter who kept swimming up to her and darting away. I will not cry. I will not cry. I have shed more than enough tears over this woman. I will not cry. One deep breath and he was able to look back up at Jo without losing control and without needing to blink back tears.

"Oh, really? Who's the lucky man?" He said with a half-smile he hoped didn't look like an anguished spasm.

Jo looked at him, head tilted at a tiny angle, as though something she was seeing didn't quite compute, some of the anger faded from her eyes. Had she noticed? She looked away and fidgeted for a moment before answering.

"Well, actually, we're just renewing our vows. We've been married for five years."

That, he hadn't known. He'd never thought to ask how long she'd been married. Andy felt the slight hold he had on his anger give. Fury bubbled to the surface, taking with it on the way the bitterness he had harbored for years.

"You've been married for five years? What the fuck! Did you run away and marry the first asshole you met?" Andy might have been shocked at intensity of the anger that took over his voice, but clearly not as shocked as Jo. She reeled back visibly, her face flooding red, her eyes flashing in anger.

"Who the hell are you to judge me?" She replied jumping up from her seat and gesturing to the kids playing in the pool. "What did you do, knock up the first girl you saw after you left me to die?"

"Left. You?" Andy had to force the words

through his clenched teeth. He was shaking as hard as Jo by now, just barely controlling his rage enough to keep his children from getting nervous. "To. Die?"

"Yes! Left me!" Tears streamed unchecked down Jo's bright flaming cheeks. "As if I could forget!" Without grabbing any of her stuff, she turned and ran, sprinting for the hotel doors.

Andy's hands dropped to his side, anger fizzled to nothing, replaced by a melancholy he could not place. He turned to look at the stricken friends who hadn't missed a word of the altercation. He glanced to make sure the kids were still oblivious to the drama.

"What did she mean?" He asked, shocked by the implication of her words. "Why does she think I'm the one who left her?"

14. Sadie

Sadie gaped, staring at Andy as though she had never seen him before. What was his deal? What was up with the anger? He was the one who had left Jo without looking back. He was the one who had never come to visit in the hospital, never called. He had even changed his number for fuck's sake. What was he so bent out of shape about?

She was the one who had picked up the pieces of her broken friend. She knew she wasn't remembering things wrong. In fact, she remembered all too well. But the despair on his face didn't make any sense. Neither did the tears pooling in the corners of his eyes.

"Andy? What do you mean? I was there, you did leave her."

Andy didn't answer, he just sat down heavily and dropped his face into his hands, shoulders hunched against the world.

"Daddy? Daddy? What wrong?"

Andy didn't look up and, after an awkward moment, Roxie jumped up and went to distract the little girl. Sadie heard them chatting but didn't focus on what they were saying. She couldn't take her eyes off of Andy. What was protocol here? Should she run after her best friend or give her a chance to cool off? Should she do something to comfort her old friend? She'd spent so long thinking of him as the bad guy, she just didn't know what to do.

His shoulders slowly unclenched, but still, he didn't look up.

"Andy?" She tried again, but he just shook his head.

"That's not what happened. I mean, I can see why she might think that. But that's not what happened at all." He shook his head. His gaunt face void of color froze the words on Sadie's lips. "It doesn't matter anyway, does it? It's too late now."

He stood up as though the weight of the world had settled on his shoulders and turned his attention to the pool. "Kids, come on. It's time to go." They started to protest, but he didn't listen, just threw their belongings in the bag, and started walking away. The little boy jumped out of the pool and grabbed Emily's hand. She resisted him for just a moment, but finally caved when she realized her father hadn't stopped to wait. The two little kids hurried after their father, dripping water as they rushed to catch up, picking up the items that were spilling out of his bag as they ran.

"What was that all about?" Roxie asked, coming back to her towel.

"I have absolutely no clue," Sadie replied, watching the three of them walk away. "No clue at all."

15. Jo

Jo rushed past the lobby to the emergency stairs. She couldn't stand to wait for the elevator, couldn't stop moving as far away as possible. The nerve! Seriously. What did he think? That she'd mope and wait for him forever? He had made it abundantly clear that he had wanted nothing more to do with her. He hadn't wanted her. He hadn't wanted their child. He hadn't wanted their Emily.

She bit back a sob and ran faster up the stairs. The hotel hadn't wasted a cent decorating stairs they assumed no one other than hotel staff would ever use. Concrete walls surrounded her on all sides, scraping her shoulders as she careened around corners too fast and bumped against the wall. The cement stairs were equally rough under her feet, giving her the traction she needed to go faster and faster. Her calves shrieked under the strain, but she pushed harder, taking the next steps three at a time, hands gripping the cool painted metal handrails on either side of her to maintain her balance. Jo just wanted to get into her bed. Bed. Bed. Bed. She couldn't let herself think about that time. She had to put all that behind her. She had found a man who loved her. A man who wanted her. A man who was desperate to have children with her.

The next sob escaped unbidden. Children. Why had it been so easy for her to get pregnant back then and so hard now? It was so unfair. Even more unfair that Andy had had two more children since. Two. When she and Jordan couldn't seem to even make one.

Jo replayed the doctor's answers in her head as she always did when the despair threatened to engulf her. Nothing wrong with either of you. No physical reason why you can't conceive. It'll happen. Give it time. Time. Time. Time. Another flight of stairs vanished beneath her. Another plain placard next to the door flashed a number as she rushed by. 4th Floor. Why was this hotel so damn big? Why was their room so damn high? Both of her legs wobbled, but Jo pushed on, desperate to get to the safety of her room.

Another sob escaped. Oh, Andy. Why did you leave me? Why did you walk away from me when I needed you most? I was so broken. I was so sad. I lost everything that day and you just left.

By the time Jo reached the landing to the 7th floor tears were cascading unchecked down her face and her sobs were echoing around the concrete stairwell. She put her hands on the heavy metal fireproof door and in a flash realized that in her haste she'd left her hotel key tucked into the beach bag she'd left by the pool. The little light at the top of the keypad next to the door blinked red on and off, a cruel reminder that the door would remain locked as long as she had no key to make it glow green. That damn key. Even though Jo's bed was just a few feet away it could have been on Mars and she wouldn't have been farther from its warm cocoon.

Jo stepped back from the door and sank onto the

first step to the next landing when her heels bumped up against it. She rested her head on the rough wall. The coolness of the concrete soothed her burning forehead even as the uneven jags dug into her tender skin. It wasn't really painful, but it was enough to send her over the edge. She gave in fully to wave of sorrow that had been building in her chest from the moment she had first heard Andy's voice the day before. She embraced the tears and the emotions that overwhelmed her, and she cried like she should have cried back then, gut wrenching sobs that shook her small frame.

16. Andy

Andy held the door open for his children and shooed them in. Emily dashed to her stack of toys in the corner of their cluttered room and started to play. She sat with her back to them, but Andy could tell from the hunch in her shoulder that she was focused on him and waiting to see what he would do. Hunter threw himself into the corner of the couch and balled himself around his game console. He too was restless, glancing over the electronic toy every few minutes to see what his father was doing.

But Andy wasn't doing anything. Just standing still, staring out the window without blinking. He didn't know what to do next. He didn't know what to think. Didn't know what to feel. He kept expecting all the old pain to rush in and fill the void it had left behind, but there was nothing but numbness and the overwhelming urge to flee. Even the most beautiful view he had ever seen wasn't countering that urge.

"Dad? Who was that? What were you fighting about?" Hunter spoke softly.

Andy didn't reply, just shook his head a bit and went back to staring at the glittering expanse of ocean that stretched as far as the eye could see.

"But, Dad? What was she so mad about?"

Andy turned to look at Hunter, blankly at first, for a second he almost didn't recognize the tan sandy haired boy looking at him so intently. He shook his head and his gaze clicked back into focus. He gave his son a half smile and made a snap decision. Coming here knowing that she'd be here had been a terrible idea. He headed to the closet and threw the doors open before replying.

"She was..." His mind went blank again for a minute. How could he explain this to a five year old when he could barely explain it to himself? He took a deep breath and continued "She's an old friend from Daddy's past. We were very close once. Then we had a big fight a long time ago. I guess we haven't gotten over it."

"You always tell me to be nice to my friends. Were you mean to her?"

Andy paused. Had he been mean? He had done the only thing possible at the time. He had done what he thought was right.

"I don't know buddy. I didn't think I was being mean. But sometimes we can be mean without realizing it."

"You also always tell me to say I'm sorry. Did you tell her you were sorry?"

Hunter's innocent questions were like lemon juice being rubbed into an already painful wound. They made Andy's urge to run even stronger than before.

"I tried. I really tried to say sorry. But it..." He didn't know how to finish that thought. Had he tried? Had he really tried hard enough? He just didn't remember any more. At the time he had felt so justified, so right. Now he just didn't know.

He leaned into the closet to pull out their large suitcase and threw it on the bed. He flung the bag open and started throwing their things into it. His thoughts wandered further. He should really find a way to tell Roxie he was leaving. He hadn't even had a chance to really say hi in person.

"Dad? What are you doing? Why are you packing?" Hunter's voice cracked and a whine threatened to break through.

"We're leaving. We... can't stay here. Bring me your things please." Hunter started to cry, immediately echoed by Emily.

"Noooooo. We just got here! I haven't even really been in the pool! We haven't ever gone in the ocean yet!"

"Hunter! Please!" Andy fought the urge to yell and instead just sighed loudly.

"Daddy. No! You please! Why do we have to leave?"

Andy closed his eyes and took a deep shuddering breath. All his emotions were crashing into each other and it was just making it all that much harder to think rationally. He had loved her so deeply and he had thought he had done the right thing. But what if he'd been wrong? What if he had been so very wrong?

He looked down at his tearful children, children who wouldn't be here if he hadn't made the decision he had made and felt a lump form in his throat. They had no part in this. Like everything else in their lives, they were just innocent bystanders getting caught in the crossfire.

He sank to his knees and opened his arms wide. "I'm sorry. I'm sorry guys." Hunter and Emily, now sobbing hard, rushed into his embrace.

"Daddy? Why crying?" Emily asked again putting her hands on her daddy's face and kissing his scratchy cheek gently. Hunter hugged him hard, patting his back the way he had always done to him when he was sad.

Andy smiled through his tears. They were so real. He hugged them both close. They'd been through so much already this year. The last thing they needed was more drama they didn't understand.

Andy swallowed a sob and sniffed back more tears. "You guys want to stay? Really?"

"Yes!" They both shouted, jumping up and down and clapping, tears drying on their cheeks. Andy smiled wider. He loved seeing them happy, hated seeing them cry.

"Fine. We'll stay. Don't worry any more. It'll be okay."

"Daddy?" Hunter said, pausing his gleeful dance for a moment.

"Yeah, buddy?"

"What about your friend? Are you going to try to say sorry again?"

Andy looked down at his astute little boy and shrugged.

"Maybe. If she lets me. Let's see how it goes. Deal?"

17. Jo

Jo leaned against the cool wall and took a deep shuddering breath. She was all cried out. Drained. Her eyes felt swollen and her face felt sticky. She turned her head to put her burning forehead on the wall. The cold felt soothing despite the roughness of the concrete, but she knew it was just making a bad situation worse. Now she'd be bright red with scratches instead of just bright red.

It was easier to focus on how frightful she must look than to take stock of the ridiculous situation she had just placed herself in. She was stuck at the top of a stairwell without a key. She probably looked like a freak. And she had zero desire to head back down to the pool to collect her things.

The mere thought of facing Andy again— letting him see how much seeing him had affected her—made her shudder. He didn't need to know he still had this kind of effect on her. She took another deep breath and felt her whole body convulse with a massive sob. Amazingly enough, despite the dread of running into Andy again, she felt better. Like all those tears had been bottled up for way too long. She felt almost cleansed. She pulled her forehead off the wall and turned around, so she was leaning back against it. She rested her head back and sighed deeply.

This was good. She had needed to get this all out. Had needed to mourn her past one last time so she could get past it once and for all. Had that crying been enough though? Was she over it? If she were really over it she probably could get up and go get her key. Right?

She stayed put.

A soft cough startled her and sent a jolt of fear through her. She hadn't heard anyone come up. She hesitated to open her eyes, scared to see who was standing there. What if... her heart jumped into her throat. So much for being over anything.

She cracked an eye open and was flooded with relief at the sight of a ridiculously good looking young man who was in no way at all Andy.

"I'm sorry, I didn't mean to disturb you. Are you stuck? These fireproof doors don't open from the stairwell if you don't have a key."

Jo snorted. "You know, I noticed that. I just hadn't quite figured out what I was going to do about it. You're just in the nick of time." Another sob escaped, startling the young man.

"Are you okay?" He asked with a worried look on his face. Tears welled in her eyes and she shook her head. She had no idea if he was worried she was going to burst into tears or if his question came from pure empathy. Either way, it made her want to sob all over again.

"Yeah," Jo lied, swiping at her eyes with the back of her hand and patting her cheeks in a halfhearted effort to cool them down. The young man raised an eyebrow. "I'm fine. Well, no, clearly I'm not okay," she corrected, gesturing needlessly towards her wrecked face, "but I'm going to be fine."

"You sure?" He asked, moving away slightly.

The thought that her kind stranger was going to vanish without rescuing her freed the tears she had been holding back.

"Uh huh. Yup, going to be just fine." She snarfled back tears and noticed that he didn't recoil in disgust. Instead, he moved her legs aside gently and sat down beside her.

"You want to talk about it? I've been told I'm a decent listener."

Despite her tears Jo couldn't help laughing. Was this guy for real? Was he trying to pick her up? Here? In this depressing stairwell while she cried her eyes out? He gave her a half of a nervous smile.

"Don't worry. I'm not hitting on you," he said, smile growing into something real. "You just look like you could use a friendly ear right now." The sincerity in his voice made Jo look a little closer. She saw echoing sadness reflected in his eyes. She shuddered again. He looked too young to be sad like her. Most people their age did. She made the split second decision to trust her gut. This was no freak weirdo.

"Hi, my name is Jo." She held her hand out to him. "If you're going to see me at my worst you might as well know my name. Right?"

"Aloha, Jo. My name is Kona, just like the city and the coffee. My parents..." He shrugged. "So, what's making you so sad even being in paradise isn't enough to cheer you up? Tell me everything, though you might have to talk fast. I have about ten minutes before my shift starts."

Jo laughed. It would take a few more than ten minutes to share her miserable story. She looked over at the guy again. He hadn't struck her as a hotel employee. Then again, everyone out here was wearing Hawaiian shirts, she hadn't looked closely enough to recognize that his was the same one she had noticed the waiters wearing earlier.

"Do you work here? In the hotel?"

"Yeah, I'm one of the bartenders. It's not the most glamorous work, but..." Kona let the sentence trail off with a quick shrug. Jo had the feeling that, like his name, there was more to the story, but she let him change the subject. "How about you, what brings you here?"

"I'm getting married," Jo said sadly. "I'm getting married to the man who came to my rescue and put me back together after my first love left me after I miscarried a baby he never even wanted."

"Oh?" Kona raised an eyebrow, clearly not impressed with her story so far.

"That's where the story gets good. That first love? The man who broke my heart? He's here. In the hotel. With his kids."

18. Jo

It had been one of those perfect spring days that make you feel like dancing or bursting into song along with the delirious sparrows. Bright flowers were blooming right and left in a breathtaking display of primary colors. The air was pleasantly warm with a promise of warmer days to come. Jo had been enjoying the feel of the warm breeze on her bare arms. It had been months since she'd been able to be outside without a jacket, let alone without a sweater. She had felt so carefree walking around in just a cute little sundress. Everything just smelled fresh and new after weeks of rain, full of possibility and rebirth. Jo had skipped home from the doctor's office, over the moon about everything.

She had just learned she was pregnant. Pregnant.

Her face had broken into a smile. They were going to have a baby. A baby. A teeny weeny little baby.

The birds had chirped as loud as possible, equally thrilled with the promise floating in the air and Jo had hurried home along the busy streets. All the shop owners had thrown their doors wide open to let in some of the fresh spring breeze. People had greeted each other from the entrances and shouted hellos to friends walking down the street. Jo had just smiled and nodded at everyone.

A bright storefront had caught Jo's eye and stopped her in her tracks. Sweet children's things were piled high in disarray, waiting to be organized into a springtime display. She had stopped and stared, taking in the tiny shoes with big bows and small frilly dresses. Would they be buying dresses or slacks? She wondered, looking over at the pile of navy pants and checkered shirts. Would it be all soccer balls and dinosaurs or ribbons and frills? Jo had placed her hand on her still very flat belly and smiled even wider. It didn't matter; either had been fine by her. She had waved at the salesgirl who had stared at her through the glass and walked on.

"I'm home!" Jo had called, pushing the front door open. "Hey, Andy? Where are you?"

"In the den!" He had called back from the next room, the only room in their tiny closet of an apartment. It was the same joke he had made every day they'd lived in the place, but for once Jo had laughed.

"Wow. You must be in a good mood," he had said, poking his head around the door. "What's up?"

Jo had taken a deep breath, suddenly shy. Her stomach had twisted. What if he wasn't happy about this? What if he got all pragmatic? This wasn't exactly a planned pregnancy and it wasn't as if they were married.

"So... you know how I've been so sick?"

"Yeah? Kinda hard to ignore all the throwing up you've been doing." Andy's forehead had creased in worry as he waited for her to go on.

"Well..., it's not a stomach bug."

"Great!" Relief had washed over his face, but just as he'd turned to go back to what he was doing, he'd spun back towards her. "Wait, what is it then? Is it bad? Why are you crying?"

"I'm crying?" Jo had asked touching her sopping wet cheeks. "Oh, look at that! I'm crying."

"What's wrong? Why are you crying?" Andy had moved towards her in one step and grabbed her arms, peering intently into her face.

"I don't know why I'm crying. I'm not sad. I'm thrilled." Jo had looked Andy straight in the eyes. "We're having a baby."

"We... we're what?" His face had paled, and he had stumbled a few feet before catching his balance on the armrest of a chair. Jo had held her breath as he stared, unspeaking, into the distance. She'd seen horror and fear cross his face and slowly, she'd seen anger replace both of those emotions.

"The hell we are!"

The sheer anger in his voice had sent Jo reeling, her happy tears suddenly congealed in her throat, choking her. She hadn't known what to expect, though she'd let herself hope for at the very least some muted excitement. She'd never expected anger. She had watched Andy pace, face flushed and hands clenching. She had hesitated and then rushed on.

"No, really, we're having a baby. I'm eight weeks along. I saw the heartbeat and everything."

Andy had whirled at her words and stared her down, eyes flashing in anger. Jo hadn't been able to detect a trace of the loving tender man she knew so well. She had shrunk farther away from him, grabbing a cushion and holding it tightly, suddenly scared.

"This can't happen. We can't have a baby. We don't even have enough to live on ourselves. How the hell are we supposed to take care of a baby! I don't even want kids! No. No. No." Andy had kicked the couch hard, making Jo jump. "This isn't happening. Not today, not ever. You're just going to have to take care of it."

Jo had peered at him from behind the cushion, tears streaming down her face, shocked by his words. She had silently willed him to start acting differently, to unclench his hands and shoulders, sit down beside her and hold her gently, to turn back into the man she loved. But after kicking the couch hard two more times he'd stormed out of the apartment, slamming the door behind him.

19. Jo

Jo looked over at Kona to see if he was still listening or if she was boring him to tears, but he was looking at her and nodding her on. For a moment she had been completely transported back to that time. She had been so young and so scared, and she had felt so alone sitting there on that couch, waiting to see if Andy would come back.

"Then what happened?" Kona's soft voice drew Jo back before she slipped back into that day.

Jo shrugged. "He came back eventually, hours later, all apologetic and loving, but still adamant that we couldn't have the baby. He kept trying to tell me how much he loved me and how scared he was that this would be the end of us. I couldn't even bring myself to speak to him for days. He finally came around when he realized that he had to choose. It was baby and me or neither of us. The baby and I won."

Once Andy had come around it had been like night and day. He had become obsessed with the baby. When they had learned that they were having a little girl he went nuts. He bought her toys and dresses, fancy things that babies never really wear.

"I don't know where he found the cash, I never

dared ask, I knew we didn't have it in the bank. But it didn't matter, I was just thrilled that he was so on board, that I wouldn't be having a baby by myself."

Kona nodded.

It had been a dream come true. Everything a girl dreams of; a supportive partner, solidly by her side during the most stressful event of a lifetime. He had come to all the doctor's appointments. They had even started talking about how they were going to decorate the baby's corner of their room.

"We didn't have enough space for her to have her own room, though we did joke about turning our tiny closet into a nursery. Actually, we really joked about turning one of the drawers in the closet into a bed for her. It was pretty much all the space we had."

"Huh." Kona's response was a little less encouraging this time.

"What?" Jo asked. She felt a flicker of annoyance at being interrupted when she had finally gotten to the happy part of her memory.

"It's just... he was really happy about all this? It seems odd that he would do a complete 180 like that."

"I don't know if he was really happy or if it was just an act. To be honest, I didn't want to question his enthusiasm and he pretended really well. There were some signs that he wasn't entirely convinced, but I never brought myself to bring them up with him."

"Like?"

"He wasn't really sleeping much. I'd wake up in the middle of the night and find him wide awake. I think he spent a lot of nights worrying about money. It was the one thing we still argued about a lot."

"Oh, so it wasn't all rainbows and sunshine?"

Kona looked a little less skeptical.

It was funny, but Jo had forgotten about the arguments. It was easier to remember the happy part of it all. But they had argued a fair amount. Every time Jo bought something for the baby Andy would freak out. He could buy stuff, but if she did he went ballistic. It was the same thing every time they talked about Jo not going back to work. That argument really sent him over the edge. Until yesterday, it was actually the last conversation they'd ever had.

"I was almost 6 months along and really starting to show, so people at work were already teasing me that they'd almost seen the last of me. We'd been looking into daycare, but I can't say that I wasn't toying with the idea of quitting and working for myself. I came home that day bursting with excitement about a project idea a coworker and I had been bantering around. It would have been great. We would both have been able to make a ton of money and stay home with our kids."

Jo had rushed home to tell Andy, but he wouldn't even listen, just started yelling at her that they didn't have the kind of money it took to start new businesses and that she'd already have her hands full with the baby and work. She had tried to reason with him, calm him down, show him their notes and share their idea, but he just got madder and madder until he had finally stormed out of the apartment, slamming the door so hard half the books on their one bookshelf had fallen off. She hadn't seen him that angry since the day she had told him she was pregnant.

"Way to overreact."

"Yeah. But, I never even had time to wonder why he lost it like that. I bent down to pick up the books and it felt like something ripped inside me. The pain was so bad I just fell on the floor. I don't remember much of what happened after that. Apparently the neighbor heard all the yelling and the door slam, then she came over to see if I was okay. I guess when Andy slammed it shut it flew right back open. She knocked a couple of times and called my name, but when I didn't reply she came in to see if she could find me. She says she expected to find me crying, instead she found me out cold, lying in a pool of blood." Jo shuddered.

"Jeez. That's horrible."

"Yeah. She called 911 and they rushed me to the hospital. They were obviously able to save me, but there was nothing they could do for the baby. I hemorrhaged so badly; they said she drowned in all that blood."

"Oh, man, I'm so sorry. That's just awful."

"I'm lucky. At least they were able to save my uterus. In theory I should be able to have more children."

"In theory?"

"Yeah, Jordan and I have been trying, but nothing has worked so far."

"Wait, who's Jordan?"

"Jordan would be my husband."

"What? Now I'm really confused. I thought you said you were here to get married."

"Remarried. We're here to have the wedding ceremony we never had. But that's a whole other story."

"Okay. Okay. Moving on. We'll get to that later. Tell me what happened after the baby died."

Jo looked at Kona, surprised that he was so interested, but he looked at her and gestured for her to continue.

"Andy never came to the hospital. He never called. Never sent flowers. Nothing."

It had been like he hadn't even existed. No one talked about him, no one would tell Jo anything when she asked about him, they just changed the subject. When Jo was finally released from the hospital, weak, tired, and without the infant she had lost, she went back to their apartment only to discover that every trace of him was gone. Someone had scrubbed the place so well that she couldn't find any sign that he'd ever lived there with her or that she'd almost died there just a few days before.

"He'd even cleaned out any sign of the baby. All of the stuff we'd bought was gone. All the pregnancy books. My vitamins, my maternity clothes. Everything was gone. It was so surreal, like none of it had ever happened. The only proof that I hadn't lost my mind and made it all up was I had was the incision on my belly and a tiny baby sock that I found under my pillow when I went to bed. I have no idea how it got there."

"Oh, Jo, wow. That's heavy shit. I don't know what   to   say."

"Sorry. I should have warned you it was a sad story."

"No, that's okay. I'm glad you were able to tell me." Kona patted her arm awkwardly and glanced quickly at his watch.

"Oh! I'm so sorry! You said you had to get back to work and I talked your ear off!"

"Eh," Kona shrugged." "No worries. This place is pretty laid back. My coworkers will cover for me until I get there. I'll go in a few minutes. I'll just tell my boss I was rescuing a damsel in distress." He shot her a heart stopping smile and squeezed her arm gently. "So, that was it? No more Andy after that?"

"Nope, no more Andy. Though I did get an odd postcard from him about 6 months later. It was sent to my workplace, the picture of a baby on a pink blanket. It wasn't signed or anything, but it said 'I miss you. More than you'll ever know.'"

"Odd. You sure it was from him?"

"Who else would have sent that? Though for a while, I kinda thought I might have sent it to myself. I was a bit of a mess. You have no idea how I missed that baby. I lost everything that day, my baby, my fiancé, my life as I knew it was gone. Poof."

"What a story!" Kona stood up slowly, apologizing profusely about needing to go. Jo stood up too, rubbing her face. This whole morning had been completely surreal. All she wanted to do was go slide herself into a hot bath and then hide in her bed for the rest of the day.

"Hey, Kona?" Jo said, as he was heading down the stairs. "Thanks. I..."

"Yes?" He paused, one hand on the railing, smiling up at her.

"I... nothing." She smiled back down.

"You're welcome," he answered with a wink. "Hey! Come to my bar later! It's the cheesy Tiki Bar in the lobby. Drinks on me! Time for a little fun, k?"

"You sure? I have to warn you, I'll be with my two best friends and one of them can drink your bar dry."

"No worries! Bring 'em," he called as he bounced down the stairs.

"Hey! Kona!" Jo called down to him.

"Yeah?"

"Uh, could you please come back up and open

the door for me?"

20. Jo

"Hey? Jo? You in here?" Sadie called as she walked in.

"Yup. Right here," Jo called back from the armchair she'd been slumped in ever since Kona had let her into her room. She'd been staring out the window at the ocean spread out beyond the palm trees, thinking of the baby she'd lost, fingering the little sock she always kept with her. When Sadie walked in she tucked the sock into her pocket, but she didn't turn around.

"Dude! Where have you been? I've been looking for you everywhere! I even looked here a while ago. You were definitely not here." Sadie came across the room and stood in front of her, fists on her hips. Her bright curly hair had frizzed even worse in the heat and framed her face like a halo, or a lion's mane. She looked torn, like she couldn't decide whether to be irritated or relieved.

"Yeah. I was with Kona," Jo said, peering up at her friend, one hand shielding her eyes from the sun streaming in through the window behind her. Maybe Sadie's hair looked more like it was on fire, Jo couldn't tell. Either way it was very impressive, even made her friend look a bit intimidating, giving her an aura of strength that was not usually noticeable.

"What? Who?" Sadie threw her hands up in the air and sighed deeply as she threw herself into the matching chair. "Who were you with? Who the heck is Kona?"

Jo lowered her hand. "A bartender here, in the hotel. He found me stranded at the top of the stairwell. I left my key with you guys when I ran off and I couldn't even open the landing door."

"So? What? He opened the door for you? That doesn't explain where you've been for the last hour!"

"I was stranded there for a while before he found me. And, when he did get there, I was a hot mess. He was sweet enough to sit and chat with me for a while."

"Uh, dear? Need I remind you that you're here to get married? And that things are plenty complicated as it is?"

"It wasn't like that at all. Though he is awfully good looking. Scratch that, he's downright hot. Like, we won't be able to keep Roxie off him hot."

"Hey! Why does Roxie always get the guys? I'm cute too!" Sadie chucked a throw pillow at Jo.

"Okay! Fine!" Jo laughed, happy to let the focus of the conversation change. "You can have him. In fact, I think you might be a better match. I couldn't put my finger on it, but he seems to have something he's dealing with too."

"What do you mean?"

"I dunno. He just looked sad."

"Ugh. Roxie can keep him. I'm done with fix-it guys. Anyway, I have my hands full enough with you this week!" Sadie laughed and threw another pillow at her.

Jo caught the pillow before it hit her and let her

mind wander as her best friend launched into the careful analysis of the drama by the pool. Every six months or so Sadie would meet a lovely sweet, somewhat troubled man, and fall head over heels in love. Inevitably she'd have met him when he was in the midst of some crisis or another and she'd hold his hand during the tough times. As soon as her latest flame was back on his feet, both physically and mentally, he'd leave her high and dry. She'd find herself heartbroken all over again with just friends to pick up the pieces.

It had been harder to be Sadie's rock and shoulder from Zambia, but, thanks to spotty internet connections and occasional phone calls, Jo had done the best she could.

"...I think he was crying when he left. You know, manly no tears crying." Sadie's words snagged Jo's wandering attention.

"What? He was crying? What the hell is that all about?"

"I don't know, Jo. His whole reaction was weird. It was like you'd left him and not the other way around. I mean, I know what happened, I was there, but this... I dunno... this was just weird."

Jo thought back to that day when she'd come home and found Andy gone. She hadn't imagined it. She wasn't the one who'd left, she'd been in the hospital, and last she'd checked it was kind of hard to clear out an apartment from a hospital bed, so what was his deal?

"That's odd. But, whatever, right? I mean, it's all water under the bridge. No? I'm married, he has kids. Does it really matter what really happened?" Jo shrugged and then pointedly ignored Sadie's quizzical frown.

"Uh, hun. Sure," Sadie murmured.

Jo could tell she didn't agree, but she was grateful that her friend didn't push the issue. She was even more grateful when she completely changed the subject. Of course, what had happened mattered, but she couldn't change anything about it, so why bother hashing it out?

"Hey, what do you want to do for dinner? It's your last night of freedom. After we eat we're going to party like you're really a bachelorette."

Jo groaned. "Really? I don't think so. I'm so not in the mood for that."

"Yes really! You're a bachelorette. We need to have a party!"

"I'm not a bachelorette. I don't need a party." Sadie's face fell. Jo looked at her best friend's usually sunny face and relented. "Fine. What did you guys have in mind?"

"Nothing naughty, honest. We'll just go out and dance and have a few drinks. Hey, maybe we can go check out this Kona of yours! Come on, we have to have fun! Tomorrow your mom gets here, and things are going to get all tense." Sadie mock shuddered and placed her hands together in a pleading gesture. She turned her face into her most irresistible pout and made little pleading noises for extra effect.

Jo laughed. Sadie wasn't kidding. Her mother was sure to arrive clutching a wad of insane lists and plans. She'd be all business and focus. Jo knew that Sadie was right. All the fun was going to have to happen tonight or wait until the wedding was over.

"Okay, fine, you win. Plus, Kona said he'd get us free drinks," she said, winking at Sadie.

"Oh! You cow! You were totally holding out on

me! I bet you were going to go out on the sly after we went to bed." Sadie hit Jo with another pillow which she promptly threw back at her, pelting her in the face and knocking her off the chair.

21. Andy

Andy watched his kids playing with a helpless little gecko on the balcony and wondered what he should do. Staying here for the duration of their trip was all fine and dandy, even considering Jo's unexpected reaction to seeing him again, but what about when they went home? What then? He sighed deeply, letting himself contemplate their return to reality.

A second ago he had been on the verge of packing up and running for home, but really, what awaited them there was no better than what he faced here. Two different aspects of his past in ruins. Here it was the distant past. There it was the recent past. Equally depressing wherever you looked. Except out there on the dais really.

Emily and Hunter were completely oblivious to their father's thoughts, absorbed by the gecko, chasing him around, trying to block his way with their hands as he tried to scurry to safety. They howled in glee every time the little lizard swatted his tail in annoyance.

"Hey, kids," he called out halfheartedly, loath to put a stop to their fun, but feeling a bit bad for the poor lizard. "You're scaring the little guy. How about giving him a bit of a breather. Don't touch him, k? He's pretty freaked out."

They grumbled a bit but dropped their hands and took a half step back. Their faces fell as the gecko made a mad dash to the topmost corner of the wall. Andy smiled at the looks on their faces. He knew exactly how they felt. He also knew that in a minute they would have found something else to do. He wished every disappointment could be as easily forgotten.

They were good kids, but that didn't make this any easier. What the hell was he going to do with them? Coming to Hawaii had been spur of the moment decision. Something to distract everyone while he figured out some sort of plan. Amber hadn't been exactly the mother of the year, but at least she'd been around some of the time. Her departure had shaken them all up. In Hawaii they could pretend that life at home was exactly the way it had always been, dysfunctional, but consistently so. He wasn't really looking forward to going home and having to face reality. Reality was going to involve lawyers and a whole lot of unpleasantness. For all that he was desperate to get away from what he was dealing with on the island, he was in no hurry to go face what awaited them at home.

He wanted to be mad at Amber. He craved the anger, wanted to feed on it, make himself feel self-righteous. But he couldn't muster the energy. He'd known who he had married. Had known from the beginning. If he were really honest with himself he had spent the last five years expecting her to leave him, he just hadn't expected her to take so long to finally walk.

He focused his attention back on Hunter and Emily. They were starting to squabble over a rock they had found under the lounge chair. He glanced at the clock. 5:00pm. They were verging on the cranky-hungry hour.

"Hey, kids?" He called again. "Who's getting hungry? Want to go get some dinner?"

"YEAH!" They both shouted, running back into the room. "Pizza! Grilled Cheese!" They screamed at the exact same time.

"Okay. Okay. Settle down." He laughed as they swarmed him. "I bet we can find that at the restaurant here."

Kids had a way of forcing you into focusing on the present. As long as they were still here it was pointless to obsess about what would happen when they got back. Here on the island, he'd focus on enjoying his kids and the vacation. And when they got home he'd worry about figuring out the rest of their lives.

22. Jo

Jo peered into the mirror and carefully brushed a thin layer of mascara onto her eyelashes. There wasn't much she could do about swollen puffy bloodshot eyes, but a little powder and some blush could go a long way towards reducing the glaring red blotches that had broken out all over her face as a result of all the crying she'd done earlier.

She hated her sensitive skin. It made it virtually impossible to keep a breakdown private. Hopefully the darkness of the bar would hide the worst of it.

"Hey, Sadie," Jo called from the bathroom. "What top are you wearing tonight?"

"I was thinking of wearing the pink sparkly one. I think it'll look great against my new tan. What do you think?" She asked, walking into the bathroom.

"Oh! Good choice. Looks hot." Jo winked at Sadie.

Jo couldn't believe how tan Sadie had gotten in such a short time. She was the only redhead Jo had ever met who looked beautiful in pink. She was also the only redhead Jo knew who got a tan instead of turning bright pink I n the sun. Jo compared their two faces peering side into the hotel mirror. She was going to look like a ghoul next to her friends. A pale splotchy ghoul. But, as Sadie carefully applied her own mascara, Jo couldn't help but smile. It was hard to stay annoyed at Sadie for long. She was too darn sweet and loving. Sadie smiled back broadly.

"So, tell me more about this Kona guy. Is he really worth all this make-up?"

"Ha! I knew you were interested!" Jo elbowed Sadie gently.

"Well, we can't let you be the only girl getting some action around here! Plus, I think a little island loving is exactly what this hopeless romantic needs!"

Jo laughed and went to rummage in her suitcase for something suitable to wear. She had planned for fancy lunches and breakfasts, typical wedding events, but she'd forgotten to think of bringing something club-worthy.

"I have nothing to wear!" Jo whined, all desire to go out gone again. She threw herself on the bed and pulled the pillow over her face. "Why don't you guys just go out without me. With my luck I'm going to run into some other ex or something and ruin the fun again anyway."

"Do you even have any other exes?" Sadie asked, pulling her friend back into a sitting position and handing her a ridiculously skimpy black halter top. "Put this on, stop whining, and get your shoes. We're going and that's that. I bet Roxie is already waiting for us."

"First I seriously doubt that Roxie is remotely ready. And second there is no way I can pull this top off. And no, I guess I don't have any other exes. Oh my God! That's terrible. I can't get married! I only have one ex!"

"Dude. Get a grip! First of all, I'm not asking you

to pull the top off, just to put it on. And second, you're already married. What the heck are you freaking out about?"

Jo didn't reply. Instead, she dropped her gaze and stared hard at the sequins on the black top clutched in her hands. She wished Sadie already knew what she hadn't dared tell anyone yet, not even Jordan. She wished she didn't have to say it out loud. The sequins shimmered dully and started to blur as her eyes filled with tears.

"What? What haven't you told me?" Sadie demanded, hands on her hips again. "I know this isn't about the top. What is it?"

Jo opened her mouth and closed it as the words didn't come.

"What? Tell me already!"

"We're not really married," Jo mumbled.

"What? You're not what?" Sadie said. "Did I hear you correctly? What does 'we're not really married' mean? Sure, you are. You got married in some sordid hut in the middle of Zambia. I saw the pictures!"

"Well, yes. We did get married. Except we didn't. That's the thing. Turns out our wedding wasn't actually valid. I found our wedding certificate the other day and I realized that both of our names are misspelled on it and the date is off by like three years and... and..." Jo took a deep breath and said the rest as fast as possible. "I checked and it's not a valid marriage license."

Jo turned her back on Sadie, unwilling to see the look on her face. She stood up and slipped on the halter top, which did after all look pretty good on her. Pretending to peer in the mirror to fluff her hair, she peeked at Sadie's reflection and held her breath. Sadie wasn't moving, just standing there gaping at her. Her mouth opening and shutting silently. Jo had never seen her speechless before. This was not a good sign.

"Sadie, say something, please," Jo pleaded, turning around to face her friend.

"I... I don't know what to say. Wow." She wrung her hands. "Does your mother know? Does Jordan know?"

Jo couldn't bring herself to answer. She had so wanted to tell Jordan, but things had been insane before she left, and she hadn't found the right time to tell him. She looked down at her chipped toenail polish and shook her head no.

"I didn't know what to say! I didn't know how to bring it up!"

"Oh. Jo. Honey. What are you going to do?" Sadie asked, eyes pulled down in a concerned frown.

"I don't know!" Jo wailed, resisting the urge to throw herself back on the bed and burrowing under the covers until it was all over. "I'm so confused. When we planned all this, we were already married. Now that we're not I feel like I have to decide all over again." She paused and took a deep breath. "Sadie? What if Jordan isn't the man of my dreams?"

Sadie's eyes narrowed. "What are you talking about? You adore Jordan."

"Well, yes. But that was before, when we were married. Now I'm not so sure." Jo shrugged miserably.

"Oh. My. God. This has nothing to do with Jordan, does it? This has everything to do with Andy! You didn't have any doubts before you saw him again, did you?"

"No! No! It has nothing to do with Andy!" Jo

protested, but Sadie just looked at her with one eyebrow raised. "Well, OK, yes, maybe it has something to do with him. But not in the way you're thinking."

"What the hell does that mean?" Sadie demanded, throwing her hands up in the air.

"Well, back when Andy left me I was a wreck, you know that." Sadie nodded. "The only way I got myself through that time was to just block everything out instead of dealing with it. I just did my best to survive. Then, when that didn't work, I just ran away."

"Right. I know all that. I was there."

"When I met Jordan, it was like I was being given a chance to start all over again. I didn't have to deal with anything, I just put it behind me and moved on. It was such a relief."

Sadie nodded, her face softening a bit.

"Well, now, seeing Andy again has opened up every single wound. It's like it all just happened yesterday instead of six years ago. And I just don't know what I feel any more."

"Oh." The fight seemed to leave Sadie in a whoosh. She moved towards Jo and wrapped her arms around her. Jo rested her forehead on her friend's shoulder and felt the tears start to flow again. Sadie rubbed her friend's back gently and rested her cheek on her head.

"And..."

"And?"

"And, well, I think I might still love Andy," Jo whispered.

"Well, that seems normal in this situation. You never stopped loving him, you just walked away."

"But I also love Jordan." Jo moaned slightly and

Sadie rubbed her back harder.

"Oh, honey. Of course, you do. He's your soul mate," Sadie said again.

Jo stood up and started pacing around the small room.

"Is he? I'm just so darn confused. I can't think straight. I mean, it turns out I'm not even married to Jordan, so if I also love Andy, is it fair to him for me to go through with the wedding?"

"Fair to him who?"

"Well, I guess for either of them!" She threw herself back onto the bed.

"But, sweetheart," Sadie pulled Jo back upright. She cupped her hand under Jo's chin and lifted it so they'd be eye to eye. "You don't even know who Andy is today. You love the boy he was six years ago. And you don't even know how Andy feels! You don't know anything about him anymore. For all you know, he's moved on completely."

"Really? You think so?"

"Well, okay, maybe not. But you can't forget, he has kids now, and we have no idea what he's been up to for the last six years. I mean, where's their mom in all this?"

"Oh, I don't know. I don't know what to think any more!"

23. Sadie

Sadie left Jo lying flat on her back, moaning softly into the pillow she had pulled over her face and escaped into the bathroom. She had never understood why hotels placed phones in the bathroom, but maybe there was a use for them after all.

"Hey, Rox? Are you ready yet?" She said softly when their friend answered her phone.

"Of course, I'm ready! I was just about to head down to the bar. Aren't you? Why are you whispering?"

"We're ready, but something's come up. I think you'd better head up to our room instead."

"What's wrong?"

Sadie hesitated. "Just come up, please? I'll tell you when you get here." Sadie didn't beg, not quite, but she was sure Roxie heard the intent in her voice. It would just be easier to explain in person, and she was sure that Roxie's legendary matter-of-factness would help them all see more clearly. Food. Food would also help. How, she had no idea, but it couldn't hurt. She picked up the phone again and called Room Service.

By the time Roxie had arrived, dressed to kill as expected in a sparkly red number, Sadie had done her best to mix up a couple drinks with what the mini bar offered. Jo was still on the bed, but she had pulled her head out from under the pillow and was instead sitting propped up against the royal blue padded headboard. She was clutching her drink in both hands and gazing into it as though the ice cubes held the answers to all her troubles.

"What's your drink of choice my dear?" Sadie asked Roxie with as much cheer as she could muster. "Teeny tiny Gin & Tonic or Teeny tiny Whiskey & Diet Coke."

Roxie laughed, "I'll take my chances with a Gin & Tonic."

"Good choice," Jo called from the bed. "It's not so bad actually! Sadie has secret bartender talents." She threw back her head and downed her drink in one gulp before handing her glass to Sadie for a refill. Roxie glanced at Sadie eyebrows raised in a silent question that Sadie was quick to answer.

Sadie gave Roxie the bare bones of the story with Jo interjecting comments and explanations here and there. The food arrived and all three girls threw themselves on the massive burgers dripping with toppings that Sadie had ordered. Roxie chewed quietly for a moment before speaking.

"Let me get this straight. This whole time you were never actually married?" Roxie asked.

"Yeah. Weird right?"

"Hell no, forget weird! It's awesome! Fantastic! Did I already say awesome?"

"Dude, seriously? This is so not the time for your 'marriage sucks' crap. It's just not constructive in this situation." Sadie groaned.

"Yes! This is the perfect time. Marriage does suck.

Jo's free! Do I have to explain all this to you guys again?" "NOOOOO," howled Sadie and Jo at the same time. They knew Roxie's stance all too well. Their friend had been raised by a very militant single mom who had been abandoned by Roxie's dad the day before she was born, just as the first contractions were making themselves felt. She had never recovered from the betrayal and had spent Roxie's entire childhood preaching the benefits of never being tied down to one man. As a result, Roxie's life had been filled with a series of Uncles Bob, Max, Billy, and whoever else happened to be taking up space in her mother's bed. Much to her mother's delight Roxie had adopted a similar lifestyle and changed boyfriends as often as she changed shoes, which was impressively often. As soon as one started to sound more or less serious about the relationship he found himself out on his ass wondering what he'd done wrong.

"Come on Rox. Don't you ever think it would be nice to get to know someone really well? Someone you could relax with at home on the weekend? Let your hair down? You know, wear sweats around?" Jo asked her old friend. "Find someone who doesn't care if you fart in bed?"

"No! Ugh. How atrocious." Roxie recoiled. "Why would I want anyone to see me in sweats? And you know I don't let men into my home. It's my space. That's where I let my hair down and relax, all by myself, without anyone watching or judging!"

"Well, I think it would be perfectly lovely to never have to impress someone on a first date ever again," Sadie said wistfully. "Seriously, Jo, isn't it nice to never have to worry about meeting the perfect someone?" She instantly wished she could take her question back and she looked quickly over at Jo. "Oh, hon, I'm sorry."

"Nah, it's OK," Jo said. "You're right, it's lovely not worrying about all that stuff. It's nice to know you don't have to wear make up all the time, or worry about always cooking fancy meals, or having to be careful about what you say or do all the time. It's what I love about Jordan. He loves me best when I'm at my most relaxed. I don't care where we are, I feel at home when I'm with him."

"See? That's what I want!" Sadie said pointing wildly at Roxie. "And see? You do love Jordan! How could you not want to marry someone who makes you feel that way?" She added turning back to Jo.

"Sure, Jordan makes me feel all safe and warm and fuzzy, but Andy, well, Andy still makes my stomach flip-flop."

"And, that my friends, is why I date lots and lots of men. I'm addicted to that flip-floppy feeling. I don't ever want it to go away. It's the promise of fun! Of excitement! Of adventure!" Roxie said, getting up from the bed. "Come on, can we please get out of this room? It smells like French fries in here and I want to go dance! What kind of a bachelorette party is this?"

"Uh, well, one for a wedding that might not happen," Sadie answered shrugging, but she stood up too. "Come on Jo, Roxie is right. We're not going to solve anything tonight. We might as well go have some fun. We'll go see the wedding planner first thing in the morning and see what she says we can do about the license. And who knows, maybe a drink or two more will help you decide what you want to do."

"That, my dear, is doubtful, but I agree, we need to get out of here. We've emptied the minibar and the fries are all soggy and cold. To the bar we go!" Jo said, jumping up and shoving her feet into her sandals. "Let's go see if Kona is going to make good on his promise!"

24. Sadie

The bar was one of those overly decorated touristy places that most of the hotels on the island boasted, with Tiki lamps and lots of fake leis draped over every possible surface. Cheap gaudy masks had been turned into candle holders and hotel guests were drinking frothy drinks through bright straws sticking out of coconuts and pineapples. The girls hesitated at the door, but the music wafting out was somewhat decent and the lure of free drinks was more than they could resist. Plus, their options were severely limited. The hotel didn't boast too many other bars and it wasn't like the island was all that big.

They stepped into the dark room and let the door shut behind them. Once engulfed in the bar it was easy to ignore the tacky decorations and just enjoy the upbeat music and vacation atmosphere that permeated the room.

Sadie looked over at the bartender Jo was waving at and did a double take. Oh, wow. She hadn't been kidding. Kona was hot! Tall, dark, with arms so buff she wasn't sure she could wrap her hands all the way around his biceps. Not that she wouldn't be thrilled to try. Sadie felt a shiver run down her back and her stomach broke into a string of crazy somersaults. She resisted the urge to run her hands through her hair as she looked him up and down again then tore her gaze away. There was no way he'd be into her. And in any case, she'd sworn that she was done with fix-it men, which was too bad, because this one looked like he might be worth the time. Sadie risked another glance and blushed furiously when she caught Kona looking her way.

"What do you guys want to drink?" Roxie asked, also looking Kona up and down. "I'll get the first round!" She winked at them suggestively.

"I'll come too!" Sadie surprised herself by cutting in. "You can't carry three drinks by yourself!" She felt drawn to Kona in a way she couldn't explain. And in any case, even if she didn't want to get caught up in his drama, she sure wasn't going to let Roxie have her way with him. Poor guy might never recover.

Roxie just laughed and grabbed Sadie's arm as she started to walk away. "Don't worry, if you like him I'll leave him to you," She teased as they walked to the bar. "Jo, grab us that table over there!" She said, pointing to a table at the edge of the dance floor. "I'll get you a Mai Tai, k?"

Sadie bristled at the notion that Roxie could just chose to "leave" someone to her. Like she didn't have it in her to win a man without her super model friend stepping out of the ring. She glared at Roxie, but her friend was 100% focused on the bartender and didn't even notice the look. Fine, two could play this game. Sadie could show Roxie that she didn't need permission to go after a man.

"No, by all means, go for it." She gave Roxie the

sweetest smile she could muster and tried not to blink when Roxie looked at her with a hint of surprise.

"Oh! Okay. If you're sure?" Sadie felt a bit bad at the genuine kindness and love she read in Roxie's eyes, but she was tired of everyone feeling sorry for her and thinking that she couldn't fend for herself.

"Sure." She smiled back. Then she threw her shoulders back and turned her attention to the bar. She had work to do.

If Kona was taken aback by two pretty girls coming at him all guns blazing, he didn't let on. He greeted them with a million dollar smile and a cheery "Aloha!" As soon as they had established that they were Jo's friends his smile grew even bigger and Sadie's resolve to not get involved melted away completely. She wanted this man, and not just because Roxie also had her sights on him. She wanted him because she could get lost in his smile and his eyes and never ever come up for air.

Sadie heard Roxie switch into high flirt mode and tore her gaze away from Kona. Roxie was pulling her best moves on the poor man, batting eyes, hand on forearm, boobs pushed up and at him. Sadie suppressed a giggle and was delighted when Kona's head instantly swiveled her way. He caught her eye and winked. She beamed at him. He wasn't taken in at all by Roxie's show. Sadie felt a swell of something she couldn't yet identify bubble up from the pit of her stomach to her throat. She giggled again and almost swooned when Kona laughed too.

"How good are your Mai Tai's?" Sadie asked with a dazzling smile of her own. "I think a couple of those would just about hit the spot!"

25. Andy

Andy closed the book he'd been trying to read for the last hour and looked down at his two sleeping kids. Emily was dressed in one of her many ruffled pink pajamas and Hunter was just wearing a pair of boxers. Ever since he'd once seen Andy sleeping in a pair he'd decided that was how he should sleep too. Andy hadn't been able to think of a single reason to say no, especially since it was so hot in their room. He could have turned on the AC, but much preferred to sleep with the window open so they could all be lulled by the sound of the surf. Apparently it had worked well on the kids.

"Hey, guys, you asleep?" He whispered loudly to see if they were really out and only got snorts in response. They were both out cold. He glanced at the clock on the nightstand. Damn. It was only 7:45. What the hell was he supposed to do for the rest of the night? It was awesome being here with the kids, but these early nights were torture. He never got tired before 10 or 11 and there was only so much bad hotel TV someone could watch before going insane. Unused to so much downtime, he had miscalculated how much reading material he needed and had managed to finish the only book he had brought with him sometime in the middle of his first quiet evening in the hotel room. He'd already read it once and was working on a second reread. He kept meaning to pick something up from the hotel store, but when he had the kids in tow he always forgot that he'd need something to read later. At home there was always some chore to occupy him. Here there was absolutely nothing to distract him from his thoughts.

His eyes roamed the room looking for something to do, but the only other reading material in sight was the hotel information binder.

Hey! Maybe room service could bring him something. Andy slipped off the bed, careful not to disturb the two children who had fallen asleep while he told them a story and grabbed the binder. Breakfast, Snacks, Dinner. Darn it. All food, nothing else. Crap.

Well, if room service was no help, maybe the actual store could bring it to his room. He flipped through the binder, looking for a page containing info about the store. With luck they'd still be open and might be willing to help. As he flipped through the pages the word 'babysitter' caught his eye. He stopped and glanced at the paragraph. Babysitting! Score! How could he have forgotten that this was one of the reasons that Amber had agreed to come here? Not all the hotels offered babysitting, but this one prided itself on it and Amber wasn't one to go somewhere that would force her to be in bed by eight pm. At the time he'd been annoyed by her insistence that they only vacation somewhere that offered the opportunity to dump the kids on someone else every second possible, but now he was grateful to get a chance to go out and stretch his legs.

He called and crossed his fingers that someone would be available on such short notice and resisted the urge to do a victory dance when the director of the program told him she'd have someone at his door in 30 minutes. He couldn't remember the last time he'd been so excited to go out.

He rushed around the room getting ready. After gently tucking the kids into their respective beds, he found his Hawaiian shirt under a pile of dirty laundry in the corner of the room. It passed the sniff test and he pulled in on, smoothing out the wrinkles as best as possible. He thought about changing out of his shorts, but he was still hot, and he couldn't be bothered to find his jeans. A quick glance in the mirror showed halfway decent hair. Good enough for the hotel bar for sure. Just a dad going out for a drink. He had no one to impress. As ready as he was going to be, he threw himself on his bed and turned on the TV. It didn't annoy him as much now that he knew he'd be doing something other than staring at it all night. He was still glad though when a soft knock interrupted a Seinfeld rerun he'd already seen a million times. He snapped off the TV and bounced to the door.

"The kids are asleep in the adjoining room, so there's really nothing much for you to do." He apologized about the mess as he let in the young girl waiting at the door. He hadn't had the heart to pick up the disaster that was their room. The kids would just tear the place apart again in the morning. "Sorry about this place. When they're awake they're like little tornadoes."

"Don't worry. I'm used to it. I have three little brothers. And don't worry, I won't be bored. I brought a book." She waved some girly looking paperback at him and smiled. He smiled back and relaxed. This was perfect. She was just the type of girl he would have hired back home.

"Okay. Well, I won't be out too late. Just going to grab a couple drinks and a bite to eat downstairs, see if there's any live music. I wrote my cell number on the pad next to the phone. Call if you need anything!" He waved and pulled the door shut behind him, heaving a sigh of relief as he found himself gloriously alone. For a few steps he felt out of sorts, like he'd forgotten something, but when he realized that he was just missing Emily and Hunter, he laughed. They were fine, he was... well, he was out, and all he needed was a drink or two to feel fine too. It had been a hell of a day.

Andy hesitated outside the hotel bar. He wasn't really all that hungry. The early dinner he'd shared with the kids felt like a rock in the pit of his stomach. When he swallowed he could still taste the greasy fries he had picked off their plates. Come to think of it, the mere thought of eating something was making him queasy. No. What he really wanted was to sit in the corner of the bar, listen to some music, and nurse a Mai Tai. He didn't harbor any hopes for the kind of bar he loved to hang out in – dark, wood paneling, deep booths, and smoky – but this place was the only bar at this hotel, and he didn't want to leave the hotel grounds while the kids were alone with a strange sitter.

He pulled the door open and hesitated. It was worse than he'd imagined. Instead of oak paneling and live jazz he'd have to make do with tacky decorations and an 80's cover band. He shrugged and went in anyway. A bar was a bar. As long as they had something he could drink he'd deal.

He pulled the door open a little more and went

into the bar. With a quick glance around the room, he spotted the perfect table off in the corner of the room, in a shadowy spot. He wouldn't be bothered back there. He headed to the table with a quick nod to a passing waitress. She followed him and took his order as he sat down. This was perfect. He'd sit here for a while and watch people dance and have fun. He always got a kick out of watching people act goofy. It was amazing how a little drink and the freedom of being on vacation made people nutty.

His gaze focused on two girls flirting outrageously with a bartender. The really hot girl was leaning forward, one hand on the guy's arm, head thrown back in a big laugh. He fantasized for a moment about running his hands through her blond hair. His eyes traveled down the length of her hair and came to rest on her ass. He couldn't see her face, but he was really enjoying the rest of her. The other girl, not quite as hot, but not bad to look at either, was acting a little more shy, but she was clearly really into the guy too. She kept titling her head in a way that made her red curls bounce around. It was cute, but he'd never been into red heads. From this angle the guy looked like he was though. Good for him. The blond chick was definitely more his style. Plus, she looked like she'd be fun to hang out with.

He watched them a little more, letting his imagination run wild. For a moment he even considered heading to the bar to see if he could chat her up. The thought had barely crossed his mind when she laughed again and turned her head a bit towards him. He felt a glimmer of recognition. It might have been dark, but those girls looked awfully familiar...

Oh shit. Roxie and Sadie. So where was...

"Hi Andy. Mind if I sit down?" His heart sank. Well, that answered that, he thought, tilting his head up and peering at Jo.

26. Andy

"Sure you want to do that?" He almost snarled but seeing her face fall made him instantly want to take back the bitterness of his tone. "I'm sorry, Jo. That was uncalled for. It's... It's just been quite a shock actually seeing you again."

Relief washed over her face and he realized that she'd probably been scared to come over and talk to him. His heart ached at the thought that she'd be scared to talk to him. At one point in their lives, they had been impossibly close. Best friends. She had been his rock and vice versa. Back then he would have been devastated if she'd had cause to be scared of him. Today... well. Things were so different, but it still made him sad. He looked up at the face he had once loved so deeply and felt a stirring deep inside him. He was still angry at her, but the tenderness and love he had once felt for her was still very much alive in him. He gave her a tentative smile and gestured to the chair in front of him.

"Yeah. You could say that. It has been quite a shock," Jo said sitting down. "And I'm sorry for the way I yelled at you this afternoon. I was out of line."

"No! No! I was out of line! Are you kidding? I went nuts!"

Jo gave a sad little half smile. "How about we just agree we were both out of line?"

"Deal." Andy smiled too and then gratefully turned his attention to the waitress handing him his drink. "Oh, hey, did you want something?" He asked Jo belatedly as the waitress walked away.

"Nah, it's okay. Sadie and Roxie are getting me a drink."

"I really don't think that's going to happen any time soon," Andy said, nodding towards the two girls draped over the bar, fighting for the bartender's attention.

"Excuse me?" He waved down a passing waitress. "Could we please have another Mai Tai?"

Jo looked over her shoulder at her two friends and snorted. They both had their elbows on the bar and their chins in their hands. They were captivated by the good looking bartender. "I see Kona has already worked his Hawaiian magic on them. Thanks for the drink."

"Kona? You already know the bartender? You move fast!"

"Yeah, well, it was a total fluke. He rescued me this afternoon. I got stranded on the stairs without my key card." Jo let her voice trail away as she glanced away.

"Well, that was nice of him." Andy didn't know what else to say. At one time he and Jo had never had any trouble talking, but he just couldn't get past the awkwardness of the situation. If the way Jo was looking anywhere but at him was any indication, clearly she felt the same way.

Andy wished he'd never come into this bar. This was just painful and pretty much the opposite of the relaxing evening he had been hoping for. Yet, he couldn't bring himself to regret it completely. He couldn't take his eyes off Jo. For years now he had hoped to see her again, even if it was just to catch a glimpse, and here she was, sitting in front of him, with him. It was like a dream come true.

She was still just as beautiful as she'd been the last time he saw her. Actually, that wasn't quite true, she was prettier. "You look amazing. So, grown up. So pretty," he blurted out. Jo looked surprised for a moment. She blushed a deep scarlet and mumbled a thank you. "I'm sorry. I didn't mean to embarrass you. It's just... I..."

Jo looked him in the eye and waited for him to finish.

"I've missed you. More than you'll ever know." He gave her a shy smile.

Jo smiled back. "You know. I carry that post card everywhere I go."

"You do?" Andy was surprised. He had sent the card out of pure selfishness. The lack of goodbye had tortured him for months. Sending it had made him feel a bit better.

"I missed you Andy. I was hurt and I was sad, but I missed you. It was the only thing of you I had after you left."

"What do you mean the only thing? I left all our photo albums, and a ton of my things behind when I left. You had all those!"

At the thought of his hasty departure Andy felt himself get angry again. He had been chased out. Chased out so fast he hadn't been able to take most of his things. Before the anger could take over completely Andy saw the look in Jo's eyes and felt flooded with guilt. Her face was contorted in pain and she seemed to be having trouble saying something.

"What?"

"There wasn't anything. Nothing at all."

"What do you mean?"

"When I came home from the hospital. There was nothing of yours in the apartment. Nothing."

Andy knew he had left behind countless things. They had lived in that tiny apartment together for a long time. He had taken the bare essentials and had left everything else behind. What Jo was saying made no sense. As he tried to work out the ramifications in his head he could see Jo get more and more agitated in front of him. Her face kept flickering between confusion and anger, and she was growing visibly more upset by the minute.

"Jo, it's okay. We can figure this out. Why don't we start at the beginning?" He watched her take a deep breath and looked around for the waitress while taking a long sip of his own drink. It didn't seem right that he could fortify himself with alcohol while Jo had nothing in her hands. Luckily the waitress arrived at just that moment.

"Hey, your friends want to make sure you're okay. Are you?" She asked kindly while putting the glass in front of Jo and pointedly ignoring Andy. He winced.

Jo smiled at the waitress through the tears that were coursing silently down her face and thanked her. "Could you please let them know that I'm fine? I'll holler if I need help, but I'm fine."

"Fine honey. If you're sure. I'm not going far so let me know if you need rescuing." The waitress patted

Jo's shoulder gently before sauntering away swinging her hips in a way that Andy was sure most patrons appreciated.

"Why do I feel like I should apologize again?" Andy asked, taking another swig.

"After you left things were... they were... well they were bad, really, really bad for a while." Jo took a deep breath and placed her hands flat on the table. The two of them stared hard at her fingers while she continued. "I think they were all scared I was going to kill myself."

Andy's head snapped up. He couldn't look away. "Were you?" He held his breath.

"No, that never crossed my mind. I mean, why bother? I was already dead inside. It would have taken too much energy to kill myself." Jo shrugged, but didn't look up, not even when Andy gently placed his hands on hers.

"Jo, I am so, so very sorry I wasn't there. I had no clue."

When Jo looked up tears were still streaming down her face. The pain in her eyes twisted his stomach and made his heart stutter. He had caused that pain.

"Of course, you had no clue. You were long gone. Why Andy? Where did you go? Why did you go?" She whispered. Her eyes were unrelenting, digging deep into his own pain.

"I had to leave," he finally said, drawing a deep breath. "When your mother called to say you'd been hurt... when she told me that you'd lost the baby and that it was my fault... all I wanted to do was run. But I couldn't leave you! You needed me! You were there, in the hospital, looking like you were dead! But your mom... she wouldn't stop. She kept telling me that it was my fault and that I had to leave. She just kept saying that over and over again. I don't know what happened. It all started to make sense. I started believing that I had hurt you. That I had almost killed you. That I had killed our baby. She told me that I had to go. I had to stop hurting you."

27. Jo

Jo watched Andy's face dissolve, but she couldn't react. His words were buzzing around her head too loud for her to form a coherent thought. How could two people live the same thing and experience it so differently? She could barely focus on the words he had said. Couldn't get them to line up in a way that made sense. And she couldn't figure out the implications of what he was saying. It was big, she knew that, but the buzzing in her head made it impossible for her to grasp at the ramifications. Jo tried to focus her mind, still the noise, but the buzzing didn't stop. She started shivering. She gently pulled her hands out from Andy's grasp and hugged her arms to her chest.

The shivering slowly stopped and as she stared hard at the half melted candle in the middle of the table the words started to make sense. What she had been unable to grasp a moment ago started to make sense.

"She told you it was your fault? My mother told you it was your fault our baby died? Why on earth would she do that?"

Her mother hadn't left her side as she recovered from the hemorrhage that had taken their unborn child and almost killed her in the process. She had been the picture of the perfect mother, doting, supportive, almost to a fault.

Jo looked deep into his eyes watching the waves of pain crash down again and again. Maybe more than just almost to a fault. She unclenched her arm and reached out her hand towards him again.

"Andy? What did she tell you exactly? How were you hurting me?"

He took her hand and held it hard. She winced a little as the bones in her knuckles rubbed together, but she didn't pull her hand back. All of this was wrong. Nothing fit her memories of what had happened. But this need to hold her tight? It felt like exactly the need she had had for him back then. And she was loath to deny him what had been denied to her.

Andy didn't meet her gaze. He stared hard at their entwined hand. He started speaking so softly that she had to lean forward to hear him clearly over the sound of the music.

"I came to see you as soon as I heard you had been taken to the hospital. I sat with you for a while, but you never woke up. I guess they had given you a ton of drugs to stop the bleeding or something. They also said you were in shock. When Sadie came to sit with you I went to get a cup of coffee and clear my head. Your mother cornered me in the waiting room. She was like a crazy woman. Hair all over the place, eyes blazing. She told me that one of the nurses had told her that only great shocks or physical abuse can cause this kind of bleed." Andy's face twisted in pain and Jo squeezed his hand harder. She didn't think she was strong enough to hear whatever he was going to say next. At the same time, she knew she wasn't strong enough to stop him.

In a deadpan voice he continued, but the tears pooling in his eyes and threatening to spill over onto his already ravaged face spoke volumes. "She said that I had done that to you. That I had put you in that bed. That I had killed our baby. I tried to argue, but she wouldn't let me talk, let me explain. She just kept repeating over and over again 'You did this. It's your fault. You almost killed her.' I was so confused. So tired. Finally, I started to believe her."

It was so painful to think he could have done that to Jo. Andy had no idea how, but Jo's mother was so convinced, so convincing, that he just started to believe her. And yet he was drawn to Jo. He believed that if he could just see her, just hold her hand, he'd know that her mother was wrong. He'd stop doubting, stop believing that maybe he had in fact put her in that hospital bed.

"She never let me go back into the room. She stood in front of the door and blocked me. Short of picking her up and throwing her aside there was no way for me to go in. Don't think I didn't consider it. But she already thought I was an abuser. I didn't want to give her any reason to confirm her thoughts."

He'd left, after wandering around the hospital for hours, hoping she would relent. That she'd let him go in. But she never did. She'd stood guard over Jo and whenever she saw him she just kept berating him, repeating herself over and over again, like a broken record set on manic.

"I eventually just went home. I think I wanted to get you some of your favorite things, do something to prove I wasn't out to hurt you. But when I got there all I could see were all the things we had ready for the baby..."

His voice faltered and he gulped some more air. Jo wanted to reach over to hug his shaking shoulders, but the table was in the way and she was frozen in place. She was shocked by what he was saying. Horrified. It didn't sound like her story. Until he had mentioned the baby she had almost forgotten that she was the one in the bed that her mother was protecting so fiercely. His last sentence brought her crashing back and she instantly felt his pain again.

It was her pain too.

Only she had never seen the baby's things again. She had been spared that particular agony, but she could imagine it all too clearly.

"So, you left," she filled in and he just nodded.

"I didn't leave right away. I headed back to the hospital again, but your mother still wouldn't let me in. I couldn't stand to be at home without you. I couldn't stand the thought of seeing you come home and have to see what I'd just seen. I knew it would hurt you so much to see all the baby's things. But there was nothing I could do about it. I couldn't stand to be in our place. Couldn't stand to touch the baby's things. So, I just left. I'm sorry. I was a coward. I should have been stronger. I should have stayed. I should have been able to protect you."

Andy lowered his face into his hands. Jo could see his shoulders strain with tension. She could feel a similar tightness in her own back. She rolled her shoulders back a bit, wincing in pain.

"But I don't understand, when did you come get your things? When did you get rid of the baby's things?" She hadn't imagined it. When she had come home everything had been cleaned out.

"Your mother's words just kept echoing in my

head. I know I never hurt you physically, but what if she'd been right? What if that fight we had caused you to lose the baby? What did I know? I was an asshole kid. And what if my terror about even having the baby made it all happen? What if I willed it somehow?" He hesitated again, staring deeply into his drink. Jo wondered if he hoped it would take him back in time to fix what had gone wrong. Or maybe that was just wishful thinking on her part.

"That's ridiculous and you know it. Just wanting something to go away never makes it really go away."

"Really? Are you sure about that?" He made an unreadable face and shrugged. How could she hold it against him? She sometimes wondered if she had made this happen. If something she had done had caused the hemorrhage. The doctors had assured her again and again that it wasn't her fault, but what did they know? The guilt didn't make it easier to deal with, but it was easier than having to rely on "shit happens."

Andy looked up and gave Jo a half apologetic smile. "I became convinced that your mother was right. I had caused you all that pain and the only way to make it right was to leave and let you get on with your life without me poisoning it anymore." Jo grasped his hand hard, like she could reach back in time and keep him from leaving.

"What? How could you have possibly thought that? How could you think that being without you then was the right thing for me?"

"I don't know. I wasn't thinking clearly. I was convinced that my mere presence was hurting you and that you'd be better off without me."

His defeatist attitude and the nonchalant way in

which he described discarding the relationship they'd had infuriated her.

"You left me! You left me alone to deal with the death of our child!" Jo heard her voice go shrill for a moment and took a deep breath to settle herself. "You left me Andy, you left me when I most needed you."

"It was the most cowardly thing I have ever done. I'm sorry Jo. I know that now. But I swear that that day, in that apartment it seemed like the only possible solution. I should have gone back to the hospital. I should have pushed your mother out of the way, barged my way in, and never left your side again. I was wrong to leave. I've never forgiven myself."

Jo shook her head a bit. She had been so angry at Andy for so long. So mad that he had left her when she most needed him. She had imagined him off somewhere living the high life, not caring a bit about her or their baby. And she had been wrong this whole time. If anything, he seemed to have punished himself worse than she would have punished him if she'd had the chance. It was hard to come to grips with this different reality. But this still didn't clear up everything.

"So, you just packed up everything and left." She shook her head a bit. "What did you do with the baby's things? Did you just throw them out?"

Andy looked a bit surprised at the question. "I told you, I didn't touch her things. I didn't even take most of my things, just a few things to see me through." He stopped and looked deeply in Jo's eyes again. "I wanted to leave you a note. Say sorry. Explain. But I couldn't find the words. So, I left the only thing that made any sense at all."

"The sock. You left her sock under my pillow.

And you took the other one." Andy just nodded. Jo was grateful that she had found the sock even if she hadn't understood its exact significance. It had seemed like such an arbitrary thing to find under her pillow at the time, but she had held on to it like a lifeline.

"When I got home... the place was cleared out. There was no trace of you or the baby's things. I'd always assumed it was you, but I guess my mother must have come by after you left. It was so surreal. It felt like none of it had ever happened. I couldn't even find a picture of you. It made me so sad. Like you had both been wiped away. Like neither of you had ever happened. Like I'd dreamed you up. I thought I was going crazy. I couldn't stand to see the place look like that, so I just went to bed. When I put my hand under the pillow I found the sock. My mother must not have thought to look there." Jo hiccupped a laugh that was half a sob. "I mean, why would she?"

Andy squeezed her hand even tighter. "I'm so sorry. I honestly thought you'd be better off. You had your friends and your family. I thought they'd support you, help you get through this." He held her gaze, not blinking, eyes filled with compassion and strength even in the face of the pain she was pouring out. She felt a flash of anger. Where had all that strength been when she had needed him? Where had it been when it counted?

"They did their best," she snapped, and just as fast the anger slipped away. Neither of them were the people they had been back then. Andy wasn't the boy he had been. This Andy was more grown up, wiser, and clearly stronger. Being mad at this man made no sense; it was his younger self who had left her in the lurch. "But they hadn't just lost a baby and a part of their lives. They couldn't understand. They just wanted me to move on, put it behind me, get over it, get over you."

Jo looked at Andy, willing herself to comprehend what he'd gone through. Wondering if he'd felt the loss the way she had. Had he been sad? Had he really mourned their baby? Or had he just been relieved that she was gone?

"I always keep that sock with me. It was what I clung to when everything else felt like it was going to float away and vanish. Now I keep it to remind myself of how far I've come."

Andy looked surprised and he jerked his hand out of hers. Jo's head snapped back. Had she offended him? She watched, bewildered as he leaned back and reached into his pocket. He pulled out his wallet, flipped it open and drew out a tiny, tattered piece of fabric.

"Oh!" She gasped and reached into her own pocket for the matching sock. Jo's was equally threadbare. They lay them next to each other gently. "You did miss her." The thought was comforting. Their baby had died long ago, and Jo had come to grips with the loss, learning to live with it. But this soothed a part of her soul that she had thought damaged forever. She hadn't mourned the baby alone. And their baby lived on in more than just one heart.

Jo and Andy both looked at the forlorn socks for a moment.

"Andy?"

"Yeah?"

"Thank you. Thank you for that. Having that sock made me feel like I hadn't gone insane. I think... I think that sock might have saved my life."

"I'm glad." He paused. "It did the same for me."

Jo looked at Andy and wondered if the sock really had meant the same to him as it had to her. She had run far away from where they'd been, all the way to the other ends of the world. She hadn't been able to run away when he did, but only because she'd been strapped to a hospital bed. If she'd been in his shoes, would she have run? There was just no way to know. She was a radically different person now than she had been back then. But she suspected that she might have been tempted to do what he did even though it made her a bit sick to her stomach to admit that to herself.

"You know, I think I get it now. I think I understand. I don't like it any more today than I did back then, but at least I understand. And I think I can forgive you."

28. Jo

A soft cough wiped the spreading look of relief off of Andy's face. They both looked around. Jo was surprised to still be in the hotel bar and for a moment she was completely disoriented. She had been a million miles away, back in their tiny apartment, surrounded by the ghosts of Andy's and the baby's things. She broke her gaze from the little socks and looked up. Andy yanked his hand back and sat up, scooping both socks up in an impressively swift and very discrete movement.

"Roxie! Hi!" The hotel bar rushed back into focus, tiki lamps, wilted leis, and all. For a moment Jo was dizzy, then the world stopped spinning and she landed softly back into the present.

"Hi Andy. Hey Jo. Can I join you guys? I feel like a third wheel over there." She motioned with her head towards the bar where Kona and Sadie were gazing deeply into each other's eyes, oblivious to the people around them. Jo looked over at the two and smiled. They looked so happy. So infatuated already. Jo envied them this fresh start. Nothing could have possibly come up yet to complicate matters. All they knew right now was the obvious attraction both felt for each other. She remembered what it was like to think that really that was all that mattered.

She watched Sadie and Kona, not really listening as Andy and Roxie chatted quietly. The two of them were leaning over the bar towards each other. They were so close their foreheads were almost touching, their fingers almost entwined, much to the annoyance of the bar patrons hankering for more drinks, clearly they were already somewhere else.

"They do look sort of smitten," Jo said with a smile. Roxie made a little face, part jealousy part annoyance. She wasn't used to being the third wheel ever. In fact, she wasn't used to not being the center of attention. Having to go find someone to hang out with had clearly unsettled her.

Jo glanced back at the bar and noticed no fewer than five men visibly lusting after her friend. That she hadn't noticed was a clear sign of how disturbed she was that Sadie had won her man. Jo stifled a snort. It wouldn't hurt Roxie to feel like everyone else for a while. She'd have recovered soon enough from striking out with Kona.

She was about to tease her about it when something in Roxie's face, something she'd never seen before stopped her. She'd never know Roxie to look sad. Pouty, annoyed, jealous, proud, yes. Sad, no. She took pity on her and patted the seat next to her.

"Come here, babe, come sit next to me. Andy and I were... just... catching up," she said with a glance at him. It was a lot to process, Jo wasn't sure she was ready to share it with anyone else yet. Andy shook his head and rubbed his face with his hands like he was trying to wipe off sticky cobwebs.

"Roxie, why don't you take my seat? I... I need to

go relieve the babysitter." He stood up and let Roxie slide into his booth. He stood next to the table, hands hanging by his side. He looked down at her, eyes filled with emotion. "Jo? Thank you."

Jo reached up and gently took his hand. "No. Thank you, Andy. I'm glad we were able to talk." He gave her a small smile, nodded at Roxie, and walked away. Jo palmed the little sock he had slipped back into her hand.

"You OK?" Roxie looked at her strangely.

"Yeah," Jo said, watching him walk away. "Yeah. I am." There was so much to say, so much to explain, but for a moment she wanted it to be her own, plus she could tell that Roxie wasn't in the mood to discuss the past.

Roxie looked around the room, searching for the waitress. Jo watched her eyes dance over the men sitting at nearby tables. As was often the case whenever she was out with Roxie, there seemed to be an inordinate amount of extremely sexy men all around them. And as usual each and every one of them had eyes only for her friend, intent clearly etched into their faces. Out of habit Roxie checked out each man, one at a time, and moved on to the next with a blink, but Jo could tell that her heart wasn't in it. Jo was actually surprised that she was being so dismissive. It wasn't like Roxie to not be on the prowl.

"Are you okay?" She asked, a little concerned. She didn't know what to make of this Roxie.

"Yeah. I don't know. I'm... bored... I guess. I don't want to do the usual thing. I just don't feel like it." Roxie shrugged, looking a bit sad, then went back to looking around the room. Even if her heart wasn't in it, Jo knew she couldn't help it. It was what she always did. Jo turned to check on Sadie. A stab of jealousy tugged at her stomach as she saw Kona's hand brush Sadie's as he passed a drink to someone sitting next to her. She wanted that again. Simple, easy love.

She had love, she reminded herself. She had a wonderful man who was on his way to see her tomorrow. On his way to come marry her! At the mere thought her stomach sank.

29. Jo

The friendly waitress brought their drinks, nodding briefly and smiling conspiratorially at Jo as she dropped off the cold glasses. Jo had no idea what the woman had imagined after overhearing some of her conversation with Andy, she really didn't care so she just smiled back and thanked her for the drinks.

Jo let the waitress walk away before taking a huge gulp. She shook her head a bit and squared back her shoulders. "Enough already! Isn't a bachelorette party supposed to be cheery and fun? This feels like a funeral! Shouldn't we dance or something?"

Roxie immediately perked up and tore her gaze from her drink. "Yeah! Let's dance! Forget exes and silly friends who dump us for the first pair of bright eyes! It's time to partay!"

Roxie and Jo danced like maniacs to every song played by the cover band, even the slow maudlin ones that others tried to slow dance to. It felt great to let go and just let the music move them. During a particularly slow number Jo stood on the dance floor and let her body sway to the music. She felt like a reed being tossed around by the sea—free and relaxed for the first time in... in, well, a long time.

Sometime during the evening, the two girls decided that it would be a fabulous idea to taste each and every one of the bar's specialty drinks, a hilarity ensuing activity which left them decidedly worse for the wear but didn't keep them from dancing their hearts out. Kona laughed at them every time they'd head back to the bar for a new drink and by the end of the night he could have been serving up dish-water and they wouldn't have known the difference.

At long last they reached the end of the menu and when they tried to start back at the top, with a gentle laugh Kona insisted that enough was enough.

"Even though you guys don't have to drive home doesn't mean I don't have the right to cut you off," he chided. "I think your heads are going to hurt plenty in the morning as it is." He handed both girls a cold bottle of water bearing the hotel's bright label and told them to call it a night. Sadie waved her friends off with a knowing smile and a wink.

"Don't wait up for me. I'll catch up later!" She said, batting her eyelashes at Kona. He beamed back at her. Even through her drunken stupor Jo could easily read the infatuation and lust in his eyes.

Roxie and Jo made pretend gagging noises and erupted into hysterical giggles. They fell into each other's arms and stumbled out of the bar, more or less holding each other up. The air outside sobered them a little and their giggles faded away.

"S'fun," Jo said, squeezing Roxie's arm a bit harder. "We should do jish more often."

Roxie nodded vehemently and almost fell over. Jo nearly caught her, but when she missed, the two of them crashed to the ground, giggling hysterically again.

Jo felt like she was hovering outside of her body, watching the two of them heaped on the floor, laughing hysterically every time one tried to stand up and fell over the other again. Even as she laughed and fell she knew they were making fools of themselves; she just couldn't bring herself to care. She was having fun. It felt good to laugh and be silly. It felt good to just be.

"I don wanna go up yet," Roxie slurred, once they'd both managed to get up and stay up. She pulled on Jo's arm and headed towards the beach. Jo couldn't think of a single urgent reason to go anywhere, but she followed her friend down the stairs.

"Where'r we goin'?" Jo asked, stumbling over a step in the dark.

"Dunno. Know when I see it."

They picked up speed until they were racing through the dark hotel grounds, stumbling over invisible obstacles and succumbing to the giggles again when Roxie squealed after almost stepping on a huge toad sitting on one of the steps leading to the pool. The toad was completely unimpressed and just puffed out his hideous throat at them, sending them into further gales of laughter. Roxie and Jo ran away from him, making pretend toad calls to each other.

Roxie came to a sudden stop just beyond the deserted glowing pool.

"Here. Found it."

"Whah? What d'ja find?" Jo asked, looking around to see what Roxie could possibly mean. All the teak pool chairs had been cleared of their cushions and didn't look very inviting without them. The hot tubs had been turned off and just looked like mini versions of the desolate pool. Then Jo saw what Roxie had been looking at and nodded wildly.

"Yesh! S'perfect! We can look at the stars!"

They climbed awkwardly into the hammock, tipping themselves out onto the sandy ground three times before finally figuring out the perfect way to both get in without flipping the whole thing over. The hysterical laughter caused by each spill slowed down the proceedings considerably.

They rocked silently for a long while. Jo could feel the alcohol's effects leaving her system slowly. The fuzziness that had clouded her brain was starting to fade, but the joy from the evening was staying, making her feel warm and loved in a way that she had missed.

"You know, it's been good seeing Andy again," Jo said, "It's helping me remember all the great things about him."

"He is a lovely, lovely man, that's for sure," Roxie agreed. Her voice was still a little slurred and Jo wasn't sure if she was still completely drunk or half asleep. She didn't care.

"Yes! That's exactly it. He's a lovely, lovely man." Jo nodded. "He's gentle and sweet, and really, really caring."

Roxie murmured her assent, but when she didn't say anything else, Jo just kept talking, following her train of thought.

"I think that the way things ended made me forget all the great things we had. We used to laugh all the time. We were such good friends. I'd almost forgotten that. But seeing him again? Talking with him today? It also reminded me of how young we were, how young he was. We were so immature. It makes me want to cry to think of those two kids having to deal with the stuff they ended up having to face."

Roxie murmured again, this time with a slightly more sympathetic tone.

"When I met Jordan, I think that's what attracted me to him. He was such a man. Not a boy, a real man. Someone who could take care of me."

"And he did," Roxie cut in.

"Yeah. It's like Andy and I were kids together. Jordan and I are grown-ups together. I just don't think I ever expected Andy to grow up too."

"But he has hasn't he?" Jo heard a hint of wistfulness in Roxie's voice. It echoed the feeling in her heart. She stared up at the stars peeking through the branches of the tree. Andy, her best friend, a grown-up. It was a perturbing thought. She had always imagined he'd always be incapable of rising to a challenge, of facing a hardship. But clearly, in his own way, he had finally learned to do that. It made him infinitely more attractive.

"Plus, he's hot." Hearing the words that had just gone through her head spoken out loud startled Jo. She twisted herself to look at Roxie, who just shrugged. "Well, he is! Don't tell me you hadn't noticed how we'll he's grown into that baby face he used to have!"

Jo poked Roxie and both girls melted into giggles. Roxie was right. Andy hadn't just grown into his face though. He'd also grown into his body. His broad shouldered body and strong arms...

Mmm," Roxie said, and Jo laughed again at hearing her thoughts come out of her friend's mouth.

The breeze picked up and made the leaves rustle above them. Jo looked up through the gently swaying branches and sighed. The moon was glowing brightly, lending a surreal glow to everything around them. Jo was still a little buzzed and everything just felt dreamlike and timeless. Here, in the hammock, lying with Roxie, she could easily pretend that they were still college girls lusting after a classmate. There was no wedding. No husbands. No lost babies. Just a warm breeze that smelled like the sea and the stars.

"Sadie doesn't know what she's missing," Jo said, sighing happily. "Does anything get better than being in paradise, in a hammock, with a good friend?"

"Jo?" Roxie asked, her voice more serious than Jo had expected. "Do you think I'll ever meet someone?"

"Well, duh, you meet someone every other day!"

"No, I mean someone special. Like you and Jordan." Jo winced at the mention. "Like Sadie and Kona. I could tell, you know? I could tell that they were connecting. There was this... this spark when they looked at each other. I don't think I've ever felt that before."

"Do you even want to feel that? What happened to little Miss I Never Want to Be Tied Down?"

"You know, I just don't know. It might be nice to feel that connected..." her voice trailed away one last time and no matter how much Jo pushed and cajoled she wouldn't say any more. After a while her silence and the gentle rocking combined with the warm breeze lulled Jo. She started to drift off, so she wasn't sure if she imagined hearing Roxie saying, "what if I found the man I'd give up my freedom for?" or if she was already asleep and dreamed it.

30. Sadie

Sadie sat perched on her bar stool and watched Kona work. It was like watching a dancer, a really, really hot dancer who owned the stage he was on. He moved from one customer to another gracefully, making each one feel noticed and important with a smile, a wink, a light touch on the arm, or just a particularly attentive gaze, never forgetting an order or spilling more than a drop. She saw the visible effect he was having on people. Everyone who came into contact with him stood a little taller, smiled a little wider. He made them feel attractive and special; it was written all over their faces and their bodies. She smiled to herself and nodded. He was having the same effect on her. When he looked at her or touched her arm she felt a million times more attractive and funnier. She finally felt like a real catch.

Every so often Kona would glance her way and shoot her a small smile or a slow wink that made her heart speed up. The way his forehead would smooth, and his eyes would light up when he saw that she was still there was making her stomach do somersaults. He'd smile and wink and she'd feel herself slip a little further under his spell. Sadie shook her head and sighed. She was so out of her league here. Men like Kona didn't fall in love with her. Heck, she didn't fall in love with men like Kona! Or rather, she did, painfully so, but they never reciprocated. No, men like the stooped-over balding man nursing a very girly looking froufrou drink over at the end of the bar fell for her. And she gave in to them, so she'd have someone by her side.

She looked away from the man, avoiding his pointed leer, and looked at Kona again. His gaze crossed hers and he beamed at her. Her heart almost stopped. He was just so incredibly good looking. His Hawaiian tan made his skin look like a warm day in the sun and his thick dark hair looked like it would be silky soft and smooth. Her eyes slipped down from his hair to his broad shoulders. Shoulders she would love to feel under her hands...

Sadie blushed furiously. What on earth was she thinking? She was not even going to think the word love in conjunction with this boy. In conjunction with this unbelievably beautiful boy. Whose eyes were captivating her. Whose smile was causing the butterflies in her stomach to fall over themselves in their haste to wake up...

She sighed. Who was she kidding? She couldn't take her eyes off him, couldn't stop thinking about him, and she knew it was nuts, but she could barely resist the urge to murmur a quiet "I love you" in his direction. It was insane. She wanted to take herself back to her room to give herself a cold shower. She had known this boy for all of an evening. An evening where she had sat and watched him work. They had exchanged all of three sentences, but she had felt such a connection the instant their eyes had met for the first time. There was no explaining this madness, but she already felt like he was a part of her.

She'd never felt this way before. She'd fallen in love plenty of times, but this was different. This wasn't passion; this was like a deep recognition. She felt like they had always known each other, just hadn't come together yet. Her romantic sappy side kept wanting to say things like their souls were finally being reunited, but her more rational brain was slapping that side upside the head and telling it to hush up fast.

And yet, she couldn't stop feeling like she'd always been searching for Kona and he'd always been waiting for her to find him. Sadie shook her head again. She was insane, she thought, as she took a sip of her coke. She'd stopped drinking an hour or so ago, determined to keep her feet on the ground, but despite the lack of alcohol she knew she was losing the battle. Already she felt like she was dancing alongside Kona, floating in his wake as he danced behind the bar.

"Hey sleeping beauty. I'm almost done here. Want to go for a walk or are you too tired?" Kona's rich voice lulled her out of her reverie, and she smiled up at his kind face.

"I'd love to go for a walk," she said. "I'm not tired, just daydreaming."

"Hope I was in that dream of yours," he teased. Sadie blushed crimson and was instantly grateful that it was dark inside the bar. Kona laughed. "I was just teasing. I'll be ready to go in a minute."

"Okay. I'm just going to run to the ladies' room. I'll be right back."

"Don't run away now. I'm really looking forward to this walk." Kona caught her hand as she went to push herself off her bar stool. He squeezed it gently, looking deep into her eyes. She got caught in the intensity of his gaze, surprised and pleased at what she saw there. He wasn't just flirting. He really wanted her to come back. Her butterflies fluttered a little harder and for a moment she did consider running away. This was sheer madness. And it was terrifying. She wasn't used to men worrying about her leaving. She was always the one who worried.

Kona squeezed her hand gently again and his face broke into a huge grin. The intensity in his eyes was joined by the sparkle that Sadie had been loving all night and her fears took a back seat to her desire to stay close to that smile.

Sadie squeezed back and smiled. "I'm really looking forward to it too." It was nothing short of the truth. She had been wondering all night what it would feel like to have Kona's arms around her and maybe his mouth against hers. Now she just might find out. She resisted the urge to skip her way to the bathroom.

In the bathroom Sadie splashed some cold water on her neck taking care not to smear her make-up and shook her head some more, trying to clear her head. As much as she was looking forward to her walk, she had to remember to keep her feet on the ground. She took a couple deep breaths and stared herself down in the mirror.

"You are not in love with this guy. You do not know him. You have just met him. Get a grip young lady," she sternly told her reflection and almost died when a teenager walked in and gave her a sideways glance. "Sorry," Sadie said to the kid. "I'm not crazy, just trying to keep myself from doing something nuts. It's all good."

The teen rolled her eyes and darted into the stall. Sadie laughed and let herself out of the restroom. Maybe the kid was right, she was ridiculous.

"What's so funny?" Kona asked, as he saw her approaching the bar, giggling.

"Nothing." She smiled at him. "Are you ready?"

"Yup!" Kona walked out from behind the bar and waved goodbye to his coworker who winked suggestively and called to them to be good. "Don't listen to him, he's an ass."

"Aw, you mean all Hawaiians aren't as nice as you?" Sadie teased, poking him playfully in the side as they headed out into the dark night.

Kona grabbed her hand and spun Sadie around. He gathered her up tightly into his arms.

"I've been waiting all night to do this," Kona murmured as he lowered his mouth to hers. His lips were both soft and firm and there was absolutely no hesitation as he kissed her at first tenderly and then increasingly passionately. She parted her lips and felt the last of her resistance melt away as their tongues met.

His arms tightened around her waist and her hands rose up to entwine themselves around his neck. Sadie had never been kissed like this before and she let herself ride the wave of passion that overtook her. Her ardor easily matched Kona's and when one of his hands started roaming down her back her own hands followed suit easily. His back was incredibly muscular and feeling the tightly bunched muscles under her probing fingers fueled her fire even further. The way his hands seemed to be enjoying discovering her own back was doing nothing to cool her down either.

They pulled apart at the same time, gasping for

breath, still clutching each other tightly.

"Whoah. Sorry I...," Kona started, but Sadie interrupted.

"Sorry nothing. That was as much me as it was you. And I'm sorry. I'm not usually so... ah... forward." Sadie blushed and tried to look down as she said that.

He smiled down at her and reluctantly took one hand off her back to use it to lift her chin. "Don't be sorry please. I'm not usually this forward either. I just can't resist you." He leaned his face towards her again and kissed her extremely gently on the lips. This light kiss was no less passionate than the last, even as his lips barely grazed hers Sadie could feel the intensity that he was holding back, could tell that he was 100% focused on her and her alone. Sadie returned the kiss and felt herself getting pulled in again. She placed a hand on Kona's chest and gently pushed him away.

He lifted his head and took a deep breath before laughing. He took her hand in his and stood there clasping it in his. "Sadie. Sadie. Sadie. What have you done to me? I don't normally have this little self-control." He pulled her closer and she felt him shudder as her thighs pushed up against his. He rested his forehead on hers and gazed deep into her eyes. She felt herself sink into the intoxicating blueness of his eyes and the darkened world around them faded even further.

This time she was the one who reached for his lips, but he pulled himself back after a short, but rather intense moment that left her knees shaking and her body craving more.

"Come on, if we don't start walking, we're never going to get anywhere."

"Now would that really be such a bad thing,"

Sadie murmured, shocked at her own forwardness, but not caring a bit.

Kona just laughed and pulled her in for another tight hug and kiss that left them even more breathless than before. He let her go and slipped his arm gently around her waist, leading her down the path towards the beach. Sadie's knees still felt wobbly, so she was grateful for the strong arm holding her up.

Sadie loved how she fit neatly into Kona's side. It all felt so natural, so normal – the kissing, the way their bodies fit together, the way she instinctively knew she could just be herself and not have to worry about what he would think of her. This was absolutely insane. She'd known him for just a couple of hours. There was no way she could possibly be feeling this way. She sighed deeply causing Kona to look down at her.

"You okay?" Even in the dark she could detect the concern in his eyes. It filled her with a warmth she hadn't expected.

"Yeah, it's just..."

"It's just that this is insane, right?"

"Yes! God! What is the matter with us?"

"I have no idea, but I really like it," Kona said as he pulled Sadie close and kissed her again. She let herself be carried off on another wave of passion. Who cared if this was insane? Who cared if there was no way this could last? It was too good to resist.

The catcalls and teasing cries of "Get a room!" from some passing hotel guests made them jump apart and Kona grabbed her hand.

"Come on!" He started to run, and she followed along, feeling like a kid. They ran through the dark hotel grounds until they reached the pool. Sadie thought that

Kona would stop by the lounge chairs that were still lined up at the water's edge, but he kept running. They sidestepped the trees sheltering the hammocks and ran on down to the beach. The sight of the brilliant moon perfectly reflected on the sparkling sea stopped them both in their tracks and made Sadie start to laugh.

At first it was just a giggle, but the laughter grew and grew until she was clutching her middle and gasping for breath. Kona was soon doubled over and laughing just as hard. "Please, please," he gasped. "Please tell me why we're laughing so hard," which made Sadie laugh even harder. She fell over into the sand and pulled Kona down with her. They alternated kissing and laughing and rolling over and over in the sand that was still warm from a long day in the sun. Whenever Sadie opened her eyes and saw where she was she felt herself get hysterical again and she'd start laughing all over again.

She finally caught her breath enough to say "Seriously, is this for real? If this were a movie I'd be irritated at how insanely corny it is!" Kona was lying on his back and she was half lying on top of him, loving the feel of his hard body under hers. Quick as a cat he grabbed her wrists and flipped her over so that he was lying on top of her and her hands were pinned above her head. He lowered his torso closer to hers and kissed her quickly all over her face – first her forehead, then her nose, her cheeks, her chin, her ears.

"Is this corny? Does this feel real?" he murmured between kisses. "Is this? How about this? And this?"

"Yes! Yes!" Sadie answered after each kiss. But as his mouth traveled lower and lower, moving from her face, to her jaw, to her neck, and then to the dip where her collar bone met her neck, her answers became less joking and more pleading. Her hands strained against the strong one holding them down, but it didn't release her. Kona finally stopped, taking pity on her, and as she gasped for breath he leaned on the other elbow and looked down at her, lust etched clearly in every detail of his face.

Sadie could feel her chest heaving and almost started laughing again at the thought that this was adding even more to the corniness of the situation instead of taking away from it.

"I'd let you go, but I don't think I can control myself if I feel your hands anywhere on my body," Kona said with a smile.

"Oh, really?" Sadie said, with the sweetest, most innocent look that she could muster. "Why don't you let me go and we'll see just how much you can stand." She batted her eyes at him for extra emphasis and with a chuckle and a deep kiss Kona released her hands.

Sadie instantly entwined her fingers in Kona's thick hair and pulled him even closer. Their kiss deepened and the last of the laughter faded. She placed her other hand low on his back and felt him shudder in response. "Wow. You weren't joking," she murmured and was rewarded with a low growl. Kona tore his mouth from hers and started kissing her neck again. Now that his hands weren't busy holding hers they started exploring her body, fueled as much by Sadie's moans and gasps as his own desire. He skirted her breasts and moved down to cover her taunt belly with more kisses and tiny maddening bites. Sadie felt like she was on fire. She wanted nothing more than to let Kona discover every inch of her body. She wanted the two of them to become so entwined that they'd never be able to be separated. As he explored her body with his soft lips she did her best to keep up with her hands and her mouth when he let her get close enough. She couldn't find a spot that wasn't a tight firm muscle. When her hands discovered a new section of his body that she hadn't yet encountered she was met with deepening growls and moans, which only motivated her to explore further.

Kona worked his way back up her body and she met his lips with her own, pulling him in for another endless kiss. They lost themselves further into each other and as the kiss went on and on Sadie let her hands roam more over Kona's back, chest, and anything else she could reach. She was thrilled by the shudders that kept tearing through his body. She'd never had such an effect on anyone before. Her hand stilled on his chest for a moment as she focused on the kiss and he grabbed her hand and held it tight. He broke away for a moment and looked into her eyes as he tried to catch his breath.

"Told you I'd have trouble resisting," he said with a smile.

"Seems to me you're doing pretty well so far," she teased back. "Let's see if I can push you any further," she added as she pulled his hand towards her breast, one of two parts of her body he'd resolutely avoided. She was aching to let herself go. She placed his hand flat against her breast and had the extreme pleasure of seeing pure lust cross his face.

With an agonized look he let his hand stay there for a moment before lifting it to cup her face. "Not yet" he murmured as he kissed her tenderly. "Soon, but not yet. You have no idea how much I want to, but even more, I want us to get to know each other first."

Tears of frustration mingled with tears of delight welled in Sadie's eyes. She was hurting for his touch, but if he wanted to get to know her then she was more than happy to let that happen. As she looked into his brilliant eyes she was stuck by the fact that she couldn't remember another man who'd ever said that to her before.

31. Sadie

Kona jumped to his feet and took a deep bow. "M'lady? May I have this walk?" He asked, mock solemnly, holding out his arm for her to take. Sadie tucked one hand under the proffered arm and held out the other one so he could help her get up. He gently pulled her to her feet and pulled her into a gentle hug as soon as she was up. He held her for a moment and looked down at her.

"You're not mad, are you?" He asked with a worried frown.

"Mad? Because you're being a gentleman and not taking advantage of me? Yes I'm very, very mad!" She teased poking him in the chest. Sadie stood on her tiptoes and placed a gentle kiss on his cheek. "No, I'm not mad at all. I'm actually quite flattered," she said, tucking her arm back under his. "Now, weren't we going to take a walk?"

He untucked her arm, and she was surprised by the wave of sadness that washed over her when he released her. She was equally surprised by the bubbles of joy that popped in her belly when instead he wrapped his own arm around her waist. She really couldn't get over how much she enjoyed being this close to him.

Before long they were walking along the glittering water, a warm breeze swirling around them. The moon shone bright, lighting their way along the deserted beach. Their footsteps were the only ones marring the immaculate sand, and if it weren't for the occasional burst of laughter floating down from the hotel they could have easily imagined they were the only couple left on earth. For a while they didn't talk. Sadie was hyper aware of every inch of Kona's body that was in contact with hers. She kept trying to match her breathing and her footsteps to his and losing track when he'd squeeze her a bit closer or stop her for a kiss.

She smiled again at the thought of the utterly corniness of the situation, but the urge to laugh hysterically had long passed. She didn't care anymore that this was like a bad romantic comedy. She just wanted to enjoy every second of it. She opened her mouth to ask Kona what he was thinking, but the words got stuck in her throat. It was all so perfect, he was so perfect, that she suddenly felt too shy to talk. What if this was a dream and speaking made her wake up?

"What? Is something wrong?" Kona looked down at her, face creased in sudden concern. "Are you okay? Are you cold?"

Sadie laughed, the shyness instantly dispelled. "I'm fine! Nothing's wrong. In fact, everything is oh so very right." She felt more than heard Kona release the breath he'd been holding. "Wait, should something be wrong?" she asked.

"No. No," he answered quickly. "I was just..."

Sadie stopped walking and turned to face him, giving him a moment to continue.

Kona looked away from her. "I was worried you

were worrying about the... you know... the fact that I work in the hotel and all."

"You mean, as in I was worried that you might get in trouble for being with me?" Sadie laughed, sliding her arm back around him.

"No! No! You know, that I'm just a lowly bartender," he stammered for a moment and then rushed on. "Because I'm not, you know!"

"You're not?" Sadie's voice rose in surprise. "Wait, that came out wrong. I mean, whatever, I don't care what you do." And she really didn't. Or at least she hadn't a second ago. Who cared what the guy you had a vacation fling did? Did it really matter in the end? Wasn't that the whole point of a fling? To just have fun? Because then you went home and went back to doing all the things you were supposed to do.

The thought caused an unbidden lump to form in her throat. She was really enjoying being with Kona. It just felt so right to be with him. Figured that she'd find the love of her life in paradise and that she'd have to leave him behind when the real world beckoned.

"No! Really! I'm not!" Kona rushed on. "Well, I mean it's complicated, and it's confidential, but I really want to tell you. I need to tell you." He stopped walking and turned her so she could face him. "It's going to sound a bit nuts, but I just need you to give me the benefit of the doubt. Okay?" Sadie nodded, and he turned his head and made a sweeping gesture towards the hotel spread out behind them. "I'm, ah, I... I own this place. Or I will. I mean I do."

"Huh?" Sadie tried hard to believe him, but he was right, she thought he was nuts. Owned the place? What kind of delusional bartender's crap was this? Kona glanced down at her and saw the look that crossed her face.

"I'm serious! You promised you'd hear me out!"

"Okay. Fine. I'm listening," Sadie said, but she took a half step away from Kona and crossed her arms in front of her. She wasn't so sure any more about this man. He had seemed so genuine and normal. But this? This was weirder than most of the stuff her past boyfriends had thrown at her. Jilted lovers she knew how to handle. Delusional minimum wage employees? Not so much.

He reached out for her hand and she almost held it back, but she had told him she'd listen, and he didn't look too crazy. Just really, really tormented right now. She compromised. She let him take her hand, but she didn't come back to stand close to him. Kona squeezed her hand and let it go. He started walking again, talking softly. She rushed to keep up. She was going to hear him out, she wasn't sure why, but her heart was pulling her towards this man and, while she definitely couldn't explain why, she felt like she owed it to herself to follow.

"My dad started this place," Kona gestured back at the hotel again, "with his best friend long before I was born. This place was his everything, especially after my mother died when I was fourteen and that best friend ran off with most of what was in the bank. He spent every moment working and I hated him for it. I missed my mom and I wanted him to miss her too. But he never talked about her. Never did anything but work on hotel business. Now I know he was just trying to save the place, but back then the only thing I saw was that there was no room for anything else, not even me. God knows I did my best to try to get his attention though." The bitterness in his tone surprised Sadie. He hadn't struck her as the bitter type. She didn't know whether to try to comfort him or give him the space he needed to continue. She settled for just moving a bit closer to him and letting him speak on without interrupting him.

At first it has been small stuff, but soon he'd been smashing windows, breaking into hotel rooms to go through people's things. He never took anything, but it pissed people off and they complained. Not that it stopped him. He would have done anything to get his father's attention, and the only thing that worked was stuff that had to do with the hotel.

"When going through people's bags got old I started helping myself to drinks in the bar. That's where my dad drew the line. He could handle the little shit that happened more or less in private, but when I started making nightly scenes in front of all the guests..." Kona's voice faded away for a moment and he stared straight ahead with unseeing eyes. Sadie couldn't resist any more. She was already falling in love with those eyes. She hated to see them darkened with pain like that. She reached out and grabbed his hand and squeezed tight. Kona squeezed her hand back gently. The tenderness in his grasp melted her heart. Here he was, reliving a painful memory, which clearly was pissing him off, but he still had enough control over himself to be gentle with her. She bit back a smile, not wanting to make him think she was laughing at him, but inside her heart sang.

"He sent me away to boarding school and after I ran away for the third time he started threatening to make me stay there over the school breaks, even during the summer. I tried hard to behave, but by then I couldn't help myself. Plus, every time I acted up I got to talk to him... He may have been an insensitive, preoccupied bastard, but he was my only family..."

His voice cracked and he stopped talking. Sadie had no idea what to do. She wanted to comfort him, but he wasn't putting out a single 'take care of me vibe.' She stopped walking and tried to give him a hug, but he pushed her back gently. She stepped back, her heart sinking. This wasn't how things went. Guys came to her broken and she fixed them. She mothered them. It was what she knew how to do. Maybe she had misread Kona and he wasn't really all that interested in her. She looked at his face, trying to read his emotions, but all she saw was the same face she had been so drawn to earlier – strong jaw, tender eyes, and a sweet smile peering out of the frown that had been there when she went to hug him.

"I'm sorry. I'm okay," he said, voice back under control. He looked down at her and smiled more broadly. "Can I tell you the rest?"

She lifted her hand and placed it gently on his chest for a moment before tucking herself back under his arm. The feel of his strong, steady heartbeat under her hand was comforting. They walked on down the beach. Sadie wasn't used to dealing with someone so tough. She had been in many relationships, but things were so different here. She was felt like a schoolgirl falling in love with the first time. This was completely uncharted territory, and she had no idea what to do next.

Then again, she didn't have to decide right then and there, she realized as Kona resumed his story.

Kona had been punished and forbidden to come home for the next two years. His father had arranged for him to work on the school grounds during the long summer. Said it would teach his son some valuable lessons. Instead, Kona had just learned that digging holes was hard work and that it was possible to miss home more than anything in the world.

"Maybe that was his goal all along. My plan was to grovel for forgiveness and beg to be allowed to come home after graduation. I was going to promise to work my tail off if I could just be allowed to come home, but just before I was able to call my dad and plead my case, I was called into the school office." Kona's voice broke again, but he didn't stop talking.

His father had died. Heart attack from working too hard and not taking care of himself well enough.

Sadie couldn't help it, she gasped. "Oh my God. What did you do?"

"What could I do? I came home. I didn't know what to expect, but it was definitely not to be the sole heir to the place. I don't know, I guess I assumed that he'd sell off the place before leaving it to me."

"So you weren't joking. You really do own the place." Sadie turned around and looked at the huge resort spread out behind them. Despite the late hour, hundreds of lights still flickered from countless windows looking for all the world like beacons in the night or stars in the sky. "Wow."

"Well, see, that's the thing. I don't own it. Yet."

Sadie turned back to Kona and raised one eyebrow in invitation to explain.

"My dad left a clause in his will. I have to work my way up through the ranks. He knew I didn't have the skills to run the place, and he still thought I was a complete fuck up so he wasn't willing to trust me with the hotel he had single-handedly saved and turned into something of a local legend. He left the board in charge, appointed an asshole of a general manager, and left strict instructions about what I'd have to do to earn my inheritance."

"Wow. That is cold."

"No. I mean, I thought so too at first. But now I know that he was right. I had no clue about how to run a business. Plus, I was so messed up and angry, I would have run the place into the ground just to spite him. It's a huge responsibility, running a place like this. I'm still not sure when I'll feel ready to take over. And, let's be honest, it's not like the employees don't know, so it's not like I don't get some special treatment." Sadie nodded, suddenly understanding why he could be so liberal with the handing out of free drinks and how easy it had been for him to leave the bar before closing. "On top of that I get a pretty decent salary and full room and board, which I guess I'm technically paying myself." He smiled down at her. "See? I told you it was a bit complicated."

Sadie gave a half giggle and shook her head a bit. "Wow. I mean. Wow. That's quite a story."

"You believe me? Don't you?" Kona frowned suddenly and he stopped her to look her in the eye as he asked.

"I believe you," Sadie murmured. "It's just... It's a lot to take in." She looked back at the impressive hotel. His impressive hotel. And shook her head again. "I think I need a stiff drink." She said, frowning herself when she realized how far they'd wandered from the spot they'd first set foot on the beach.

Kona took in her gaze and her concerned look and seemed to instantly understand. "Hey! No worries," he said, pulling her towards the trees lining the far end of the beach. Sadie hesitated and tried to pull back "Really! It's okay. I promise! It's safe. Come on, you've trusted me this far! Why stop now?" Sadie still didn't move so he turned to her and hugged her gently. "Sadie. Tell me, what's your gut telling you right now? Is it telling you to run, or is it telling you to trust me?"

She gazed up at him and felt herself slip into his deep gaze. Her brain was yelling at her to run, shouting stats and replaying bloody horror movie sequences to her. This guy had just told her a really, really farfetched story. For all she knew he wasn't an eccentric heir, he was a serial killer of sorts. She knew how the perfect scene on the beach ended on the big screen. It ended with missing limbs and heads, that's how.

But that was just what the voices in her head were screaming. Her usually very expressive gut was calm. She knew instinctively that Kona was no fake and that he wasn't insane. She felt no fear as he pulled her gently into the trees.

Even so, the floodlights that instantly turned on helped to quiet her overactive imagination and the adorable squat little bungalow that she spotted at the edge of the lights brought a smile to her face.

"Yeah. I mentioned there were some perks, didn't I?" Kona laughed at the rapid slideshow of emotions that must have been flying across her face. "This is one of them. I get to live on one of the prettiest beaches in the world, in one of Hawaii's fanciest resort bungalows."

The tiny house was whitewashed with light green plantation shutters. All the windows were wide open, but her view of the inside was obstructed by billowy white curtains. There was a little wraparound deck, decorated with colorful Adirondack chairs, not exactly traditional Hawaiian, but they somehow worked perfectly here.

"It's so... lovely," Sadie whispered as she let Kona lead her inside his home. The bungalow was expertly decorated, just like their hotel rooms—white, plush couch and chairs, weathered wood furniture—but had many more personal touches—photographs, books, gorgeous paintings of island scenes that brought it to life. Bright cushions and throws livened up the classy, but plain hotel decor. Sadie instantly felt at home in the space and she followed Kona into his compact little kitchen when he headed there to get her a drink.

She was surprised to see that the space was fully outfitted with every kitchen appliance a person could dream of, including a beautiful set of serious pots and pans hanging from the ceiling.

"You cook!" She said.

"Yeah. I had to learn. All this fancy hotel food... after a while it gets old, you know?"

"Uh, no." Sadie had just been saying to Jo that she'd be happy to eat at the hotel restaurant every day for the rest of her life, she couldn't fathom ever getting sick of it. "Wait a minute, just how long have you been working your way up the ranks of this hotel?"

It had just struck her that if he had inherited the hotel right after high school, there was an unexplained time lag in his story. Kona looked young, but he didn't look 18.

"Uh," Kona thought for a moment. "Four years. I didn't start right away. I traveled for a bit before."

"Shit! Four years?" Sadie said. "Wow! And you're only a bartender?"

"Yeah, I told you, my dad really wanted me to

earn the job. I have to work every single job in the place for at least three months before I can move on."

"Every job?"

"Yeah. Trust me. I never want to clean another toilet in my life!" Kona laughed again. Sadie looked at him with newfound respect. She would have been livid if someone had made her do menial tasks like cleaning bathrooms in a hotel she technically owned. But Kona seemed more than just fine with it.

"I'm impressed. Really."

"You are?"

"Yes. It takes a big man to do what you're doing." She nodded appreciatively.

Kona looked solemnly out the window at his hotel for a moment before looking back at her. "Well? It's worth it, don't you think? Look at this place. It's mine. And it deserves this kind of sacrifice." Sadie looked out the window at his little slice of paradise. He was right, it was worth it, even if scrubbing toilets had been part of the price.

"Now my dear, may I give you the grand tour?" Sadie nodded and laughed when instead of taking her hand, he reached down and swept her into his arms. He held her close and looked down at her, suddenly serious again. He kissed her gently and carried her into the only other room in his home where he carefully laid her in the plush center of his large white bed.

32. Sadie

They made love gently at first, then more passionately the second time. Despite being unbelievably tired, they couldn't get enough of each other, couldn't stop touching each other. Finally, they lay spent, not a speck of energy left between the two of them, not a square inch of either body left undiscovered.

They rested on the huge white bed, Sadie's head resting on Kona's muscular shoulder, his arm wrapped possessively around her, tired, but unwilling to sleep. Their two hands danced in the air above them, taking turns tracing the lines in each other's palms.

It was still dark outside, but Sadie could see the moon shining bright over the ocean through the bedroom's sheer white curtains. The bed was strategically positioned so that you could see a vast expanse of beach and ocean without ever lifting your head off the bed. It was breathtaking. Sadie couldn't imagine ever getting tired of waking up to that sight. Having it be the last thing you saw every day wouldn't be half bad either.

"You know, I meant what I said about wanting to know more about you," Kona gently said. "I'm sorry I couldn't wait to ravage you," he said, "but now that I can focus on something other than my deep dark secret and how you're going to take it, and you're no longer throwing yourself at me like a horny beast, I'd love to know more about the mysterious Sadie."

"Oh, you would, would you?" She teased back, poking him in the side and causing him to squirm. "And I was no hornier than you!"

"Okay. Fine. That may be true." He laughed "But still? What's the story behind that gorgeous face?"

Sadie and Kona talked until the horizon turned a pale then brilliant pink and the sun started streaming in through the sheer curtains. If you had asked her if she had a story to share, she would have shrugged and said no, but as Sadie recounted her idyllic childhood, her attentive parents, her uneventful life since school, she found she couldn't stop talking. Kona's attention never wavered, and she felt a need to feed his clear fascination. She even caught herself going into more details about her terrible habit of hooking up with men who just needed her to fix them so they could go off and find true love with someone else. She held her breath after saying this and refused to look at Kona's face, terrified at what she might see in his eyes. But he quietly squeezed her and told her that he would never, under no uncertain terms, do that to her.

Her stomach lurched. She believed him. She had seen it the night before when he had opened up to her and shared his story with her. He was past that point in his life, was already on the mend and looking to move on. She knew it was unlikely, seeing as he had to stay here in paradise and she had to go home in a week, but she couldn't help hoping that she would play a role somewhere in the next chapter of his life, as more than just a paragraph or a footnote.

"So? What do you say?" Kona repeated the question that she hadn't heard.

"Huh?" She asked pulling herself back from the brink of sleep.

"Swim? Morning? Sunrise? Now?" Kona murmured suggestively in her ear.

"No suit," she murmured, snuggling into his shoulder, ready to let herself drift back off to sleep.

"No suit, no worries!" Kona laughed. "We're at the far end of the beach at a luxury resort where guests tend to sleep very, very late! Come on sleepyhead! It'll be fun."

Sadie lifted a sleepy eyebrow at Kona and looked at him carefully to see if he was joking. He leaned over and kissed her frown.

"I love it when you do that thing with your eyebrow."

Sadie's heart skipped a beat. She had been sure for a moment that he'd been about to say that he loved her. And, as crazy as that guy was, she was sure it would have come as naturally from him as her instantly echoed reply would have been from her.

"Deal! Swim!" She said, sprinting up to banish the weirdness that had just gripped her. "Last one in is a rotten egg!" She said, dashing out of the house in the direction of the ocean, Kona hot on her heels. The beach was breathtaking in the morning light. The pink and gold rays of the sunrise turned the sand into gently shimmering jewels, each one looking like it had been placed precisely there for her enjoyment. She took it all in as she made a beeline for the glittering water, its huge empty expanse so inviting in the early warmth of the day. Kona nearly ran into her when she came to a dead stop at the very edge of the sea. He came to a standstill behind her and slipped his arms around her waist. He leaned in and nibbled on her neck before murmuring into her ear.

"Pretty isn't it?" He leaned his head against hers and looked out in the same direction as her.

"Look! Is that a dolphin?" Sadie said, cupping her hand around her eyes so she could see better into the glare of the morning sun. She pointed to a dark speck in the distance.

"Where?" Kona asked, gazing into the direction her finger was pointing. Right away his body froze, and every trace of laughter evaporated. "No. That's no dolphin." His body tensed as he turned to run to the bungalow. "That's a shark. We have to close the beach! Don't go in the water!" He called back before vanishing through the door.

Sadie called after him as he ran back to the bungalow. "Shark? What? Close the beach? Wait. You don't mean actually close the BEACH? Right? Kona? Kona?"

She looked out at the water where the black speck was slowly growing until it was a clearly visible triangle of fin cutting through the water, heading her way.

Sadie took a hesitant step back away from the edge of the water. There was no way the shark could have reached her, but she felt the urge to get away from its menacing shape.

Sadie watched the shark swim towards the shore. It was a good thing the wedding was still two days away. This stretch of beach was exactly where it was scheduled to take place. By then the shark would surely be gone. The fin glided closer and Sadie took another step back. She could almost make out scars on the shiny black skin. She didn't know anything about sharks, but she was suddenly very glad that she had paused at the water's edge to take in the beautiful sunrise.

She eyed the shark uneasily. He had to be gone in two days. At least she really hoped he would be. She had no idea how Jo would take the news of the beach being closed.

The sound of a plane circling overhead her heart made her look up. Her stomach lurched as she realized who must be on that plane.

Forget Jo! Maryanne was not going to like hearing that the beach was closed.

33. Jordan

The airplane circled the island lazily, banking to give all the passengers a glimpse of the orange rising sun showering the blue water in shimmering light. There was a collective sigh from passengers followed by hushed chatter. Jordan couldn't tear his eyes away from the beauty spread out below them. It was very different from the sights he had grown accustomed to in Zambia, but it was awakening the part of his heart that had shut down when he and Jo had arrived in urban America. For the first time since they'd left Africa he felt his heart lift. He glanced over at his mother in law who was also staring out the window intently. He couldn't quite read the expression on her face, but it was definitely one he had never seen before. She had been tense ever since they had gotten onto the plane, reluctant to talk or do much of anything else. After a few tries at engaging her in a conversation, Jordan had given up and focused on a book he had picked up at the airport.

"It's amazing, isn't it?" He said as gently as possible, but she still startled at the sound of his voice. She just nodded, not taking her eyes off the window. "Bet you're glad you brought all that sunscreen!" He teased. He wasn't used to this quiet version of his mother-in-law. She was usually the chattiest person in the room.

His gentle ribbing had no more effect on her than it had had at the start of the flight, so he turned his attention back to the window. The plane was now coming in for a landing and the resorts lining the coast were growing in front of their eyes.

He looked at the vast hotels spread out below them. Each looked more luxurious than the next. His heart sank a bit. He'd hoped that he'd be able to discover a bit of the natural beauty of the island. When he had first seen the island appear in the distance he had imagined a rugged wild place that would remind him of his chosen home, but the resorts looked nothing like what he had imagined. They looked like little bits of modern America imposing themselves on a land with no regard to the local history or culture.

He took a deep breath and pushed his mounting irritation aside. It was impossible to tell from up here, maybe he should give the resorts a chance before damning them all to the hell he reserved for most of America. Maybe a stiff island drink or two would help. That, and getting to see Jo again.

At the thought of his fiancée his stomach lurched. It had been almost a relief when she had decided that she was going to leave early for Hawaii. Things had been off kilter ever since they'd left Zambia, ever since they'd arrived in her hometown.

He pictured her face and couldn't stop a small smile from tugging at the corners of his mouth. He loved that woman, had loved her from the first moment he laid eyes on her, but the woman he'd been living with since they had gotten back was a shadow of the woman he had fallen in love with. He couldn't remember when they had last had a real conversation. Heck, he could barely remember how to talk to her. She seemed angry at him all the time. Like he was solely responsible for what was eating her alive. It broke his heart.

At least it had at first. Now he was just tired. Tired of a job he hated. Tired of living in a place that drained his will to live. And tired of always being the bad guy. He wished he'd been stronger when they'd first met and had followed his gut.

From the day they'd met, Jo had occupied a special place in his heart and his head. He had fought the attraction he felt for her, had been rude, obnoxious, and had done his best to turn her off. For years he'd managed to stay distant from the people around him, but Jo? With one glowering look at him and her 'don't mess with me' attitude she had broken right through every defense he had spent years erecting. He had been fascinated by her. During those first months in the compound, she'd often wavered between being angry at everything and everyone, vibrantly alive in her anger, to, well, nothing. The days she shut down, it was as though all that was left her was a shell of a person. Then, a day or two later she'd be back. Vibrant and alive all over again.

His fascination with her had terrified him and had made him want to run. But he'd stayed put. Every day he spent trying to figure her out found him even more attracted and unable to walk away. Now the thought of a life without Jo seemed impossible, even if it was starting to feel like life with Jo was equally impossible.

The plane bounced down onto the small runway and the pilot welcomed them to Hawaii with a resounding ALOHA! The passengers erupted into loud cheers and Jordan felt drawn out of his morose musings. They weren't stateside anymore. Maybe things would be different here. Maybe Jo would be different here. Maybe the two of them could recapture a bit of the something that had drawn them to each other when they had first met. Even his mother-in-law smiled broadly and seemed to relax a bit, proof that island magic wasn't just a myth.

"Oh, I hate flying!" She said with a bit of a shaky breath. "It's good to be back on the ground! Now I can worry about the wedding instead of fearing for our lives." She let go of the armrest and massaged her hands, wincing as she worked the cramps out of her fingers. Jordan hadn't realized just how hard she had been clutching the armrests and felt a stab of remorse which was washed away at the mere thought of the wedding.

This whole wedding was going to be a disaster, he was sure of it. It would have been one thing if their relationship had been in a great place. But truth be told, they just weren't, and going through this rigmarole of a wedding was ridiculous and an outrageous waste of money. He couldn't for the life of him remember how he had even agreed to the ordeal. One minute they had been joking with Maryanne about how she had missed their incredibly fancy mud hut wedding and the next they had been picking music and choosing between caviar on blinis and smoked salmon toast points.

He had no idea what else had been planned. He'd opted to let himself get sidetracked by work and now the mere mention of the wedding was enough to make him crave a drink. From the start he'd had a sinking feeling that the whole thing was going to end badly. There was just no way it couldn't. If a simple wedding ceremony held at the spot they had first met, honoring their love for each other, witnessed by people who truly believed that they were soul mates hadn't been enough to ensure their enduring happiness, there was no way that an overblown and insincere ceremony in a place that meant nothing to either of them could do a better job.

34. Jordan

"Jorrrrrrdan!" Sadie's voice sang out through the hotel lobby, bringing a small smile to Jordan's face and making every guest turn to see who was being greeted so enthusiastically. They hadn't known each other for long, but it was hard not to instantly love Sadie once you met her. Her enthusiasm for life was contagious. She had a knack for seeing the good in everything and everyone. Even better, she had the knack for making people around her want to see the good in everything and everyone.

Just watching her hurry towards him, smile spread across her face, eyes gleaming in delight, lifted his spirits. It struck him that if they had never left Zambia he would have been reduced to only seeing Sadie if and when she was able to come visit, and a stab of sadness filled his heart. He spent so much time hating everything about the States that he had forgotten that there had been some good to moving to Jo's childhood hometown. Meeting Sadie had been like discovering the little sister he'd never had.

Jordan braced himself as Sadie flung herself into his arms, catching her in a huge bear hug and just barely stopping her from bowling him over. He held her tight for a moment before reluctantly putting her down. She smelled like suntan lotion and sun. Holding her was like hugging a summer vacation.

"Well, hello there! That was quite a welcome!" He said, smiling broadly. He pulled back for a moment. Her face was tan, glowing, just a few freckles peering through the reddened nose and her eyes were shining bright, alive with a twinkle he had never noticed before. She looked exhausted, dark circles lined her eyes, but happier than he'd ever seen her. An unexpected warmth filled his chest. Jordan hugged Sadie again, only letting go when he heard a quiet cough. He looked around and finally noticed the guy standing patiently next to her.

"Oh! I'm so sorry! How rude of me!" Sadie said. "Jordan, I'd like for you to meet Kona, Kona, this is Jordan." Sadie blushed furiously and slid her hand into Kona's. Her adoring gaze up at the guy made Jordan smile. Mystery of the glow explained.

"Hi Kona, good to meet you, man," he said, holding out his hand. Kona shook his hand firmly and with more confidence than Jordan had expected. For some reason with the tan look, messy hair, and the Hawaiian shirt he'd assumed this guy would be some sort of laid back surfer type. The handshake didn't quite mesh with that image.

Jordan studied Kona out of the corner of his eye while Sadie prattled on about the rooms and the hotel. He hadn't gotten very far in his observation before Sadie grabbed his arm.

"Wait! Where's Maryanne? Please don't tell me you forgot Jo's mom!"

"No, I did not forget Jo's mom. Are you insane? I'm here to get married, not divorced!" Jordan said. "She ran to the restroom while I checked us in. Probably wanted to make sure she was wearing enough sunscreen."

"Young man! It is not polite to poke fun at your mother-in-law like that!" Maryanne said. She caught up to the group and pulled Sadie into a big hug before holding her at arm's length and peering at her closely. "Sadie, honey! You look amazing! Your skin is actually glowing. Have you been wearing enough sunscreen?"

Sadie blushed even harder than Kona thought possible and she visibly squirmed in Maryanne's grasp. She stammered and introduced Kona to Jo's mother. There was a brief moment of awkwardness that Kona dispelled with a warm welcome. Jordan was impressed. Maryanne was a nice woman, but she wasn't exactly easy to win over. She'd definitely made it hard for him at first. Some days he even wondered if he'd ever be able to win her over completely. But there was Kona, already arm in arm with her, pointing out the hotel's finer points and making her giggle like a kid. Though that wasn't nearly as disturbing as the way she kept rubbing her hand up and down his arm.

"Well, well. Look who's having a little Hawaiian fling!" Jordan teased after Kona politely untangled himself from Maryanne's grip and excused himself to go work.

"He does look like a nice young man," Maryanne said. Her cheeks were a bit more flushed than usual and she couldn't take her eyes off Kona as he hurried away. "Is he a local? What does he do?"

"Well, that's actually pretty complicated," Sadie said, not making eye contact with any of them. "But you must be tired and in need of some freshening up! Are you all checked in? Let's go drop off your bags and then we can go find Jo and get something to eat. I can't wait to show you around the hotel. It's amazing here!"

She grabbed Maryanne's carry-on and headed for the elevator bank. "Jordan, hope you're ready for some golf! We reserved a 3 o'clock tee time for this afternoon."

Jordan grinned. "I could probably handle a round!" Between the sun, the thought of a tasty lunch, and the potential of a round of golf his mood was improving by the minute. First world living did have its perks.

35. Jo

The door opened with a crash, jerking Jo awake. She lifted her head off the pillow and frowned at the clock on the night table.

"What? What's going on?" Jo mumbled. She wiped the drool from her mouth and looked around to see who had come in. She struggled against the fog of way too many drinks and definitely not enough sleep and focused her bleary eyes. Her heart jumped and she fought the swell of tears in her eyes, when she saw who was at the door. She rolled herself out of bed and ran to Jordan just as he called out a cheery "Rise and shine!"

"You're here!" Jo threw her arms around him. Her stomach flipped at the smell of him and for a moment she couldn't tell if it was excitement, nerves, or just the alcohol sloshing around in there. Jordan's arms tightened around her and she smiled. She felt nauseous and disgusting, but it was beyond good to be in his arms again. A groan from the other bed made her turn her head away from the comforting crook of Jordan's neck.

"Hey! Who's in my bed?" Sadie had been half a step behind Jordan, but in her excitement at seeing her husband, Jo hadn't even noticed her yet. Jo hadn't spotted who was behind Sadie either.

"Good morning darling!" said Jo's mother, her voice grating on Jo's hung-over nerves. "Yes, pray tell, who is in Sadie's bed?"

In answer, the mass of blankets heaved, and a slightly disheveled person emerged.

"Me. I'm in Sadie's bed." Roxie ran her hands through her luscious locks and buried her face in her hands before groaning again. "Though I don't really remember why."

"Roxie!" Sadie cried, jumping onto her bed. "Did you see? Everyone's here!"

"Yes. I saw. And now I'm going to go to my own room to finish sleeping, after which I will be delighted to catch up with each and every one of you." She nodded and smiled weakly at all the newcomers before standing up unsteadily, wrapping the sheet around her as best as she could, and slinking out of the room. Jo watched her go, slightly envious of the sleep she'd be getting. She was delighted to see Jordan, but she had no idea what time they'd made it back to the room. It felt like it had only been five minutes ago.

The door slammed shut and Jo stifled a groan that her mother still heard.

"Honey? Are you OK?"

Jo nodded and kept her eyes shut tight, resting her throbbing head back on Jordan's shoulder. She wondered for a moment if she kept them shut long enough they'd think she was asleep and put her back to bed. Maybe they'd all disappear, preferably leaving Jordan behind to hold her while she slept. She wouldn't have to face her mother and have to deal with what she'd learned last night. She wouldn't have to worry about wedding licenses. She could just pretend everything was perfect. Her arms tightened around his neck a bit; he smelled so damn good. No matter where they were he always smelled the same to her; woodsy and fresh, with a hint of sunshine. Her head was spinning like mad, but in his arms Jo felt grounded.

She almost did doze off, standing there in his arms, but she startled when he pulled back a bit and looked at her face. He was frowning slightly, though she couldn't tell if he was irritated or concerned.

"Just how much did you drink last night? You smell like you bathed in gin."

"Lots, and lots, and lots, and then some more. I think. It's all a bit fuzzy," Jo said before bolting for the bathroom. The sheer thought of the amount of alcohol they had drunk the night before had churned her stomach. She barely made it to the toilet in time.

She rested her head on her hands for a moment, waiting to see if her stomach was done emptying itself. She didn't want to rush back out there. She knew even without seeing their faces exactly what both Jordan and her mother were thinking. He was mad at her for getting so drunk. He didn't much approve of public drunkenness or even private drunkenness for that matter. And her mother, well, her mother would have a hopeful look in her eyes. She'd be wondering if maybe, just maybe the nausea was pregnancy induced.

Her stomach seized again, sending a fresh wave of bile cascading into the toilet and tears springing to her eyes. Nope Mom. Sorry, Mom. Not pregnant. Not now, not yesterday, not tomorrow. Haven't been pregnant in years. In fact, seems I can't get pregnant. Oops. Sorry to disappoint again. Another wave of bile hit the toilet with a satisfying splat and Jo grabbed some toilet paper to wipe her mouth and her eyes. She rested her forehead on the cool toilet seat this time and closed her eyes. She was pretty sure that her stomach was empty, but tears were still rolling down her face and she just wasn't ready to step back outside.

36. Jo

The smell of the toilet soon overpowered the soothing coolness of the ceramic and Jo finally pulled herself off the floor. It didn't help that she'd caught a whiff of herself while curled around the toilet and she had to agree with Jordan's assessment. Frankly, he'd been quite nice. She reeked, pure and simple. She turned on the shower and stepped into the hot stream.

Once her body smelled more like Dove and less like bar swill, she stepped out of the shower and took her time pulling the rest of herself together. With minty fresh breath, scrubbed and shining face, wet hair pulled neatly back in a ponytail, and morose thoughts shoved back into a dark recess of her brain, she finally felt ready to go face the chaos that was her life. Jo tightened the belt of the plush hotel robe and left the safe confines of the bathroom.

Jordan was sitting up in her bed, propped up against the headboard, flipping through the TV channels. The rest of the room was blissfully empty. A stab of dismay shot through her. If her mom had left why hadn't he come join her in the shower? It wasn't like him to turn down an opportunity like that. Especially after a long flight. Was he punishing her for the drinking? But he didn't look mad, he looked... she had no idea how to describe how he looked. He just didn't look like himself. Any trace of joy at seeing her had evaporated from his face.

"Hi," Jo said. She felt suddenly shy, though she couldn't explain why. This was her husband. The man she loved. She'd seem him at his worst, grubby, wet, miserable in torrential downpours. She'd also seen him at his best and in every stage in between. She could have sworn that she knew him better than she even knew herself, but standing there in this hotel robe that was ten times too big, she felt naked when he turned his head towards her and hesitated before saying hi back. Even now that he was looking at her she still couldn't read the expression in his eyes, couldn't decipher his face, and she hated feeling so shut out. When he patted the spot on the bed next to him she didn't hesitate. She scrambled onto the bed and hid her face in his shoulder. His smell was familiar and comforting even if the look in his eye wasn't.

"Baby. Are you okay?" Maryanne hurried over and placed her hand on her daughter's forehead after they walked into the hotel lobby. Jo wanted to be mad, wanted to stay mad, wanted to channel the anger that had erupted last night when she had learned what her mother had done to Andy, had done to her. But the urge to be angry faded as the overwhelming feeling of comfort washed over Jo. Whenever she had felt lost and broken her mother had been there to make everything better. Giving in to that child's need for comfort was more than she could fight at that moment.

She let go of Jordan's hand, noticing that he made

no show of holding her back. She still couldn't figure out what was going on. Back in the room he hadn't kissed her, hadn't made any advances. He'd hugged her hard and then had gone to take a shower, leaving her to get dressed in the empty room. He was holding back from her in a way he hadn't done since they'd first met, and it made her stomach hurt.

"I'm fine mom," Jo said. She pulled her mother into a tight hug, relishing the feeling of welcoming arms around her and the love she could see in her mother's eyes. "I'm glad you're here." Things were going to get complicated and ugly when she finally found a way to talk to her mother about what she had learned. But right this second, she could just pretend it hadn't happened.

Her mother hugged her back tightly, fully taking advantage of the rare show of affection. Jo quelled a rush of irritation. She needed the love, and her mother was always more than eager to dispense it. It was the reproach that Jo could sense in every loving gesture that tended to drive Jo mad. A hug was never just a hug, it always felt like a "finally you're letting me hug you hug."

"I'm glad to be here too," her mother said, putting both her hands on Jo's face and kissing her quickly on the forehead. "Now, you probably know this, but a good hearty breakfast is the best hangover cure in the world. Shall we go down and see what the hotel has to offer?"

Jo rolled her eyes, of course she knew that. How did her mom think she'd gotten through college? She bit her tongue though, if only to quell a bout of nausea. Breakfast sounded like the last thing she could stomach, but it was better than hanging around the lobby putting off one conversation while wishing she could have one with Jordan about what was eating him. She trailed after her mother and Jordan as they made their way to the hotel restaurant located in the middle of the lower lobby on a balcony that overlooked the hotel grounds and the beach. Now that they weren't alone any more Jordan was acting more like his usual gregarious self. He pointed out trees and flowers telling her mother some arcane facts about them that Jo would bet even the hotel staff didn't know. He smiled at people they passed and seemed to all extents and purposes like a guy thrilled to be on vacation in Hawaii. Jo really wanted to believe that she'd been imagining things in the bedroom, but if everything had been completely normal, her ear would have been the one he would have been talking off, not her mother's.

As it turned out, her mother had been annoyingly right. After a bit of breakfast and a large mimosa Jo was well on the way to feeling like herself again. She sipped a second one slowly while watching Sadie chatter. She was perky and happy, which was both awesome to see and annoying to witness when bleary eyed and hung over.

Judging by the glow in her friend's face, it had been quite a night. Sadie caught Jo staring at her and winked. Quite a night indeed then.

"Is there anything you need help with today? I was thinking of playing golf with Sadie and Kona," Jordan said, bringing her train of thought back to the restaurant patio and away from the night before. It was the first time he'd addressed her directly and his question caught her off guard.

"Help? Why would I need help?" Jo pictured the

pool waiting for her.

"Yes? Help? You know, with wedding stuff?"

His words snapped Jo back to the present and with a vicious twist her stomach caught up fast. All thoughts of the relaxing pool flew right out of her mind, instantly replaced by panic over the wedding license situation. How could she possibly have forgotten?

Jo felt herself grow hot and hoped no one would notice. She grabbed a menu and fanned herself in what she hoped looked like a languid manner. "Oh! No, I've got all that covered. It's all good. Really." She looked at Sadie frantically. "In fact, what time is it? I need to go check in with the wedding planner to make sure that everything is hunky dory. Sadie? Are you coming?"

"Hunky dory?" Jordan asked as both he and Sadie looked at Jo, one eyebrow raised. If she hadn't been so panicked she might have laughed at their identical faces, as it was she felt a bubble of hysterical laughter threaten to take over.

"Oh, whatever! You know what I mean! Sadie?" Jo said, standing up, ready to bolt for the wedding planner's office, though with her stomach doing flips the way it was she might have to make a quick detour towards the bathroom again. She covered up a moan with what she hoped passed for a cheerful and happy laugh.

"Oh! Perfect timing! I have a few details to go over with her," her mother said, sending Jo's stomach into an even faster spiral. All she needed right now was for her mother to find out what a mess she'd made of things. Yes, clearly that would make this moment perfect. Jo shot another crazed look at Sadie, who this time caught the hint.

"Oh, Maryanne, don't you want to rest for a moment before you get bogged down in last minute wedding details? I'm sure Jo will come get you if anything has come up. You really have to see the pool. It's amazing. Jo? You go ahead, I'll take everyone down to the pool to show them around. I'll catch up with you later before I go golf."

Jo mouthed a quiet thank you to Sadie and gave Jordan a quick glance before hurrying off towards the main lobby. She wished she could have spent a few moments alone with him to see if she could pry out what was bothering him. But he clearly had no desire to talk and if she didn't sort out the fiasco that she had created the whole thing might be moot anyway. She had a hunch that he wouldn't be too pleased to learn that this whole wedding might not work out according to plan. He'd been annoyed enough at the expense and at being forced to take a group vacation with his mother-in-law and all of Jo's best friends.

37. Jo

Jo knocked timidly on the door to the wedding planner's office and sent up another wordless plea to any wedding gods who might be in attendance. Please, please let her be here. Please, please, let her be able to fix this. When she didn't hear anything, she took a deep breath gave the heavy wooden door a hearty shove. The door swung open silently.

"Jo! What a lovely surprise! What can I do for you?" Kelli was sitting behind her massive desk looking just as perfectly put together as she had every single time Jo had seen her, which wasn't all that many come to think of it. "How come you aren't by the pool enjoying yourself?"

Jo was already out of sorts and upset, but the fact that Kelli's words and tone didn't match her facial expression at all destabilized her even more. The woman looked annoyed and downright pissed about something. Jo hesitated.

"Hi Kelli. I... ah... we.... Right. I really have no idea how to say this, but we have a bit of a situation. I really need your help."

"Oh?" Kelli cocked her head to the side and waited for Jo to continue, small fake smile still plastered in place, eyes narrowing.

I feel like I'm meeting with my shrink, Jo thought, not my very expensive and not so helpful wedding planner. Well, maybe that wasn't very fair. Up until this moment she hadn't had a ton to do. Maryanne had handled pretty much all the planning despite the distance and the time difference. She'd just had to put all of Maryanne's requests into effect. Which granted might not have been a piece of cake, but certainly didn't warrant the level of hostility the woman was putting out.

"Well, ah, it seems that Jordan and I aren't actually already married. Well, we are. But we aren't. I'm not making any sense. Sorry."

"No, you're not." Kelli's painted smile started to lose its luster.

"Just before we got here I discovered that our marriage license wasn't valid. I haven't actually told Jordan yet. I'm going to. Soon! Honest!" What did this woman care about that anyway? Jo wondered, still unable to stop herself from justifying herself. "But first I really need you to tell me what we need to do to get a license in time for the wedding."

Jo held her breath as she waited for Kelli to answer. The wedding planner cocked her head a bit further and pursed her lips tightly, waiting to see if Jo had anything to add. This really was like being with a shrink! Jo rushed to fill the silence.

"I really, really need you to tell me that this is going to be okay, because I might cry if you tell me that there's a two week waiting period in Hawaii." Jo held her breath again and cringed, waiting for Kelli's answer. She expected the worst, instead she got a laugh. A bitter, angry, totally uncomforting laugh.

Jo slowly opened one eye and peered at Kelli. She hadn't yet seen her laugh. Not once. Fake flat smiles, yes. Laughter, no. Not even bitter strange laughter. But she hadn't heard wrong. Kelli was laughing, laughing hard. The bitterness in the laugh was fading, replaced by true mirth. Jo stopped cringing and stood up straighter. Seriously, how rude could a person get? The story wasn't that crazy! Seeing Jo throw back her shoulders and raise her chin made Kelli laugh even harder, tears streaming down her face.

"Kelli? Please? This isn't funny. I'm begging. I really need your help here." Jo hated the lump that formed in her throat and the tears that pooled in her eyes. She hated that she had to rely on this madwoman to get her life back into order. Hated that she was begging for something from a woman who clearly didn't give a rat's ass about her situation.

"Of course, you do. Everyone needs my help. The brides, the grooms, the mothers of the bride. You all need my help, day and night, all the time, for every little detail. Though I have to hand it to you, this isn't as small a detail as most. Who ever heard of a rededication ceremony where the couple isn't even married yet?" Her voice cracked and Jo cut in quickly before she could start laughing again, her own voice cracking for a completely different reason.

"Fine. Whatever. Can you help me or are you just going to laugh at me?"

"Of course, I can help," Kelli snapped, instantly sour and bitter again. "But after this I'm done."

"What the heck is that supposed to mean? You're the wedding planner! You can't be done. Not until the wedding is over!"

"I'm the ex-wedding planner. I quit this morning. I promised my boss that I'd stay through until your event was done, but you know what? I don't think I want to. What's he going to do? Fire me?" Kelli sneered and shrugged her shoulders, her plastic little smile finally completely wiped from her face.

Jo stood in front of her now ex-wedding planner and her jaw dropped. This woman was insane. She was going to make her insane. But she had no choice. There wouldn't even be a wedding without the marriage license!

"Okay! Fine! Whatever! You help get me a marriage license; we'll figure out the rest. What do I need to do?"

Jo tried not to think of the planning that had gone into this event. She had no idea what she had just agreed to; her mother had made all the arrangements. She'd gotten married barefoot in a mud field. What did she know about fancy resort weddings?

But this was going to be fine. It had to be. Her mother would help; she knew all the plans anyway. Stupid wedding planner. Who needed her anyway?

"Great!" Kelli said, fake smile plastered back onto her face as though they'd just discussed what hors d'oeuvres were going to be served. "Actually, there's nothing you need to do. We'll just tell the officiant and she'll bring the license. You and Jordan can sign it just before the ceremony." She shrugged again and gave Jo the biggest fake smile she'd given her yet.

Jo felt her eye widen and her jaw drop again. Her fists clenched, itching to make contact with Kelli's smug know-it-all face.

"That's it! That's all? You just got me to agree to taking over the rest of the wedding planning and you didn't have to do anything? You... you... I... I..."

"What? What are you going to do? Report me? Have me fired?" Kelli's eyes glinted dangerously. She threw back her head and laughed. They both knew there was nothing Jo could do. Jo gritted her teeth and growled.

"Fine. Whatever. Call the officiant. I'll take care of the rest." She turned to leave and abruptly turned back. "Do you at least have a file or something, so I'll know what still needs to be done?"

Moments later Jo was standing back in the hall, thick file with her name embossed on it clutched under her arm. She shook her head slightly. What had just happened here? What had happened to her no fuss, no stress, island paradise wedding?

38. Jo

Jo pushed open the door to the room and called out to Sadie before remembering that she was off golfing. She let the door slam shut and stood surveying the chaos in their room. They'd rushed out the night before without cleaning up a thing, so rejected outfits were strewn over every possible surface. A tornado couldn't have made a bigger mess. Jo chucked the thick file onto the desk and threw herself onto the bed. Papers spilled out everywhere as she swallowed back the tears that threatened to overflow.

It was all just too much. Seeing Andy again was one thing. A big, big thing. The wedding was another. All she had wanted to do was put on a pretty dress, let someone else put her hair up, say a couple words, and then party with her friends. Was that really too much to ask?

Now her husband was barely speaking to her, though she still had no idea why. Her wedding planner had quit. Her ex-fiancé was lurking around the hotel. Jo couldn't wrap her brain around any of it.

She let her mind wander to the event she had imagined when she had first brought up the idea to Jordan and her mom a few months ago. She hadn't cared about any of the details. She's just wanted to enjoy the end result. Soft sandy beach, barefoot bridesmaids, softly lapping ocean, and brilliant white dress shining in the sun. In her mind the event was stress free and fun for everyone involved. In reality it had turned into a nightmare almost instantly. Her mother had gone into hysterical planning mode. Jordan had taken himself so far out of the planning that some days she wondered if he even planned to come. And now even being on the island was proving to be more complicated than she had anticipated.

As she stewed about how her dream event had turned sour something nagged at her brain like a tongue poking at a sore tooth. She tried to focus. What thought had tripped her up?

Oh crap. The dress! Where was the dress? The dress that was supposed to shine brightly in the sunshine. Where was it?

Jo remembered grabbing it as she got off the plane and she could vaguely remember that it had been in the car when she had arrived at the hotel. Beyond that moment though she was drawing a blank.

Jo couldn't believe she didn't even know where her dress was. Whose wedding was this? She grabbed the phone and tried to get through to Kelli, but the phone rang and rang before cutting off. The stupid woman hadn't even turned on her answering machine before skipping off into the sunset. Just as she was about to hurl the phone through the room in frustration, her eyes fell on a business card that had spilled out of the folder.

Debbie's Dress Shop

Debbie's! Jo vaguely remembered Sadie mentioning something about the dressmaker who was ready to make the final alteration. She had bought the dress off the rack, marveling at how well it fitted. It had only needed a tiny alteration in the back so, based on the wedding store's recommendation, Jo had agreed to wait until she arrived on the island to have the dress fitted. Kelli had assured them that there was a seamstress at the hotel who would be able to help.

Wait! Wasn't the appointment for today? Why hadn't anyone reminded her?

"SADIE!!" Jo howled.

The only response she got was an answering bang on the wall from the neighbor. Jo grimaced and picked up the phone again. She had no idea what time the fitting had been scheduled for. Luckily, Debbie answered the phone after just one ring. Unfortunately, it was because Jo was already over half an hour late for the fitting and she'd been about to call her.

Shit. Shit. Shit. Shit. Jo thought running out the door, making sure to grab her key card and Kelli's binder before letting the door slam shut. What else was she missing? Did she have a meeting set up with the florist? With the music coordinator? Was there even such a thing? Jo pounded on the elevator button, but just as it arrived her brain finally caught up to her feet. Duh. Sadie might be out golfing, but presumably her mom was somewhere in the hotel! She'd know what had been scheduled!

39. Jo

Jo stepped into the elevator, glad to be moving in the direction of a solution to her problems. She looked at the rows of elevator buttons and realized that she had no idea what to push. How did she not know what room her own mother was in? And why did she have to have so much to drink last night? Jo rested her pounding forehead on the cool metal of the elevator door and tried to will the information into popping into her head. While she was at it she begged her stomach to stop reeling. Had someone mentioned the room number at some point during breakfast? A floor? When nothing came to mind, Jo reluctantly pushed the button to the lobby. She'd have to get someone from the front desk to call her mother and have her meet her at Debbie's.

The relief of finally having made one tiny decision flooded through Jo. One step at a time, she told herself. One step at a time, starting with the step out of this elevator. The doors opened and Jo walked out.

Five minutes later she pushed open the door to Debbie's little boutique, grateful that it was located right off the lobby and not at the other end of the resort. The receptionist's assurances that they would find her mother and have her go straight to the dressmaker's had eased some of Jo's panic and the soothing decor inside the tiny boutique calmed her even further. The walls were painted a quiet eggshell and the thick burgundy carpet cushioned her hesitant footfalls. Jo didn't see Debbie right away, distracted by the racks of gorgeous dresses that lined the tiny store. She finally heard hum of a sewing machine that seemed to be coming from behind a lavish crimson Chinese screen.

Jo cleared her throat, but the hum of the machine didn't stop. She coughed a bit louder and attempted a quiet "Hello?" The noise stopped and a stunning petite Asian woman popped out from behind the screen.

"Jo? Jo Fleming?" Her perfect, unaccented English caught Jo unawares and she mentally kicked herself for assuming that all Asian people would speak with an accent.

"Yes. I'm so sorry I'm so late. I had no..."

"Better late than never!" Debbie cut Jo off cheerfully. "Do you have the dress?"

Jo's heart stopped and she looked around frantically.

Debbie laughed. "I'm sorry. It's my favorite joke. I have the dress, don't worry."

Jo smiled weakly and sank down onto a nearby chair. This woman had no idea how close she had just been to having a hysterical bride on her hands.

"I'm sorry. I didn't mean to upset you!" Debbie was instantly all genuine smiles and comforting pats on the shoulder. She rushed over and helped Jo stand up. "Don't worry! It's all going to be fine. Your dress is gorgeous, and I can already tell that it barely needs any work! Come, let's go try it on."

She took Jo's hand and pulled her to the back of

the little boutique, behind the screen, where the dress hung against the wall. Jo gasped. She hadn't seen it since the day she'd bought it and had forgotten just how pretty it was. She loved its utter simplicity. The bodice was a beautiful light cream raw silk, a perfect contrast to the rich silky satin of the skirt. The cap sleeves that had caught her eyes at the store made her smile; they were just as adorable as Jo remembered them. The tiny pearl sequins that swirled around the skirt glinted in the shop's lights, reminding her why she'd picked this dress over all the others. She'd imagined the sun making the whole thing glitter, exactly the way she'd dreamed.

"It's going to be okay. Right?" Jo asked Debbie, who just nodded and smiled wisely in response as she shooed her into the changing room. She was probably used to dealing with irrational brides and their cryptic questions.

"Take off your clothes and call me. I'll help you put on the dress."

Jo shot the dressmaker a grateful smile and did as she asked. For a moment she was going to pretend that everything was going exactly according to plan.

40. Jo

"Jo! You look..." Her mother's voice trailed off and Jo caught her eye in the mirror. She stood in the door of the boutique, mouth wide open, eyes shimmering with tears. Jo smiled at her and she stepped in and let the door glide shut behind her. "Stunning. You look absolutely stunning."

"Really? You think so?" Jo looked at her mother and grinned.

"Yes. Yes. It's perfect. It's so you. However, did you find such a perfect dress?"

Her mother had been so mad when Jo hadn't let her come dress shopping, but she had clearly been forgiven. Jo hadn't wanted it to turn into a huge event and had gone alone and had stopped after just one boutique. Come to think of it, Jo had only tried on three dresses before realizing that the first dress she had seen was the one she really wanted. At first she had thought that it was just because she didn't want to deal with the dress shopping, didn't think the dress was all that big of a deal, but seeing herself in the mirror here made her think that maybe it was just because this was the perfect dress after all.

Jo nervously smoothed down the front of the

skirt, fingering the sequins her fingers encountered. Debbie swatted her hand away.

"No touch!" She mumbled from behind the pins trapped between her lips. "I'll stick you!" Jo raised her arms back up to where Debbie had asked her to keep them and shrugged slightly. Her mother sat down in the chair Jo had just been pulled out of and suddenly looked serious.

Jo could tell she was dying to ask what was going on. Could tell that she was torn as usual when dealing with Jo. It made her want to scream the way her mom always seemed to walk on eggshells around her. As though one out of place word could make their whole precarious relationship disintegrate.

She had no idea what to say so she just watched her mother in the mirror. She couldn't read her mother's expression as her eyes took in the dress. Jo looked at herself. In this dress everything looked just right. She looked like a bride about to enjoy her wedding. She didn't look like a bride who had a huge mess to clean up before she could do just that. Jo ignored the tiny voice in her head that whispered that she didn't look like a bride who might never get to enjoy her wedding day. Instead, she took a deep breath and met the reflection of her mother's eyes.

Jo stood still as Debbie futzed and fretted about the dress, tucking in a bit there, pulling on another here. In between sharp intakes of breath when pins got a bit close for comfort and sharp orders to turn this way or that, Jo finally filled her mother in. She held her gaze as she confessed about the wedding license and vented about the way the wedding planner had just dumped the whole event into her lap.

She'd been holding in the wedding license secret for weeks, unable to come to grips with that it meant. A part of her had been terrified that both her mother and Jordan would insist on calling off the wedding if they knew that the renewal ceremony was a sham. A tiny voice in her head had insinuated that maybe she thought that because that's what she wanted herself. The days had passed, and Jo had never found the nerve to speak up, either to herself or to anyone else. And then they'd been packing, and she hadn't been able to say anything because she was so mortified she hadn't had the nerve to face the situation.

Jo sighed. She could have saved them all a world of trouble if she'd just had faith in herself and in her husband.

During the whole tirade Debbie shook her head and mumbled nasty asides about Kelli.

"So, let me get this right. She told you she was done, gave you the file, and then kicked you out of her office?" Jo nodded at her mother and then stopped when Debbie poked her with another pin.

"Yes. It's going to be okay, Mom, right? Please tell me it's going to be okay." Jo heard her voice crack and hated herself for it, but she couldn't stop it in time.

"Of course, it's going to be okay! Don't be silly. The whole thing is pretty much planned. As long as she did everything I asked her to do ahead of time, we'll be fine. But she's not getting away with this! As soon as we're done here I'm going to see the manager about getting a serious refund on this wedding. This is absolutely inexcusable!"

Jo heaved a sigh of relief. She'd hoped her mother would take charge, but she hadn't realized just how much she'd wanted her to. It felt like a weight had been lifted from her shoulders and her chest. The only thing keeping her from doing a silly giddy dance was Debbie and her evil pins.

Now if only she had the guts to also mention the minor issue of Andy's presence in the hotel. One quick glance at her mother's flushed reflection convinced Jo that now was not the ideal time to open that particular can of worms. Her mother was stomping around the room, grumbling about customer service not being what it used to be. Every so often she'd stop to finger one of the sequined gowns hanging on plush hangers then she'd turn and growl before rattling off another thing she hoped Kelli had done. Debbie just snorted and focused hard on the dress.

Jo let her mother rant for a few minutes, knowing full well from experience that it was too early to even attempt to redirect her anger. A longer pause than usual in front of an aquamarine full length sheath was the moment that Jo had been waiting for.

"I like the neckline on that. It reminds me of that dress you got me for Prom."

Her mother looked down at the dress she'd been fingering like she'd had no idea she had anything in her hand. She focused her eyes and looked at the dress. A hint of a smile pulled at the corner of her frown and she nodded slightly.

"Speaking of dresses, Jo, did you check that the girls all brought theirs?" Jo shot a panicked look at Debbie who assured them that not only had the dresses arrived, but they had already been altered to fit the bridesmaids and were just waiting to be picked up.

"Good. Good! At least that's something. No one

will be naked at the wedding. Now we just have to figure out the seating arrangements, assemble the center pieces and the wedding favors... Oh! And check in with the florist and the DJ. You don't happen to have their numbers, do you honey?"

Grateful that the ranting was over and that her mother had flipped into organization mode, Jo relaxed a little more and pointed to the thick binder she'd placed on the corner of the counter when she had come in. Her mother pounced on it like a lion seizing its prey. More frantic mumbling list making followed, but none of it was aimed at Jo and Debbie.

Content to let her mother take charge, Jo turned her attention to the dressmaker kneeling in front of her working on the hem of the dress.

"Is it ok? Are you going to have to make a lot of changes?"

"Oh! It's fine! It's really amazing how well it already fits you. You could walk down the aisle right now and no one would notice anything amiss. But I'm a perfectionist. I see the teeny tiny things that could be just a bit better."

Jo had to admit the dress really was gorgeous on her. It hugged her in all the right places, accentuating the waist that had remained slim even after they had returned to the land of junk food and all the chocolate you could eat. Her smallish chest was artfully framed and looked perfectly plump and inviting. Even her shoulders looked cute in the little cap sleeves.

"Your wedding is in two days, right?" Debbie asked Jo, who nodded yes only to be rewarded with a sharp poke with a pin in her ankle.

"Ouch. Yes, in two days. Are you going to have

time to finish the alterations?"

"Oh, yeah. I'm not worried about that. I'll probably be done tonight. No, I'm just hoping that the shark clears out in time. You are getting married on the beach, aren't you?"

"What shark?"

"I heard there was a shark in the water. Usually, it's not an issue. There are always little sharks around. But when it's one of the big sharks they have to close the beach entirely. I hope the coast guards will allow the hotel to open it again in time for the wedding."

"They close the beach? Why would they have to do that? It's not like we're going in the water!" Jo's voice squeaked and her mother raised her head to see what they were discussing.

"What? What's wrong now? Is it the dress?"

"Debbie says there's a shark in the water and that the beach is closed! It might not be open in time for the wedding!" Jo wailed, feeling like a cranky kid and not caring a tiny bit.

"Oh, for crying out loud!" Jo's mother stormed over to where she had scattered the contents of the binder and started grabbing at papers and shoving them back in haphazardly. "That's it! I'm going to see the manager right now. This is absolutely ridiculous."

She stormed out of the boutique and let the door slam shut behind her. Debbie and Jo heard her heels clicking angrily on the stone tiles in the hall.

"Well then... I wouldn't want to be in Anthony's shoes right about now," Debbie said before turning her attention back to the dress.

Jo glanced in the direction of the door and shook her head. "Me neither. I've been on the receiving end of that anger."

41. Andy

The kids had woken up early, way, way too early this morning and had only agreed to get back into bed after Andy had promised them pancakes for breakfast and found them some cartoons for them to watch while he slunk back under his own covers, leaving the door between their two rooms open so he could hear if they got up again.

Once the sun had actually peeked over the horizon he had taken them to the breakfast buffet and was now letting them gorge themselves on pancakes and pineapple. He nursed a strong cup of coffee and ruminated on the previous evening.

It was hard to be bitter about losing Jo, he thought as he watched his two children fight for the last piece of bacon on the plate. If he and Jo hadn't broken up he would never have gotten together with their mother and they would never have been born. That was another story that had ended, or rather was ending disastrously, but at least he had Emily and Hunter to show for it. They were so much better than a sad little sock.

Amber had been a waitress at his and Jo's favorite diner and for a while she'd been the closest thing to a friend that he could find. She always had a smile and a comforting pat on the shoulder for him when he stumbled in early every morning, half dead from grief and exhaustion and, yes, often on the wrong end of a terrible hangover. He hadn't slept for months after Jo lost the baby. Every time he closed his eyes all he could see was Jo lying in her hospital bed, looking dead. Instead, he drank until he passed out. Then he woke up with a blinding headache and an unquenchable craving for coffee.

After a few weeks of shy smiles Amber had started talking to him, bringing him more substantial breakfasts than his standard black coffee. They had started shooting the breeze about nothing at first and then eventually about everything. Slowly Andy had realized that he didn't want to spend his evenings drinking anymore and that he was actually looking forward to his morning stop at the diner.

He'd waited a few more weeks before asking Amber out to dinner and a few more weeks after that before taking her out on another date. Theirs had definitely been a slow courtship, one that had sped up radically the day she'd told him she was pregnant.

Andy looked at that baby now, carefully spreading butter on his little sister's pancakes and smiled. Hunter's birth had given meaning to Andy's life. He'd found a real reason to get up in the morning and he didn't regret for a moment agreeing to marry Amber.

The first time Andy held Hunter, moments after he was born, he'd gazed in his son's deep gray eyes and seen a glint in there. Hunter had blinked slowly and then given Andy a half smile before sighing and falling into that deep trusting sleep in which newborns excel. Andy had watched the tiny infant sleep and had felt forgiven.

A weight had lifted from his shoulders and he'd made a silent promise to this child that he'd always be there for him. That he wouldn't let anything bad happen to him, ever.

With this baby in his arms, he couldn't understand why he'd been so panicked that day Jo had first told him she was pregnant. It had seemed so ridiculous he had almost laughed out loud. Only the fear of disturbing the sleeping infant had silenced the laugh before it crossed his lips.

Things had gotten bad with Amber right away. They had squabbled over everything and anything. Truth was, if she hadn't gotten pregnant they probably would have soon gone their own separate ways, but Hunter's arrival had changed things. Andy had been determined to stick around and make things work so when Amber had started working longer and longer hours and had stopped coming home every night he hadn't said anything. She hadn't exactly been mother-of-the-year material. When she was home it wasn't like she did anything to help with the baby, so it was almost easier when she stayed out. There was less fighting at least. Andy had done everything for Hunter and when Amber got pregnant again, he'd been there for that baby too, even though he hadn't been 100% convinced that the baby was his.

He hadn't doubted for long. Just as with Hunter, as soon as he had held her he had known he was Emily's father. It was a miracle considering how many people Amber had been sleeping with at the time, but he wasn't going to quibble. Especially since she'd radically changed her ways right after the baby's arrival. Or so he'd thought at the time.

For a while everything had been postcard perfect. Amber had managed to care for Emily the way he'd often wished she'd care for Hunter and she'd even found it in her heart to show their firstborn the attention he deserved. There had been days he'd caught himself thinking that he really had it made – beautiful and attentive wife, healthy happy kids, decent job – total American dream. It was what had made her recent announcement that she was running off with her asshole of a boss even more shocking.

In one afternoon, she had cleaned out all her things and pealed out of the driveway as if she were being chased. The dust was still settling when Hunter's school bus pulled up at the end of the street. He'd hardly known what to say to the kids that night. For a while he'd hoped that she'd realize what she'd done and come back with her tail between her legs, so he didn't want to go into any details about her being gone. But he didn't need to worry about that; she didn't even call for the first two weeks. He'd kidded with the kids about the vacation mommy had gone on, one where there were no phones of any kind, but they weren't dumb, they knew something had happened. They'd eventually stopped asking and the three of them had fallen into a routine of sorts. Luckily, he worked from home, so their days weren't much affected. The rest had felt just like the early days when it had been just him and Hunter.

When Amber had reappeared, months later, demanding custody, it had thrown them all for a loop. The kids didn't know what to do, they were torn between being thrilled to see their mom and their loyalty to him. He hadn't known what to think or do either. In the middle of all that he'd gotten the Orbitz reminder about his upcoming vacation. Vacation they'd planned together long before their family had disintegrated. He'd figured that there was no reason not to go, they could go be just as upset about the future in the sun as they could in their home.

Then, when Roxie had mentioned that she and the gang would be there too, any hesitation had vanished. He hadn't exactly anticipated how it would go. He would probably have been better off staying home and finding a kick-ass custody lawyer who would make sure his soon to be ex-wife had to beg for the right to so much as set eyes on his kids.

A loud crash startled him, and he looked up to see both his children frozen in shock with their mouths hanging open. He spotted the water stain spreading over the tablecloth and resisted a groan.

"It's okay guys, accidents happen. Let's clear up this mess." The kids scrambled to grab napkins to help him mop up the puddle they had just made. "Have you guys eaten enough? Are you ready to head to the pool? I think we have a bit of time before Hunter has to get to camp."

As the three of them headed back to their hotel room to gather bathing suits and pool toys, the kids ran ahead, checking back periodically to see if their dad, walking carefully so he wouldn't spill the cup of coffee he'd poured himself before leaving the restaurant, was following. They rushed around shouting with glee over the pretty stones they kept finding on the path and laughing at the antics of the colorful bird chirping down at them from the trees. Andy smiled as he watched them dart from one treasure to the next. It was hard to stay indignant or angry when he was around these two.

A familiar voice stopped him in his tracks. He held his breath and listened. Had he heard the voice correctly? The kids glanced at him and ran back when they saw that he'd stopped. Of course, being kids, they got sidetracked by something in a bush. As luck would have it they picked the very bush that was shielding them from the voices Andy was trying to identify. He stood stock still and willed the children to stay quiet. He was sure there were two people talking, though he couldn't hear the other person. There was no mistaking the person he could hear though. He still heard that sharp, bitter voice in some of his more upsetting dreams.

"I am telling you, sir, we will not stand for this!" Maryanne's voice dripped with sarcasm and anger and it made Andy shudder even though, for once, the bitterness was not directed at him. "It is unacceptable! Have you no control over your staff or your property? We came a long way to have the paradise wedding you promised us, at a very steep price, I might add, and we are getting nothing of what was promised to us, sir."

Andy motioned to the children and started to move away as quietly as possible both so the people on the other side of the bush wouldn't hear him and so he could keep listening. He didn't want to admit it, but the thought of Jo's wedding going up in flames made his heart jump a little.

"Ma'am, there's absolutely nothing we can do about the shark, my control of my property doesn't extend to the ocean," Maryanne had met her match in sarcasm apparently, Andy swallowed a snort of laughter, "but I guarantee that we will set you and your party up in a beautiful location. As for Kelli, you have my humble apology for the way she has handled this situation and I promise that I will personally take over your event to make sure that nothing else goes wrong. In fact, I shall go get started right away. If you'll excuse me..."

Andy heard the man's hasty footsteps retreat and he froze. He really didn't want to speak to Maryanne, especially not while she was this riled up. For a minute he hoped that she might walk away and let them go by undetected.

The thought of the kids made him realize that they'd fallen silent. He looked around to see what they were up to. Time slipped into that painful movie slow-motion feel and Andy knew before he'd even started running that he wouldn't get there in time. With a horrible crash Emily, then Hunter, tripped up by his sister's flailing feet, fell loudly into the very bushes that were the only thing protecting him from his once-upon-a-time-almost-might-have-been-nightmare-of-a-mother-in-law.

Somebody screamed, he wasn't quite sure who. It could have been Maryanne, it could have been the kids, but it could also very well have been him. For a split second he stood frozen to the spot and watched as the kids shoved each other out of the dense bushes. The sight of a bright red gash on Emily's forehead and the sound of her escalating wail finally unglued his feet and he sprinted.

"Are you okay?" Andy asked both kids, kneeling in front of them and looking them up and down for more signs of trauma. Hunter was unscathed and looked indignant as he brushed leaves and dirt off his hands, but Emily's mouth was wide open and she was screeching, tears streaming down her face. She clawed at him, trying to bury her face in his neck, but Andy held her back, looking closely at her face. He let out the breath he'd been holding in tightly. It was just a scratch, a tiny scratch that was barely bleeding. More fear than harm. He let Emily bury her face in his shirt and hugged her tight.

"Are they okay?" The familiar voice came from behind. Maryanne must have come around from the end of the bushes. Andy considered just nodding for a moment and walking away with the kids, but Emily was still crying hysterically around the thumb that she'd jammed into her mouth and Hunter was kicking his toe angrily into the dirt. There was no way he could make a fast clean get away with these two at his side.

Andy steeled himself. "Yes, thank you. They're fine. It's just a tiny scratch and a bruised ego I think."

"Oh, good. I'm so glad. It was such a crash I thought for sure there'd be a broken bone or two."

Andy glanced quickly at Emily's arms and ran his hands up and down them just to double check. He hadn't even considered broken bones! Hunter had moved on to shadow punching the bushes, clearly he was fine.

"Yeah, well, curiosity might have killed the cat, but it only bruised these kids." Andy still hadn't turned around to look at Maryanne. He wanted to avoid it as long as possible. He turned his attention to Hunter. "What were you guys looking for anyway? Another gecko?"

The kids nodded sheepishly.

"He gotsaway," Emily mumbled around her thumb. Maryanne's arrival had done more to calm her down than all the hugging and back patting Andy had tried as a first recourse.

"Yeah, he ran when Emily fell. He was really cool too. He had a purple stripe down his back!" Hunter chimed in.

"Sounds pretty cool. Not sure it was worth almost breaking an arm for, but cool. Maybe we can look him up on the computer when we get back to the room," said Andy, reluctantly standing up. He held his breath again, waiting for Maryanne to recognize him, but she only had eyes for the kids.

"Have you seen lots of neat lizards at the resort?"

Hunter glanced at his dad to see if it was okay to answer the stranger, and when Andy nodded yes, he quickly he launched into a complete description of all the geckos they'd seen since the day they arrived.

Andy let Hunter ramble on through the description of the first five geckos they'd seen, all within two hours of their arrival on the island, before taking pity on Maryanne. Hunter could go on for hours at this rate.

"Right, buddy, that's enough. Let's let Mrs. Hunter get back to what she was doing."

"Hey! That's my name too!"

"I'm sorry, do we know each other?"

Hunter and Maryanne spoke at the same time and Andy mentally kicked himself for the slip-up. He wished he could find a massive hole and hide away. Hunter was so very much just Hunter to him now that he at times forgot where he'd gotten the inspiration for his name. Opening that can of worms wasn't something he'd been planning on this morning.

"Hello, Maryanne," Andy said finally, looking her straight in the eye. "Long time no see."

Maryanne's eyebrows furrowed for a minute as she looked into Andy's face, then they shot straight up in the air as she recognized him. Had he really changed that much? He thought about this woman almost every day. Had she really forgotten him that quickly?

"Andrew! Andrew Sullivan. Well. I never." She gaped at him, mouth opening and closing.

"Wow, Maryanne. I've never known you to be at a loss for words."

"Uh. Ah. Well, I don't know what to say!"

"Dad! Dad! Did you hear that? She has the same name as me!" Hunter bounced up and down in delight at this unexpected coincidence.

"I know buddy. I know. You're actually kinda named after this lady." Andy felt his face flush. Maryanne visibly stiffened.

"You named your son after me?" Her brows furrowed again, and her neck flushed a deep red. Anger? Embarrassment? Andy couldn't tell.

"No Maryanne, I did not name my son after you. I named him after your daughter. And I named my daughter, Emily, after the child Jo and I lost." Andy watched Maryanne flinch at the mention of the baby and had to suppress the urge to smile. It wasn't fair, he knew, she had lost her first grandchild when Jo had miscarried, but that seemed so insignificant compared to his and Jo's loss.

Maryanne's head snapped up. "Oh! Jo! Does she know you're here?"

"Yes, Jo knows I'm here." Andy wanted so badly to say that Jo had invited him, but who knew what that would lead to. Probably no good for Jo, or for him, in the end.

"Does she know about the children?" Maryanne's voice dipped at the end of her sentence so that she whispered the last two words like they were dirty naughty words that should never be mentioned aloud.

Andy leaned in and whispered back. "Yes, Jo knows about the children. She kinda met them at the pool yesterday." The thought of that encounter made him cringe. Not his best moment.

"Oh." Maryanne was once again at a loss for words. She glanced at her bare wrist and frowned again. "Oh. I. Well, I have to run. Jo's waiting for me. Problems with..." She stopped herself and looked at Andy.

"Problems with the wedding?" He finished for her, biting back a smirk. "Something wrong?"

"Oh, if it was just one thing!" Maryanne threw up her hands. "I have to run. It was... interesting to see you again. Are you staying long?"

"Yes, we're going to be here for the week. In fact, Jo invited us to the wedding, so we'll definitely be seeing you again soon." Andy smiled as sweetly as possible and pretended he didn't see the look of horror that crossed Maryanne's face. He was enjoying this much more than he should. "Okay kids. Let's go! Hey! Get away from that bush! Do you want to fall in again?"

Andy nodded at Maryanne as he pulled Emily and Hunter away from the bush they were determined to crawl into again.

"Let's go, guys. Time to hit the pool. Let's go see if they have bandages down there for Emily." He hurried on ahead and with giggles the kids rushed to catch up.

"Hey, Dad? Was I really named after that lady?"

"Well, yeah, a bit. You're named after her

daughter."

"Her daughter's name is Hunter? That's a funny name for a girl!"

"No, silly, Hunter was her last name. Her first name is Jo."

"Well, that's a silly name too. It's a dumb name for a girl. Jo's a boy's name!"

Andy laughed. "Yeah, it's a bit silly, but it suits her. She's a silly girl. Okay, who wants to race?" He pretended to fumble and watched his children race ahead. They might have been named after the ghosts of his past, but they were so alive that it had been easy to forget that the names had once belonged to others before them.

42. Jo

"Jo? Jo? Are you here?" Maryanne knocked loudly on the door.

Jo dropped the shirt she had just picked up and went to open the door for her mother. She was itching to go for a run, but first she needed to know what her mother had managed to arrange. She was dressed and ready to go, just killing time by tidying up.

"So? What did the manager say?" She asked as her mother came into the room and scooped up the shirt from the floor.

"The who? Oh! The manager. He was no help at all. Well, that's not entirely true. He said he'd see what he could do. Whatever that means. I'm not holding my breath. We'll figure something out, I'm sure."

"Oh. Good. I guess."

Jo moved to the side of the bed where she had thrown all the clothes she'd gathered from the floor. Her mother joined her on the other side, and both started sorting through the pile, folding what was obviously clean and setting aside the rest.

"Jo?"

"Mom?" Jo's gut twisted. She'd been enjoying the quiet and she wasn't quite ready for the talk she and her mom needed to have.

When her mother didn't say anything, Jo looked up from the red top she was folding. Her mother, usually obsessively neat and attentive, was twisting a shirt in her hands. Jo frowned. The wedding couldn't be causing her mother's angst; the woman could plan a party in her sleep. Only one thing could cause that level of stress. Even without asking Jo knew what was wrong. Her heart sank. She would have much preferred being the instigator of the confrontation.

"Mom?"

"I ran into him in the lobby."

"Oh."

"Yes. Oh."

"I'm sorry. I should have told you he was here. I... I didn't know how to bring it up." She stared down at the pile of clothes, refusing to make eye contact with her mother. They'd never talked about Andy. Before last night Jo had always thought it was because her mother was trying to spare her the thought of him, now she suspected that it had a whole lot more to do with guilt. She felt a flash of anger and gripped a shirt tightly.

"Jo. I..." Her mother's voice trailed away, and Jo felt her anger melt into a ball of anxiety that settled in the pit of her stomach. What was she going to hear? Excuses? Apologies? Recriminations? Lies? More lies? Whatever it was she knew with utter certainty that she didn't want to hear it. She and her mother had reached a certain status quo over the years. Their relationship was anything but perfect, yet it worked in its weird little way. Jo didn't really want it to change. And this? This was going to change everything.

She watched her mother's hands frenetically

folding and unfolding the clothes in front of her. With every one of her mother's nervous gestures Jo felt the ball of anxiety grow until it filled her stomach and chest and started to burn.

"What, mom? What?" Jo stopped herself a second too late. She could taste bile in her throat, and she fought to keep her stomach in check, but her mother had heard the anger lacing her words.

Jo waited to see if her mom would finally say something, but her mother stood frozen in front of her, mouth opening and shutting like a guppy. The sight of that softly padded jaw, the perfect lipstick, the mouth she loved so much, but that never said what she was always dying to hear, turned all of Jo's anxiety into pure brilliant anger. She could hold her breath forever, but her mother was never going to say what she needed her to say. Never. Her mother's mouth shut, and her lips disappeared into a thin pink line.

"You lied to me! How could you lie to me?" Jo erupted, balling her fists as tightly as possible so she wouldn't give into the urge to punch something.

"I never actually lied," Jo's mother almost whispered. The outburst had unzipped her lips but hadn't snapped her out of her torpor. She already looked defeated. Her hunched shoulders and refusal to fight back angered Jo even more.

"Fine, whatever. Want to split hairs? No problem. How could you let me believe that Andy left me? How could you? What kind of a cruel monster does that to her own grieving daughter? I needed him mom! I needed him by my side! And you... you...," Jo faltered, overwhelmed by the need to cry, shout, and throw up all at the same time. There were simply no words for what her mother had done. It felt like the ultimate betrayal by the person she'd clung to her like her savior at the time.

"You did not need that... that... boy!" Now that Jo had run out of her words her mother was finally fighting back. She spat the word boy out like it was poisonous. She had drawn her shoulders back and was holding her chin up so high Jo was having trouble seeing her eyes. What little she could see was shiny and bright. Tears or anger? Jo couldn't tell, but the slight tremor in those shoulders held so high was unmistakable. Her mother was crying.

Jo felt all the fight go out of her.

"Yes, mom. Yes, I did need him," Jo whispered. "He was the father of the baby I lost. We needed to mourn together. I needed to mourn with him."

"I did what I had to do to protect you!" It was the last bastion of defense. The justification that had always made her feel like she was in the right. Anything was acceptable as long as it was to protect Jo. It had driven Jo crazy her entire childhood and it was no different now.

"Oh? Really? Do tell, mother, how could isolating me from the only person who could possibly understand what I was going through, help me?" Jo could feel herself get pulled back into the argument. Could feel the anger build up again. She wanted to stop, wanted to turn away, but the whole situation was infuriating. Just admit you're wrong already! For once, admit you're wrong! Jo thought angrily.

"I knew what you were going through! He was just hurting you!"

"He was not hurting me! Andy never did

anything to hurt me. Ever! What on earth gave you that idea?"

"The nurses... they said..." Her mother faltered, shoulders coming down half an inch or so, confusion crossing her face.

"I don't care what they said! You should have known better! For crying out loud! You knew Andy. He was part of the family! And you know me; I would have come to you if he'd been hurting me."

"The nurses... the nurses said that to miscarry like that someone must have hit you. That young, healthy women, don't just suffer from placental abruption for no good reason."

"That's what you've thought all these years? Really?" The revelation stunned her. Jo looked at her mom and imagined how crazed she must have been to think that her soon to be son-in-law had beaten her so brutally that she'd lost a baby over it. "I leaned over, mom. I leaned over and something ripped. It was an accident. No one was hurting me."

"I know that old story. I thought... I thought you were covering up for him! And then when he left, when he didn't fight to see you harder... I thought it was like a confession. Like he was guilty." Her mother's shoulders drew back again, but Jo could tell she was starting to falter. Jo wanted so badly to reach out and hug her tightly, she couldn't wrap her brain around the burden her mother had carried all these years. But something held her back. Years of baggage stood between them, preventing her from being the bigger person here.

"It doesn't really matter what you thought in the end. Does it?"

"It doesn't?" Her mom looked up, confusion

etched deeply into her frown.

"No, it really doesn't. It wasn't your fight. It wasn't up to you to decide what would happen. You drove Andy away and it wasn't your fight. You meddled. You meddled like you always meddle."

"I did not meddle!" The shoulders drew up a few inches higher and the chin started to go up too. They were on familiar ground here. This was a fight they'd had so often they could have recited it by memory. "Okay, maybe I meddled a bit. But it was my fight! You're my baby and someone was hurting you! It's my job to protect you!"

"Oh! My! God!" Jo yelled at her mother. "I am not your baby anymore! I am a grown woman! It is not your job to fix everything anymore! I'm not six, for crying out loud! It wasn't a bully in the playground who pushed me over and made my knee bleed! He was almost my husband! I lost our baby! You meddled and it wasn't your fight! You drove him away when I needed him most. It wasn't you I needed it was him! What you did almost killed me! You hurt me way more than anything Andy ever did!"

As the words left her mouth Jo knew she'd gone too far. Even as the words were forming she wanted to call them back, but they had a mind of their own and they flew out unbidden. Her hurried apology was too late, too quiet, and wouldn't have done any good anyway even if her mother had heard it. As soon as the hurtful accusation had come out her mother's lips had sealed tight and her face had shut down.

"I'm sorry you feel that way," she said "Don't worry. I won't be meddling anymore. You want to be on your own? Fine. Be on your own."

She walked to the door and left, the only indication of her anger and hurt were the quaking shoulders and clenched fists.

Jo stood glued to her spot until the door slammed shut. Then she lunged. She wanted to apologize. Cry. Hug her mother and say sorry, say she understood, that she hadn't meant what she'd said. But deep in her heart she knew she had meant every word and that she couldn't take them back, so her feet slowed, and she stopped moving before she ever got to the door.

All her mother had done since her father had died, leaving them, a widow and a five year old, alone to face the world, was do her best to protect Jo. She had inserted herself into every single part of Jo's life, was the favorite mom of all her friends, the den mother to her scout's clan, the class mom for every class. She had spent a full week in a nearby hotel when Jo had started college. It had been stifling and overwhelming and yet, now that Jo had told her to stop, she felt lost. Was there anything to their relationship if there was no protection needed? Had she just lost her mother?

Jo went back into her now very tidy room and sat on the bed. She couldn't wrap her brain around what had just happened. She couldn't think past the hurt, broken look in her mother's eyes as she walked out of the room. She had to get out of this room, had to stop seeing that image. She pulled the door open and sprinted out of the room like it was on fire. She would run, that's what she would do, she would run, and run, and run. And when she got back, everything would be okay again. Kelli would be back at work, her mother wouldn't be mad at her, and Jordan and Sadie would be back from the golf course. She knew in her heart that only one of those things was possible, but she ran anyway, just in case miracles could happen.

43. Jo

"Jo's high tech sneakers pounded the hard sand at the edge of the water in a very satisfying and completely different way than they pounded the pavement at home. This was the closest she had ever come to recreating the sensation she had fallen in love with when she'd started running again shortly after arriving in Zambia. Back then running had made her feel like she was back in control of her life, and here it was working the same magic.

She stretched her legs into increasingly longer strides, loving the feel of her muscles reacting to the pressure. The sun was hot and even though the sweat was already pouring down her back in warm sticky streams she didn't care. She pushed herself harder and harder until all that was left was the sound of her feet hitting the hard sand and the crash of the waves trying to catch them as they flew by.

Jo ran until her lungs felt like they would burst, and all the stress had oozed away. She slowed down to catch her breath and came to a stop. So much had happened since she'd arrived that she hadn't had time to fully appreciate the beauty of the island during the day. Now that the run had cleared her head and lightened her heart she finally noticed her surroundings. She leaned forward, hands on her knees, and breathed slowly, giving her body a moment to recover. She had come far from the hotel; she'd need the strength to get back.

A group of massive rocks jutted out into the ocean and the sun glittered tantalizingly off the water. Jo looked around wondering if anyone would notice if she stripped off her clothes and dove in. The hotel was pretty far away, but was she daring enough to skinny dip in the daylight?

"Jo? Is that you?"

Jo jumped straight up and yelped. She turned around to see who had just talked to her, hand at her throat, feeling her heart pounding, both from the hard run and the fright she had just had. A dark figure stood at the edge of the palm trees that lined the beach. She moved her hand from her chest to her forehead and squinted to see better.

The man stepped forward into the sun. "It's okay. It's just me, Kona."

"Oh!" laughed Jo. "You scared the crap out of me." She fanned her face with her hands, hoping that she wasn't blushing too hard. What if he had come out five minutes later? There was a good chance he would have caught her completely in the nude.

"You sure you're okay? You look a little flustered. What are you doing so far from the hotel?"

By now Kona had reached her and Jo sat down on the warm sand, inviting him to join her as she gazed out at the sea. The sweat still felt sticky on her back, but at least she wasn't heaving anymore.

"I needed to get out. I needed to run."

"What's going on?" Ever the compassionate one, Kona reached over to pat her shoulder, but Jo moved out of the way just before his hand made contact. It was more than enough that he was seeing her looking like shit again. He really didn't need to feel just how sweaty she was.

"Oh, please don't. I'm all sweaty and nasty. You really don't want to touch me right now. Say, anyway, how come you aren't out golfing? I thought you were going to go with Sadie and Jordan."

Kona explained that he'd been all set to go and that he'd even taken them to the course to show them around and help them find another duo to play with, but in the end he'd thought it wise to stay back and help with the shark situation.

"What's the shark to you?" Jo asked, glad that he had stepped out right then. She eyed the still water she had been about to dive into and shuddered. She had completely forgotten the damn shark.

"Didn't Sadie tell you?"

"Tell me what? I barely got a chance to talk to her after we left you two last night." Jo winked suggestively and elbowed Kona in the side. "Say, how did it go last night? You guys had a good time, did you?"

This time she had the satisfaction of seeing Kona blush a deep mahogany and she didn't feel so self-conscious about her own hot cheeks.

"Sadie. She's really different. Special, you know?" Kona stared intently at the sand between his feet. "Thank you for bringing her last night."

Jo looked at him sideways, she had assumed that Kona and Sadie were having a fling, a vacation thing, but that wasn't the vibe she was picking up. She wondered if Sadie felt the same way. It would definitely explain the glow she had been emanating earlier that morning. At the time she'd assumed it was just a post-sex glow, but maybe there was more to it.

"My pleasure." She patted his arm gently. "You're right, Sadie is special. She's the best friend I've ever had. She's been there for me through so much and she's suffered an unfair number of heartbreaks."

Kona smiled at the thinly veiled warning. "Don't worry, I have no intention of hurting her. Ever."

They both stared out at the water for a quiet moment.

"So, this shark? How come he falls under your jurisdiction?"

"It's kind of complicated actually, but I'm just helping out. To the hotel patrons a shark is a mere nuisance that keeps them from swimming, but there are more ramifications than you can imagine." He shrugged. "You actually shouldn't be on the beach right now, you know? Didn't you see the sign when you came down from the hotel?"

Jo had been so lost in the storm raging in her head that she hadn't noticed any signs at all near the entrance to the beach let alone ones about a shark. She shook her head no.

"Nope, no signs, not that that means they weren't there! I was a bit wrapped up in myself. But seriously? No one on the beach at all? I can understand the no water thing, but the beach too?"

"People can't resist the water. First it's just the beach, then they dip their toe in, then their ankles... They always assume that they're safe since the water is so clear, but those sharks move fast, and they're mean. We just want to keep everyone safe."

Jo nodded. She was one of those people. Even now, knowing full well that a huge shark was lurking in the translucent blue water, she felt the urge to take off her shoes and dip her toes. In fact, even if she hadn't had the guts to go skinny dipping, she probably would have walked back to the hotel with her feet in the water.

"So, the theory is that you know better, so you get to be on the beach all you want?"

"No, I live back there behind the palm trees. I saw you out here and I came to warn you not to go in." Kona laughed. "Don't know why, but I got the distinct impression that you were about to go in." It was his turn to elbow her in the side and make her blush hard. At the sight of her flushed face Kona laughed even harder. He had a wonderful, contagious laugh, and Jo couldn't resist grinning.

"So, anyway, what were you running from?" Kona asked.

Jo sighed and looked out at the water again. Maybe she should have gone in. Knowing what was waiting for her back at the hotel made a shark attack seem almost inviting.

44. Jo

Kona listened patiently while Jo ranted on and on about Kelli and the shark who were apparently conspiring to destroy her barefoot-on-the-beach wedding plans. He didn't interrupt when she vented about how her mother didn't know when too much meddling was simply too much. He just nodded and made sympathetic noises in all the right places until Jo had unburdened everything that was weighing her down and she felt downright silly for monopolizing the conversation once again. She stopped herself and took a deep breath. She felt better. Silly and mildly embarrassed, but better. And now that she'd said everything aloud it all seemed like a lot of silly nonsense to be getting so upset about. She sighed.

"Feel better?" Kona asked, patting her shoulder.

"Yeah. I'm sorry. I don't know why I keep doing this to you! You know more about me and my pathetic life than anyone I know, and I still hardly know anything about you. Have you ever thought of becoming a shrink?"

Kona smiled. "It's okay, really, and your life is not pathetic."

"It's not?"

"Does all of this really matter to you in the end?" Jo nodded and shook her head at the same time. "If it matters to you, then it's not pathetic. But you have to ask yourself: what is it that's really upsetting you in this situation?"

Jo gazed out at the sea, searching for a sign of the shark, searching for an answer to all her problems, searching for the problem itself. What was really upsetting her? She wasn't mad at her mom. Not really. Her mother had just been doing what she always did, trying to protect her. Was she upset that Andy was here? That was disturbing for sure, but she wasn't really upset about it. It had been good to see him again and it was really good to finally know what had happened. So, what was it?

"I really can't put my finger on it. I think I just wanted all this to be easy. I just wanted to come to paradise, get married, and go home. Instead, I..." Jo faltered, unsure of how to finish her sentence. "Instead, everything is so complicated."

"Wouldn't be worth it if it weren't complicated."

"I guess." She shrugged. Complicated didn't usually faze her. Not being able to identify what was bothering her did.

"Life isn't scripted like the movies and in the end you can only ever run so far before you catch up to yourself."

Jo looked around. In her dreams this was the kind of place she always escaped to. The sounds of the birds, the ocean, and the wind whistling through the palm trees soothed her racing mind. The warm sand she kept scooping up and drizzling over her toes made her feel grounded and safe, and the heat of the sun beating down on her back felt like a comforting blanket.

She'd always thought she'd be safest and happiest on a desert island. That it would be the only place she'd be isolated from all the things that scared her, made her sad, or threatened to upset the delicate balance she'd managed to find. She had never considered the fact that, a million miles away from the day to day distractions that kept her from the dark scary parts of her mind, the only thing that would be left to ponder would be exactly the thing she thought she was running from. She had come to her island paradise and all her nightmares had come with her, and without any distractions there was nowhere else to go except to turn around and face them head on. She had run away from the hotel and everything that was going wrong. Now it was time to go back and take charge of her life again.

45. Andy

Andy sidestepped the massive yellow and black sign warning beach goers of the presence of a man eating shark. He had no intention of going into the sea, he just wanted to sit on the beach and enjoy the short child free moment he had just been granted. Two rescue Zodiacs bounced around, tethered to huge stakes in the sand and he fantasized about jumping into one and gunning the engine. It would feel amazing to fly over the water, free and alone. He sighed. He hadn't been able to give in to an impulse like that in years, not with the kids to consider.

Just as he'd glanced at his watch for the fifteenth time in a half an hour, wondering just how soon he could finally put Emily down for her nap, Roxie had shown up at the pool, looking just as perfect and gorgeous as always.

She had put her towel down on the chair next to theirs and, instead of laying back and ignoring everyone around her like he had expected, she had instantly started chatting up Emily. Within minutes of her arrival the two girls, one small, pudgy, and awkward in her water wings, the other sleek and gorgeous in her wonderfully skimpy bikini, had been splashing together in the shallow end, seeing how high they could make water squirt out of their hands. Andy had never taken Roxie for the kind of girl who would splash around in a pool. She'd always struck him as the type who wouldn't want to get her make-up or her hair messed up, but there she was, throwing her head back and laughing when the water squirted her in the face. He had laughed at her when Emily had jumped onto her back and ducked her under, and when Roxie had come up, spluttering and laughing, she had splashed him and laughed with him. He hadn't thought it was possible, but she was even more beautiful sopping wet and bedraggled than she was when she was fully dressed and put together and it had nothing to do with how her wet bikini clung to her perfect body. There was just something so approachable about her like this, so much more appealing than the vibe she usually put out. This was the girl he'd gotten to know online over the last couple of months. The girl he'd already started to really appreciate.

The two girls had been having so much fun together that he felt comfortable asking Roxie to watch Emily for a few moments while he took a quick walk to the edge of the water. She had waved him off with a smile and a splash, which he had ducked easily as he turned away. He was still adjusting to this new relaxed Roxie, but apparently Emily was already a big fan.

The fine sand felt like heaven between his toes and he stood for a moment letting his feet sink into the soft warmth. This was not the sand of his childhood, not the coarse sand of the Hamptons beaches he had spent countless summers sculpting into sandcastles, tunnels, or whatever structure he was determined to master during that vacation.

It was probably where his love of architecture had blossomed. He was pretty glad he had graduated from sand as a construction material though; it was unpredictable at best. Sometimes it wasn't even adequate. Take the stuff on this beach for example. He wasn't sure he'd be able to build anything here. The sand was too soft, too fine. It would be like trying to build something out of flour or fine sugar. He walked closer to the edge of the water to see if the wet sand was any more malleable, but a shout caught his attention before he got too close.

He peered down the beach to see who was calling to him, a spark of annoyance flaring up inside him. He had really just wanted one short moment to himself to catch his breath and try to sort out the chaos in his head. He'd hoped that on a deserted beach, where the access was restricted, he'd be able to find the quiet he craved.

"Andy! Don't!"

He strained his eyes harder, wondering who it could possibly be. Not that many people at the hotel knew his name. The person calling his name was running hard, arms pumping fast, legs stretching. The shape of the body and the intensity of the runner collided with a memory in his head. Jo. Jo running a half marathon shortly before she got pregnant and had to stop running. He had been awed by the sheer power of her body as she ran that day, not winning, but definitely not finishing last either. The sight of her powerful body hard at work had made him fall in love with her all over again.

Today he watched her run towards him, and he was again awed by her strength, but this time the overwhelming rush of love didn't follow. He could have been watching anyone run and he would have felt the same appreciation for the art and the way the body was moving, without any personal feelings getting in the way.

This lack of emotion shocked him. For years he had intently studied every runner he saw in the distance, searching for the exact recognition he had just felt. He had willed each and every one of them to turn into Jo, turn into the woman he pined for even as he was married to another and carried another's child on his shoulders. But until today those distant shapes had resolutely refused to morph into the woman he saw running in so many of his dreams. And now, there she was, the real thing, and he didn't even feel a glimpse of the flutter in his chest that he'd experienced with each ghostly encounter.

He forced a smile and waved at Jo, who, seeing that he had stopped moving towards the water, slowed down to a regular running pace. He could see that she was breathing hard and he wondered how hard she had pushed herself to come warn him away from the sea.

"I saw the sign!" He called to her, gesturing to the ocean. "I wasn't going to go in!"

She must not have heard him properly because she shook her head no and waved her arms frantically as she sped up again.

"No! No! It's okay!" He called louder and she finally heard him. She slowed to a stop and leaned over, hands on her thighs. Even from where he was standing he could see how hard she was heaving. He was touched that she'd been so concerned for him, and then he realized how odd a thought that was. Of course, she'd be concerned. It wasn't like he was some guy she had just met. They had history together. Even if finally seeing her again had freed him from the feeling that had tethered him to her ghost for so long didn't mean that there was nothing between them. He looked at her tenderly. There would always be something between them.

His feet sank into the soft sand as he moved forward. He glanced at the wet sand near the water, still wondering if it would be good building sand, but he didn't head in that direction. Instead, he headed towards Jo.

As he drew closer that feeling of tenderness grew and when she smiled at him he finally felt the telltale flutter in his stomach. Maybe he'd been a bit hasty to rejoice in being over her. Now that he was within an arm's reach he had trouble resisting the urge to touch her. Would it feel the same to hold her in his arms? Would their bodies recognize each other?

"Good run?"

"I... was... worried..." Jo struggled to catch her breath even as she nodded in response to his question. She stood up tall and took three deep breaths that she let out slowly. She closed her eyes and he saw her willing her breath to slow. He smiled. She had always been mistress of her emotions and body. It was another thing he had always admired, and he told her as much.

"I was? I am?" She looked confused for a moment, but she had her breath in check, and she spoke normally. "I sure never feel in control."

"You are. Or at least you used to be. You're a fighter. The Jo I remember always got what she wanted."

She dropped into a runner's lunge and Andy's

heart lurched as he watched her tight body move. She was still breathtaking, maybe even more so than before. The wisdom and pain etched into her face and reflected in her eyes gave her a depth that he had never seen in her before, not even last night when they had...

What was it exactly that they had done? Reopened old wounds? Cauterized them? Jo stood up tall and stretched her hands above her head and in a gesture that Andy couldn't control any more than he could control his own breathing, he reached for her and hugged her tight body to his. His mouth found hers instinctively and he kissed her with all the passion and longing that he'd kept bottled in since the day he had said a silent goodbye to her as he left their little home.

Jo fought him for an instant and then he felt her melt into his kiss. It felt exactly as he'd imagined again and again. Like being home again. And yet it was different. She dropped her hands around his neck, and he hugged her closer and kissed her deeper.

Her body felt the same and her mouth tasted exactly like he remembered. But he felt none of the fire that had warmed them in the past. He felt none of the passion ignite. In fact, he felt like he was kissing a good friend and it felt a bit wrong. Now that he noticed the difference he realized that her body didn't feel as familiar in his arms as he had first thought, like a puzzle piece that used to fit, but has been warped by water or exposure to the sun. You could hammer it into place with a well-positioned fist, but it would never quite be the perfect fit it had once been.

He released her at the exact moment that he felt her pull back.

"That was...," Jo started.

"Weird?" Andy finished.

"Yeah. Weird, exactly. I mean, don't get me wrong," she laughed, putting a hand on his forearm. "You're still a great kisser. But I craved that kiss for the longest time and it just didn't... it wasn't..."

"It wasn't right," Andy finished again, lifting his hands from her waist and placing them on either side of her face. He kissed her gently, tenderly on the lips and it was the kiss he should have given her in the first place. A goodbye kiss to their past and a hello to their new friendship.

Andy's hands fell to his side and they stepped away from each other. For the first time since he had first spotted Sadie near the elevator banks early the day before Andy felt at peace. He had been so scared about what seeing Jo again might mean. And now it was turning out to be the best thing he could have imagined. He felt lighter and happier than he had felt in years. The sun shone brighter, the water glimmered more vibrantly, and the colors seemed to come to life.

"You know what, Jo?" He said, laughing.

"What?" She asked warily.

"I am not in love with you!" She stopped walking and looked at him, both eyebrows raised straight up. She laughed, a huge laugh that grew and grew leaving her breathless again. Andy laughed too and for a moment neither of them spoke, letting the laughter finish the healing that had started the night before in the dark bar. Finally, Jo caught her breath and spoke.

"Andy?"

"Yeah?"

"I'm not in love with you either!"

They started laughing all over again and it was a

while before they managed to stumble back towards the hotel, holding each other up with an arm around each other's waists and stopping frequently as more giggles took their breath away.

46. Jo

Jo walked Andy back to the pool where Roxie and Emily both greeted him enthusiastically. She smiled as she watched him jump into the water, splashing both girls as soon as he reached them. The way Roxie's face lit up made her smile even wider. She was probably imagining things, but the picture was so idyllic that she let herself daydream a happy ending for both Roxie and Andy. Anything was possible, even a world where they lived happily ever after, a perfect couple with perfect kids.

Nah, maybe not for Roxie. She thought, shaking her head, as she strolled towards her room. It was one thing for Roxie to be wistful about romance and marriage, a whole other thing for her to embrace parenthood all at the same time. Jo giggled at the thought of her good friend, ever the paragon of style and fashion, wiping boogie noses, changing diapers, or doing messy arts and crafts projects. Doubtful. Not Roxie.

She took the steps up to the lobby two by two and felt her legs protest under the added strain. It had been a hard run and, while she had enjoyed the feel of pushing her muscles to their full potential, the effort was starting to take its toll. She ached to sink into a hot tub to ease the soreness away.

Despite her now throbbing legs, the run had been exactly what she had needed. She felt more in control and less overwhelmed than she had since she had arrived. And the kiss with Andy? Well, that had snapped everything back into perspective. Even with Andy's lips on hers all she'd craved was Jordan's touch. She didn't care about Kelli or the damn wedding details. She wasn't even mad at her mother anymore. She was in paradise and everything was just as it should be. She had been confused for a while, but now she knew exactly why she was there, to reaffirm her vows to the love of her life. She couldn't wait to look Jordan in the eye and tell him once again just how much she loved him. That they'd actually be getting married for real this time was just icing on the cake.

She started humming the wedding march as she bounced to the top of the sprawling staircase and broke into a light jog as she reached the top step. She was anxious to shower so she could be presentable, or at the very least huggable, when Jordan and Sadie returned from the golf course.

She stepped into the open lobby and glimpsed Jordan's familiar shape our of the corner of her eye. He was leaning on the banister, looking towards the beach. Her heart lurched. He was so good looking. She couldn't fathom that she'd ever doubted her love for him. Just seeing him there, framed in the glowing sunlight, made her heart swell.

She glanced down at herself. Damn it. She wasn't going to have time to clean up. Then again, he'd seen her looking much, much worse. A little sweat probably wouldn't faze him. She headed towards him but slowed and then stopped as she looked beyond his actual shape and took in exactly where Jordan was staring. His fingers were gripping the railing so hard that she could see the whites of his knuckles from where she stood, frozen on the spot.

Jordan's face was drained of color and his shoulders were bunched up in tight balls under his t-shirt. He radiated anger. More anger than she had ever seen from him. He was angrier even than when the local authorities had blocked essential shipments of medicine and food that the children at their orphanage had desperately needed, angrier than when his medical jeep had been stolen and trashed by stupid kids from the village. And his reputation back in Zambia had been founded on those two events. For miles he was known as the guy you just didn't want to mess with.

She stood rock still and her heart felt like it might stop as she watched him stare unflinching at the exact spot on the beach where, just moments before, she had been kissing Andy.

47. Sadie

A full 18 holes on the golf course following her long night with Kona had left Sadie bone tired and ready to crash. All she wanted to do was sink into a hot bath and snooze until the water turned cold. Then she wanted to put on a plush hotel bathrobe and finish her nap in her ridiculously squishy hotel bed. Instead, she was sitting behind a huge potted plant in the corner of the lobby, feeling like an idiot and stewing over how stupid she'd been to hook up with the first hot bartender she'd run into. The first hot, lying, bartender she had run into.

She felt like such an ass. She'd bought Kona's story hook, line, and sinker and she could kick herself. She was smarter than that! She'd been around the block a couple times. She knew that guys lied to get girls into bed and that the more farfetched the story the better off they were. The really great stories bought them extra bragging rights in the locker room.

As mad as she was at herself she still wanted to curl up and cry. She had truly thought that there was something special about this one. She'd let herself believe that maybe, just maybe...

Sadie shook her head hard and punched the floor

as quietly as possible. She had to stop thinking those kinds of thoughts. He was a lying bastard just like all the rest. He didn't deserve her heart or any more of her thoughts. And to think that if she hadn't decided to go find him for one tiny little kiss before going to shower she would never have known the truth...

She'd barely pulled open the door to the main office when the yelling had made her pause. She hadn't really been able to see into the room, but she had spotted Kona, head hung low, getting chewed out from what clearly must have been a manager.

It hadn't been the kind of reprimand reserved for the boss's son. It had been the kind of telling off reserved for errant bartenders who misbehave and are about to lose their job. The noise of the lobby fountain and the crash of the surf below had muffled the sounds so that she had no idea what he was being berated for, but she didn't really need to hear, his body language said it all. There was no doubt, he was the employee here, not the boss, and she was just a big fat idiot who had been taken in again. She had let the door slide shut again before she was spotted and she'd since been sitting here, behind this plant, not really sure what she was going to do next.

No wonder he couldn't go play golf with them; it would have been inappropriate for the bartender to be seen on the green. And he probably had to work, make up the hours he had missed the day before.

Sadie tried to keep feeding her anger, but the overwhelming sadness that threatened to engulf her kept interrupting her train of thought. He was just so damn nice. Such a good listener. He had those soft hands and that smile. And while she was at it she might as well admit how great a lover he'd been. And she'd really,

really believed him.

She moaned and shook her head again. What was she going to do, sit behind this plant all day? Wait for Kona to come out of the office and explain himself? What good would that do? It wasn't like he couldn't just lie some more. And clearly when she was around him she couldn't think straight. It was that damn smile and those blasted eyes. When he was around, she lost her head. Ha! If he came out right now she probably wouldn't even care if he lied to her again, she'd just want to kiss him again.

The quiet swoosh of the office door swinging open surprised her. There had been no movement at all since she'd slipped herself behind the plant who knows how long ago. Sadie leaned forward and peered through the leaves. It wasn't Kona though and her heart sank. Instead, a tall girl in a hotel blazer, long blond hair cascading down her shapely back stepped out into the lobby. Sadie sighed and stifled a bitter laugh. What was she doing here? Spying on the guy? How far could she possibly...

The door opened wider and this time Kona stepped out, right on the girl's heels. He caught her arm and held her back. He spoke intently, but the pounding ocean at her back kept Sadie from hearing a word he was saying. Her heart sank further when he pulled the beautiful girl into a tight embrace. Sadie choked on the acid bile that bubbled into her throat. She couldn't have been more wrong about this guy. Not only was he a liar, but he was a cheat too. She let herself sink back to the ground and dropped her head into her lap. She was such a stupid, stupid girl.

48. Jo

Jordan turned as though he felt Jo's eyes boring into his back. If she'd been scared by how angry she thought he looked, now she was positively terrified. His face was sheer white, and the warmth that had always laced his eyes had been replaced by an icy glare that chilled her to her core.

"Jordan," Jo didn't say any more than that. Her hand floated up towards him and hung there in midair. She wanted to say something, go to him, hug him, but she couldn't. She didn't know what to say. Didn't know how to cross the endless space between them. What had he seen? What was he thinking? She dropped her arm and crossed both in front of her. Her hands rubbed her arms to warm them up, but it did no good. It was Jordan's embrace that she needed, and it didn't look like she'd be welcomed into his arms any time soon.

Jordan just stared at her with that cold unreadable stare. The left corner of his lip jerked up into a disgusted sneer and he turned and walked away. Jo stood frozen to the spot, staring at his stiff back as he moved farther and farther away from her.

Even as he walked away too angry to even look her in the eye, too disgusted to even talk to her she couldn't help but feel a surge of love at the sight of his broad back.

The day before she had thought she was ready to throw their relationship to the wind, ready to let it slide between her fingers like the sand on the beach. She had been convinced that maybe their time together had run its course, that they weren't meant to be together and that the snafu with the license had been a sign. But now that he was walking away from her, she was terrified that he was walking away forever. Her throat tightened as she tried to call his name, but the words caught, and a mere gurgle slipped out. She raised her hand again, reaching towards his departing figure like a drowning woman reaching for a savior.

Jordan didn't notice her distress, or if he did, he didn't show it. He just kept walking, not even slowing at the sound of her gurgled anguish. The sight of him vanishing into the dark hallway at the end of the lobby spurred Jo into action. Andy was right, the girl she had been didn't give up. She didn't let others decide for her. She had forgotten that she had once been a decisive woman who called the shots and let others follow. That part of her had vanished with her baby. It was time to reclaim it. She wasn't going to let Jordan go without a fight. She didn't know how they'd gotten here, to this point where he wouldn't even fight for her. But she wasn't ready to give up.

She ran after him, strained legs protesting with every stride, but she pushed through the pain, determined to catch up to her husband, because he was her husband, even if the damn papers didn't agree. He'd been by her side through better and worse, sickness and health, definitely through poverty, and as far as she knew neither of them was dead yet.

49. Jo

Jo caught up to Jordan just as he stepped into the elevator. It was a good thing since she suddenly realized she had no idea what room he was staying in. Her mother had insisted they stay in separate rooms until after the ceremony to make it seem that much more authentic. He saw her coming and jabbed the close door button, staring her straight in the eye, mouth a thin forbidding line. Lucky for Jo the elevator wasn't the most responsive and she reached him before the door closed all the way.

She jammed her foot against the closing door and stood there, her hand on her chest, heaving, trying to catch her breath again.

"Move your foot," Jordan said, in a deadpan voice which startled Jo. It was the first thing he'd said so far. She hated the tone. She could deal with passion or anger; she didn't know what to do with this void of emotion.

"Jordan. No. Wait..." Jo's voice threatened to break, and she struggled to get control of herself. She knew Jordan well and turning into a crying hysterical woman wouldn't help her case at all. "We need to talk.

That... That wasn't what you think that was."

Jordan stepped back into the elevator and crossed his arms. His lip folded itself back into the same sneer she had just witnessed. It stabbed Jo in the heart.

"Oh. Really? You're telling me I didn't just see you kissing another man two days before we're scheduled to renew our wedding vows?" Jordan asked, his words laced with sarcasm. "Because from where I was standing, that's exactly what it looked like you were doing."

"Well, yes. But no," Jo stammered, still flustered by his cold demeanor. "I was... That was..."

"What, Jo? What could you possibly say that would allow me to forgive that." A flash of anger crossed Jordan's face as he gestured back towards the lobby. Jo felt a hint of relief at the sight of the emotion, anger was better than nothing. Anger meant that at least he still cared a bit.

"That.... That was Andy," Jo whispered, looking down. The door to the elevator kept bumping against her foot, straining to shut, but she didn't move.

When Jordan didn't reply she looked up. Anger and exasperation were toying with his features, but she finally saw what she had been looking for in his eyes. Hurt, he was hurt. He was angry and hurt because he thought she had betrayed him. A sigh of relief escaped her lips. Hurt was better than nothing. Hurt she could work with. All she had to do was explain what had happened and everything would be alright again. He would forgive her; there was no way he couldn't.

Her sigh wiped the traces of emotions from his face and the cold mask fell back into place.

"What? So, you think that makes it okay? You

think that because it's your old lover that you were kissing that I'm going to be fine with all this? What the f—k is wrong with you? Who do you think I am, just the guy you were biding your time with until he came back into your life? Well fine then! Go! Go back to him! Knock yourself out." He pushed the button again and pushed against her foot with his.

"What? No! No!" Jo shouted. Her cries caused Jordan's face to grow even darker. She struggled to control herself. "No. Jordan, please, no. That's not it at all. Please? Can we please just go talk? I swear I can explain. I swear."

Jordan hesitated and Jo held her breath. She honestly didn't know how he would react. For a moment he struggled too, his foot stayed near hers and she watched it carefully to see what he would do. Without saying a word, he stepped back. She stepped into the elevator after him.

They rode up in silence. Jordan had reached past her to push the 7 on the console. It was her only clue to where his room might be. Jo held her breath as she watched the numbers above the door. A tiny wistful childlike part of her thought maybe if she could hold her breath all the way up then everything would be okay.

The doors slid open silently on the 7th floor, her floor, and Jo let out her breath. Maybe a shared floor was a sign of sorts. Jordan gestured for her to go, and for a short moment she wondered if he was just trying to get her out of the door so he could hit another number and escape into the depth of the hotel.

"Just go already. This really is my floor, it's not a trick."

Jo tried to play off her hesitation, but both Jordan

and she knew that it was no use. He had always known what she was thinking.

That's what was really confusing her here. From the first moment they had met he had been able to read her mind. He could read her like a book. It had driven her crazy at first. When she had arrived in Zambia, she had been desperate to be left alone in her head, left alone with her dark thoughts. To a certain extent he had given her the space he craved, but whenever the darkness lifted he had been right there, waiting. It had been unnerving, and for a while it had irked her, but after a while she had stopped resenting his presence and had started welcoming it. It was soothing to be with someone so in tune with her emotions, he always knew exactly how she wanted or needed to be treated.

So, if he could read her mind, why was he so angry? How could he not be picking up on the fact that she had no feelings left for Andy?

Jordan stepped out of the elevator behind her and relief flooded through her. Despite his assurances, she really had wondered if he'd try to ditch her.

"I told you this was my floor," he snapped before striding away to the left without looking to see if she would follow. She raced after him, trying hard to keep up with his long strides. Before she caught up to him he stopped abruptly in front of a door and slid his key smoothly into the lock. The door swung open as if by magic. Clearly she was the only one challenged by the key system in the hotel.

Jo stepped in behind him and stood awkwardly by the door, not really knowing what to do with herself. She didn't think throwing herself on the bed would go over very well, neither would throwing herself at

Jordan's feet.

He wasn't exactly making it easy on her. After coming into the room, he had made a beeline for the bathroom, coming out with his toiletry kit in hand. He zipped it shut and threw it into the open suitcase in the corner of the room. He grabbed the few things he'd tossed onto the armchair and threw those into the suitcase too. Jo had no idea what to do. Did she just start talking? Did she help him fold his clothes? At home she would have been chiding him for how he was packing, but right now it really didn't seem like the appropriate thing to do. She shifted from one foot to the next and Jordan finally looked up from the binder he had just flipped over. He looked genuinely surprised and almost annoyed that she was standing there inside the room.

"What Jo? What is it you have to say? Say it fast. I need to figure out when the next flight out leaves." Jordan placed his hand on the phone and waited.

"Jordan. Please. No." He gestured for her to go on. "Please. At least hear me out before you call."

"Fine. Talk." Jordan removed his hand from the phone and stood, arms crossed in front of his chest, staring at her unflinchingly.

Jordan didn't sit down or invite her to, so she stood there, facing him, one of the two beds in the room separating them. She longed to reach across the bed and grab him. She wanted nothing more than to kiss him hard and tell him that he was everything she had ever wanted, that she had never been so sure of anything in her life. But it felt like there was more than just a bed between them, there was a whole painful gulf to be crossed and she wasn't sure she had it in her to make it across.

"I... I... kissed Andy."

"Thank you, Sherlock," Jordan spat the words at her. "I saw that part. Any other pointless confessions you want to make or are we done here?" Jordan was so rarely sarcastic or openly mean that Jo faltered. She blinked away tears pooling in her eyes, took a breath, and tried again.

"Yes, I kissed Andy." Jordan grimaced, but she pressed on, determined not to let him stop her this time. "BUT! But it wasn't that kind of kiss. It was a goodbye. An ending. It was... I guess it was the closure that we never had."

"You kissed another man, two days before our wedding. Is there really any story that excuses that? You can't change the simple fact that you kissed another man."

"Yes. Fine! You're right. I fucked up." Jo heard her voice get shrill and forced herself to take a breath. If she yelled, the conversation would be over. Nothing made Jordan shut down faster than raised voices. It took him right back to his terrifying childhood. "I'm sorry. I fucked up. I truly did. I should never have kissed Andy. But Jordan, it's you I love. It's you I want to be with forever and ever and ever. I know that now."

"I'm sorry? You know that now?"

Even before Jordan recoiled as if she'd slapped him Jo knew that she'd made a mistake. She had never let on to Jordan that she'd had doubts about them. He had no reason to know what she'd been thinking. Fuck. He didn't even know about the wedding license issue.

"What?" Jordan instantly caught what she knew was a guilty look flashing across her face. "What aren't you telling me? Did you sleep with him?" This time it was Jordan's voice that was getting shrill. Jo flinched.

"NO! God! I swear! I didn't sleep with him! The kiss was it. One kiss. Nothing more. One goodbye kiss!"

"Then... why... do... you... look... so... damn... guilty?" Jordan accentuated every word in his question, pausing between each, as if she was a slow child being reprimanded.

"It has nothing to do with Andy! I swear!"

"Then what is it?" Jordan balled up his fists and glared at Jo.

She looked down at her feet, swallowed, and told him. She started with the license and having crossed that bridge, explained how she had imagined that it was a sign that maybe they shouldn't be together. She told him about running into Andy the instant she had arrived on the island and how she had thought that it might just be another sign. And once she had told him about that it was easy to tell him about her mother's betrayal, all those years past and how learning about all of it had made her feel closer to Andy, had made her miss the life they'd had. The life they could have had.

"I was confused, Jordan. All that stuff... it came back up and threw me for a loop. But that kiss... it was like kissing a friend... a brother almost. It felt so wrong, I can't even explain it. And the whole time I was just thinking about you and about how when you kiss me I can feel it all the way down to my toes. How it fills my heart and makes me feel like I can do anything in the whole world because you love me and we're together."

Her words had rushed out, everything at one, one big jumbled up confession and Jordan had listened to every word, not nodding, not moving, not saying anything. When she was done, she sat down heavily on the bed. She was spent. It had been a roller coaster of a day and she didn't know if she had the stamina to keep going. She stared at the carpet and waited for Jordan to speak or move. She didn't dare look at his face, terrified at what she would see etched on the features that she so loved.

He opened his mouth to speak and she held her breath.

"So, what you're saying is that we're not actually married?" Jo nodded silently, still not looking up. "We're not married, and you weren't sure you wanted to be married to me anyway, but everything is okay now because you saw the love of your life again, only he's not really the love of your life anymore, I am?"

Jo hesitated and then nodded. It was a bit simply put, but she couldn't argue that that was exactly what had happened.

"I don't know what to say. I really don't."

Jo ventured a look at his face, but what she saw there didn't reassure her in the slightest. The anger and frustration that had been painted there since she'd stopped the elevator door was gone, replaced once more by the white mask of nothing that she had first encountered at the top of the stairs.

"I'm tempted to lead with fuck you and follow it up with fuck off for good measure."

Jo reeled. If Jordan rarely used sarcasm, he definitely never swore, especially in such an impassive voice.

"Do you have any idea what this last year has been like for me? We left everything so you could come home. And then? Then you stopped speaking to me, but not before coming up with this fucked up wedding plan.

You are so damn full of yourself aren't you? You thought you could bring us both here and then just pick and choose once you could size us up against each other? Well, you know what? The choice isn't yours to make. I'm done living my life according to your latest whim. I'm leaving. Get out."

"Jordan! What? No! That's not it at all! That is not what happened!" Jo stammered, blindsided by the accusation that she'd manipulated a comparison.

"I said get out. This conversation is over. I'm not talking about this anymore. Get. Out."

Jordan turned his back on her and picked up the phone to call the front desk. Jo stood there, eyes boring into his back, gaping. She had no idea what she could say. Didn't know which accusation to address first. She knew she had botched her explanation, but this... this went way beyond what had just happened.

"Jordan? Please?"

But Jordan hunched his shoulders and didn't turn around. When she heard him tell the receptionist that he would be checking out early and asking her to book him onto the next flight back to the mainland, Jo turned and left the room noiselessly.

50. Andy

Andy bounded up the stairs to the lobby taking them four by four. He was flying high on excitement, joy, and just pure adrenaline. This was turning out to be quite the vacation. He reached the top and danced over the last step. The words to the old 80's classic, I'm walking on sunshine, looped around his head and he started to hum as he danced around the lobby furniture.

He had left Emily with Roxie again for a moment, so he could run to their room to grab her back carrier. The two of them had decided to go for a walk before picking up Hunter from camp and he knew that Emily wouldn't make it far before becoming a whiny mess. He figured that in the back carrier she just might fall asleep, leaving him and Roxie virtually alone for the first time. The mere thought of being alone with Roxie made him want to sing out loud instead of just humming.

He spotted the concierge's desk and made a split second decision. He wheeled around and tried to slow to a more regular walk as he headed towards the concierge. A tall man approached from the other direction, laptop case slung across his back, worn duffel clasped in his hand. The two men reached the desk at exactly the same time and the concierge looked at both of them. Andy nodded and smiled.

"Go ahead. I can wait." He stepped away a bit to give the man some privacy. The desk was lined with thick glossy brochures advertising all the activities vacationers could distract themselves with. Rock climbing, Quad excursions, Parasailing, Helicopter ride to the nearby volcano. He grabbed the one showing the spewing volcano and snapped it open. It seemed cool enough. He was surprised to realize he was hoping Roxie might be interested in going with him. He laughed at himself, last thing he needed was another girl in his life, but he had no control over the infatuation he was feeling. Roxie was a girl he had known forever, but the girl he was seeing this weekend seemed like a completely new version of the one he'd known for years, and he really, really liked what he was discovering. She was funny, she was smart, obviously she was beautiful, but it was more than just the beauty he had always assumed was barely skin deep. He was discovering that she was a lot kinder and less shallow than he had always presumed. He smiled and hummed a couple more bars.

"F.L.E.M.I.N.G. And the first name is J.O.R.D.A.N." The irritated tone and the words caught Andy's attention. Wasn't Jo's husband named Jordan? This couldn't be him. This guy was clearly leaving; he was asking the woman about shuttles to the airport. Andy glanced over at the man and realized that he didn't have a hint of color in his face, not even the pale pink of someone who had lathered up careful layers of sunscreen before heading into the hot Hawaiian sun, just the paleness of a guy who has been in an office too much and hasn't seen the sun enough. This guy might be leaving, but it looked like he had only just gotten here.

The date on the airline tags attached to his duffel confirmed Andy's suspicion. This guy had just arrived that morning.

The concierge was busy at the computer and the man was fidgeting, agitated over something. Neither of them were paying him any mind, leaving him plenty of time to conduct his little investigation. He had no facts to back up his gut feeling but Andy was convinced that this was Jo's guy.

"Leaving so soon?" Andy's voice surprised him as much as the traveler. The guy didn't even look up before answering.

"Yeah. I... I have to get back."

"I'm sorry to hear that. It's a fabulous hotel." Andy sauntered closer, trying to get the guy to engage in some sort of conversation. He had no idea what had happened but couldn't resist. This was the man Jo had married. This was the guy who had taken his place. The concierge was still tapping away at her keyboard. The guy glanced around the lobby and shrugged.

"Whatever, it's nice enough I guess." He shrugged again and turned his back on the breathtaking view.

Andy wasn't usually the type to meddle, but he couldn't understand why this guy would be running away two days before his wedding. There was a time he would have given his right arm to be walking Jo down the aisle. Now he was more than just curious. There had to have been a reason Jo fell in love with this jackass, but for the life of him, Andy couldn't figure out what. He seemed like a real piece of work. Condescending and rude didn't even start to cover it. The concierge found a satisfactory flight and Jordan handed her his credit card.

Asshole or not, Jo had chosen this man and he knew she was a great judge of character. There had to be something more to the situation than Andy could see.

"Listen, I don't mean to pry. But aren't you supposed to be getting married in two days?"

The man turned on Andy, lips barred in a fierce looking scowl.

"Who the fuck are you?" Recognition dawned and the scowled deepened, his fists clenched at his sides.

Instead of taking the step back that he really wanted to take, Andy stepped forward and held out his hand as if to shake Jordan's. He felt like an ass himself, but damned if he knew what this particular situation called for.

"Andy. Andy Sullivan."

The look of disgust that took possession of Jordan's face made Andy finally take that step back. This was way more than he had bargained for. This guy wasn't just rude, he was violent, or at the very least he looked like he wanted to be violent. Andy had no idea why, but he had the distinct feeling that he was about to get punched in the face. Hard. He waved his hands is front of him, warding off the impending blow.

"Dude, sorry. Didn't mean to meddle. Sorry. I'll go over there. You finish your transaction. Safe flight and all."

Jordan audibly growled and stepped towards him. Andy took another step back and found himself pushed up against the desk, unable to get out of the way. Jordan's face was purple with anger and Andy could see every vein in his forehead bulging as he finally started speaking.

"You're sorry? You're sorry you fucking

meddled? You fucking kissed my fiancée two days before our wedding and you're fucking sorry you meddled? Are you fucking kidding me?"

Andy tried to step back again and bumped up hard against the desk. He sidestepped, anything to get out of the way of the finger that Jordan was jabbing into his chest. He resisted the urge to grab the finger and bend it back. No need to piss the guy off any further. Adding a broken finger to the situation wouldn't help anyone, least of all him.

"Listen, man, that's not what happened. That's not what happened at all!"

"Don't you man me! I fucking saw you kiss her!"

"Sir? I need your signature." The concierge interjected, in a faint attempt to diffuse the situation, but Jordan ignored her. He and Andy stared each other down, neither of them flinching or saying anything else. Jordan's finger dug deep into Andy's chest. All Andy could do was stare deep into Jordan's eyes. He couldn't see the man Jo had fallen in love with. Couldn't see what she saw in this pissed off jackass. All he could see was his own pain reflected deep in Jordan's eyes. He knew that pain. He remembered what it felt like to be losing Jo. He understood where the anger was coming from.

"Don't do it," he said quietly, breaking the silence. "Don't leave. I never forgave myself. It's taken me all these years to be able to deal with the pain of leaving her. I've missed her every single day since I left. Don't make the mistake I made."

Anger flashed in Jordan's eyes and then went out. His shoulders drooped and he released the finger that had probably left a bruise on Andy's chest. His hand dropped by his side and he stood there, defeated, the fight gone out of him.

"Well, now you can have her. That's what you both want, isn't it?"

Now that the anger had left his eyes, Andy could see the pain even more clearly than before. This guy was already mourning Jo.

"No, it's not what she wants." He reached out and gripped Jordan's upper arm. "And really, it's not what I want either." As Andy spoke he knew the words were true. For the first time in five years, he honestly and truly didn't want Jo. He loved her, sure. He always would in some dark part of his heart where he'd buried his youth, but he was free of her pull. It really had been a goodbye kiss. He was more than ready to move on. "It's you she wants. It's you she always wanted. Even when we were together a part of me knew that I wasn't who she was supposed to be with. Maybe she was waiting for you all along."

A look of utter confusion crossed Jordan's face and he looked at Andy like he might be insane. Andy just shrugged and squeezed his arm harder.

"Whatever. It doesn't matter. Just... don't leave her. Not like this. Trust me."

51. Sadie

Kona gave the tall blond girl a final hug and slowly let go. She walked away with a bit of a spring in her step and he watched her go, his back to Sadie so she couldn't get a good read on his emotions. She could tell his shoulders were drooping though. Her stomach twisted painfully.

Once the girl was out of sight Kona turned and headed in the opposite direction, passing dangerously close to Sadie on his way. She shrunk back towards the wall and held her breath. Sadie felt her face grow hot at the mere thought of being found out. Who hides behind plants in hotel lobbies anyway? Kona moved out of hearing range and Sadie let out her breath. When she could no longer see him, she let herself sag back against the wall. There was no longer any reason for her to stay behind the plant, but she couldn't seem to muster enough strength to stand up.

She'd just watched the guy, her guy, kiss another girl and she still felt torn about how she felt about him. Last night had been so magical and amazing. And this morning... Well, this morning had been nothing other than nightmarish, but still, she couldn't get past last night. Tears welled up in her eyes and she tried to swallow the lump that had formed in her throat. For a brief magical evening she had let herself believe that she might have ended her streak of terrible luck. Now she was sitting behind a plant, in a lobby, and she had nothing to get up for.

Sadie completely lost track of time. She heard people come and go, sometimes stop and chat. She heard all the sounds you would expect in a busy hotel lobby. People checking in, their excited chatter increasing as they discovered the ornate decor and the stunning view. Others checking out, their words more muted, sedate, already mournful. Yet others, still in the middle of their stay, stopping in to check in with the concierge or the front desk for information or excursion reservations.

Considering how hard it had been to overhear Kona's earlier conversations Sadie was a bit surprised that now she could hear almost everything that was going on around her. Maybe the sound of the blood rushing through her ears had slowed down. Or maybe being so much closer to the ground was affecting the way sound was reaching her. Whatever. Sadie shrugged. She didn't really care about what she was hearing.

If she crawled out of her hiding place, she'd have to face her friends. What would she tell Jo? "Uh, yeah. So that guy. He was awesome. We really connected, we talked all night then we hooked up. Turns out he was lying the whole time. Surprise!"

She didn't know what would be worse, the supportive hug Jo was bound to give her or the knowing look that would definitely be in Roxie's eye. Poor stupid Sadie, always falling for the wrong guy. Always letting the guy walk all over her and manipulate her. Poor little

Sadie. She shuddered and bit back a sob. It didn't help that her friends would be right.

"I'll be checking out early."

Out of all the chatter, surrounding noise, and self-pity that was washing over Sadie, Jordan's voice rang out clearly and her head popped up off her knees. Jordan? Checking out early? She must have heard wrong.

Curiosity got the best of her and she slipped onto her knees to peer out through the plant's leaves. She hadn't heard wrong. That was Jordan, and he definitely had his luggage with him. Wait. She'd only left him, well, however long she'd been sitting here. It couldn't possibly be more than an hour or so. Could it? What could possibly have happened since they'd gotten back? Jordan hadn't been particularly chatty during the golf game, but she hadn't picked up on anything being really off. She definitely hadn't thought he'd want to leave. Then again, she'd been in a completely different place while they'd been golfing. Maybe her head had been too high in the clouds to notice that something was wrong.

Sadie started to slide out of her hiding place, but Andy's abrupt arrival on the scene stopped her in her tracks. She slipped back to her original spot and parted the leaves again. It had felt weird to spy on Kona, but now she just felt like she was in some low budget spy movie. But there was no way to step out there. Not now. She watched the two men, the only two men that Jo had ever really loved stare each other down. She had no idea what had happened or what was happening in front of her, but the tension was so thick it almost made the air around them shimmer.

She couldn't hear what Andy was saying, he

spoke too low, but she assumed he was trying to convince Jordan to stay. It was painful to see the confusion and sadness in Jordan's eyes and it was finally what motivated her to stand up and step out from behind the plant when Andy turned away to speak to the concierge. The need to go comfort him was too strong to fight. Jordan didn't move or look away from the ocean when she stepped out quietly and came to stand beside him.

She placed her hand gently on his arm and he looked down at her, not questioning where she'd come from.

"He's right, you know. You shouldn't leave."

"You think?" Jordan's eyes didn't really connect with hers. She wasn't even sure he'd really seen her. It was a genuine question, not one laced with sarcasm or bitterness.

"Jo loves you. She'd do anything for you. The two of you are meant to be together."

Jordan shrugged, and stared back out at the sea. "I'm not so sure anymore."

Andy turned away from the concierge and looked surprised to see Sadie standing with Jordan. She stammered out a story about seeing them both as she was walking through. Andy shrugged and turned his attention back to Jordan.

"So? Have you made a decision?"

"I..." Jordan paused, eyes still glued to the sea. "I think I'll stay. You're right. I can't leave her. Not like this."

Andy and Sadie looked at each other. Sadie heaved a sigh of relief. She still had no idea what was going on, but she liked feeling the tension dissipate.

Jordan spoke quietly to the receptionist and checked back into the hotel. Sadie and Andy looked on, not really knowing what to say. He drifted back towards them when the transaction was completed.

"You hungry?" Andy asked. Jordan shrugged. "Let me take you to lunch. It's the least I can do." Jordan shrugged again. Sadie was sure he was going to say no, especially after Andy explained that the kids and probably Roxie would have to come too. But, when Andy turned to leave, Jordan asked the receptionist to take his bag back to his room and he followed along in his wake.

52. Jo

"Jo! Jo?!" The voice startled her, and she fought the urge to duck around the corner. Footsteps hurried her way, and she forced her mouth into a smile before looking up. Her shoulders sagged gratefully as she saw that it was Roxie hurrying her way. "Babe? You OK?"

Jo didn't know how it could be possible, but she knew without a shadow of a doubt that Roxie knew what was wrong. She'd been hopeful that a shower would help her regain control of her emotions, but it hadn't worked nearly as well as she'd hoped. She'd washed off all the sand and salt from her run, but she still had no clue about what to do with her life or even her day. Roxie caught up with her and pulled her into a bear hug. For the first time ever Jo appreciated the fact that Roxie was taller and nestled her head in her friend's shoulder.

"Honey, I'm sorry. What happened?" Roxie rubbed Jo's back tenderly and hugged her close.

Jo bit back a sob but was unable to check the tears that had finally broken through. "Well, that depends. What do you know? It's been such a crappy morning it's kind of hard to know where to start."

Roxie patted her back. "All I know is that Andy

251

ran into Jordan as he was booking a flight off the island."

"So, he's... he's... really gone?" Jo felt all the hope she'd been clutching seep away. She moaned. He'd said he was leaving, but part of her had had refused to believe it until this very moment.

"Well actually, no. Andy convinced him to stay."

"Huh? Really?" Jo looked up to see if Roxie was telling her the truth. "He did? Jordan's still here?"

"All I know is that Jordan canceled the flight out."

"Oh my god. I have to talk to him. I have to. Right now. Do you know where he went?"

"He and Andy took the kids to grab some lunch. Give them a moment to settle before you rush down there."

Jo nodded. With a little luck and a bit of time on their own Andy would help convince Jordan of what she'd been unable to make him see.

Roxie and Jo walked to the lobby to see what they could do about finding a cup of coffee. The morning's emotions combined with the sheer quantity of alcohol they had consumed the night before had left Jo with a raging headache that was making it hard to think clearly. Maybe if her head stopped pounding she'd be able to see her way to taking control of this nightmare.

Jo slipped her arm into the crook of Roxie's arm and tried to pretend that she wasn't clinging on for dear life. She filled Roxie in on the all the details of her horrible morning. Her friend made all the appropriate noises and patted her arm gently when Jo choked on her sobs, but as Jo told her story again, for the third time now, each rendition getting longer and more depressing, she realized that the common thread in all these situations was that she'd failed time and time again to take control. She'd let things happen to her. She vowed that this was it. The story wasn't going to get worse before she had time to tell it again.

"You know, I don't know if this wedding is going to happen. Maybe it doesn't matter. Maybe you've been right all along and being single is where it's at."

"No!" Roxie's sharp protest stopped Jo in her tracks.

"No? You the über feminist, is telling me that being married is better than being single? I was just saying that it might be time for me to learn to stand on my own two feet so I can remember what it's like to rely on myself instead of others."

"Well, fine, maybe that part is good, but you don't have to be single to do that."

"I don't?" Jo raised an eyebrow. This was so unlike Roxie. "What do you mean?"

"You know Jo, maybe my mother was wrong all this time. Maybe being in a committed relationship doesn't mean you have to give up the thing that makes you yourself."

"Well, duh, Sadie and I have been telling you that all along."

"Okay, good. So clearly you don't have to give up on Jordan to find that part of yourself again."

Jo thought about how, from the moment they met, Jordan had always been by her side. She had always relied on him and he had let her, she wondered if he'd be just as supportive if she wanted to stand on her own two feet. She suspected that he would be, but what if she needed to really be on her own to see if she could handle that pressure?

She shrugged. "I'm not sure about that. Anyway,

what brought on this change of heart on your part?"

"You know, it's the strangest thing. I've always been so wrapped up in not letting myself fall in love that I've forgotten how nice it can be. Maybe there's something in the air here, or maybe it's watching Sadie and Kona, but I want that too. I want to let go."

"And you've found the man you want to do it with?" Jo teased, as she elbowed her friend lightly.

"I have." Roxie blushed and Jo giggled. Roxie squeezed her hand in concern. "You don't mind do you? There's something there. Something I never felt before."

"Of course, I don't mind!" Jo threw her arms around Roxie and hugged her hard. "I want you to be happy and I want Andy to be happy and I can't think of anything that would make me happier than the two of you being happy together. But are you really sure? There's a lot of baggage there."

"You mean the kids?"

"Well, yeah." Jo shrugged. "And then some."

"Funny thing is that I really like the kids. They're part of the whole package. And the rest? Maybe it's time for all of us to put the past behind us. Plus, it's not like I don't come with my own baggage!"

53. Sadie

Sadie hurried to the elevator and found herself ducking behind an ornate marble pillar as she spotted Maryanne stepping out of one into the lobby.

Shit. Shit. Shit. Shit. Sadie looked frantically for a better place to hide, but the bush that had done her such good service earlier was too far away and there was nothing but a huge expanse of lobby separating her from Jo's mother. Maybe if she dashed for it, she could get to the stairwell leading down to the pool area before Maryanne got too close. Then again, maybe the dash would make her easier to spot. Maybe the trick was just to stay put, standing as still as possible, and hope that Maryanne would head down the stairs leading to the beach. She just couldn't face Jo's mother right now; not until she had a better sense of what had just happened between Jordan and Jo.

Sadie froze and held her breath. It turned out to be a good thing. Instead of choking on her breath she was able to stay stock still as the good looking older man who had stepped out of the elevator behind Maryanne placed his hand on her lower back and leaned in closer to hear what she had to say. They both laughed.

Sadie watched the two head towards the stairs

and felt the need to rub her eyes to make sure she was seeing clearly. She'd never seen Maryanne with a man. As far as she knew Maryanne had never dated anyone since her husband had died. But this was no mere elevator acquaintance. Maryanne seemed comfortable with this man, she was clearly welcoming his hand on her back, and in fact now she was tucking her hand in the crook of his arm as they walked down the stairs.

Maybe there was something wrong with this hotel. Maybe they were piping some sort of drug into the air vents, because no one, absolutely no one was behaving the way they usually did.

Maryanne and her mysterious companion vanished down the stairs, leaving nothing separating Sadie from the elevator. She waited an extra second to make sure that Maryanne wasn't going to come back up. When no one reappeared, Sadie hurried, determined not to be stopped again and almost made it to the elevator before a voice called out to her.

Seriously? Was she being punished for something? Was her punishment that she'd have to stay in this hotel lobby for the rest of her life?

She turned towards the voice that had been muffled by the sound of the elevator door opening. Her heart skipped a beat when she saw Kona hurrying towards her.

"Sadie? Wait up!"

She glared at him and stepped into the elevator. She pushed the close door button a second too late. Kona jumped into the tiny space just as the doors slid shut.

"Didn't you hear me? Why did you run?" Kona reached for her, clearly intent on picking up where they'd left off earlier that morning. Sadie backed away

Jessica Rosenberg

from him, putting her hands up for protection. She shook her head, but she had no idea what to say.

What was appropriate in this situation? She didn't want to yell. The fight had gone out of her. She was just sad really and she didn't have the heart to argue. She really just wanted him to leave her alone.

"What's wrong? Are you mad that I didn't come play golf?" Kona seemed genuinely confused and Sadie hesitated. Was it possible that she'd misread the situation?

No! No, she hadn't! She was done being swindled. Of course, he was acting like this. He had no idea she knew about the other girl. She glowered at Kona who took a hasty step back.

"Of course, I'm not mad about the golf you... you... Jerk!"

Kona looked like she'd slapped him, which made her almost wish that she had slapped him for real. It would have felt great to feel her hand connect with his cheek, his strong, smooth cheek. Sadie caught herself gazing longingly at Kona's smooth cheek and shook her head angrily. No wonder the man was confused. She didn't know what she was doing here.

"For someone who's not angry, you're acting awfully mad you know." Kona reached out a hand towards her making Sadie slink back even further. Her back was up against the elevator wall and she felt completely trapped. Kona was in front of the door so it wasn't even as though she could rush past him to get out when the door opened. He would for sure catch her as she brushed past. The tingling in her breasts at the thought of brushing up against him angered her even more. He was just so darn good looking. It was hard to be mad at him. Hard to say no.

"I didn't say I wasn't mad. I said I wasn't mad about the golf."

"Okay. So, you're mad. What did I do? Did I hurt you last night?" His face fell.

Sadie stopped and looked at Kona carefully. He really did look confused. Maybe... No! He just didn't know that she'd seen him! The constant back and forth was wearing her down. She was just so damn tired. She wished she could have gotten a bit of sleep before having this discussion. There was no way she'd be able to win an argument in this state.

Sadie crossed her arms carefully in front of her and focused on a stain on the wall to the right of where Kona was standing. If she didn't look right at him this might be easier.

"I am mad because you..." She paused. What was she mad about exactly? How could she possibly explain? She'd eavesdropped and heard him get reamed by his boss? Then she saw him virtually make out with a tall blond? Sadie let out an angry sigh and stamped her foot. She hated this so much.

"Sadie, what? Seriously, what's wrong?" Kona stepped closer and tried to take her hand. She tucked them both closer to her body. "I don't know what happened, but I'm sorry. I know we haven't known each other long, but... but, and this is utterly crazy, but I'm crazy about you. So I'm sorry if I did anything to piss you off. I'd hate to have screwed things up between us."

Against her will Sadie looked up at Kona's face. His deep blue eyes were looking intently down at her and she found herself appeased by the kindness she saw in there. She hung onto his every word. She wanted nothing more than to believe him, to let herself fall into his arms, and to let those soft lips kiss her until she had forgotten this whole horrendous day. But she knew what she'd seen. She couldn't let herself fall into his smooth talking trap again. She had to be strong.

She forced herself to break her gaze and she looked down at her feet.

"You... you..."

"What? What did I do?"

"You're not who you told me you were. I heard you get yelled at this morning. I know you lied." Sadie held her breath and then rushed on, determined to get it all out at once. "And then I saw you kiss that girl. You're a liar and a cheat," she finished on a whisper and waited to see what he would say, hating the tears that leaked down her cheeks.

Kona's laugh erupted into the heavy silence, surprising Sadie and stopping her tears in their tracks. She looked up, enraged. How dare he laugh at her! But the condescending look she was expecting was nowhere on Kona's face. All she saw in his eyes was tenderness, gut wrenching tenderness. There wasn't a trace of malice in his deep gray eyes.

"Why are you laughing at me? It's not funny!" Sadie growled. First he'd been dismissive. Now he was laughing at her. And looking down at her like she was some cute little confused puppy or something.

Kona stopped laughing instantly and without hesitation or warning grabbed her and pulled her to him. Before she had a second to protest his soft warm mouth was pressed tightly to hers and he was kissing her with a passion that made their previous evening's activities pale in comparison. Any complaint that Sadie was about to utter was instantly lost in the kiss she hungrily returned. She wanted to fight him, wanted to push him off and get to the bottom of what he'd done, but once his arms encircled her she found herself completely powerless. Instead of pushing him away her hands snaked up behind his back and she held him tight, relishing the feel of his strong muscles rippling under her hands. The feel of his tight torso pressing up against him didn't feel half bad either.

Sadie's brain screamed at her to get away just as her body responded to Kona's touch and she moved against him. He kissed her harder in response, using his strong arms to hold her even closer. Just as she was about to start sneaking her hands up the back of his shirt he pulled away abruptly, moving his hands to either side of her face. She moaned in protest and tried pull his face down to hers so she could kiss him again, but he resisted. He stared her down, looking intently into her eyes.

"Is that what you saw earlier?"

Mutely Sadie shook her head.

"You are the only person I want to kiss today, the only person I have kissed today. And if that didn't convince you I don't know what will."

Sadie whimpered and reached for him again. Her brain had stopped its screaming and had given in entirely to her body's desires. She no longer really cared if Kona was the biggest cheat in Hawaii. She wanted his mouth on hers and his hands on her skin. She moaned and tried again to pull him close, her eyes focused on his mouth. Their kiss had turned his lips red like a handful of crushed berries, and she wanted to see if they tasted as good as they looked.

"Sadie. I'm serious."

"OK. Fine. Whatever you say. Just kiss me again," she murmured.

"No, no more kisses until you believe me."

Sadie stopped struggling to get back into his arms and took a step back out of his intoxicating pull. She looked up from his lips and searched deep in his eyes. He was right. She needed to focus. She wanted to believe him, and not just so he'd kiss her again. She wanted this to be the real thing. There was something between them, something more than the pure electricity that was filling the elevator.

She looked at him, hunted for any trace of deviousness, of manipulation. She searched for anything that seemed off. Of course, these things were easy for the truly duplicitous men to hide, but over the years she'd learned to recognize a common thread in all the men she'd dated who turned out to be liars, cheats, or worse. If she gazed deeply enough into their eyes they all had a part in there that was hidden, a piece of their soul that they kept from everyone else. They were never all there with her.

Kona's eyes were deep, clear, and 100% focused on her. In fact, the sheer intensity of his gaze was terrifying. There was nowhere to go. It wasn't impossible that she'd always taken some comfort in the fact that her particular brand of two timing, manipulative men wouldn't care if she didn't give herself wholly to them. She could always hold back a piece of herself too, a piece they couldn't get to, couldn't sully, couldn't destroy. It was how she had managed to survive heartbreak after heartbreak.

If she gave herself over to Kona, it would have to

be all or nothing. He wasn't holding back, and neither could she. She didn't know if she had the strength to give herself over to someone like that, didn't know if she would survive the fall.

Kona's gaze softened and his thumbs caressed her cheeks. "So?" He almost whispered.

Sadie looked even deeper into the clear lakes that were his eyes and leaned forward. She answered him with her lips, placing them at first gently on his mouth and then harder as she let herself dive in completely.

"You never did explain who that girl was or why you were kissing her," Sadie said as nonchalantly as possible as she and Kona walked towards her room. She had briefly explained the issue with Jo and her urgent need to find her friend.

"I was not kissing her," Kona corrected. "I was hugging her. She'd just gotten yelled at and she was upset."

"Oh... OH!"

"Yes, oh."

"You mean she was the one getting yelled at, not you?" Sadie had already committed herself, but she still felt her shoulders unclench as relief flooded her body. Of course, it had been someone else who was getting yelled at. How could she never have considered that option?

"Yes. Anthony, the manager, he might love pretending to be my boss, but there's an invisible line that he knows not to cross. One day I'll be his boss and he doesn't forget it. He might yell at me like that, if he really thought I needed it, but he'd never do it somewhere where others might overhear. No, he was yelling at Kelli. About Jo's wedding."

"Why? What happened? What's going on with the wedding? Is that why Jordan was leaving?"

Kona filled Sadie in on everything he knew. Her heart sank as she thought of Jo. Without realizing it, Sadie started walking faster and Kona placed a restraining hand on her arm.

"It's okay. We'll get there soon enough. Let me fill you in on the rest."

"You mean there's more? A shark, a wedding planner who quits on the job, and a groom who's doing a runner? What else can go wrong?"

"No, I mean I want to discuss with you how we're going to make it better for Jo. I do have some power here; we can turn this around for her. I just need your input."

54. Jo

The girls meandered their way to the pool and instantly spotted Andy, Jordan, and the children sitting at a bar table. Jo stopped in her tracks.

"Oh, babe. I'm sorry. Let's go somewhere else." Roxie glanced at Jo with a worried frown. The men hadn't seen them yet and they ducked behind a shelf of pool towels so they could decide what to do. Even as Roxie offered to leave the area Jo saw the longing in her eyes. She wanted to be with Andy, that much was clear.

Jo looked at her husband sitting with her ex. They seemed to be in the middle of an animated conversation that involved a lot of arm waving and head nodding. She couldn't for the life of her imagine what the two of them could possibly be discussing that would have them both so excited. She was itching to go over there and perch herself on Jordan's lap so she could join in the chatter while letting him hug her and kiss her. Any other day he would have pulled her to him and held her there for hours. Today though she knew her welcome wouldn't be as warm and fuzzy as she was hoping. She couldn't face being rejected. Frankly she wasn't quite ready to face Jordan. What if her turned those cold eyes on her again?

"You go," she said to Roxie. "I think I need a moment to myself."

"You sure?" Roxie asked, but she was already inching away even as she threw Jo a sad, guilty smile. Jo nodded as she waved her friend away. As miserable as she felt, she couldn't keep herself from smiling at the skip in Roxie's bouncing step and Andy's gleeful welcome.

Jo stayed behind her rack of towels and watched the small group for a moment before moving to a spot at the bar that wasn't easily visible from their table. She wanted to earn the right to be back in Jordan's arms and before she could do that she felt like she had to do something about taking control of her life again. Most urgent issue? The wedding. If she was going to go beg Jordan to marry her she wanted to feel like she had a handle on the actual event before she approached him. While she was at it, she might as well figure out what it was she actually wanted.

She ordered a soda and asked the bartender if he had a pad of paper and a pen. Making lists had always made her feel in control. When was the last time she'd made one? Could it be possible it hadn't been since she'd lost the baby? After that, nothing had felt important enough to write down and she'd gotten out of the habit of making a daily to-do list. It just seemed easier to just go from one thing to the next and not think too hard about what was going to happen next. Then, overseas, there was no need for a list, or even time to make one. There was always something that needed to be done and it was all equally urgent while being comfortingly predictable.

Jo looked down at the blank page in front of her.

The possibilities were endless. What did she want for herself? She looked out at the vast ocean spread out behind the bar and realized for the first time that she really could be in charge. The rest of her life was a blank slate with no responsibilities or requirements. Technically there was nothing holding her back. Jordan was ready to walk away. She'd have to fight to keep him, but what if instead she were the one to walk away? She could go anywhere. Be anyone. The thought was intoxicating.

So where would she go if she could go anywhere? The unbidden image of Jordan meeting her tiny plane came to mind. She hadn't cared about the destination back then. She'd just wanted to leave, so when she saw a TV special about the Mothers Without Borders organization it had seemed like the ideal opportunity for her. She was a mother without a baby, she had lots of love to give and no one to give it to, and even more importantly it was far, far away. She had signed up for their two week tourist special, the program designed to make wealthy women feel like they were giving back. She wasn't particularly wealthy, but not going out or living for over six months had left her enough cash to make the trip. She hadn't expected to fall in love, with the place, the kids, or with Jordan.

Would she go somewhere less... muggy? Hot? She tried to picture herself somewhere other than her hometown, but the only place that came to mind was Zambia. She had known nothing whatsoever about the place before she'd packed up and left. She'd done a cursory Google search, but she barely knew more than its vague location within Africa and its relative safety. She hadn't cared. But, once there, the beauty of the place and the people had blown her away and now, if she was honest, she really missed it.

When her two weeks had been up she had been so desperate to stay, or rather so reluctant to go home, that she had begged the camp organizers to let her become a full time employee. With Jordan's backing they'd offered her a position and she'd stayed on as Volunteer Coordinator. She had loved the challenge of helping new volunteers settle in every two weeks, making their transition as smooth as possible, and appeasing the ones who had trouble adjusting to the hardships of life in a rustic, muggy country where communication with the outside world was spotty at best and nonexistent for the most part.

She had fought her attraction to Jordan as long as she could by throwing herself into her work and into caring for the kids. There was always something to be done, someone to be cuddled or cared for. It had been easy to stay away from him, but she'd unconsciously always known where he was. He had also always been hyper aware of her presence and the more they danced around each other's periphery the more the rest of the staff had worked to throw them together.

Jo hadn't known what had brought Jordan to the camp, but she'd recognized the wary looks that he gave her. He had the same haunted eyes that she hid behind thick sunglasses and wide brim hats. Later, long after they'd finally given up and stopped fighting the mutual attraction, he had confided in her that he had also landed there in a desperate attempt to escape a destructive relationship. In his case he was running from his mother, a vicious, destructive, conniving woman who was determined to make his life as miserable as hers had always been. His mother had alienated every person he had ever loved and when she had physically attacked the woman he had hoped to marry he had cut all ties with her and run for Africa.

They had been careful around each other for a long, long time, ignoring their growing attraction and acting out the roles of good friends to perfection, until one day Jo had slipped up and had told Jordan that she loved him. Not only hadn't he answered, but he hadn't talked to her for days, throwing her back into the deep depression that had sent her running in the first place. She had started to make plans to go home, realizing that her relationship with Jordan was the main reason she had stayed in Zambia. It was what made putting up with all the hardships bearable.

On a nasty rainy day not long after, during an errand trip to a nearby town, her jeep had hit a hole in the road and she'd burst a tire, stranding her miles from anywhere. She'd had to attempt fixing the thing herself. She had been covered in mud from head to toe, desperate for a hot shower and an even hotter cup of tea, cursing at the rain, the jeep, and the blasted pothole that had put her there in the first place when Jordan had miraculously passed that way on his way back to camp from an extended trip away. He'd pulled up next to her and had wordlessly gotten out to help. Sheer relief at the help and at seeing him again had made her cry, but when he'd resolutely refused to speak to her, her silent tears had turned to stifled sobs.

He had turned around after putting the spare tire on the car and had seen her standing in the rain, tears streaming down her face, and finally the stiff, frozen look on his face had melted. He had taken two purposeful steps in her direction, had pulled her tight to him, and had kissed her harder and more passionately than she'd ever been kissed before. It was their first kiss, and she could still feel her entire body tingle at the memory. He had pulled back and in one breath had told her that he loved her and had asked her to marry him. And right there, covered in mud, drenched in rainwater, she had sobbed out a yes and they had kissed again.

Everyone at the camp had cheered and hooted. No one had been surprised. They had arranged a low key, wonderfully warm wedding that had been in every way perfect, from the home grown food to the hand sewn gown. One of the village elders had performed the ceremony and everyone had brought their instrument and their joy to the celebration. The lot of them had danced around a bonfire until dawn. It had been clichéd and utterly perfect. Except for the part where it apparently had been neither real nor valid.

Jo sighed. Maybe that's what was wrong here. This wedding was the antithesis of their original event. Everything that had felt simple and true was getting lost in the details of this fancy materialistic event.

Then again maybe it wasn't just the wedding. Nothing had felt exactly right between her and Jordan since they had left Zambia and come back to the States. He was more guarded and stressed here and she, well, she was a bit the same. They had come home because it felt wise to be in America to have a baby. After all, they knew firsthand about the risks of childbirth in a third world country. But once home they'd been confronted with all the materialism and judgmental mindset that America has to offer. Their relationship clearly had suffered. Add to that the fact that she had been completely incapable of getting pregnant despite all the doctor's assurances that absolutely nothing was wrong, and it was really no surprise that they had grown so far apart.

Jo sighed again. She didn't just miss Zambia, she missed who she and Jordan had been back there. She looked down at her paper and frowned when she saw what she had doodled. "I want to go home" was written over and over again. The whole page was covered in the words.

They had come home and that was the problem. She closed her eyes and thought of home, but instead of the square brick house that she'd grown up in, the image that came to mind was the makeshift hut that had been their first home. It had been rustic to say the least and the roof leaked so badly in the rainy season that they'd lovingly referred to it as the shower. More often than not they had to make do without electricity or running water, but neither of them had ever been as happy as they had been when they'd spent long evenings huddled under a thick blanket weaving elaborate fairy tales for each other.

They hadn't told each other a single story since they'd gotten back. Jordan had gone to work at the Mothers Without Borders headquarters, hoping that he'd still be able to make a difference, even from far away. Jo had taken the doctor's orders to heart and had started a strict regime of lying around resting. He had been stressed by the work and the painful bureaucracy; she had gotten frantic with boredom and loneliness, which meant that he came home spent and desperate for peace and quiet just when she was most in need of someone to talk to.

Jo shook her head and sighed again. They had no business getting married, had no business having kids. This wedding was a farce. She drained her soda and stood up, bringing the small lunch party into view again. Jordan's familiar head was leaned towards little Emily, listening intently to her speak. Jo's heart lurched and her stomach twisted. She loved him so much it hurt. She yearned to see him lean his head like that towards their child. She knew every inch of his body and she couldn't imagine never again resting her hand on the back of his neck and hearing his warm voice say her name.

She could go anywhere in the world, be anyone she wanted to be, but she really only wanted to be by his side.

Jordan turned slowly towards her and looked straight at her. Her heart jumped again at the sight of his warm gaze filled with love, then crashed as confusion crossed his face and his eyes settled into the tight angry look that he'd turned on her earlier today. She felt her own eyes fill with tears and she turned and ran from the bar. She didn't want to see that look, didn't want to see Jordan looking at her without love in his eyes. She'd rather never see him again than see that.

55. Andy

The sun played with Roxie's hair, turning it into fine strands of gold. Andy couldn't take his eyes off her. Her skin glowed and her smile made him want to burst into song. He knew he was making a fool of himself, but he really couldn't look away. Each one of her movements caught his eye, making it impossible to focus on anything else. It had been so long since he'd been really attracted to someone he hardly knew how to act.

A splash of freezing liquid hitting his lap finally snapped him back. He jumped and looked down then at the table where Emily's glass lay on its side, the contents slowly dripping onto the growing stain on his shorts. His daughter's stricken face stopped the angry tirade from bursting out of him. Instead, he made soothing noises as he grabbed a stack of napkins from the table.

"It's okay honey. It's okay. It was an accident. Accidents happen." Far from being comforted, Emily's eyes filled with tears and her lower lip started to quiver. "No! No crying! It's fine. Really. We'll get you more water. Maybe this time with a lid. Huh? What do you say?" Emily nodded slightly but the quiver didn't stop.

There was no salvaging his shorts, they were

soaked through and through, the wet material clinging uncomfortably to his thighs, looking for all the world like he's peed his pants. Any other time he might have run back to their room to change, but the food was about to arrive, and the kids were finally settled. He glanced at the hot sun and reasoned that he'd be dry soon enough.

He made a face at Roxie who just smiled back, looking for all the world like she was trying to swallow her laughter. "Andy? Want me to stay with the kids while you go change? That has to be uncomfortable." Roxie flashed him a mischievous smile and he melted all over again as he looked deeper in her eyes and saw only empathy tinged with amusement. "Unless you want me to come help you?"

"Daddy? Why would you need help changing your pants?" Hunter asked with all the innocence of a five-year-old. "Aren't you big enough to do it yourself?"

Andy blushed and mumbled a hasty answer to his son before distracting him with the crayons that were scattered all over the table.

"Roxie! Can you draw a plane?" Hunter turned his attention to the new guest and beamed in delight when she grabbed the crayon and attempted a crude aircraft on the place mat.

"So? What do you think?" Roxie glanced up at Andy and gestured to where Jordan had just run off to catch Jo. "Think they'll work it out?"

"I hope so. I'd hate to think I might have…" Andy looked away, embarrassed. He wasn't thrilled that Jordan had caught them kissing, but he doubted that their one, rather innocent, kiss had been the entire reason behind the guy's attempted escape. The catalyst maybe, the excuse possibly, but it couldn't be the reason.

"I don't think so," Roxie answered. "If an innocent kiss caused him to run, there had to have been something else lurking below."

Andy did a double take and stared at Roxie. "Wait, you mean you know?"

"Of course. No secrets between girlfriends. Jo told me while we were walking down here. It didn't mean anything to you either, right?"

Andy shook his head. "We needed to get closure I think." He looked towards the beach. "Just closure." He flashed a bright smile at Roxie. "I hope they can work it out. I like thinking of her as being happy. He's a nice guy and he really seemed to love her. Sucks that things got all muddled up."

The food arrived and Andy busied himself with getting the kids set up with just the right amount of ketchup, salt, napkins, and waters that they needed so they could nibble and then reject their chicken nuggets and fries. It never failed. They were only ever starving until the food actually arrived. Once their plates were in front of them they were instantly too full to eat. At times he was tempted to tell them to suck it up and stop acting like babies, but with Roxie's quick smile and even faster distractions, the meal passed without any raised voices. He even managed to tuck into his own burger before it congealed. A definite first in the presence of his kids.

"You're a natural at this, you know." Andy watched Roxie help Emily deal with her food. She blushed pale pink and looked down at the girl's plate. "No, seriously. You have a natural way around kids. I would have never guessed."

"Thank you. I have to admit I'm surprised myself." They smiled at each other and Andy's stomach flipped over as he felt Roxie's foot pressing gently against his ankle. He looked at her sharply and tilted his head slightly. She blushed hard and rubbed her foot against his ankle again in response.

"Daddy! Daddy!" Andy forced himself to look away from Roxie who was now doing something magical to his ankle with her toes and turned his attention on Emily who was clamoring for more water.

Despite his best intentions to stay focused, Roxie's inquisitive foot kept Andy from noticing that Emily was trying to grab a very full glass of water perched at the edge of the table. The second cascade of cold water sluicing onto his lap caught his attention and made him gasp. Roxie jumped up and squealed just as Andy jumped up and groaned. The kids were laughing so hard they were almost falling out of their chairs.

Somehow the water had splashed all over him and all over Roxie who was trying to dab the water off her dress with a tiny cocktail napkin. All the larger napkins were already soaked from their first spill. She was having no effect on the spreading stain and, even as he hurried to grab some bigger napkins from a nearby table, his eyes appreciatively took in the way the wet material clung to her curves. The sight of her tiny waist and rounded ass brought back to life what the second glass of water had squelched, and he shifted uncomfortably in his own wet shorts. It was very much time for this lunch to be over.

Instead of handing her the napkins, Andy helped Roxie dab at the stain on her dress. Her body was as tight as he had imagined and he smiled when he realized that instead of pushing his hand away she was pressing her hand against his, holding his palm against her flat belly.

He couldn't remember the last time a woman hadn't just welcomed his advances but had actively encouraged them. He looked into her eyes and saw his own passion and desire reflected in the deep blue. She winked suggestively and poked her tongue out between her lips. Andy grinned back.

"Okay, kids! Everyone done with their lunch? I think it's time for Hunter to get back to Kid Club and for Emily to take a nap!" He winked back at Roxie. "Rox? Can Emily and I walk you back to your room so you can change?"

"Oh, no, that's okay!" She said. "How about instead I walk you guys back to your room and help tuck in Emily?"

Emily's squeals of delight answered that rhetorical question and Andy squeezed Roxie's hand appreciatively. She left her hand in his as they walked back towards the hotel. Her hand felt so fragile and so strong at the same time, delicate, but tough. Andy loved the feel of her palm against his. He sneaked a glance at her face and blushed when he saw her looking back. He played it off by pulling her closer and sliding his arm around her waist. It wasn't until he felt the weight of her head come to rest against his shoulder that he realized how long he'd been craving this kind of closeness with someone.

He let go of Roxie reluctantly as they neared the day camp so he could sign Hunter in for the afternoon. The path back to the hotel was too narrow for all three of them to walk side by side, so he wasn't able to pull her back into his arms until Emily was safely tucked into her bed. He and Roxie backed their way out of the kids' room and pulled the door shut. Before the latch had clicked Roxie's arms had made their way around his neck and he leaned down to place the softest, most tender kiss he could muster onto her warm waiting lips. Her lips felt as much like home as her hand had felt and he felt an answering smile form on her mouth. She parted her lips slightly and their tongues met as their kiss deepened. He led Roxie to his waiting bed and quietly prayed that Emily would sleep a good long while.

Roxie lay back on the bed, looking up at him with unmasked desire. He held himself back, willing himself to take it all in, just in case it turned out to be some phenomenal dream. It almost had to be a dream. Stuff like this didn't happen to Andy Sullivan. He just didn't have that kind of luck. Then Roxie pulled him down to her and he stopped thinking about anything at all.

56. Jo

Jo just ran. Anything to get away from that stony face. Without consciously deciding it she found herself headed straight for the beach. The "Beach Closed" sign loomed in front of her, slowing her pace to a more sedate jog. The thing was huge, so big it really was surprising that she'd missed it earlier that morning. She considered the implication for a second but ran on. She wasn't going near the water. She wasn't putting herself in danger. She just needed to feel warm sand between her toes. It was hard to feel threatened by the shark when all she could think about was the sand.

Now that she had slowed her crazy pace and could finally hear beyond the blood pounding in her ears, she realized that her footsteps weren't the only ones echoing on the path. Her heart sank. She hadn't even had a chance to pull off her shoes and dig her feet into the sand. She prepared a silly excuse for ignoring the sign and plastered her most winning smile on her face. Maybe the hotel employee would be swayed and let her sit on the sand for a minute.

"Jo?" Jordan's soft voice made her heart leap into her throat and wiped the fake smile off her face. She whirled to face him and stood there, frozen. She didn't know what to do. Jump in his arms? Run away again? Should she be ready to fight? To defend herself? Or was he here to make peace? Her chest clenched at the thought. She had been so convinced that he would never want to speak to her again. She couldn't believe that he was standing there in front of her. Couldn't let herself hope that it was for more than to say a more final goodbye.

He wasn't smiling. In fact, he was frowning, and Jo was glad she'd tramped down the flicker of hope that had flared in her heart. He was clearly not here to make up. Her heart dropped out of her throat only to be replaced by a huge lump she couldn't dislodge. She looked down at her toes and tried hard to swallow. Her nail polish was still chipped beyond repair, but it didn't matter. There would be no wedding. No cute peep toe sandals. No need for a pedicure.

"Jo? Look up. Please."

Jo couldn't bring herself to do what he asked. She didn't want to see his eyes if no love was going to be reflected there. His face had always been a source of comfort for her. She hated seeing it void of emotion.

The feel of his hand on her chin made her heart flutter and her stomach jump. His fingers were as soft as a calloused hand could be. Jordan had never been one to slack when work had to be done. He was a trained doctor, but back in Zambia he was just as likely to be working in the clinic as digging a trench in a local field. Jo wanted to lift her hand to his so she could feel more than the one finger touching her jaw.

Jordan increased the pressure on her chin and she finally stopped resisting. Maybe one last look at his face would be a good thing. She could memorize that, too. To her surprise she didn't see any of the coldness that had been in his eyes before. Instead, Jordan's face was contorted in confusion and sadness, so much so that she wanted to hug him tight to her and comfort him.

He had always been the strong one. Seeing him this tortured was agonizing.

"Can we sit?" He motioned to a weather-beaten log at the edge of the beach.

Jo just nodded and didn't fight him when he, as if out of habit, took her hand tenderly in his as he passed her. They sat down, side by side, knees touching, without a word. Jordan didn't let her hand go, but he stared straight ahead at the ocean. Jo didn't speak either. She didn't know what he wanted to hear. She didn't know what she wanted to say.

"Jordan," Jo stopped and took a deep breath. "I'm going home. You don't owe me anything, and frankly I'll understand if you say no, but I hope you'll choose to come with me." She stared at the sand at her feet, refusing to look at his face. The silence stretched between them and Jo held her breath until she heard Jordan open his mouth. She closed her eyes.

"Jo." Her heart lifted a hair at the sound of her name. The warmth she'd come to expect from him was once again present in his voice. "I love you. I love you like I've never let myself love anyone before." Jo's heart lifted further. He wasn't using the past tense. "But..."

"Yes?"

"When I got to Zambia, I wasn't the man you met when you arrived. I was the shell of that guy. I was terrified to let anyone get close, terrified to let myself get close to anyone." Jo turned and opened her mouth. Jordan lifted a hand. "I know you know all this, but, please, hear me out. When you arrived, I'd already come a long way. I had made friends. Friends! It was the first time I'd had real friends who cared about me. Then you got there, and I got scared again. I saw instantly that I could lose myself to you and that there would be no coming back from that."

Jo nodded. He was right, she knew all this. Had known it right away. She opened her mouth to speak again, but Jordan squeezed her hand and she stopped.

"I tried to fight it. I even tried to leave. But I couldn't stay away from you. That day? In the rain? I didn't find you by accident. I was looking for you. I wanted to tell you that I was leaving forever, but when I saw you drenched and trying your damnedest to fix that tire I realized that I couldn't leave. Life without you wouldn't have been worth living."

This Jo hadn't known. She had truly thought that he had come upon her by complete accident. She squeezed his hand back. She knew how he had felt. She had felt the same way.

"Jo. I still feel that way. Life without you isn't worth living. But what we've been doing? It's not living, and it's not working. I know that it wasn't all your doing. I'm sorry I accused you of that earlier. I thought coming back was a good idea. I was wrong."

Jo nodded silently. He was right, things hadn't gone quite the way they'd hoped.

"So, what does 'go home' mean?" Jordan looked down at her. "Which home do you want to go to? Because I don't think I can come if you mean in the US."

He finally stopped, but now that she was free to talk she found that the words couldn't come out. She looked out at the quiet ocean that hid untold nightmares and miracles.

"Zambia. With you. If you'll come." The words hung in the air. "There's nowhere else I want to be, no one else I want to be with. Can we please go back to our home, to the place where we're happy?"

Jordan's deep sigh startled her, and she turned her head to see his face. Pure relief was spread all over his face and his eyes shone with unshed tears. He had been holding his breath, waiting for her to speak.

"Really? Are you sure?" He asked, hesitantly, squeezing her hand hard as if he didn't believe she was really there with him.

"Yes. I'm really sure. We came here to start a family, instead we lost each other."

"So? We go back? We give up on a baby?" Jordan released her hands and pulled away. The wall between them that was starting to crumble threatened to come back up and Jo rushed to push it back down.

"No! No! We don't give up. We just don't do it here."

Jordan's shoulders relaxed and he picked up her hand again.

Jo felt a laugh building in her. After all this, after all the uncertainty, after all the stress, this was what he was worried about? She smiled and nodded.

"I want a baby. With you. A little Zambian baby. A baby who won't know what a mega mall looks like and won't ever even so much as taste a Happy Meal."

Jordan leapt from the log and landed in front of Jo. Keeping a tight grip on her hand he lowered one knee to the ground and looked at her intently. Jo's stomach flip-flopped and she started to protest, but stopped when Jordan opened his mouth.

"Jo? My love? Will you do me the honor of marrying me? For real this time?" Jo let her laugh escape. Jordan's solemnity barely cracked, just a hint of a smile appeared at the corners of his mouth. "And then, will you do me the honor of sharing a life of poverty, excitement, adventure, and love in Zambia with me?" By the time he was done asking she had slipped off the log and had come to rest on her knees in front of him. Through her laughter and the relieved tears that had broken free she choked out an answer.

"Yes Jordan, I will marry you and I will come back to Zambia with you, to whatever life awaits us there." Then she threw her arms around his neck and placed her mouth on his. She smiled as he kissed her back. This was the kiss she had been craving all day. This was the kiss that felt more right than anything she could possibly imagine. She let herself sink into the home that was his embrace.

57. Jo

They walked down the beach slowly, taking turns talking and listening. Catching up. It felt like they hadn't talked in months instead of just the few days since they had last seen each other. But Jo realized, as she heard Jordan explain what made him so sad and angry — the way America had become insanely materialistic and self-absorbed, how he felt cut off from the help he was delivering through work, and the disconnect between the two worlds he straddled every day — that they hadn't really talked since they had left Africa. She had no idea that Jordan had been so painfully unhappy since their move. He had clearly worked hard to keep it all from her, probably out of conviction that she was happier where they were. Jo's heart swelled and tears choked her. She couldn't believe he'd make such a sacrifice for her.

"Jordan?" She asked, interrupting a rant about malls and teenagers who already had more than they could possibly know what to do with and yet were never happy.

"Yes, babe?" He answered without skipping a beat.

"Promise me we'll never stop talking again. OK?"

Jordan stopped walking and looked down at her. He placed his hands on either side of her face and kissed her. "I promise."

Jo kissed him back and for a moment she didn't even care that their wedding plans had all gone up in smoke. She had her Jordan back and that was all that mattered. She'd be happy just walking up and down this beach for the next week, ignoring the entire world, just enjoying feeling close to Jordan again.

A loud whine caught her attention and she looked up as a plane started taxiing towards the island.

Guests.

She'd be happy to wander around the island like a lovesick teenager for the rest of the week, but she probably had guests on that plane. Wedding guests, who probably wouldn't mind not having a party to go to, but who might be perplexed if they landed and heard that the whole thing had been canceled.

She groaned as she tried to think of all the things that had to get done if they were going to get married in two days.

At Jordan's gentle prodding Jo explained. Amazingly enough, he hadn't heard about any of the wedding drama, but he listened patiently as she rattled off everything that had gone wrong even before it had gone really wrong.

Suddenly he stopped and looked down at her.

"Jo? Does any of it really matter?"

Jo shrugged. It certainly didn't matter to her.

"Why can't we have a simple ceremony like we did the first time?"

"I wish! But my mother would have a snit. This is her big event." Jo's heart sank as she remembered their earlier fight. "Though maybe now she won't care either."

Jordan just laughed and hugged Jo. She buried her face in his chest and inhaled deeply. Now that she was thinking about the actual wedding she realized that after nearly losing him she didn't care how it happened, she just wanted to be really, honestly, truly, and most importantly forever married to Jordan.

"I know! Let's just call the whole thing off. Let's elope!" She said with more than just a hint of hopefulness in her voice.

"Yeah! Let's run away to Hawaii and get married!" Jordan said. He leaned down and kissed her, gently at first, then increasingly hard. The urgency of his embrace pushed all thoughts of petit fours and appetizers right out of her mind. Her hands reached up and pulled his face closer to hers and he responded by holding her tighter.

Their bodies knew each other so well they instinctively came together until Jo couldn't tell where her skin left off and Jordan's started, but today things felt different, more urgent, like they needed to drive out the very memory of having almost been separated forever. Jordan's hands moved over her back and sides like he was making sure he recognized every inch of her body. Jo herself focused on Jordan's face and the sweet smell of his skin. His taste and his smell mingled together and finished bringing her back to herself. This was what mattered. This and only this. She didn't need a wedding. Didn't need a fancy party. She needed her other half, by her side, preferably touching her this closely all the time.

Her body rubbed against his and she felt rather

than heard, the low growl that her movements elicited. She growled right back. She wanted him, right there and then. She didn't want to wait. She needed to feel connected to him in a way that she would never be connected to anyone else ever again. She smiled at the thought and Jordan pulled back to see why. He didn't ask, just looked down at her, arousal written all over his face, head cocked to the side, waiting to see if she would share her thought or if he could continue to lavish attention on her body.

"It's nothing..." She smiled again, and he cocked his head a little further to the side. "It's just that I'm never going to kiss another person again." Jordan's face fell and she laughed. "No! That's a good thing. I never want to kiss another person. Ever! And I never want to do this to anyone else," she said, squeezing his butt.

Instead of answering, Jordan pulled her close and showed her that she wasn't giving up anything by vowing to only ever kiss him and no one else. And when he moved on to show her what else she was agreeing to Jo would have gladly dropped to the ground right there to show him that she was completely on board. A very familiar voice, just on the other side of the bushes, froze them both in place.

Her skin felt naked without the feel of his warm hand pressed up against it, but even Jo was willing to admit that it might not be ideal to be caught half naked by her mother. She reached up to kiss Jordan and then pushed him away.

"Your room or mine?" He murmured with a half-smile.

"Yours definitely. Last thing I want is to be interrupted again. I have lots of things to show you. All the things you're never going to get to do with anyone else ever again."

"Oh? Really?" He asked, both eyebrows raised. "Care to tell, or are you just willing to show?"

She stretched to the tips of her toes and whispered a few key hints into his ear. It was in this rather uncompromising position, but with very dirty thoughts and bright red faces that Jo's mother found them when she finally came out from behind the bushes. She was disheveled and flushed herself and she blushed further to a furious crimson when she realized who she had disturbed.

The thoughts of what she wanted to do to Jordan right then and there mingled with the thoughts of guilt and sadness over the fight she'd had with her mom caused Jo to completely lose the ability to speak for a moment. She painfully chased all thoughts of sex out of her head and tried to focus on her mother's face. It was surprisingly unlike her to be unkempt and Jo couldn't remember a single time she'd ever seen her mother blush. The sight was so mesmerizing that it took a small noise, immediately to her mother's right for Jo to notice that she hadn't emerged from the bushes alone.

Jo gaped as she took in the tall older man standing next to her mother. He had one hand protectively resting on her waist and he smiled nonchalantly through his trim beard. His broad shoulders and kind face made her skin crawl. The way his fingers hugged her mother's waist made Jo want to throw up.

"Babe, close your mouth, you're going to swallow a fly," Jordan whispered, his own arm wrapped tightly around her waist. He reached past her and held out his hand to the stranger.

"Hi, Jordan Fleming, the, ah, son-in-law." He said, nodding to Maryanne who stood with her mouth open in the perfect image of her daughter. "And this speechless beauty here is my wife, Jo. Jo, say hello to your mother's friend." Jordan pushed her forward.

Jo stammered a hello and stared wide eyed at her mother. She had never, ever seen her mother with a man other than her father. She tried hard to think back, but since he'd died, to her recollection, there had never been anyone. Surely she had to be wrong. Her mother must have had needs, she was a healthy, handsome woman, but Jo couldn't picture her with any man. What else had she not known about her mother's life? Because clearly? This man was no stranger met on the beach. There was no awkwardness in the way he held her and there was an aura of familiarity between the two that Jo was sure she wasn't imagining.

Completely ignoring the two women who were staring like they'd never seen each other before, the man reached past Maryanne and shook Jordan's hand firmly.

"Hi. Richard Wallace. Nice to meet you."

The two men looked each other up and down and waited for Jo and Maryanne to stop gawking. After a few more uncomfortable moments Jordan nudged Jo gently. "Babe? If you're not going to say anything, maybe we should give Richard and your mom some... space?"

Jo wanted to speak; she had the opposite of nothing to say. A million questions were fighting their way out of her throat and getting stuck, not one finding its way out. Even if one question had triumphed over the rest, she wasn't sure she could get her mouth to work and she was pretty sure she had no idea where to start.

With an apology for the way she had acted earlier? Should she ask about Richard? Her eyes darted back and forth from her mother's frozen face to the concerned face of the stranger standing next to her.

Maryanne's face softened as she finally recovered from her own shock and registered Jo's confusion. She reached out a worn hand and rested it on Jo's forearm. Their eyes met and she added a wink to a tiny knowing smile. "We'll talk later? Okay, baby? I'm sorry for this morning."

"I'm sorry, too, mom," Jo stammered out, grabbing her mother's hand and squeezing it. There was a happiness and a glow in her mother's eyes that she'd never noticed before. If this man was causing that then he couldn't be all bad. She found that the million questions had given way to just one thought. She wished she could tell her mother that she was happy that she had someone to be with, she wanted to give them her blessing, but there was no way to get the words out and definitely no way to do so without mortifying everyone. She hoped that the quick squeeze would transmit her intentions. The gleam in her mother's eye grew and a second tiny wink indicated that she had understood.

"Lovely to meet you, Richard," Jo said with a smile to the good looking man. "I look forward to getting to know you." she couldn't help adding with a pointed look at her mother.

As they walked away a sound she had never heard before followed them.

"Jordan?"

"Yeah, babe?"

"Was my mother just giggling?"

"Yep. I think so," Jordan answered as he pulled

Jo into a run. Jo hoped that the sound of their own giggles wouldn't reach Maryanne and Richard's ears.

58. Jo

They raced to the elevator bank and this time Jordan pulled Jo in with him as soon as the doors opened. As they rose their way up to the seventh floor, he resumed exactly where they had been interrupted on the beach and Jo welcomed the feel of his hands molding onto her skin again. He toyed with the snap on her bra and she squirmed against his hand, trying to help him take it off her. She wanted nothing more than to feel her nipples rub against his broad chest. Once they were nice and hard she wanted him to first rub them gently between his fingers before taking them firmly into his mouth. She told him as much and had the extreme satisfaction of feeling him grow hard against her in response. She reached between them and grabbed him, making him groan and kiss her deeper.

"Want to know what I'm going to do to you while you take care of my nipples?" She asked in an unintentionally throaty voice.

The feel of Jordan's large hand cupping her heavy breast and his thumb teasing her right nipple to life answered that question and she happily complied. She took his earlobe into her mouth and suckled it gently. "I'm going to do a little of that," she whispered. "And a little of this," she said, rubbing his crotch. "Then we'll see where that takes us."

Jordan growled again and rubbed himself harder against her hand. Jo laughed. Then she laughed harder when the doors to the elevator opened and Jordan swung her up into his arms. He carried her to the door to his room, smiling at a passing elderly couple.

"We just got married," he explained in response to their bemused look.

"Now, now, honey, don't lie to these nice people," Jo drawled as she smiled mischievously at them. "We're not married yet!" She laughed as their bemusement turned to shock and Jordan thankfully let the door slam behind them.

He lay her gently on the bed and remained poised over her. "So, it's sin you want, is it?" He murmured. "You want to do this in sin one last time before we get married?" he smiled and grabbed her hands to pin them above her head. Jo pretended to struggle, but she gave in quickly as Jordan skipped everything she had asked for and jumped straight to the part where he took her nipples into his mouth. The fact that her shirt was still draped over her chest didn't seem to be disturbing him in the least, and it wasn't bothering her at all either.

Moans filled the small room and Jo had no idea if they were hers or his. Her thigh had found Jordan's crotch and she was intently rubbing him back to the state he had been in in the elevator. His growls of desire vibrated against her sensitive nipples and she ached to feel his lips on her skin instead of on her shirt.

"Please? Jordan? Please?" She struggled against his hands, but he held her tight. He showed some mercy though and started to unbutton her shirt, with his teeth and his tongue. Each flick of his tongue and nip of his teeth against her fiery skin caused another moan to escape. By the time he had unbuttoned her entire shirt she was frantic to feel his mouth on her. Luckily for her, the sight of her naked chest distracted Jordan and he released her hands.

He gazed down at her body, a mixture of awe and desire ravaging his face. "You are so beautiful. So sexy," he said in a hushed whisper. Jo sat up, silently thanking all the ab work she had done to prepare her body for her wedding day and reached for his shirt. In one fell swoop she had pulled it over his head and was running her own hands hungrily over his muscular chest.

"Been working out, have you?" she murmured, coming in to nuzzle at his neck.

"I could say the same to you," Jordan answered as he placed a longing hand on her taunt belly. She gasped and he smiled. "Now come here. I have a couple things to show you too."

Much later, Jo lay next to Jordan listening to his soft snores. For the first time since they had first started trying to have a baby she forgot to tilt her hips skyward. The small move, rumored to help the sperm reach their destination, had become routine instantly. It had been a subtle sign that they had moved from sex just for the sake of lovemaking to sex with a purpose. Eventually the gesture had become the ultimate goal of their lovemaking. She had been obsessed with the baby they were trying to create and wanted to do everything in her power to give the sperm every chance to reach that one elusive egg. She had stopped thinking of Jordan as the man who made her heart jump and had started thinking of him as the means to an end; sex with him had somehow become just a necessary pit stop on the road to motherhood rather than a testimony to their love for each other.

Today she didn't think about the pelvic tilt more than just in passing. The sex had been mind-blowing, better than ever before, and her head and heart were filled with thoughts of Jordan and herself, nothing more, nothing less. Her nose was filled with his scent and her body still tingled everywhere he had touched her. She felt like she was home again, like she was back with the Jordan she had first fallen in love with. She turned to him, tucking herself under his arm. She rested her hand on his chest, then as the proximity to his body stirred her, let her hand travel further south until his snores had once again turned to low moans.

59. Andy

Not far from his lounger, Roxie and Emily had been splashing in the water for forever now and neither girl seemed to either mind or to be getting tired of the endless games. Andy was lying on his stomach, chin resting on his hands watching Emily and Roxie, barely closing his eyes long enough to blink.

Andy wasn't sure if he was more grateful for Roxie's willingness to play with his daughter, the fact that she seemed to like kids, or the fact that she looked so damn hot sitting there in a tiny bikini. Either way he was really enjoying the view, not to mention the break from being his daughter's sole source of entertainment.

Every so often one of them would look up at him and he'd wave or blow a kiss. He had no desire to get up and go play with them. Watching them was way more entertaining. In fact, he was happy he was lying on his stomach. He could have been causing a scandal if he had been on his back.

"Boy, I'm beat!" Roxie's voice slashed through the beginning of a fantasy. She stood up and stretched and guilt flooded Andy as he felt his face flush. He sat up quickly, remembering at the last minute to pull the towel onto his lap. "Kids sure do take a lot out of you." She made a face at him.

"Oh, man! I didn't realize! I'm sorry."

"Yeah, it's been kind of a long afternoon," Roxie smiled, but it looked a bit more strained than usual. "I think I'm going to head up to my room for a bit of a lie down."

"I know! Why don't you and Emily wait here, and Hunter and I will come back for you. Then we can all have a rest together!"

Roxie didn't answer right away, she just looked at Andy. He stared back, wondering why she wasn't answering. Then he caught on.

"Oh! Right. Sorry."

She smiled again, this time with even less warmth. More guilt flooded through him and he felt himself flush hotter. He was such an ass. There he'd been enjoying himself and essentially treating her like a glorified sitter. A free one at that.

"Rox, I'm so sorry. I wasn't thinking."

"Clearly," she mumbled, but he could see that she was pleased he had figured out why she was upset.

"Let me make it up to you. Please? I'll get a hotel sitter tonight and take you out to a really nice dinner."

Roxie hesitated and Andy pleaded some more, promising lobster and local delicacies until she caved reluctantly. She gave him a quick peck on the cheek before turning away too fast for him to grab her so he could give her a more substantial kiss.

She walked away, tucking a hotel towel around her tiny waist. She stopped by the pool where Emily was still splashing and gave her a little wave before blowing her a kiss. Andy watched her go with a rock in the pit of his stomach. You don't get a million chances with women like Roxie. You get one. Maybe two if you're extremely, extremely lucky.

Her long hair swayed back and forth against her bare back in perfect time with her shapely hips. He really hoped he was lucky.

"Right kiddo, hop on out of the pool," Andy called to Emily. Before she could start whining about having to leave the water he dangled the biggest enticement he could. "Let's go get your brother! The two of you can swim some more after we collect him."

Emily scrambled out of the pool and came to be wiped dry without a fuss. She looked tired from all the time she had spent playing, but she also seemed content, something Andy could easily understand. Roxie made him relaxed and happy too.

The little flip-flops that Emily had insisted he buy at the gift store clacked against the stone walkway, making more noise than her tiny footsteps warranted. It was a good thing they were picking Hunter up early. Every other day this week they'd been on the cusp of being late.

Emily stopped and checked out every little thing along the way and, for once, Andy enjoyed taking the toddler observation route. three-year-olds noticed things he would never have taken the time to look at, colorful leaves, pretty bugs, even the occasional interesting crack in the pavement. By the time they arrived at the camp Andy was feeling very Zen and in touch with the nature around them.

He whistled a little ditty he'd heard at the bar the night before as he walked up to the camp's cheery white picket gate. As vacations went, Hawaii was a nice place to relax for a bit.

Jessica Rosenberg

The utter surprise on the counselor's face when she saw him behind the door temporarily froze the whistle on his lips. They weren't all that early, not early enough to warrant that amount of surprise.

"Hi, Mr Sullivan!" She beamed at him and he smiled back. "Are you here to get Hunter? You daddies are all the same!" Now she was downright teasing, though Andy had no idea what was so funny about a dad showing up an hour early to pick up his kid. Before he could ask she cut in. "His mommy picked him up, like, ten minutes ago."

"What? His mom? What are you talking about? His mom isn't on the island with us. Are you sure you don't mean a friend?"

Even as he spoke, he knew that didn't make sense. Roxie had been with him until a minute ago and there was no one else in the hotel who would have picked up Hunter unless he'd asked them. A bubble of panic started to form in his chest.

"No, no. Definitely his mother, or at least that's how Hunter referred to her. Called her mom and ran to her when she arrived. He was totally excited to see her. We, like, just assumed she had just arrived and hadn't had a chance to be put on the pick-up list... She was his mother... We weren't supposed to let him go with her?"

The girl prattled on, color draining from her face, as Andy just stared at her, jaw hanging open.

Tears welled in her eyes and he finally closed his mouth and patted her on the arm. He reassured her that she hadn't done anything wrong but asked her to please not let anyone else pick up Hunter in the future.

He knew she was crying as he led Emily away, but he had no time to console her. He had to find Hunter and figure out what the hell Amber was doing in Hawaii.

60. Sadie

Kelli hadn't just quit on the job leaving them high and dry with the last of the planning, the bitch had done nothing. Zip. Nada. Nothing. Sadie and Kona had gone to find the manager to see what they could do to help Jo and had discovered that exactly none of Maryanne's requests had been carried out. None. No flowers ordered, no food selected. Nothing at all. Even the order for the cake had been ignored!

Sadie groaned. After all the drama they'd just gone through, how was she supposed to tell Jo? The only thing they had was a gorgeous wedding dress.

"Babe. It's going to be okay. You'll see. We'll figure something out." Kona wrapped his arms around her and hugged her. She buried her face in his chest and moaned.

"I have to tell Maryanne. She's going to be so…" Sadie couldn't find the words to adequately explain just how irate Maryanne would be. "She doesn't like it when things don't go her way."

"Let's sit down for a minute and see what we can figure out. It's always better to show up with bad news and a plan to fix things than with just bad news." Kona took her hand and led her to a plush couch near the plant where she'd hidden just hours earlier. Sadie blushed at the thought. What an idiot she'd been.

"They can get us any number of leis that we want, but nothing else. I'm sorry." Kona snapped his phone shut and made a face.

Damn, Sadie thought with a mental stamp of her foot. Instead of elegant Calla Lilies, Maryanne would have to make do with a host of terrible inappropriate jokes about people getting laid right and left. She groaned and Kona gave her a quick hug.

In a minute she'd have to go find Jo and Maryanne and tell them the bad news. Sadie looked up at Kona and sighed. He hugged her again in response. He had really pulled every string possible, had tried to cajole the hotel restaurant into pulling a miracle out of their chefs' hats, but the kitchen staffers had said no emphatically. Short of roasting a couple whole pigs in the imu pits and building a tower of tropical fruit there was little they could do. Appetizers and fancy mainland dishes took prep, lots and lots of prep, and in 48 hours there was just no time. So, unless they were willing to turn the fancy party into a laid back luau they were out of luck.

Sadie did not relish the thought of telling Maryanne that her precious wedding could only take place if it became a traditional Hawaiian feast, fire pit and all. She had been hearing wedding plans and details for months now, years if you counted all the lamenting Maryanne had done when she'd heard that Jo gotten married in a dirt hut. Jo's mom thought that weddings should be refined events that featured tiny delicate finger foods, fine linens (that Kelli had forgotten to reserve and were now being used by a retirement party taking place on the same day), even finer dinnerware (forgotten as well, also being used by the retirement party), and of course a five piece band. And no, her ideal band didn't involve either a steel drum or a ukulele, the only two types of music that the hotel manager had been able to locate on such short notice.

Sadie was kissing Kona one last time, working up the courage to haul herself out of the couch to go find Jo and Maryanne when Andy burst into the room, Emily perched awkwardly on his hip. His face was pale, and he was sweating hard, much harder than the weather called for.

"Ma'am? Ma'am?" Andy called to the concierge who was in the middle of helping a guest.

"Just a minute sir. I'll be right with you!" The lady shot him a warm smile.

"No. Now. My son is missing. I need help now!" Andy's voice rose and sounded like it was dangerously close to cracking.

A second later Sadie and Kona were by his side.

"Andy? What's wrong? What do you mean Hunter is missing?" Emily stuck her thumb in her mouth and lowered her head to her daddy's shoulder.

"He's… gone. He wasn't at the Kid Club when we went to pick him up. They say his mom came to get him, but Amber isn't here. Well, she shouldn't be here." Andy looked confused and freaked out. Sadie reached out and placed her hand on his arm.

"Breathe. We're going to figure this out."

Kona stepped behind the desk and jiggled the computer mouse. "What's her name? Let's see if she checked in."

"Amber... uh... Amber Sullivan. We're technically still married. She still has my name."

Andy didn't take his eyes off Kona as he typed. Sadie didn't take her eyes off Andy. Emily slurped on her thumb.

"Okay. I have it. She checked in just an hour ago. Her name was still on your reservation, so she was able to check herself into your room and get a key."

"Oh? Are you looking up Mrs. Sullivan? Such a nice lady!" The concierge had just finished up with the guest and was standing behind Kona, looking over his shoulder. "She asked me about the boats down on the beach. She wanted to take her son out on the water. I told her about the shark, and how, even if they'd been available to the guests, she wouldn't have been able to go out until he left. Such a nice lady," the concierge repeated, "is she your wife?"

Andy just stared at the woman, his jaw hanging open. Sadie turned her head to look out at the sea. She took a few steps closer to the balcony railing.

"Andy... look." She pointed out to the water's edge where a woman was trying desperately to push one of the rescue Zodiac boats into the water, her red hair gleaming in the sun.

61. Andy

Andy stumbled to the railing and clutched it with his one free hand. From this vantage point the beach stretched out endlessly. A detached part of his brain wondered if this was where Jordan had stood and watched him kiss Jo. The rest of his brain tried to process what the woman was doing.

She turned to look back at the hotel and suddenly his brain started working properly again.

"Oh god. That's Amber. She has Hunter. She has Hunter and she's taking him out on the water. Why? Why would she do that?" Even as he asked, Amber shoved the boat hard and jumped in as it moved away from the shore. Andy looked down at Emily and back at the beach. He had to go rescue Hunter, but he couldn't just leave Emily.

"Go! I'll watch Emily! Go!" Sadie plucked the little girl out of his arms and shoved Andy towards the stairs. He started running before she even stopped speaking.

Andy raced down the curving staircase leaping down three stairs at a time. Now that he was away from the balcony, he could no longer see the beach, could no longer see Amber or Hunter. His imagination went into overdrive.

Please god, let me get there in time. He can't swim well in the ocean. He can barely swim in a pool. Visions of his son flailing in the water as a shark circled closer and closer made him run even faster.

Pounding feet behind him caught up and he glanced up to see Kona racing beside him.

"There's another boat. If she gets out on to the water we'll catch her."

They raced around the pool and onto the sand, but by the time they reached the edge of the water the only boat on the beach was empty. The sound of a motor reached them from the ocean.

"There!" Kona pointed to a dot not too far in the distance. "She's heading for the next island! Help me get this boat in the water!"

"Andy? Kona? What's going on?" Maryanne called from the edge of the beach.

Andy didn't even stop to wonder why she was there or to answer. He couldn't tear his eyes away from the rapidly diminishing dot in the distance. He and Kona each grabbed a side of the motorboat and heaved it into the water. As they climbed in Kona called back to Maryanne.

"Mrs. Hunter? Could you please run to the pool bar and have them call the Coast Guard? Tell them a woman on one of the hotel's rescue Zodiacs has kidnapped a child." He grabbed the engine's starter and pulled back hard. Maryanne gaped at him. "Please? Go now? It's urgent."

The engine started with a roar and the boat leapt

forward. Maryanne shook her head and ran.

62. Sadie

From their vantage point at the lobby railing Sadie and Emily watched Kona and Andy burst onto the beach and launch the boat into the water. By the time she heard the engine roar to life she could no longer see the first boat in the distance. She closed her eyes. Please get there in time. Please get there before something bad happens.

"Where daddy go?" Emily mumbled around her thumb.

"He had to go get Hunter baby. How about we go get a snack next to the pool?" Emily nodded. Sadie had spotted Maryanne talking to Kona and Andy and she wondered what they had told her.

She had only recognized Maryanne thanks to the hideous leopard print one piece suit that she had bought to embarrass the young Jo and Sadie on a long ago vacation. The girls had failed to rise to the bait, too mortified to even mention the monstrosity, and Maryanne had taken a liking to the suit and now wore it whenever she could.

"Uh, miss?" Sadie turned around and glanced at the concierge. The woman was looking her way, a concerned look on her face. "Do you think I should call the Coast Guard? Just in case?"

"Yeah, that might be a good idea."

"It'll take them a while to get here from the big island, but it can't hurt, right?"

"Right."

By the time Sadie and Emily reached the pool bar Maryanne was standing there, wringing her hands, and staring out to the sea. Her mystery friend was standing behind her, rubbing her shoulders and upper arms with broad muscular hands. Sadie cringed and felt her face grow hot. Maybe the hotel was pumping an aphrodisiac into the air instead of crazy juice. She looked away. This was her best friend's mother. Almost a second mom to her. Seeing her being pawed by a virtual stranger wasn't exactly something she wanted to witness.

She cleared her throat quietly, but neither head turned in her direction. She did it again, a bit louder.

"You're de lady with my broder's name!" Emily plopped her thumb out of her mouth and beamed at Maryanne who finally turned her head.

"Oh, baby," Maryanne gave Emily a sad smile.

"Where's my broder?" Emily asked Sadie.

The three grownups looked out at the sea where now even the second boat was shrinking to a faint dot.

"He's... uh... he's out on a boat!" Maryanne tried to make it sound like he was off having fun and only seemed to realize her mistake when Emily's face fell.

"I wanna go ona boat too!" Emily's face screwed into a tight pout and Sadie cringed.

"Hey! Fries! You want some fries?" She pointed at a plate being prepared at the bar. "Oh! And a milkshake? How about a pink one?" Emily hesitated and then nodded.

Everyone let out the breath they'd been holding, and the bartender smiled. He ushered them to a table and quickly brought a plate of fries and a strawberry milkshake topped with a cheery paper umbrella. Emily tucked into her snack and ignored the three grownups around her.

They'd positioned Emily with her back to the water so they could all see if anything happened all while shielding the little girl from any potentially traumatizing sights.

Sadie scrutinized the horizon, but she couldn't see anything other than brilliant blue water glimmering under the sun. It was such a peaceful, beautiful sight. It was hard to fathom that something terrifying and possibly devastating could be taking place just beyond what she could see.

"Ugh. This is so frustrating!" She groaned.

"Now, now, dear. We just have to be patient. I'm sure everything will be fine. He's such a sweet boy."

Maryanne's logic made zero sense and just made Sadie want to growl, but she was right, there was nothing to do but be patient. She tried to snatch a fry off of Emily's plate, but the little girl shooed her hand away.

"Fine, I'll get my own. Maryanne would you like something? How about you, uh..." Sadie looked at Maryanne's friend and faltered.

"Richard, Richard Wallace." He stood up and held out his hand. "Why don't I get us all some drinks and snacks?" He smiled.

Maryanne and Sadie eyed each other warily. Sadie wasn't sure how to navigate a conversation about her best friend's mother's lover when he was only a few feet away buying her fries. Instead of even trying she opted for the safety of small talk.

"So, how are you enjoying your time in Hawaii?"

Maryanne gave her a look and sighed. "It's a beautiful place. Things have just been more... complicated than I anticipated." She looked down at her hands, knotted together on the table.

"You mean with the wedding?" Sadie had no idea how Maryanne could possibly know about Kelli's treachery, but she was grateful she wasn't going to be the one to have to break the news to her.

Maryanne's head snapped up. "The wedding? What's wrong with the wedding? I thought I had sorted everything out with that idiot of a manager."

Damn. She's walked right into that one. "Never mind. It seems silly to be worrying about it at a time like this."

"What? Tell me. What happened?"

"Nothing. Nothing happened."

"Then what's the problem?"

"That is the problem. The wedding planner didn't do any of the things she told you she did. Nothing has been ordered. Nothing has been prepared. We can't have the wedding you planned. We don't have food, flowers, cake, or even an officiant. All we have is booze, lots and lots of booze, and one perfect wedding dress."

Sadie cringed, waiting for Maryanne's reaction. Jo's mother had poured an insane amount of energy into this event and Sadie knew how important it was to her. This was a woman who freaked out if everything wasn't picture perfect when her daughter's old college buddies came over for a post movie snack. She had been known to send people out in blizzards to get that last tiny item that would make her Christmas table centerpiece just right. She was not going to be fine with the ideal wedding being anything less than magazine photo perfect.

Maryanne's face turned beet red, her lips pursed tightly, and her shoulders rose up a mile in silent indignation.

"That fucking bastard," she hissed. "Damn hotel manager never let on that so little had been done." Sadie reeled at the language Maryanne let loose. She wasn't sure what she'd expected, but it definitely wasn't this.

Just as Maryanne was getting started on her tirade, Richard came back with a tray loaded with appetizers. He set it down on the table before slipping his arms around Maryanne's shoulders and kissing her neck gently. He whispered something too quiet for Sadie to hear into her ear and the tense shoulders unclenched slowly. Maryanne let out a deep sigh.

Sadie stopped cringing and peered at Maryanne through creased eyes. This also wasn't what she'd expected. For a second Maryanne still looked livid, and then the turmoil of emotions that had been in her face just vanished. Instead of anger and frustration, all Sadie could see was resignation. She didn't know what to make of resignation. Anger she could have possibly handled. Even maybe more swearing. This was just plain weird.

"Oh well. Whatever will be will be," Maryanne shrugged.

Sadie's eyebrows shot up in surprise. This was not the Maryanne she had always known.

"Good girl," the man crooned softly into

Maryanne's ear making her smile slightly. Sadie's eyebrows went up even higher. He slipped himself into his chair and started dispensing appetizers and drinks. Maryanne took a few sips of her soda before speaking.

"Sadie, I'm sorry. It's just that this is Jo's problem now. She made it quite clear this morning that she doesn't need or even want my meddling," Maryanne shrugged. "Frankly, she's right. This is her wedding. She should be in charge of planning it." She relaxed back against her chair with a hint of a smile.

Jo had said those exact words to her mother for years. She had pleaded, cajoled, begged her mother for more personal space, more freedom, but Maryanne had always stayed close. Jo hadn't been allowed to go away to college, and even when she had finally moved out, finding a place just two blocks away, Maryanne had called multiple times a day and stopped by for frequent visits.

When Jo had finally run away to Zambia, Maryanne had taken it upon herself to take care of the life Jo had left behind. Bills were paid like clockwork; obligations were met as though Jo had been there to care for them herself. Even the houseplants hadn't been allowed to perish.

So why on earth would Maryanne finally decide to release her hold on Jo's life just when they needed her to step in and save the day?

Maryanne smiled at Sadie, true warmth and love radiating from her eyes.

"Honey, I know this isn't what you wanted to hear. But Jo's right. I've always meddled. I've always done everything, and it hasn't done anything but bring her sorrow. So, I'm done. I'll be at the wedding, if you guys manage to pull one together. I'll even walk her down the aisle if she still wants me to, but it's her wedding and I need to let her take care of it."

"You're... you're serious," Sadie said, realization dawning.

"Of course, she's serious," Richard answered in a deeper and more confident voice than Sadie had expected. "She has spent the last 20 years doing and being everything for Jo. It's time for everyone to live their own life now. Right, babe?" His eyes blazed in fierce support and Sadie saw what she hadn't noticed before: deep, deep love. Maryanne just nodded in response.

"I love her you know. I just need to do this for me. And for her. It's time."

"Okay, but just so you understand, at this point we think the only event we might be able to pull together is a really casual luau themed event."

"That sounds lovely. I'm sure Jo will be thrilled."

63. Andy

The grey boat flew across the water bucking against the waves. There were handles on top of the inflatable tubes all around the boat and Andy held on for dear life. It wouldn't help his son any if he fell overboard. Kona sat at the back of the boat wielding the little engine, stone-faced, eyes never wavering from the dot they were pursuing.

As they gained on the first boat the dot grew slowly and gradually started to take shape.

"Do you think he's in any danger with her?" Kona asked. Andy could tell he was trying to keep his voice neutral, but there was a bit of an edge to the question.

"No... I don't think so. I mean, she's just not a violent person. I can't fathom what possessed her." Andy shrugged. "I'm a pretty reasonable guy. I just imagine what she could have been thinking. Why go to the extreme of kidnapping him? Why not try to talk to me first?"

His stomach clenched as the boat hit a wave and rocked back and forth.

"Can you go any faster?"

"I can't, I'm sorry. I'm already pushing this thing faster than it's ever been pushed before." In response to

Kona's comment, the engine coughed twice and then resumed its low roar when he hit it with the heel of his hand. "I just hope we catch them before it gives out completely."

Andy looked forward again. He could now make out the two people on the little boat ahead of them. Amber was sitting at the back manning the engine. Hunter was in the middle, moving back and forth to peer over the sides.

"Can he swim?"

"No, not really. You know, he can get himself from one side of the pool to the other, but I wouldn't exactly call it swimming and he definitely couldn't do it in the ocean." Andy looked down into the clear blue water. He couldn't see the bottom, but he could see fish swimming around. He could all too easily imagine Hunter sinking below the surface, too fast for him to be able to catch him. He shook his head and looked at the other boat again.

"Daaad! Daaaad!" Hunter was standing in the middle of the boat, waving at them, beaming with excitement. Amber glanced back at them and paled.

"Hold on buddy! We're almost there!" Andy called back. In response Amber gunned the engine and their boat jumped forward. Hunter stumbled and fell to his knees. From where he sat, Andy could see surprise and confusion cross his son's face. He turned and looked at Kona.

"I know dude, but we're already going as fast as we can. Don't worry. We'll catch them." Kona's face was grim with determination. He leaned forward as if that would help the boat go faster. Andy turned back to face Hunter.

The boy had regained his footing and was now sitting in the middle of the boat. His broad smile had been replaced with a mild look of concern and he was watching his mother warily.

Amber glanced back at them and tried to gun the boat again, but she'd maxed out her engine as well. Her hair was standing on end and she had a wild look in her eyes. Her gaze crossed Andy's and he mouthed a silent "why?" She shrugged and looked away.

They'd nearly reached her boat when it jerked again. This time Amber looked as surprised as Hunter. The two of them looked over the side and screamed.

"What? What is it?" Andy yelled.

The boat jerked again. Harder this time.

Time slipped into slow motion and Andy reached his arms forward as if it could possibly help, but he wasn't able to stop Hunter from bouncing out of the relatively safe spot in the middle of the boat.

Hunter landed on the inflated edge of the boat and hung there, clutching a handle. He locked eyes with Andy and didn't blink.

"Daaaaad! There's a shark! He keeps bumping our boat!" His voice shook.

Andy's heart stopped. After the second jerk Amber had let the engine stutter to a stop and was sitting in the boat, both hands clamped over her mouth. Her eyes were following something swimming around and around them. Now that she was no longer moving it took Andy and Kona barely any time to finally catch up. Their boat pulled up alongside just as a huge grey shadow swam under the two boats.

"Daaaad!" Hunter stood up and reached for Andy.

"NO! Stay put!" Andy yelled, but he could tell that Hunter was desperate to come to him now that he was almost within arm's reach. Andy was the safe parent, the one they went to when they were scared. They'd learned early on that Amber was next to useless in a crisis. He glanced at her and watched as her eyes widened. She was staring into the water on the other side of the boat, the side he couldn't see, but whatever she was seeing there wasn't good.

"Hunter! SIT DOWN AND HOLD ON!" Andy howled, but Hunter was too panicked to hear. When the shark bumped the boat again he had one leg over the side of the boat and was reaching for Andy and Kona's boat.

"Oh god," Andy moaned. He lunged across the boat and reached for Hunter's arm. If the boy had been wearing a jacket he would have been able to grab him, but he'd spent the afternoon at Kid Club playing in the pool. He was only wearing a bathing suit and he was coated in sunscreen. Hunter's arm slipped right from Andy's grasp and their boat swung away.

Hunter flailed for Andy, his fingers grasping in the air. Kona reached for the other boat, but they were just too far to grab it.

"It's okay! I'm going to get you. Hold on," Andy called to him.

The shark loomed, easily the size of one of the boats. It swam up a little and Andy felt its dorsal fin graze the underside of their boat as it passed under them. His stomach dropped and suddenly he was just as desperate as Hunter to have his son in his arms. Kona gestured to something at Andy's feet.

"Grab that thing! Give it to me!"

Andy looked where he was pointing. A fishing gaff was wedged under the center seat. It was perfect. They could use the hook at the end to catch the other boat and bring it closer.

"Amber! Swing the boat closer!" She looked at him, eyes glazed with fear, and shook her head. A wave did the work for her and the boat bobbed closer just as the shark vanished again with a menacing swish of his tail. Kona swung the gaff and caught one of the boat's handles. He pulled and brought the boats together.

"Okay Hunter. I've got you!" Andy wrapped his arms around Hunter and held on tight. There was no time to get him onto their Zodiac. They braced for the jolt of the shark hitting the boat again, but it never came. Instead, Amber shrieked as the shark's head came out of the water, mouth wide open, teeth gleaming. Its massive jaws closed around the boat's side and it jerked its head to the side, wrenching the boats away from each other.

One second Hunter had been safe in Andy's arms, the next he was flailing, falling over the side of the boat. Andy hit the water mere seconds after Hunter fell in. He tried not to think about the monster swimming around in the water with them. He had to find Hunter, had to catch him. He ducked under the water and saw a pale form thrashing just a foot away from him. He swam to Hunter and grabbed him. Hunter spun to face him, mouth open in a soundless scream, eyes wide in terror. Underwater there was no way to reassure him. Andy just pulled him tight and held on. He kicked towards the sun and broke water a few feet away from the boat.

Kona was frantically looking in the water for them, holding the gaff in his hand like a fishing spear.

"Hurry! Swim back!"

"Where's the shark? Do you see it?"

Amber shrieked and pointed in the water. The shark had spotted them and was losing interest in the boat now that easier prey was in sight.

The boat was only a few feet away, but in waterlogged clothes and with a terrified child pawing at him, it might as well have been miles farther. He had to try though. He couldn't just sit in the water and wait for the inevitable.

Andy shifted his hold on Hunter so that the boy was on his side and started to swim. He spotted a dark shadow to the left of the boat.

"There!" He shouted to Kona.

A flurry of activity ensued, but Andy just focused on getting to the boat. Every time he kicked, Hunter whimpered. It only made him kick harder. He glanced at Kona and saw him leaning over the side, repeatedly jabbing the gaff into the water. The shadow was staying put. The distraction was helping.

"Okay buddy, we're almost there." The boat was only a couple more kicks away. "Kona! Help me get him into the boat!"

One more kick and he was close enough for Kona to put his arm in the water to reach for Hunter. The boy whimpered and held on tight.

"You have to let go babe, you have to. We need to get out of the water, and I can't get you into the boat if you don't let go."

Reluctantly Hunter released his hold and Kona hauled him overboard.

Amber shrieked again. The shark had taken advantage of Kona's momentary distraction to make a lunge for her boat again. Kona reached back into the water and grabbed Andy's arm. With considerably more effort than it had taken to get Hunter into the boat, he hauled Andy in.

Hunter lunged at his father and wrapped his arms around his waist. Andy held him tight. He closed his eyes and let out a deep shuddering breath.

"Dude. We're not home free quite yet!" Kona said.

Andy opened his eyes. Half of Amber's boat was floating away, and the shark was nosing her feet as she clutched at the engine and screamed. Kona was leaning over the side of their boat, trying to get her to let go and grab his hand. She was having none of it.

"No! NO! It'll grab me! NO!"

Andy moved to Kona's side. "Amber, honey, listen." He didn't want to be calling her honey or anything endearing. He had half a mind to let the shark have his way with her, but the thought of Hunter witnessing his mother's death like that made his stomach roil more than the thought of having to be nice to her, so he forced himself. "Babe, you have to let go. You're starting to sink and in a second you're going to be in the water with that thing. You HAVE to take my hand."

Kona had gone back to jabbing at the shark with the gaff and with a loud snap they realized the shark had had enough. The gaff splintered in two and the shark made off with the pointy end.

"NOW Amber! NOW!"

She must have heard the terror in his voice because she closed her eyes tight and lunged towards him. Kona grabbed one arm and he grabbed the other and in one swift move they hauled her onto the boat where she collapsed in a heaving sobbing pile on the bottom.

"Go! Go! Go!" Andy shouted at Kona who was already getting the engine started. The black mass was already turning to swim towards them, moving faster by the second.

64. Andy

The engine sputtered twice and finally caught, spinning the boat in a circle before Kona steadied it and aimed for the shore. Andy clutched Hunter to him and frantically looked over the sides of the boat to see if he could spot the shark. It wouldn't take much for their boat to also be reduced to shreds.

Just as he spotted what looked like a menacing shadow heading towards them, a much louder engine roared in the distance. Kona looked around and heaved a sigh of relief.

"Thank god. It's the Coast Guard." He spun the boat around and headed in their direction. "We can reach them faster than we'll get to the shore. Plus, they have spear guns on board."

At the same time, he and Andy glanced down at what was left of their fishing gaff. If the shark decided he wasn't done with them yet there was no way they'd be able to fight him off again.

"AHOY!" The Coast Guard ship had arrived even faster than Andy had dared hope. "Are you lot in trouble down there? We've had a report of a suspected kidnapping!"

Kona and Andy waved the rescue ship closer

until they thought they might be heard without a megaphone.

"SHARK. There's a shark. We've been attacked! HELP!"

Without wasting any more time, the coastguardsmen dropped a ladder over the side of their boat and started helping them aboard. Andy tried to get Hunter to go first, but the little boy wouldn't let go.

"Go on, take him up there. I'll stay here until someone helps her up." Kona gestured to Amber who hadn't moved from her spot at the bottom of the boat. "Hurry up though. I'd rather not wait around any longer than we need to." He glanced into the water, but the shark was nowhere to be seen.

Somehow Andy managed to clamber up the ladder without dropping Hunter. Big hands grabbed the both of them at the top and wrapped them in a blanket.

"You guys okay? Need anything?" Andy shook his head. "K, sit there. Don't move." The coastguardsman gestured to a bench at the side of the boat. Andy sank down and pulled Hunter closer. The boy buried his head in his father's shoulder and let out a huge shuddering sob. Andy felt tears pool in his own eyes. So close. He'd come so close to losing his son.

"Don't let her out of your sight," Kona warned as a coastguardsman gently helped Amber up the ladder. "She's the kidnapper you're looking for." Instantly the man's demeanor changed, and he stopped being as gentle and patient as he'd been.

"Come on lady. Let's go."

Once he had her on board, he pushed her into a sitting position on the deck near the bench where Andy and Hunter huddled. She lunged at Hunter, but the guard held her back.

Andy glared at her and turned Hunter away. Her face was twisted in agony, tears streaming from both eyes, but he felt no pity.

"No. You do not get to hug him. You do not get to come near him. We almost lost him because of you." The last words were almost lost in a sob and he turned so that he couldn't see her face. He could all too well imagine the pain she was feeling, but he couldn't bring himself to be kind.

"Is there any way we can tow the boat? We already lost one today." Kona was on board and gesturing to the Zodiac still bobbing around below.

"Yeah, I don't see why not," the coastguardsman shrugged and tied the lead to the back of their boat. "So, what happened exactly?"

65. Jo

"You know, maybe this wedding just wasn't meant to be."

Jordan didn't answer right away, but he did slowly roll towards her and cracked open a sleepy eye.

"Seriously. Could more have gone wrong with this whole plan? What were we thinking anyway? We're not fancy resort wedding people."

Jordan snorted. Jo smiled down at him. They were the antithesis of fancy resort people, something he'd been saying since the beginning. They were beer and bonfire people, not martinis-and-peep-toe-sandals-poolside people.

"I just felt guilty. But really, guilt is a terrible reason to let someone talk you into a wedding that doesn't feel right. Isn't it? I just felt so bad for running away like that and getting married without mom. Having her plan the wedding felt like giving her the best gift. Remember how her face lit up when I asked for her help?"

Instead of answering Jordan inched his way towards Jo and rested his head on her lap. They were still in bed, but she had dragged herself up so that she was leaning up against the fabric covered headboard. Jo started running her hands through Jordan's wavy hair and he closed his eyes. She smiled down at him. This was what she had been missing. This closeness with him. Without the distraction like TV, computers, phones, and everything else that just wasn't available in Zambia they had spent so much time talking and walking and dreaming together. They had been so close. Board games had been one of their favorite pastimes. It was amazing how much you could actually connect over a fast and furious game of battleship.

"Know what I miss?" Jordan mumbled without opening his eyes.

"Scrabble?"

"Yeah! How'd you know?" His eyes snapped open and he peered up at Jo suspiciously.

"Because I was just thinking the same thing. We haven't played a single game since we moved back to the states."

"We haven't taken any walks either. Or spent an evening just reading or talking."

Jo nodded. The worst of it was that neither of them had noticed. Or at least she hadn't. It had been so exciting to be home, to be able to see her friends and do all the things she used to do. Even better it had been so nice to just have modern amenities again. But all the stuff she had thought she had missed were really just that, stuff. And now that she was away from them again, even if it was just for a short time, she felt free. Relieved even.

As though he could hear her thoughts Jordan reached for her other hand and brought it to his lips for a gentle kiss.

"This is nice. This quiet. Without the distractions.

I don't just miss the Scrabble, I miss you. I miss us." He peered up at her. "Jo?"

"Yeah?"

"Are you serious? Will you really go back with me? Will you give all this up again?"

Jo didn't answer right away. She looked out of the window at the gorgeous expanse spread outside. Zambia was beautiful too and the people were amazing, but there life there hadn't been easy. It had been simple, but far from easy. It was challenging to have to learn to do without the modern amenities she had grown up taking for granted, especially since the Internet and phone were so spotty. It was brutal being so far from her mother and her friends. And yes, there was the fear of giving birth to a baby a zillion miles from the sterile hospitals she had always assumed would be available when she delivered her children.

But in the end it was the thought of that baby that pushed her to answer. Clean delivery rooms were one thing, a simple wholesome life with the man of her dreams was a whole other.

She nodded again and answered Jordan. She would go back to Zambia with him. For real this time. They would build a home and a life there. Their children wouldn't have the childhood she had, but that was fine. Even if they stayed in the States they wouldn't have her childhood. The world had changed too much for that.

Jo sat still, her fingers still entwined in Jordan's hair, searching her heart and her head for signs of unrest or anxiety, but this felt right. She wasn't running, she was choosing, and it felt right.

While she was at it, there was one last thing she needed to take control of. One last thing she had to do.

66. Sadie

"I'm calling off the wedding," Jo said, beaming at Sadie as she bounced down the stairs, just before turning as if she was going to drop that bomb and just dance away. Sadie paused, one hand on the stair railing. She was making her way up the stairs back to the lobby to see if there was any news about Hunter. She'd lost sight of the boats from the beach and she was anxious to hear what had happened. She hadn't expected to run into Jo.

"Wait. What?" Sadie said, raising her hand to stop her friend before she vanished again. She shook her head. This was all wrong. What was wrong with this island? Why did every single situation turn itself completely upside down? "What do you mean you're calling off the wedding? Are you and Jordan breaking up?"

Jo shook her head and smiled.

"No. Never. I love Jordan. I know that now. I love him with every microfiber of my body and mind. Even the parts that were scared to be in love with him before are now glowing. But this wedding?" She gestured around the hotel. "It's not us. It's mom. It's never been right for us. We all kinda knew it, right?" Sadie nodded. "Everything that has gone wrong could. I think it's a sign that this was never supposed to happen this way. Jordan and I talked. We want what we had the first time. We're going home and we're starting over again."

"But, but, what about the guests?" Sadie wailed, refusing to even consider what Jo had just said about them leaving again.

Jo just shrugged. "Whatever. They're in paradise. We gave them the perfect excuse to take a vacation. They won't care that there isn't a wedding to interrupt their fun."

Sadie let herself fall back against the stair railing and squeezed her eyes tight to keep the tears from pouring over. All that stress for nothing. She took a few deep breaths until she was relatively sure she wouldn't cry then she opened her eyes again.

"So, no wedding? For real?"

"We'll get married. Just not like this. We want something simple. Something real. Something that's all about us and not at all about the pomp and circumstance. I have to go find the manager to let him know." Jo started moving up the stairs again, but Sadie grabbed her arm.

"No need. There's no wedding to cancel. Kelli didn't do any of the stuff she was supposed to do. Nothing's been ordered, nothing's been prepped. I was on my way to tell you when..." Sadie's voice trailed away. Her brain had finally processed the words 'We're going home.' "What do you mean home?"

"Home. Zambia." She gave Sadie a sad look. "I know. It's far, but it's where we're happy. It's where everything feels right to us." Her face shone with delight as she said it and Sadie knew it was true even though her own heart was breaking at the thought.

"Really? She did nothing? What a bitch!" Jo shrugged and then laughed. Sadie watched Jo and finally had to smile too. Before long she was laughing too. This wedding had been cursed from the beginning. It felt right to be letting it go. It was just such a relief to see Jo happy, even if it meant she was losing her friend all over again.

Jo walked over, still laughing, and pulled Sadie into a hug. She hugged her hard and whispered a quiet thank you in her ear. Sadie hugged her back, but this time no amount of swallowing or blinking could stop the tears. She had finally felt like she was part of Jo's life again. Now they were going off again, leaving her behind. As happy as she was for them, it was lonely having her best friend live on the other side of the world. But there was just no way to say that. It wouldn't be fair to put that on Jo.

"I just really wanted to be your maid of honor," she almost sobbed into Jo's shoulder.

Jo patted her back.

"You'll just have to come to Zambia for the wedding. You'll love it there. I bet Kona will love it too."

It was only as she watched Jo bounce her way back up the stairs, all of her old exuberance showing again, that Sadie realized she'd never told her about Hunter. Just the thought reminded her of her original mission, and she shook all images of mud hut weddings out of her head and hurried up the stairs.

67. Jo

Her knuckles hovered over Jordan's door. For the first time since they had first kissed, Jo was struck shy by the prospect of seeing her husband. Maybe he had reconsidered. Or maybe she had imagined the whole thing and he was in there packing and getting ready to leave.

Before she had time to stop psyching herself out the door crashed open. Jordan stood there, just wearing his favorite pair of faded jeans, goofy smile on his tan face, hair still mussed from their earlier activities.

"You coming in? Or are you going to hover outside my door for another hour?" He teased as he grabbed her hand and pulled her into the room, letting the heavy door slam shut behind her. Their smiles connected and dissolved into a kiss that made Jo's toes curl up in her sandals. Her heart thudded and her stomach clenched when Jordan's hands started fumbling with the buttons on her shirt. He undid one, then the next, and she couldn't wait any longer. She needed to feel her skin against his again. Needed to be chest to chest, heart to heart with him. In one impatient gesture that made him laugh she took matters into her own hands, interrupting their kiss just long enough to pull her shirt over her head.

Before the shirt had hit the ground Jordan had swooped her into his arms. Oh, how she loved it when he showed off his brute strength like that. She wrapped her hand around his bicep marveling at how small it felt against his bulging muscle and felt the flutters in her stomach move further south. Jordan held her tighter and kissed her again before carrying her over to the bed, which still showed signs of their earlier lovemaking. She giggled, for a couple who hadn't made love in weeks, twice in one day was quite surprising. She ran her hands over his tight chest and had the immense satisfaction of feeling his whole body quiver.

He bounced her onto the crumpled sheets and threw himself onto the bed besides her. Leaning on one elbow he towered over her, making her feel both incredibly vulnerable and unbelievably turned on. She arched up towards him, inviting him to put his arm around her, but he ignored the invitation, instead tracing her body with an unbearably light touch, letting gentle kisses follow his fingertips down her torso. By the time he reached the tender spot just below her belly button but just above the edge of her shorts she was begging for him to finish undressing her.

The world slipped away until all that was left were his mouth and her body.

Jordan's finger slipped between the coarse fabric of her shorts and the sensitive skin underneath and she gasped. His moist mouth moved to that same spot and she moaned and placed her hands to the snap on the shorts. She wanted nothing more than to take them off. Well, technically that wasn't true, but what she wanted wouldn't happen until she took them off.

"Tut, tut." Jordan's teasing disapproving voice rumbled against her belly, making her moan even harder. This was torture. Pure, unadulterated torture. Didn't he understand how badly she wanted him?

Jo tried to sit up, determined to take control of the situation, but Jordan pushed her back down and pulled himself up so that they were head to head again. She fought him again, and he kissed her hard and pushed her head back onto the pillow. She tried one more time, this time changing tactics, but Jordan pulled her hand away from his belt buckle and held it gently in his.

"Relax," he murmured into her ear. "Relax and let me take care of you." He took her earlobe in his mouth and nibbled on it gently.

His hand moved back down to her snap and in one barely noticeable gesture he had unsnapped her shorts, pulled them down, and was doing something that she was more than willing to relax and enjoy.

"We can't stay in here forever, you know."

Jo couldn't see why not. With a room service menu and a working bathroom less than a foot away, she didn't see why they'd ever have to leave. They could just stay locked away in here, enjoying each other's bodies the way they had already done twice more – Twice! – since she had gotten back. She was sore in spots she didn't even know she had, but it was a great kind of sore, the kind of sore that feels, well, like you've just had mind blowing sex again and again.

"We might have to. I don't know if I can walk anymore." She lifted her head from Jordan's broad chest and smiled at him. He beamed down at her and winked.

"Too much sex?"

"Not enough sex," she replied, showing him that she was more than willing to take care of the problem if he agreed with her.

"Mercy! Mercy!" Jordan moaned, laughing. "Please! I'm not the young stud I once was!"

Jo took mercy and stopped doing what she had been doing with her hand. "Fine, you can have ten minutes to recover. I'm going to shower."

Three minutes later, in the shower, she proved to Jordan that he was still quite a stud, and again when they were back in the bedroom supposedly getting dressed. Even then her body wasn't ready to quit. She couldn't get enough of him. It felt like she was taking possession of his body again and she wouldn't feel satiated or at ease until she had tasted and touched ever tiny bit of him. She reached for him again, letting her hand trail on his chest and down the side of his body to his thigh.

"Babe?" Jordan said gently, pinning her hand to his body and entwining his fingers with hers. "I'm not going anywhere. We have the rest of our lives to do this, again, and again, and again. But it doesn't have to all be today."

She smiled up at him, feeling shy for an instant. He could always see right through to the part of her mind where she hid the truly scary stuff that she was too anxious to look at very closely. He was always right, and he had always known what to say to calm her fears.

"Promise?" she asked, voice quivering.

"Promise," he answered, lifting her hand to his mouth and sealing his promise with a gentle kiss.

"Jo?" He hadn't said anything else in the long moments that had followed, and she had wondered if he had fallen asleep. She had been too comfortable with her head resting on his chest, feeling the gentle rise and fall of his breathing, listening to the strong rhythmic beats of his heart to lift her head to check. His voice startled her. She glanced up at him, surprised to see a hint of a frown cross his face.

"What is it? What's wrong?"

"You need to go talk to your mom." He grimaced to show that he knew she wouldn't find the prospect pleasant, but she saw in his eyes that he wouldn't let her not go. She groaned and matched his frown. "I know. I know you don't want to, but you need to go talk to her, clear the air, especially if we move soon. I don't want you to regret leaving things unfinished with her."

He was right. If they left before she and her mother had talked things out it would be damn near impossible to take care of from Zambia. It was hard enough to maintain regular communication from there, patching things up would be more than just awkward. Plus, she didn't think she could leave without getting her mother's blessing. Until they settled their differences she didn't think she'd really get it.

"Does it have to be now?" she whined, suddenly exhausted. "Can't we pretend there's no one else in the world, just us for another hour or two."

"Yeah, it sorta does have to be now. She called a couple times while you were out talking to Sadie. She said she would meet you in the bar around six."

Jo glanced at the clock and jumped up. It was ten to six. She had all of five minutes to make herself somewhat presentable. She held back the flash of irritation that nipped at her.

"Maybe give me an extra 30 seconds of warning

next time? K? I'm never going to be ready in time."

Jordan reached over and rumpled her hair.

"There. Looks great. No need for a brush." He kissed her deeply. "And now your cheeks are adorably flushed, no need for any make-up." He looked at her more seriously. "I'm not kidding, you look amazing."

Jo scowled and pushed him away before scrambling off the bed. A quick glance in the bathroom mirror confirmed that Jordan was delusional from lack of something, her hair was a complete mess, and her face was blotchy, not adorable. She splashed some water onto her face and used her wet hands to pull her hair back into a sloppy ponytail. She'd just have to hope that her mom would assume she had just come from the beach or the pool.

She hurried back out of the bathroom and slipped into her crumpled clothes. Maybe her mom would even be willing to believe she'd been swimming in them, Jo thought ruefully. One hand on the door she paused to say goodbye to Jordan, but the sight of him stopped her. He truly was the best looking man she had ever known. His entire body radiated strength and self-confidence even as he lay there, vulnerable and slipping into sleep. He had had enough strength for the both of them for the last five years. Now she wanted nothing more than to match it.

She opened the door as quietly as possible and smiled. He was right, he wasn't going anywhere, she had the rest of her life to enjoy and be with him.

68. Andy

"Sir? How would you like us to proceed? Would you like to press charges?" The coast guardsman looked at Andy and waited for him to reply. "If you do, we can radio the police and have them meet us here."

The Coast Guard ship had just pulled into the dock near the hotel and Kona was taking care of getting the Zodiac unmoored. The last thing Andy wanted to do was to decide what to do about Amber. He just wanted to get Hunter on dry land and put the whole event behind him. Amber had barely moved since they'd pulled her on board. She'd just sat and stared out to sea, tears streaming down her face. While they'd been at sea Andy had focused his attention on Hunter; he couldn't bring himself to even look her way. By some miracle they were all safe and sound, not a scratch among them, but every time he thought about the danger she'd put their son in, his blood started to boil.

He wanted so badly to have her thrown in jail, wanted this to be on the record for all the lawyers to see. It would make his life easier in the end if she had an arrest record for kidnapping. It would work in his favor during the custody hearings.

"Dad?" Hunter pulled at his arm.

"Yeah, buddy?" One of the officers had found him a dry Coast Guard t-shirt to change into. It was huge on him and hung down below his knees and made him look ridiculously small and vulnerable. Andy shuddered at the thought that he had almost lost him.

"What does 'press charges' mean?" Hunter looked up at him with a little worried frown and then looked over at Amber. "Is someone going to hurt Mommy? Because she didn't mean to get us into trouble! We were just playing a trick on you. Honest!"

It took all of Andy's self-control to not tear into Amber right then and there. Tears welled in Hunters eyes and, when one overflowed, Andy forced himself to breathe deeply. He turned and glared at his soon-to-be ex-wife.

"Amber? What do you have to say for yourself? What should I do here?"

She looked up and him and started crying in earnest.

"I'm so sorry Andy. I never meant to put him in harm's way. It was so stupid. I'm sorry. I'm sorry. Don't let them take me away. I'll do anything you ask. Anything." By the time she was done speaking she was on her knees, hands clasped in front of her. She looked so pathetic it made Andy's stomach hurt.

Hunter ran to her and put his arms around her. She wrapped her arms around him, buried her face against him, and sobbed. "It's okay Mommy. It's okay. Don't cry. See? I'm fine! Daddy, tell her I'm fine!"

"Alright. Alright! Enough. Amber, get up. You're scaring Hunter." Andy walked over and tried to pull Hunter away, but the boy clutched his mother tighter. "Fine." He turned to look at the officer who was still waiting for instructions. "Officer, I don't think I'll be pressing charges. Not this time. No one was hurt. I think we all just need to put this behind us." He reached out and squeezed the man's arm. "Thank you for all you've done. Really. I don't think we would have made it if you hadn't arrived when you did."

The officer nodded and walked away.

"Amber, this isn't over, you hear me? There's a lot we have to talk about, a lot you have to answer for." She nodded without lifting her head from Hunter's chest. "But, right now, let's just go get cleaned up."

69. Jo

The bar was just as badly lit as it had been the evening before. It wasn't all that surprising, but it had been such a long day, it was jarring to realize that less than 24 hours had passed and that the world around her hadn't been affected in the least. The decorations were still just as cheesy and the music just as good, the only difference was that Kona wasn't behind the bar. She smiled at the bartender who was there in his place and asked for a Mai Tai.

"Would you mind sending my drink to that table over there?" she asked when she spotted her mom at a table in the back.

The bar was still relatively empty, and her footsteps echoed throughout the tacky room as she walked all the way to the back. Her mother never turned her head and as she got closer she realized that her shoulders were hunched in what had to be a painful shrug.

Her mother was dreading this as much as she was.

The revelation shot through Jo like a lightning bolt splitting an ancient tree, leaving her feeling vulnerable and raw. For the first time she realized how hard this had to be on her mother. All the anger that she had been nursing since the fight earlier that morning had vanished in a puff when they had met on the beach, but they still had so much that needed to be said. Before they started though, she wanted nothing more than to hug her mother and bury her face in her scratchy sweater like she had as a child whenever life became too hard or too unfair to handle.

But she wasn't that child anymore, and her mother was wearing a t-shirt, not one of the many shapeless, hand knit, sweaters that she had sported through Jo's childhood. They were meeting here as equals: two grownups who needed to figure out how to make their relationship change so it could survive.

Jo placed a gentle hand on her mother's bony shoulder and gave a small squeeze before leaning down and placing a timid kiss on the familiar cheek.

"Hey, Mom."

The two of them stared at each other warily. They had never fought like this before, not really, so this was all new territory. Jo wished she could throw herself at her mother's feet and beg for forgiveness, but there was a new proud tilt to her mother's chin that made her hold back.

Jo slid into the booth just as the waitress arrived with her drink and a few macadamia nuts for them to munch on. Both stared at the bowl for a long while, waiting for the other to start first.

Jo had grown up in the midst of her mother's constant chatter. Whenever she walked into a room her mother peppered her with questions, nonstop questions, about her day, her life, her thoughts. This complete absence of words from her mother was making her want to squirm like a little kid awaiting punishment.

She risked a glance at her mother and caught her gaze. She was surprised to see a hint of sadness in her mother's eyes. Anger yes, pride for sure, but also more sadness than she had expected to see. Jo reached out a tentative hand and covered her mother's. Both women smiled and squeezed gently at the same time.

"I'm sorry," Jo murmured.

"Me too," Her mother replied. Both of them fell silent again.

This was too hard. Jo didn't know how to handle it. Her mother had always been in control of their conversations; she had no clue how to get her to talk now that she was in charge. Maybe she'd have to turn the tables and start peppering her with questions.

"So? Richard?" She ventured. Her mother blushed a deep crimson and started to pull her hands away, but she didn't say anything. Jo watched, waiting for an answer or even a hint that she'd start talking sooner or later.

She knew her mother's face so well, had looked at it so many times before that, if she'd had an ounce of artistic talent, she could have drawn it with her eyes closed. The bright eyes and soft cheeks had always been exactly the same. The same make up, the same hair style. A comforting constant in her life. But as she studied this face that she knew so well, Jo realized that she knew virtually nothing about the woman behind it.

She felt her forehead crease in puzzlement. She had to know her mom. Right? The woman never ever stopped talking, yammering on about something or other all the time. She knew what her mother liked to eat, which books she preferred to read, and even what movies she enjoyed watching. She had a vague notion of her mother's current political leanings and how she felt about a few random news events, but she knew nothing about the real woman inside.

Who had her mother been before she became a wife, a mother, and then a widow? What had she studied in school? What did she do when Jo wasn't around?

Her mother was a master of deflection. Answering just enough questions to make it seem as though she were sharing but turning the tables so that people were the ones confiding in her.

How was it possible that Jo had never wondered why her mother had never been on a date?

Jo felt her forehead crease further. All those years that Jo had felt comforted and loved, her terrible high school years, her painful post stillbirth recovery, she had never once wondered if her mother was lonely or sad. Had never thought to ask. She looked at her mother again and it was like looking at a complete stranger.

Instead of giving into the panic that threatened to engulf her Jo cleared her throat and pursued her inquiry. Better late than never. She could start getting to know her mother now. Maybe it was the first step in the direction of whatever the future held for them.

"Mom?" She jiggled the hand that she still held clasped in her own and her mother jumped a little as though startled out of a dream. "Richard?"

Her mother looked up at her, a moment of confusion crossing her face, then her eyes focused and she smiled. The transformation to her face was magical. It was as though she had instantly lost twenty years. Whoever this Richard was he clearly made her mother feel special and happy. Jo smiled at the life that was flooding her mother's face. This wasn't a version of her mom that she had ever known. The face she knew always had worried crinkles in the corners of the eyes, but this was a face that filled her heart with warmth. It was impossible not to be uplifted by the joy that shone out of those eyes.

"Richard. Richard... is... Oh, it's going to sound corny." Her mother blushed and tried to pull her hand away again. She shook her head and the worried look returned. "And anyway, it has nothing to do with you. I don't want to worry you with it."

Jo bit back a frustrated growl. It wasn't her fault that she knew nothing about her mother's life. She had never been invited into the inner sanctuary of her mother's mind. Clearly, that wasn't about to change.

Anger started to course through her as she placed her hands on the slightly sticky table and went to stand up.

"Of course, it has something to do with me! Damn it mom! Some people have normal relationships with their mothers! Some people chat about life, and relationships, and yes, even sex!" She hadn't meant to shout the last word and the horror on her mother's face shut her up. She almost sat down, almost apologized, but instead she lowered her voice and finished. She was tired of only being exposed to her mother's sad face. She wanted to know the happier version of her mother. "Why do you shut me out? Why won't you talk to me?"

Her hands shook as she stood there, looking down at her mother still sitting on the bench. Her vision blurred, but even as her eyes filled with tears she saw fear cross her mother's face. Fear and sadness etched into the worn and tired lines that she knew so well. Jo sat back down, all her anger spent. She reached for her mother's hand again.

"Mom. Talk to me. What is it you're so afraid of?"

Her mother's shoulders rose in a hesitant shrug. She looked down and shook her head.

"I don't know," she said. "Maybe that you'll disapprove? You were young when your father died. It was hard being the only parent. You know, when kids have two parents they can afford to be mad at one, because there's always another to go to for comfort or help or advice. But I was all you had. So, I had to be perfect, so you'd never have a reason to turn away."

Jo tried to speak, but her mother was on a roll and didn't let her interrupt.

"I tried so hard. I never dated because I didn't want you to have to get attached to anyone and maybe have to say goodbye again. Plus, I always wanted to be available for you. And I tried hard to be fair, to give you some freedom, all while keeping you safe too. And with all that, there was really never any time to do anything else."

Jo picked at a tender cuticle on her pinky. She couldn't look at her mother. Couldn't face the raw emotion that was pouring out. She had known that her mother was more present and involved than her friends' mothers, but she had never guessed at the motivation behind it. Guilt flooded her chest, making it hard to breathe. Her mother had given up her life for her. And how had she repaid her? By being an ordinary pain in the ass teenager?

This time it was her mother's hand that reached out and grabbed hers.

"I'm not sorry Jo. I wanted to be there for you. It was a choice I made." Jo blushed. The guilt must have been all over her face. "I'm serious!" Her mother insisted, gripping her hand. "I don't know, maybe I needed to fill my life with yours so I wouldn't have to deal with losing your dad. As long as I kept myself busy with you I could pretend his death wasn't real. Or at least..." She shrugged and let the sentence hang.

She didn't need to fill in the blank. Jo had played a similar version of the "Daddy's just at work and will be home later" game her whole life. Pretending he was just away on business had been her way of pretending she was a normal kid with two parents like all her friends. She sometimes even told people that that was why he was never around. She had only stopped when some of her friends' parents had started getting divorces. After a while, living with just one parent became the norm and the thing that made her different was that her mom didn't go on embarrassing dates with loser boyfriends.

"I messed up, didn't I? I did it all wrong." Jo's mother looked at her with an even sadder look on her face. Jo wished they could rewind to early that morning when she hadn't made her mother cry and hadn't opened this particular can of worms.

"No. No, you didn't mess up. You did the best you could in a crappy situation." Her mother winced at the language, but Jo continued. "You wanted to protect me, and you thought you were doing the right thing." All she got as a response was a sad little nod. "But Mom, I'm not a little kid anymore. I don't need someone to protect me and watch over me and guide my every move anymore." She hesitated when she saw her mother stiffen slightly. "Mom? I want you. I want a mother who's my friend and my confidant. I want to get to know you. It's been all about me all these years, don't you think it's time for that to change?"

Jo watched as her mother shifted in her seat, never looking up. She pulled her hand away from Jo's and crossed her arms in front of her. This wasn't good. Jo's heart sank. Maybe she wasn't meant to have a mom she could be pals with. Maybe this was just a sign that, instead of changing, their relationship was destined to end, or at least become a cold, distant one punctuated with periodic cards and emails detailing the goings on in the neighborhood. Jo took one last swig of her drink and started to stand up again.

"Don't go. Please?"

She hadn't expected to hear anything else from her mother. With her, conversation that ended unpleasantly usually just ended with no closure or resolution. She looked up warily. Her arms were no longer crossed, but her mother's shoulders were still hunched forward in an uninviting way. She was toying with a stray nut that had fallen on the table and was trying hard not to look at Jo.

"I don't know how to make it work." She took a shaky breath and finally looked up at Jo. She looked terrified. "But I want that. I really, really want that too. I miss you."

Jo stood up, but instead of leaving, she came over to her mother's side of the booth and slid in next to her. She took her mother's quivering hand and bumped her shoulder playfully. "It'll be okay. We'll take it slow. Hey! You know what would help? A drink!"

Her mother drew a shaky breath and laughed.

"Let's make that two. Breaking old habits is going to be hard, but there's really a lot I want to share. I mean, isn't Richard...?" She giggled, eyes shining bright suddenly.

Both of them laughed and leaned their heads together. Jo waved over the waitress and asked her to bring them both a refill. While they waited for their drinks her mother started to tell Jo about Richard and how they'd met, and Jo listened as the floodgates burst open.

70. Jo

"Ten years!" Jo burst into the room making Jordan jump. "Ten years they've been together!"

She had kept it together while her mother had told her all about her relationship with Richard, how they'd met at a bookstore, how he'd taken her for coffee, and then wooed her relentlessly for months before Maryanne had finally capitulated and allowed him to take her out again. They had seen each other on the sly, never letting Jo catch on.

"Ten freaking years! And I never knew! No! And there I was feeling sorry for her! Sorry that she was alone for so long! Ten years!"

Jordan's answering chuckle stopped the next rant about to burst forth and she looked over at her husband whose face was creased in laughter.

"What? What the hell is do damn funny?" She smashed her fists against her hip bones and stared him down. If anything, the stern glare just made him laugh harder.

"Nothing. You're just cute when you're angry." Jo bristled and he stopped in mid stride on his way to hug her. She glared even harder at him and he laughed again. "Okay. Fine. What is it exactly that you are angry about? That she's been in a committed relationship for ten years? That she's happy?"

"Noooo..." Jo's anger subsided a bit. Maybe she was overreacting a tad. But ten years!

Jordan inched closer to her and reached for her. She let herself drift into his arms and rested her forehead on his warm chest. She was surprised to feel tears working their way out of her eyes.

"You've been living in a different country for five of those and before that you had quite a bit on your plate yourself. Could it be that you're mad that she's kept it from you? And maybe that she's finally moving on?" The sob that escaped was answer enough for both him and Jo.

"He's gone. And she's forgetting him." Even as she sobbed Jo knew how silly she sounded. Her father had been dead for twenty years. But she couldn't stop the tears or the feelings of betrayal that coursed through her. "So, what? Now I get a new daddy? And I'm supposed to just forget the old one?" She sobbed harder for a moment and Jordan hugged her closer.

"Now you're just being silly." He kissed the top of her head and pulled her back so he could look her in the eye. "Don't you see why she didn't tell you all this time?"

"Yes. No." Jo shrugged and sniffled hard. "I guess." Indignation grew again. "Well! Well! She should have trusted me! I would have gotten over it! I'm getting over it now aren't I?"

"Well, sure," Jordan patted her head patronizingly. "Now that you're married, or almost, and getting on with your own life. But ten years ago, maybe it wouldn't have been as easy."

Jo shrugged again and snorted. "Yeah. I guess it wasn't the best time for either of us. I guess… I guess…"

"Yes?"

"I guess I'm glad she's happy. I'm glad she has someone who makes her feel as loved as I feel when I'm with you. Everyone should have that."

Jessica Rosenberg

71. Andy

He let Hunter drag Amber by the hand and show her all of his favorite spots between the beach and the main hotel lobby while he followed along at a more sedate pace. After everything that had happened today he wasn't worried that Amber would try to make a break for it again. She kept glancing back at him with a worried look and a shy smile, but he didn't smile back.

Andy tried to stay calm for Hunter's sake, but inside he was mess of emotions. What the hell was she doing here? You don't dump someone, leave home, and then crash their vacation, try to steal their kid and then expect immediate forgiveness. That was just so... so....

Amber.

Hunter had kneeled down to show her a gecko and Amber had knelt down beside him. Between the high speed chase, the shark attack, and everything else he hadn't yet really looked at her. He hadn't expected to be so moved by the sight of her auburn hair glinting in the sun and the shape of the body he knew so well. She had been his savior at a time when he had thought no one could save him. Despite their less than ideal relationship, when she had walked out on them a month earlier, it had shaken not just kids' worlds, but his world

353

too.

He had more or less rolled with the punch, had fielded their questions about Mommy and where she had gone, had gotten the kids to where they needed to be, had kept them fed, clothed, clean, and more or less in their regular routine. They were used to her not being around, so they hadn't really realized that things had changed completely. Amber had sent all of one post card, begging for time, had called exactly once.

They had just begun to feel stable again, and here she was, throwing everything off kilter again. She looked up at him and smiled. His heart twisted painfully.

He loved her. Loved this woman, the mother of his children. But the rational part of his brain just kept repeating "She left you. She left them. She tried to kidnap him. She only cares about herself. You can't trust her. She's done it before. She'll do it again." Over and over again.

All of a sudden Andy felt exhausted. He just wanted to lie down and go to sleep. He wanted to forget today had ever happened, but he managed to stay upright.

"Amber. What are you doing here?" He asked, interrupting the peaceful moment.

She smiled at him again and shrugged. "We planned this vacation together, didn't we?"

Her flippant answer woke him up again and fueled the anger that the sight of her had dampened. He threw his shoulders back, filled with fury.

"No. I'm sorry, but no." He reached forward to pull Hunter away from her. "You don't get to come back like this. You don't get to walk back into our lives, try to kidnap our son, and act like nothing happened." Hunter squirmed under his grasp, but he held tight. "I don't know what I was thinking. You're leaving. Today."

Hunter looked up at his father, a horrified look on his face. He opened his mouth to argue, but Amber spoke first.

"Andy, please." Her voice was low and desperate, but her face betrayed no emotion. She smiled at Hunter like nothing was wrong. Andy wanted to scream, kick something, maybe even break something. He needed to get himself away from her, get his son away. He didn't want Emily to see her, didn't want Hunter to be around her anymore. They were doing fine without her. Fine.

In his heart he knew he was going to lose this fight. If he didn't get the children away from her right now he'd lose his children to her. If he stayed, he worried he'd even lose himself. All those years he'd put up with her behavior. He was powerless when she was around.

"Please. Calm down. You're scaring Hunter. It's okay baby, Daddy didn't mean it."

Andy's gut screamed to hold on tight to Hunter's hand, to walk away without looking back. He could call a lawyer and have this all settled by morning. Amber had abandoned them. He had witnesses who would testify to years of terrible mothering. She'd even shown up here with the sole intent to steal their son. There were witnesses to that too. She didn't deserve to be a part of their lives. They deserved someone they could count on to be there forever.

"Please? Andy? Can't we at least talk?" While he struggled to figure out what to do, Amber had gotten up and now she stood in front of him. When she placed her hand gently on his forearm all the fight went out of him again. He looked down into her eyes and saw none of the bravado that she had just been putting on. He just saw a reflection of the confusion he was sure she saw in his own eyes.

"MAMA! MAMA! MAMA!" Emily's squeals bounced off the stone walk around them and increased as she got closer. Andy's heart sank. He'd hoped he could spare Emily the confusion of seeing her mother. He glanced at Sadie who just shrugged.

"I thought taking her for a swim would distract her. I'm sorry."

72. Andy

In the end Andy consented to ordering dinner to go for the children and to head back to their room to feed them. No matter how reluctant he was to actually deal with Amber, Andy was overwhelmed by the chaos in his head. There was no way he could handle talking to her while dealing with two hysterical kids in a busy restaurant. Someone might start screaming and odds were it wouldn't be either of the half-pints.

The kids ran ahead showing their mother all the cool things they had discovered in the hotel. She was treated to a demonstration of the elevator buttons, the door key, and every single light switch in the suite.

Andy was amazed that she stayed so patient through each minute explanation and demonstration. It made him want to scream. He stepped out onto the lanais, figuring that he could catch his breath while setting up an impromptu dining area for the kids on the little balcony. He took his time arranging chairs around the tiny table that sat out there then putting out their simple chicken finger, mac and cheese dinner. He had purposefully chosen something they would both eat without needing to be cajoled. He just didn't have it in him tonight to beg anyone to eat anything green.

The kids finally spotted him outside and dragged Amber to the door. There was no gecko to show off, but dinner provided a handy distraction, leaving the grownups free to step back into the bedroom for the conversation Andy was dreading. Every minute they spent pretending to be a happy family was messing with his head a little more.

"Amber. Seriously. What the hell?" He asked as he slid the door shut. He glanced at the kids who were happily tucking into their dinner before turning around to face her.

"I... ah..." Amber looked down at her hands and he had to strain to hear her answer. "I miss you. I screwed up. I'm sorry. I want to come home."

"And you come here and kidnap Hunter as a way to show me that's how you feel? What the hell Amber? Are you insane?"

Amber's face twisted in pain. "No! That wasn't the plan! I swear! I just... I saw him... And I couldn't stop myself. I'm sorry!"

"But really? What were you thinking? You were going to speed off into the sunset with him? What Amber? What exactly was the plan?"

"There was no plan. I just... I wanted to be with him. When you're around he only has eyes for you." The bitterness in her voice surprised Andy.

"Of course, he only has eyes for me! You were never there for him! He doesn't know any better!"

"How could I be there for him when Andy the Wonderdad was always rushing to the rescue? I never stood a chance!"

Her words froze Andy on the spot. Was she right? Had he never given her a chance? Andy thought back to

Hunter's infancy and tried to see it through Amber's eyes.

"You're full of shit, you know that?" He almost whispered the words. "You were never there. You went out all the time. I don't know what you were dealing with back then, but you can't pin it on me. I just did what I had to do to keep the kid safe and happy. Don't you dare try to rewrite the story to make me the bad guy."

Amber had clearly expected an argument. She didn't quite know what to make of the quiet steely voice Andy was using. He watched her struggle to find the right words and was shocked to realize he still felt absolutely no compassion for her.

She was the mother of his children. She had been his savior. He had loved her. Once. But he looked at her standing there and he couldn't bring himself to love her again, or even to believe what she was saying.

"You left, Amber. You left me high and dry. You left us high and dry. You lulled us into thinking that we could be a happy family and just when we were starting to believe it, you walked. I just don't think I have it in me to forgive you again." Andy looked away and sat down heavily on the little sofa. He had sat here not three days before, lamenting his sad situation, wishing Amber back, and now that she was, and he had in his reach the potential to fix his life he realized he had no desire to go back. He didn't want her. "You've done it again and again. This might have been the first time you actually left home, but you've never been really there. They're my kids. You didn't want them. And now you've made it quite clear you don't want me either. You don't get to come back whenever you get lonely. You don't get to swoop in and rewrite history to suit your delusions."

Amber gave him an unreadable stare then went outside to sit with the kids. Their laughter followed him around the room as he got the children's nighttime things ready.

She had left him. She had left without a word, without giving him a chance to talk, to try to win her back. She had just walked out. And here she was just walking back in. He stole glances at her as she played around with Hunter and Emily. It was hard to admit, but they glowed around her in a way that they didn't around him.

Maybe he was just being too harsh on her. Maybe he should be thinking more about the kids than himself. It was good for kids to have a mom and a dad. All the studies showed that kids with two parents did better in pretty much everything. With a slight sinking of his heart, he wondered if for them he should dig deep and try to forgive her.

But when it came time to put them to bed it was him they asked for. They begged him to tuck them in and to read their stories. Emily even demanded that Amber wait in the adjoining room. He went through the routine that he had perfected over the years and kissed them both before turning out the light. He stood in the dark and breathed a few deep breaths before leaving them. She hadn't just left him, she'd left them all, and despite their earlier excitement, clearly Hunter and Emily didn't trust her either.

As soon as the door closed between the two rooms Amber launched into him, in turn pleading, cajoling, and demanding that he give her another chance. Andy didn't give in, but he listened. They talked, going around and around in circles for what seemed like forever. All Andy wanted was to be alone, in his room, preferably with a stiff drink in his hand. He wished Amber would just leave, go back to her room, and let him just think.

Wait, no, that wasn't even true. He just wished she would shut up for five minutes so he could catch his breath and clear the noise in his head. Noise that she was putting there.

Heck, that wasn't even it. He wanted her to leave so he could go see Roxie. Things just felt better, easier around Roxie.

The knock at the door startled them both.

"Were you expecting someone?" Amber asked.

"SHIT!" Andy jumped out of his seat. The bedside clock glowed brightly. 8:25. On his way to pick up Hunter he'd managed to call the front desk to reserve a sitter for his date with Roxie. That must be who was at the door. But Roxie...

He had never called her. She had no idea what had happened that afternoon. She was probably thinking he'd stood her up. Andy groaned as he walked to the door. What the hell was he going to do? There was no way Roxie would give him yet another chance.

"... because I'm not giving up without a fight, you know. When you want something, you fight for it. And I'm going to fight..." The knock at the door had barely slowed Amber's diatribe. Her words filtered through the cloud that had darkened his mind for a moment. He played them over and over again in his head. Her tone didn't match the words. She must have been reciting something she's been told to say, but the words resonated in him. She was right. She was 100% right. With his hand on the door, he turned and looked at her, which she took as encouragement and redoubled her efforts.

"You're right, you know," he interrupted her flow, and she stopped, not sure what direction the conversation was going to take.

"What? How am I right?" She moved towards him hesitantly.

"When you really want something, you have to fight for it."

Her face brightened. "Yes! Yes! That's right! You have to fight!"

He couldn't fault her for looking confused as he opened the door and let in the same sitter who had watched the kids the previous night. He smiled at the teenager before turning a more serious face towards his soon-to-be ex-wife.

"Amber, it's time for you to go. If you ever want a chance at being involved in their lives at all you will do this one thing for me. You will leave without a fuss right now."

"Uh, okay." Amber nodded looking perplexed. "But where are you going? Why can't I stay with the kids?"

"I'm going to fight for what I want. And if you don't know why I can't trust you to be alone with the children, well, then I really don't know what to tell you."

73. Sadie

After a long day of running around trying to throw together a last minute wedding, watching a child she barely knew, and worrying about her friend's safety, Sadie figured she had earned a kiss or two. Kona had called her to say they were back safe and sound, child in hand, and that he was late for his shift at the bar. She couldn't wait to set eyes, hands, and lips on him again.

She hesitated after leaving her room. Was it worth stopping by Roxie's room to see if she wanted to join her? Odds were good that she'd be with Andy. Whatever. She'd stop by on the off chance that Andy had chosen to spend the evening close to Hunter now that he had him back.

She tapped the door lightly and, the instant her hand connected with the wood, the door flew open.

"Finally! I thought you'd forgotten me!" Roxie stood there, dressed to kill in a tiny glittering gold dress that hugged all her curves as if it had been painted on. Her hair was perfectly done up in a style designed to look like it had taken mere seconds to assemble, but which, knowing Roxie, must have taken the better part of an hour to perfect.

Her beautifully made up face darkened

dangerously when she saw that the person on the other side of the door was clearly not the person she had been expecting.

"Oh. It's you."

"Sorry to disappoint!" Sadie replied as cheerily as possible. "I'm headed to the bar. Want to join me?"

It took a little convincing, but Roxie finally consented to leaving her room. She was torn between wanting to mope over being stood up and wanting to go out and have fun so that, should Andy eventually come looking for her, he would see she wasn't pining away for him in her room.

"I just don't get it, you know?" Roxie shook her head. "Guys go after me. I'm never the one who waits around."

Sadie made a couple clucking sounds that she hoped sounded supportive and comforting. But really, Roxie was going to have to figure out this one for herself.

"Well, it's not like he exactly planned what happened this afternoon."

"What do you mean? What happened? You mean the part where he treated me like a babysitter all afternoon while he lounged around and then made vague promises about a fancy dinner?"

"Uh, no. I mean the part when his ex showed up and kidnapped their son and ran off on a boat and almost got eaten by a shark."

"What?!" Roxie turned to see if Sadie was joking. "You're shitting me."

"No, I'm not. It really happened."

"Well, he could have called!" Roxie growled in frustration. "They're okay, though, right?"

"Yes, they're fine. And clearly he hasn't stood you

up. Not really. Not if they were vague plans. You know, when kids are involved you can't always count on everything going the way you anticipated."

"The crazy thing is that I don't even mind the kid thing all that much! I mean, I pretended to mind being left to babysit all morning because, sheesh, dude, take advantage much? But I was perfectly happy in that kiddy pool with that kid. Sadie? What is wrong with me?" She wailed.

"Nothing that a stiff drink or two won't fix," was all that Sadie could answer because she knew all too well what was wrong with her friend, she just didn't think her friend was ready to hear it yet.

Three nameless drinks later, each mixed by Kona who chuckled as he added this and that to the shaker, and she was ready.

"I mean? Is this love? Is that what this is?"

Sadie just nodded sagely, not trusting herself to not slur a response.

"But this sucks! I'm miserable! I thought love was all puppy dogs and pink puffy hearts. This? This just..." Roxie tried shaking her head, but instead almost fell off her bar stool. Instead, she stood up and made her way unsteadily towards the restroom. Whether or not she would get there without falling over was a toss-up. Whether she'd be able to make her way back was even more doubtful. Sadie settled in for a long moment of bartender gazing. Even in her drunken state she still sharply felt her need to be close to Kona. Unlike Roxie however, she didn't mind the feeling and was thoroughly enjoying falling in love with the man. She was just heartbroken that she'd have to say goodbye to him so soon.

At the very thought of saying farewell to Kona tears welled in Sadie's eyes. She struggled to swallow the lump that had formed in her throat. Just as she was about to start weeping noisily into her fresh drink she noticed a familiar figure stepping into the bar. She waved Andy over and he made his way through the crowd towards her.

"You are in So. Much. Trouble. Dude." She shook her head mock seriously. Andy's face fell.

"I royally fucked up, didn't I?" Sadie just nodded in response. "Is she here? Did you tell her what happened?"

Sadie wasn't too drunk to notice the flurry of emotions that took over his face. She took pity on the guy.

"She's here. She just went to the bathroom." She nodded towards the back of the restaurant. "I told her what happened, but she was pretty upset about being stood up. Now, though, she's just pretty drunk."

Before she had even finished her sentence Andy was gone, halfway to the back of the bar. Sadie smiled as he walked away, bumping into people and apologizing as he went. She hoped he'd find the right words. It would be a shame if they couldn't work things out. She turned her attention back to Kona, the thought echoing in her head.

Jessica Rosenberg

74. Andy

Was it creepy to wait right outside the bathroom? Andy wondered as he leaned as nonchalantly as possible against the wall right next to the entrance to the Wahine's room. He didn't actually care one way or another; he just didn't want to miss Roxie.

When she still hadn't come out after a good ten minutes he started to worry. What if she had left before he had even arrived at the bar? Sadie seemed pretty drunk and distracted by her bartender; she might not have noticed Roxie leaving. What if she'd left with another guy?

A hot flash of jealousy slammed through him and he almost punched the wall, he resisted though, not wanting to get thrown out. If he'd lost his chance with her it was his own damn fault. The very least he could have done was give her a freaking call. He wanted to hit his head against the wall, but he wasn't sure that made him any less of a nut than punching it so he settled for just resting his forehead against the well-worn wood instead.

"Are you okay?" A cute short woman, who would have totally been his type if he had been able to get either Roxie or Amber out of his head for a nanosecond, paused with her hand on the door and looked at him with a slightly concerned look on her face.

"Yeah. Yeah," Andy mumbled, lifting his head off the wall. "Hey! Actually?" she stopped with the door cracked open. "Could you do me a favor? Could you tell me if a tall blonde is in there?" She shrugged and nodded before going in quickly.

An endless five minutes later she came back out. "Yeah. She's in there. She's sitting on one of the couches crying." She shot him a dirty look and sauntered away.

What was the right thing to do here? He was frozen by the conflicting desire to rush into comfort Roxie and the age old restriction on going into a woman's bathroom. Roxie won and with a quick glance all around him, Andy slipped through the door.

Whatever he had expected it wasn't what he found. Instead of a bathroom, he was standing it what looked like a tiny living room, complete with a plush couch, matching armchair, and a little coffee table.

"Where are the stalls?" he blurted out, which, while not being exactly as smooth as he had hoped, did have the advantage of startling Roxie.

Tears still running down her face she nodded at another door he hadn't yet noticed.

"Why are you here?" She demanded, looking back at him.

"Because that girl told me you were crying." He hadn't really planned what he was going to say, and so far he was striking out, but he figured it was best to just be cautious and see where he stood before trying to improve his game.

"No, numbnuts, why are you here, at the bar? Don't you have something better to be doing?" She attempted a sneer, but something, either the alcohol or the tears, interfered and all she managed was a perfectly adorable and unreadable expression.

Andy forgot all about being cautious and threw himself on his knees in front of her.

"I am so, so sorry," he started, grabbing her hands in his. "I... I..."

There were a million excuses he could have come up with. He could think of a million spins to his story that would make Roxie feel sorry for him, but sitting there, or rather kneeling there, at her feet, he didn't want to try. He didn't want to be that guy with Roxie.

"I forgot. Amber showed up. She... she grabbed Hunter and... I forgot everything else. I'm so sorry. I should have called." He looked down at their entwined hands, encouraged by the fact that she hadn't yanked hers away, but still not daring to look up.

"Is he okay?"

"Yes, he's fine. He's asleep in his bed. Safe and sound. I left the kids with a sitter."

"Tell me something Andy. She knew where to come. Were you expecting her?" Roxie had left her hands in his, but they were slack. She stared down and he couldn't see what emotions were on her face, but her quiet resigned tone scared him.

Roxie knew the story about how Amber had left. He had told her earlier in the week, but he wasn't surprised that she was confused. Fuck. He was confused.

"No. I didn't think she'd come. She planned this vacation with me, but when she left, I... I just assumed she wouldn't come."

"So why is she here? What does she want?" Her

voice trembled and he looked up into her brilliant eyes. They were guarded, more so than he had ever seen them and he hesitated before answering.

"She says she wants... me. And the kids. She says she wants to come home."

"Oh." Roxie pulled her hands out of his grasp and Andy let her. He didn't stop her when she stood up and walked away from him either. He stayed on his knees, willing her to come back. He couldn't bear to watch her walk away. Andy stared hard at the couch where Roxie has been sitting and it was only when he heard the door open that he spoke.

"I told her no, Roxie. I told her she couldn't have another chance." He turned to face her. "Roxie. Please. It's you I want." She balked more visibly at this than she had at the announcement that his ex had come back. Her arms came up protectively and she took one more step back.

"No. That's not what I meant." He stood up and took a step towards her. "I mean, yes, that is what I meant, but there's no rush. We have all the time in the world." The wall kept her from going back any further, but he could sense her urge to flee. He took a step back and sat down on the couch to give her a bit more space. Roxie's shoulders unclenched a bit, and her stance became a tiny bit less defensive.

The door swung open to let in a portly older lady who gave Andy a surprised look before checking the door to make sure she was in the right place. She hesitated then hurried past them into the second part of the rest room.

"She's the mother of your children Andy. I can't compete with that." Roxie's voice was quiet, sad, and

Andy realized she wasn't angry, but resigned. She was giving up before the fight even started.

"No!" He spoke more loudly than either of them had expected and she jumped. "I mean, yes, of course she's the mother of my children, but no, I'm not giving up."

Unable to resist any further he stood up and came close to her. Reaching for her hands again he spoke more softly.

"Roxie. I haven't felt like this about anyone since... No. That's not true either. I've never felt like this about anyone." As he said the words he realized they were true. "I loved Jo. I thought I loved her more than life itself. But when push came to shove, I wasn't willing to fight. For you? I will fight. And I won't give up."

75. Sadie

"Shhh! They're coming!" Roxie turned to hush the crowd gathered on the beach, using wild arm gestures to get the attention of the ones chatting too loudly to hear her hoarse whisper. Andy and Kona spotted her frantic motions and quickly moved through the crowd settling everyone down.

People hurried to hide behind the palm trees that thickly lined the beach. Their bright festive clothing only noticeable if someone was staring right at them. Even then they blended pretty well with the flowers. Sadie looked away from the still chattering group. She wasn't really worried that they'd be noticed. She was pretty sure that Jo would spot the chairs carefully arranged in front of the simple wedding canopy that they had set up in a secluded corner of the beach long before she'd see the guests.

The seclusion wasn't necessary, it was just an added precaution. The beach was deserted, hotel guests still forbidden to set foot on the sand because of the shark. Sadie's eyes drifted to the glittering ocean, looking to see if she could spot him, but the sea was calm, not a single fin in sight. She shivered. They'd come so close to losing Hunter and Andy to that beast. And yet, there they both were, looking radiant and so very alive in the sun. She looked around some more, trying to spot Kona in the crowd. She saw his broad back as he shooed a guest back further behind a palm tree. Sleeping with the future owner of the place definitely had its advantages.

He had negotiated special permission from the coast guards for them to hold the wedding on the beach after all. The thick bright red ribbon separating the clustered white chairs from the ocean had been the one injunction they hadn't been able to negotiate on. Adorned with white flowers it didn't look half bad. To the untrained eye it even looked like it was a planned part of the decorations.

They hadn't wanted to take any risks though and they had made it abundantly clear to the guests that they were, on no uncertain terms, allowed to go past the ribbon or get near the water. The extra staff members that Kona had roped into the event were charged with making sure that none of the guests ignored the request.

Out of the corner of her eye Sadie saw Roxie stop waving her arms and duck out of sight of the stairs leading to the beach. She hurried over to join her.

"Where are they?" She whispered.

"At the top of the last flight of stairs. They'll be here any second."

"Ready?" Sadie glanced at her friend, winking. They had spent the last 24 hours moving heaven and earth to make this the perfect wedding for Jo and Jordan. It wasn't Zambia, but it was rustic, simple, an all about the people. Sadie took a deep breath. She really hoped they liked it.

Roxie grabbed her hand and squeezed. "Ready,"

she whispered back as they heard Jo and Jordan's voices grow louder.

Sadie stepped out from the shadows but had to clear her throat before the two of them even noticed her. She was dressed in a simple sundress that she and Roxie had found in the hotel store. They'd gone shopping after unanimously agreeing that the fancy bridesmaids' dresses that Maryanne had picked out would be all wrong for the low key wedding that they were organizing. They hadn't even picked out shoes; Jo would love seeing them barefoot. The only concession to the festive event was the bright garland of plumerias that crowned their heads. This was what Jo stared at quizzically as Sadie stepped forward.

"Jo," Sadie started, stammering a bit. What if after all that work, Jo got mad? Wasn't this just more meddling? "Jo, Jordan." She stopped again, then continued in a rush when she saw that Jo was about to speak. "We all came here to see two of our favorite people renew their vows. Nothing has happened the way we meant it to, but we've done our best to fix what we could." She stepped out of the way and let the engaged couple take in the scene.

The white chairs were all covered in more bright plumerias, and the center aisle was highlighted with even more of the same, lining the sand in the middle. The wedding canopy was made of soft white tulle studded with even more bright blooms. The effect was surreal and beautiful. Paradise within paradise.

Jo gasped and grabbed Jordan's hand. His jaw had fallen open as he looked at what they had set up. Sadie gestured behind her back and right on command Kona and Andy started leading people out from behind the trees. One by one the guests stepped out into the sun. Friends and family took turns taking their place in the sand. Each was dressed in simple but beautiful clothing. More something they would have worn to a pool party than a wedding, but the effect was miraculous.

"We didn't tell you just how many people had originally RSVP'd. Your mother and I wanted to keep some of them a surprise. We all agreed that we couldn't let you not get married here."

Sadie looked at Jo and Jordan, a worried frown pulling at the tight skin on her forehead. They had been out in the sun a lot over the last couple of days and she had managed to let herself burn a bit more than she had intended. The frown smarted, but it didn't distract her or lessen the worry growing in her belly.

"Please. Please, say something," she begged the stunned pair.

"But I thought you said that nothing had been ordered or prepared?" Jo tore her eyes from the crowd gathered at the edge of the beach.

"It hadn't. Kona pulled as many strings as possible to help me get everything ready. It's not going to be fancy, but that's not what you wanted anyway. We got a singer with a ukulele for the ceremony and after we're going to have a local steel drum band play. We convinced a pastor who was going next door for another wedding to come here before." She turned and gestured to another cordoned off spot further down the beach. "We're roasting a pig down there."

She looked at them again and held her breath. Jo and Jordan looked at each other. Smiles playing in the corners of their mouths and dancing across their eyes.

"Do you...?"

"Is this...?"

They spoke at the same time and laughed. Jordan dropped to one knee and held Jo's hand tightly.

"Jo Hunter, will you do me the honor of becoming my wife, right here, today, among all these friends who love and clearly know us so well?"

Jo dropped to both her knees in front of him and threw her arms around him in a tight embrace. She placed her small hands on either side of his face and kissed him tenderly.

"Yes. Yes, I will."

The crowd of guests cheered loudly and rushed the happy couple.

"Oh! Oh!" Jo cried, standing up and looking down at her crumpled shorts and t-shirt. She looked around wildly for Sadie who winked and beckoned from behind the mass of people that had pushed her aside to get to Jo.

"It's okay. I have the dress. It's right in there." She gestured to a rickety hut hidden in the shadows on the other side of the stairs. Jo smiled brightly before letting herself be whisked away.

The dress almost filled the tiny hut that had been assembled as a makeshift bride's room, but the two girls still managed to squeeze in. They gazed in awe at the dress that Debbie had finished just in time.

"Do you like the changes?" Sadie asked, her voice betraying how worried she really was. Jo had adored the dress the way it had been. Sadie had thought it would be a good idea to alter it a bit to reflect the changed wedding. Debbie had shortened it so that Jo would be able to wear it barefoot and had removed a couple of the extra layers that had made it extra billowy. Then, as a final touch, she had carefully hand sown among the beading more of the same Hawaiian flowers that they had used to decorate everything else. The end result was a stunningly simple and beautiful dress.

Jo swiped at her eyes and Sadie's heart sank. She hated it. She opened her mouth to apologize, but, before she could get a word out, Jo turned to her and hugged her hard.

"Thank you. Thank you so much. It's perfect. Everything is perfect." She pulled away from Sadie and wiped more tears out of her eyes.

Sadie felt her face flush. She swiped away a couple of her own tears and tried to clear her throat a bit.

"No more crying now. Let's see how it fits. OK?" She shoved Jo gently and laughed when her friend shoved back. "Debbie's here to help you get dressed." She stepped out of the tiny room to let the dressmaker take her place and she gratefully took the outstretched hand that Kona held out to her as she set foot on the sand.

"All good?" he asked, squeezing her hand tight.

"All good," she answered, squeezing tight back.

76. Jo

They had somehow managed to rig a full length mirror on one wall of the tiny changing room and Jo scrutinized herself from head to toe. The dress was perfect. Unlike so many wedding dresses it didn't just poof out and sit there, it actually hugged her body in flattering waves of silk. The changes that Sadie had asked Debbie to make were exactly those that she would have asked had she been thinking at all clearly.

Thanks to the last couple of days spent in the sun her face was nicely tanned, so she could easily do without makeup, but her hair... that was a whole other story. Jo lifted her hands to her head. In sections her locks had fallen flat in response to the heat while in other spots the humidity had caused little tendrils to frizz. There was really not much that could be done. She dragged the brush that Sadie had thoughtfully brought down, slicked back the worst of the frizz with a little leave-in conditioner that she found next to the brush, and pinned what she could back with the little barrettes with matching flowers that Debbie had left for her to use.

"Something borrowed...," she thought as she pushed the last one in place. She looked herself over in the mirror. It wasn't perfect, but it was definitely good enough. In fact the slightly messy do, the shorter dress, and the rosy tan skin all blended together perfectly. She looked just like a bride should look on her barefoot-in-the-sand beach wedding day.

The guests outside the door mingled and chatted and Jo smiled. Her friends were out there. Her friends and family. People who loved her and wanted to see her happy. She started to step towards the door when a splash of blue caught her eye. The lei hung over the edge of the door, presumably left there by Sadie. Jo reached out and unhooked it gently. It wasn't a traditional lei, made with bright Hawaiian flowers. This was a gentle string of brilliant blue forget-me-nots. Jo fingered the delicate blossoms and slipped it over her head. She had no idea where Sadie had found this marvel at the last minute, but it was perfect. The flower garland added a final touch of whimsy to her outfit which made her smile.

"Plus, now I have something blue..." She turned to the door which swung open a crack as her foot pushed down on a loose floorboard. She froze as her thoughts finished themselves. "Something old and something new."

Jordan and Andy stood together under a tree no more than a foot or two away, both looking dapper in matching Hawaiian shirts. Presumably someone had brought down Jordan's; Jo had never seen it before. Jordan wore his own lei around his neck – a more manly version made of woven leaves that looked beautiful against the bright shirt. He was smiling and laughing as he chatted with Andy. Seeing her two loves, the first and the last, talking, made her heart skip a beat.

Both were so good looking. Each in his own way. And both made her heart sing a special tune. Andy would never hold her tight again. Would never place his soft lips on hers. For a moment she longed to be in his arms and to have him hold her tight, wished things had never gone bad. Her stomach twisted as she strained to remember what it felt like to be in his arms, but two different sets of arms confused themselves in her head. She looked back and forth from one man to the other. One made her feel safe and loved, but the other had always made her blood pulse faster. What if she was making the wrong decision? What if she was being too hasty?

Sadie called to her from the other side of the door, but Jo was unable to answer. She clutched her stomach, crushing the gentle flowers against her dress. She couldn't go out there. If she was still having these kinds of doubts, she couldn't marry Jordan. It would be a mistake. One big, horrible mistake.

"Jo?" Sadie called again and Jo backed up away from the door. The wall of the tiny hut stopped her from going any further. She looked around her wildly. There was nowhere to go. She was trapped. Trapped in a tiny room with a million people waiting for her to come out. She looked around again, wishing for an unnoticed back door to appear.

"Jo? Babe? I'm coming in."

Before she could squeak out a no, Sadie had already stepped in the door and was looking at her with a worried frown.

"You OK?" She asked in her best worried friend voice. Jo tried to smile, but all that came out was a twisted grimace. "Jo? What's wrong?"

"I can't do this." Jo's voice cracked and tears threatened. Nothing had ever felt more wrong. She couldn't step out there, couldn't walk up to Jordan and reach for his hand. Couldn't marry him. Not while Andy stood there too, and a part of her heart still ached for him. "I can't Sadie. I can't do this." She nodded to the door and felt a tear roll down her face.

She blinked furiously to stop the rest from falling and she felt Sadie grab her hands and squeeze tight. She looked down at their four hands and was surprised to see that the floor was littered with tiny blue petals. The bottom of the lei was in tatters, more torn petals covering both her hands.

She looked back up at Sadie's familiar face. Her friend's eyes were filled with warmth and concern. Jo attempted a smile, but only half came out. Sadie responded with a tiny smile of her own.

"Wanna talk about it?" She asked as though a huge crowd of guests weren't standing just on the other side of the door wondering why they were hiding in a tiny hut just about big enough for two children, not two grown women and a wedding gown. A panicked giggle threatened to follow the errant tear, but Jo checked herself. If she started she wouldn't be able to stop and she'd have to be carried out of here.

"I just... I just... What if I'm making the wrong choice?" She whispered. Terrified to put into words what her heart was screaming. "I loved Andy as much as I love Jordan and look what happened. It could happen again."

"Jo! Look at me! No, wait, look at them!" Sadie pointed to the two men through the crack in the door. Jo's heart jumped and her stomach flipped again.

Feeling suddenly nauseous, she raised a hand to her mouth, worried that she was about throw up from all the stress. Instead, the petals still covering her hand made her sneeze, a huge loud sneeze that startled a number of the guests standing around outside the hut.

Jordan's head swiveled towards her and she caught his eye briefly. More tears welled up. Even through the tiny crack and the veil of her tears she could see the concern etched in his eyes. More than that though, she could see the love for her that lived there. She sobbed and gasped at the same time, a strange, strangled sound that made Sadie squeeze her hand even tighter.

"I can't do this Sadie. What if I don't love him enough? What if I let him down?"

"Jo, please," Sadie begged quietly. "Look at him. Look at him carefully. Can you imagine not waking up to his face every morning for the rest of your life?"

Jo didn't answer. She stared at Jordan and then at Andy. At one time she had thought she couldn't live without Andy, couldn't start each day without seeing his smile. She had been willing to die for him, had, in fact, nearly died for him. But she had survived and had proven that she could live without him. Her eyes settled on Jordan's worried face and her heart filled with love. She knew she could live without Jordan, knew she had it in her to start again, but she didn't want to. Her life had been exponentially better since she had first met him. He challenged her in ways she'd never been challenged and stood there by her side, never expecting more out of her than to be by his side, exploring and experiencing the world together. Andy had relied on her the way she had relied on him. They had held each other up until one of them had been unable to handle the burden any longer. With Jordan things felt different, better, healthier, like they could stand on their own two feet and just enjoy knowing they had each other's backs.

She looked out at Jordan's face and her stomach settled. Sadie saw it in her face at the same time as Jo felt it in her heart. She squeezed Sadie's hand tightly.

"Are you sure?" Sadie still looked worried, but when Jo nodded firmly, she squeezed her hand one last time and pushed the door open.

Jordan was her partner, not her life support system, and she wanted to wake up every morning with him rather than needed it. She was choosing him.

Jo wiped away the last tear and smiled. Then she stepped out to face the music.

77. Jo

Their eyes met long before their hands connected and the world around them faded. There was nothing beyond the deep ocean of his eyes and Jo let herself look more deeply in them than ever before. She let herself see their future in there, a future that held her and their children. A future that held untold promises and joy. More importantly she saw joy, and love, and acceptance, and support. Buckets and buckets of undying support.

She could be herself with this man. She could grow and thrive buoyed by his kind of love and support. She drank in more of what she found deep in his eyes and by the time their hands had met, and their fingers had intertwined tightly, she was once again full of his love. It filled her to her toes and made her feel warm and alive to the tips of her fingers.

"You are mesmerizing," he whispered, and she smiled. "I have never seen you look so beautiful." She blushed deeply and tried to tear her gaze away, but his eyes and smile didn't let her waver.

She wanted to tell him about her doubts, wanted to explain her fears and hesitation. She looked at his trusting face and wondered if by not telling him she was lying to him, to herself, to both of them. She parted her lips to say something, anything, she wasn't quite sure what, but she never figured it out, because his lips came to rest gently against hers and the kiss blew away the last of her doubts and with it even the remote desire to voice them out loud.

To think that she had almost given up the right to ever taste his delicious mouth ever again. The bolt of fear that shot through Jo at this thought made her deepen her kiss and he laughed as he pulled away.

"How about we save some of that for the honeymoon?" he teased, pulling her close again for another short kiss.

Someone nearby coughed gently, and Jo jumped, much to the crowd's amusement. She blushed furiously again and looked around her. How she had forgotten that she was surrounded by a large crowd of friends and family was beyond her. Now that she turned her head this way and that she noticed that each and every one had gathered around the hut waiting for her to make her grand appearance.

Her eyes searched out and found Andy. He leaned against a tree, watching the proceedings with a half-smile on his face. His eyes looked sad to her and she smiled at him. He tipped an imaginary hat in her direction and winked as he shot her a bright and encouraging smile.

She was relieved to feel nothing other than friendship flood her heart. She had loved him deeply for a long, long time, and she had hated him for almost as long. Today she was at peace with their story. She looked back at Jordan, now standing by her side, and was almost blinded by the love that flooded her. She was making the right decision, no doubt about it. She glanced back at Andy and felt even more warmth fill her heart as she saw Roxie come stand near him. As if he'd done it every day of his life, Andy leaned in towards her and slipped his arm around her waist. Her heart fluttered as she glimpsed the future they could have together. Maybe everyone would find happiness here today.

Jo squeezed Jordan's hand making him look down at her. She looked up and smiled then looked around for Sadie.

"So? Are we doing this or what?" She teased.

"Actually, there's one last issue," Sadie answered. "We need someone to walk you down the aisle."

"Why? Where's my mother?" Jo searched the crowd frantically. How had she possibly missed the fact that her mother wasn't there? It had been a rough couple of days, but she felt good about where they'd left things. She couldn't fathom that her mother would stand her up at her own wedding.

"I'm sorry Jo. We tried hard to find her to tell her about the wedding, but the concierge said that she and Richard had rented a car to go see the volcano. We sent word to come back ASAP, we even broadcasted a message on the local radio, but I don't know if they heard. They might not be back in time."

She looked around at all the friends surrounding her, especially at the friends who had moved heaven and earth to make this happen. She didn't want to get married without her mother, but more than anything she didn't want to not get married.

"I'll do it. I'll walk you up the aisle." Andy's familiar voice made her smile. "It seems fitting." Jo couldn't think of anything more appropriate. The smile on Sadie and Jordan's face echoed her feelings. She had already left her childhood behind long before, having the man who symbolized her past life walk her to meet her present one seemed absolutely perfect.

"Shall we?" She asked. Andy bowed gently and slipped his hand into the crook of her elbow.

Sadie started herding people to their seats and ushered Jordan to the front of the altar.

"He's right you know," Andy whispered. "You do look beautiful. He's a lucky man." Jo beamed and looked at her fiancé, waiting for her expectantly, his eyes never leaving hers.

"No," she whispered back. "I'm the lucky one."

The sight of Jordan standing in front of the flower adorned altar made Jo breathless for a moment. The setting sun shone a perfect halo behind his head and illuminated the rest of the guests. Jo had to laugh, this was all so perfect, if she had planned it like this it couldn't have turned out better. Kona and Sadie had set up the chairs so that everyone would be able to see the sun setting around Jo and Jordan.

"If this was a movie we'd be groaning at the cheesiness of it all," Andy whispered down to her and she laughed because she had been thinking the exact same thing.

The crowd settled down and the ukulele player struck a chord and started playing What a Wonderful World. Jo and Andy groaned and laughed at the same time, but when Andy tugged her arm gently and she took a first step all traces of giggles vanished.

"Wait. I need a second," she whispered to Andy. "I want to remember this moment forever." Deep, deep breaths, she reminded herself. She paused, foot raised slightly and let the warm breeze flow over her bare arms and her face. The air was filled with the scent of flowers and sunscreen. She could smell the ocean and the sun in the air. She closed her eyes and focused on just breathing it all in.

She wanted to remember this exactly the way it was. She wanted to remember the cheesiness and the perfection of it all. Weddings were supposed to be stereotypical. That's how you knew your dreams were really coming true.

"OK. I'm ready."

Andy and Jo started walking and the ukulele player switched to a Hawaiian sounding wedding march.

"What the HELL is going on here!"

The shriek coming from the path leading to the beach caused everyone to jump and turn around to see who was interrupting the processional. The music trailed off mid bar. The hotel's irate manager stood at the end of the path, hands on his hips, purple face contorted in anger. He raised a hand and shook his finger at the gathering.

"This beach is CLOSED. CLOSED. Don't you people know what that means?" He pointed angrily at the sign indicating that the beach was closed to the public and strode purposefully towards the crowd.

The guests shrunk back in their seats and Jo looked frantically towards Kona and Sadie. She heard him whisper something to her friend but couldn't hear the actual words. Time stood still as Kona walked calmly towards his manager. He got there in a few long strides and placed what should have been a soothing hand on the angry man's arm.

The manager shook it off, refusing to be appeased.

"No! Dammit. I will not calm down!" He shouted in reply to something that Kona had murmured to him. "You're fucking DONE. I've put up with your shit long enough!"

Kona reeled back as if he'd been slapped. Jo was close enough to wish she hadn't been. His eyes narrowed and his lips thinned and without looking Jo knew that his fists were curling up into tight balls. He didn't yell back. Instead, he spoke very clearly and calmly.

"Excuse me?"

Everyone who overheard his icy tone shrunk away, but the manager was too far gone to realize that he had stepped into very dangerous territory. He poked his finger in Kona's face, pausing mere millimeters from his nose.

"I said, You're. DONE. What, are you deaf as well as dumb?"

The movement was so fast it caught everyone by surprise. The manager was instantly on his knees, the finger than Kona had grabbed was bent backward at a painful looking angle. The guests gasped, but Kona didn't flinch.

"You know what?" He said, in the same extremely calm voice. "I am done. I'm done taking orders from you. I'm done paying my dues. I'm taking over, right now, and I'm going to start by dealing with you. Later. In the meantime, I want you to go back to your cozy little office and think good and hard about what you would like your role in my hotel to be now that I'm taking charge.

"But before you go, you're going to apologize to these wonderful people, guests at my hotel, for the ugly disturbance you have caused on their special day."

The manager somehow managed to sneer despite the pain that was contorting his face, but Kona bent his finger back further and he finally nodded. Kona let him stand up and gave him a moment to collect himself. He made a big show of brushing off his suit before looking up at the group of gaping onlookers. Still, he didn't say anything. His face was purple with rage, and, Jo assumed, mortification.

He turned as if to leave and Kona spoke in that same voice.

"Anthony? Wasn't there something you wanted to add?"

The man whirled around and hissed an apology before striding off.

Kona turned around, his face split by a huge grin. He apologized profusely to the group and stepped over to Jo.

"I'm sorry," he said in a tone reserved for her ears alone. "I really wish that hadn't happened." He squeezed her hand gently and moved away nodding to the ukulele player on the way back to his place next to Sadie. Jo wasn't sure what they had witnessed, she caught Sadie's eye, but her friend just shrugged before patting Kona's arm when he reached her. She glanced at Jordan and got the same shrug followed by a nod towards the central aisle. It wasn't their fight, not their worry, they were here for something quite different. She'd have to wait to get the full story.

She turned her head to look at Andy who hadn't

moved from her side, but her eye snagged on a bright gaudy hat perched on the head of a woman sneaking into a seat in the front row. Who in the world...?

A smile erupted on Jo's face. Jo had no idea where she had found that monstrous hat, but her mother wore it with pride. She sat there, beaming at her daughter, arm nestled cozily in the crook of Richard's arm. He was also wearing an ornate, though more manly hat and Jo had to giggle at the sight of the two of them. Never during her childhood or even her teen years had her mother ever worn something that wasn't conservative or solemn. Her colors were beige, black, or navy blue, not fuchsia, orange, and what was that? Jo squinted and tried to focus on the cacophony of colors mixed together on the floppy hat. Teal? Ugh. She shuddered a bit and laughed again.

"Wait? Is that your mother?" Andy asked.

"Yeah."

"What the hell is she wearing?"

"I think it's a hat. Or someone dumped buckets of paint on her head. But she sure looks happy doesn't she?"

Andy nodded and laughed a bit, but his reply was interrupted by the ukulele player's energetic relaunch into his special wedding march.

"Ready again?" he murmured, and Jo nodded. One step down the aisle and the whole disturbance had been forgotten. All that was left was her fiancé waiting for her at the altar and the few steps that separated her from their future together.

"Oh! Oh!" The startled and excited cries stopped Jo's procession one more time and she had to stop herself from stomping her foot in irritation. She'd been to other weddings. Most people didn't have this much trouble walking to the altar.

"Look!" Andy shook her arm anxiously and pointed in the distance. Jo stopped her internal rant and looked at what was causing the new commotion. At first she just saw the ocean and shrugged in irritation. So, what, everyone knew there was a shark in the water. Whatever. She squinted a bit to see if she could spot him too, but instead of seeing one dark fin swimming out there she saw five. No, six. Wait! Eight!

Despite herself she felt a bubble of joy start to push away her frustration at the hold-up. She squinted harder and peered out at the still water. One of the silver dolphins chose that moment to start showing off. As his shining body launched itself out of the water and into a perfect back flip the guests gasped and clapped. Even Jo found herself hopping up and down in glee. She had always loved dolphins. Had always wanted to see some in the wild. And here they were, getting closer by the minute.

The wedding was all but forgotten for the time being, all the guests were standing up, straining to get a better look at the dolphins without leaving their spots. Jo laughed.

"Well! Come on!" She called to the guests as she made a run for the water. "You'll get a better view from here!" She called to her friends and family.

Jordan caught up with her just as she reached the edge.

"Jo! Watch out!" He caught her arm and pulled her out of the way of a wave that threatened to wet her feet. "Remember? Shark?"

She laughed again. "It's okay! Dolphins mean the

shark is long gone." She took a determined step forward and giggled as the water lapped at her feet. "We got our beach back, just in time."

Jordan rolled up the cuffs of his pants and came to stand next to her. Jo was fully conscious that they must have made an odd sight, her in a formal wedding gown, albeit shortened, veil and flower crown perched on her head, Jordan pants rolled up, looking like any Hawaiian beach goer, except for the formal lei draped over his shoulders. She felt the wind start to play with her veil and heard her friends come gather around her. She leaned against Jordan and sighed.

"Now. Now it's perfect." He hugged her tight to him and without looking she knew he was nodding and smiling right along with her.

The dolphins had noticed they had a full audience and were acting accordingly. That first flip was soon followed by countless others, some dolphins showing off by doing double or triple loops. The guests were entranced by the beauty of the wild creatures and clapped and cheered after every trick. They could have all stood there for the rest of the evening, but the sun was quickly going down, making it harder and harder to see the dolphin's entertaining antics.

"Excuse me?" A quiet voice caught Jo's attention. The officiant stood by her side, looking a bit anxious despite the delight that crossed her face whenever another dolphin would jump out of the water. "I know this is amazing, but it's just that I have to run in a few minutes, and I'd hate to have to leave before I marry you."

"Oh! Oh!" Jo and Jordan looked at each other and laughed. "The wedding. Right!" Jo knew without conferring with him that Jordan would agree with her before she even finished getting the sentence out. "Here. Let's do it right here."

"Well, yes, that was the plan." The officiant nodded towards the chairs and altar set up not 20 feet from where they were standing.

"No. Right here. Feet in the water. Friends by our sides."

The officiant looked dubious, but Jo and Jordan nodded energetically. Sadie came over and as soon as she heard the revised plan her head started bobbing in time with theirs.

"Whatever. It's your wedding." The pastor pulled out the book she had been preparing to read from and stood officiously in front of the couple. The guests noticed that something was happening and gathered closer.

The ceremony was short and poignant. Filled with references to the ocean and the mountains that surrounded them on all sides. The water swirled around their ankles and Jo smiled as she dug her toes into the wet sand. Any residual anxiety she had previously felt about this wedding had vanished the instant the water had covered her feet.

This was how she was meant to get married to Jordan. In this wedding that was all about them and not at all about ceremony. She had been wrong. What had been special about their first wedding hadn't been the foreignness of it, it had been that the whole thing had been stripped down to the bare essential nature of what brought them together.

Weddings should be about two people committing to love and support each other forever, surrounded by friends and family, not about lobster thermidor and expensive flowers. Jo looked up at Jordan and found him looking down at her. She could see her thoughts reflected in his eyes and she squeezed his hand tightly. Their mouths were almost touching when the officiant laughed and said, "Well then! I guess now is as good a time as any to say, 'I now pronounce you husband and wife and you may now kiss the bride.'"

The crowd laughed cheered as their lips finally touched.

78. Sadie

The dolphins stayed by the beach for a long while, frolicking under the bright moon that had risen moments after the ceremony had ended. Sadie found herself gazing at them frequently as the party unfolded. They symbolized everything that she had tried so hard to orchestrate. This wasn't the wedding she had thought she would be attending when she first got on the plane. Heck, this hadn't been the week she had thought she would be having when she first got on that plane, but it had all turned out beautifully in the end.

Her gaze strayed from the dolphins to the dancers near the fire. Andy, Roxie, Hunter, and Emily were holding hands and spinning around and around, heads thrown back, laughing as they spun. The light from the fire made their hair shine and their eyes glint.

Maryanne and Richard were dancing more sedately nearby, swaying gently to the music. They seemed lost to the world around them, perfectly happy in their bubble until Hunter stumbled out of the spin and bumped into them. Both of them looked down at him and smiled before helping him back to his feet. It didn't last long, but Sadie caught the smiles exchanged between Andy and Maryanne when the little boy bounced back to his dad. Maybe even those two had found a way to make peace this week. Wonders would never cease.

Her eyes sought out Kona and found him walking purposefully towards her. He kept getting stopped by grateful and curious guests who just had to know more about the good looking mysterious man who had been yelled at so outrageously. Every time he was stopped he threw Sadie a desperate glance and she finally took pity on him and went to rescue him.

"Excuse me," she kindly asked one of Jo's aunts. "Do you mind if I steal him away for a moment?" The aunt giggled and winked as she patted Sadie's arm knowingly, but she finally let the two of them escape into the dark that surrounded the festivities.

Once safely hidden in the shadows they turned around to watch the party. Kona pulled Sadie into his arms and held her tightly to him. She rested her back and her head against his broad chest and sighed. It felt good to be in his arms like this. Safe, natural, and best of all completely uncomplicated. She was going to miss it terribly when she got on that plane in two days.

Jo and Jordan floated around the campfires, hugging guests, grabbing bites to eat whenever they could, and taking a couple of impromptu dance steps whenever the ukulele's upbeat tunes moved them. Sadie smiled as she watched them. She envied them their future together. They were done with the hard part. Now, whatever the future threw at them, they would have each other to help get through it.

Without Jo, the last couple of years had been lonely for Sadie. Her self-absorbed string of bad boyfriends hadn't been of any support when she had needed them and with her best friend lost in the wilderness on the other side of the world she had had to rely on herself more than she cared to remember.

Spending these couple of days side by side with Kona had made her feel lonelier than she had ever felt before. When he was near her she felt whole, but when he stepped away, even for a moment, she was reminded that she was going home alone, without his warm comforting presence. She had thought she was lonely before, but now that she knew what being with the right person felt like, she didn't know if she had the strength to face her solitary life again.

She didn't feel the tears drop from her eyes, but Kona felt them fall on the arm that he had wrapped tightly around her chest. He turned her around gently and cupped her chin with his hand to make her look up at him. Gently he wiped away the tears that rolled down her face.

"Hey! Why so sad?"

Sadie was unable to force an answer past the lump that formed in her throat. What was she supposed to tell this man she had met a mere four days before? That she loved him and she couldn't face leaving him? He would think she was insane.

"I don't want you to leave either," he murmured surprising her. "I don't want to say goodbye."

The lump grew even bigger so instead of answering Sadie just nodded helplessly.

"You know, we do have an opening for a wedding planner. You did a pretty fantastic job pulling this one together... If you were maybe interested I could possibly put in a good word with the owner of the resort..." Kona smiled down at her and Sadie's eyes widened of their own accord. She held her breath as he squeezed her hands tightly. "I know that we've only known each other for a handful of days Sadie, but I already can't fathom a life without you by my side. In all seriousness, is there any chance you might consider staying?"

The guests all clapped and cheered, but when Sadie looked around she realized that they were once again caught up in the dolphins' show. She looked back at Kona who was still looking at her expectantly. She could do this. She could leave her life behind. She glanced at Jo, laughing in the moonlight. Her friend had done it and survived. Who could say she wouldn't do just as well.

"What? Live here with you in paradise?" She teased as she reached up and wrapped her arms around him. "I think I just might be able to come to terms with that idea," she replied and sealed her promise with a kiss.

Epilogue

The call to buckle seat belts and place trays upright came over the loudspeaker. Jo fumbled around under her blanket until she found both ends of the belt and snapped them together with a satisfying click. She grabbed the loose end and pulled the belt snugly, but not too snugly around her waist. It was a crazy thought, but she had a hunch she should be gentle.

"What's that smile for?" Jordan asked her tenderly, looking over at her from the seat next to hers. His belt was already fastened, and his tray had never been lowered. He pushed the center armrest upright and gently took her hand as he pulled her towards him. She snuggled up to his shoulder and slipped her fingers through his. Her other hand, hidden by the flimsy airline blanket, rested protectively on her belly.

As much as she knew how happy he would be to hear about her hunch, she wasn't ready to share quite yet.

"Nothing. I'm just..." She looked out the window at the lush land spread out below them, then turned back towards him with a smile. "I'm just happy."

Jessica Rosenberg

Acknowledgements

I spent countless hours thinking about this book, writing this book, editing this book, dreaming about this book, talking about this book, and doing more editing of this book. In all that time, I never once stopped to picture myself writing the acknowledgements at the end of the book. Crazy, right? So here I am, writing the acknowledgements and worrying that I'm going to forget someone crucial. Can't I just go back to editing the more some more? No? OK then...

I'd like to thank my original Beta reader, my husband, who had to read the book in a different room than the one I was in because every time he laughed I'd beg him to tell me what part he was reading, as well as my older sister and a few of my closest friends, for taking the plunge and reading the first draft, before I did much of the editing I mentioned above. I'd also like to thank the second round of Beta readers who got to read the book many versions later when I had polished it and fixed many key parts. This book wouldn't be the book it is without any of you.

I'd like to thank Tory Hartman, my original publisher, for taking a leap of faith with me and for agreeing to publish Aloha Also Means Goodbye (and for letting me call it that!).

I'd like to also thank the lovely people at my local Starbucks where most of this book was written. I'm eternally grateful that they never once asked me to vacate a table.

I'd like to thank my online community and my friends for always believing in me, for reading countless blog posts, Facebook posts, and tweets about the challenges joys of writing a novel. Every word of this book was written with you in mind. I can't wait to finally let you enjoy it.

And last, but not least, I'd like to thank my children for their unwavering belief in me. I started writing this book when the youngest was an infant sleeping in her car seat next to me. Today they're both quick to brag to people that their mommy is a writer. Nothing fills me with more pride than having tangible proof that they're right.

Aloha Also Means Goodbye

www.ingramcontent.com/pod-product-compliance
Lightning Source LLC
Chambersburg PA
CBHW051521100726
47898CB00005B/1539